THE YEAR of ENDINGS

The Conclusion of *The Continental Divide*

Alanson Rand

Acknowledgments

Special thanks to Joey Clark and Debbie Witt for pointing out when I was making no sense.

ISBN (print edition): 978-1-946843-11-1

Also by Alanson Rand:

<u>*The Continental Divide*</u>
Waking in Ruins
Anarchista
The American Main
Wednesday's Children
Eighteen Hells
The Year of Endings

<u>*A Drive with Auntie (coming 2021)*</u>
East to Eden
The Shores of Distant Time

KEY FIGURES IN THE REVOLUTION OF 2043

Victoria Lang MD, a former director of Chalys Pharmaceuticals
Ada Lang, her daughter
Krista Warner, Activist leader
Arista Molle, a television journalist
Sergeant Mark Mason, a highway patrol officer
Tiara King, a newsfeed reporter for NewsPulse Los Angeles
Timmie Topuha, a videographer for NewsPulse Los Angeles
Lt. Jon Gilsig, Platoon Leader, First Platoon, Bravo Company, 184th Infantry

Rear Admiral Adam Harris, Commander, Submarine Force, US Pacific Fleet
Captain Zachary Caldwell, Admiral Harris' Chief of Staff
Captain Juliette Bricker, Commander, USS *Patrick Henry*
Commander Ennis Quinn, Executive Officer, USS *Patrick Henry*
Lt. Commander Tala Ripley, Strategic Warfare Officer, *USS Patrick Henry*

Gabriel Cheyn, President of the United States
Sara Hogue, former NSF Tactical Chief
Noah Hayborn, Speaker of the House
Enrico DaCosta, Governor of the State of California

Maryann Heilmann, (a.k.a. Mother Mary Ann Christ), mother of The Profit Joseph
The Profit Joseph, Archangelist leader, purportedly the son of Jesus Christ

National Security Forces
Bob Downs, Former Watcher
Raphael Vinola, Watcher
Philip Cochon, Deputy Watcher
Ari Stein, Night Chief – Intelligence
Hideki Buta, Day Chief – Acquisition
Ryan Beckmann, Night Chief – Acquisition
Piet Vark, Day Chief – Tactical Operations
Tom Riddick, Night Chief – Tactical Operations
Peter Mochyn, Day Chief – Cybermeasures

DIRE STRAIT

Day 57
Wednesday morning, October 14, 2043
Pacific Ocean, 235 miles WNW of Cape Flattery, Washington

Captain Julie Bricker strode into the Control Room followed by Commander Ennis Quinn, Lieutenant Commander Tala Ripley, and an assortment of missile and instrumentation technicians.

Bricker sat in the command station chair and scanned the status monitors for two numbers: One estimated the boat's depth using gravimetry from the inertial navigation system, and the other indicated the falsified reading of the fourteen depth sensors. Both showed a depth of 300 meters below the surface, enough to keep the four nuclear missiles from launching – for now. They were about to find out how effective Ripley's workaround was. "Pilot, up bubble two, make your depth 240 meters," she said.

Ripley shooed technicians away from the Strategic Warfare console and took her seat. The Control Room was filled with spectators; whether the depth sensor falsing worked or not was critical because most sailors on board would be exiled on the Falkland Islands if it failed. They'd live in fear and anonymity on that barren rock, forever wanted for the destruction of Sacramento.

On the other hand, if the sensors worked, the sailors might see their loved ones again, assuming they could slip undetected beneath the USS *John Jacob Astor* and through the Strait of Juan de Fuca. There'd only be one chance for that – two warships were an hour behind the *Astor*, and two more were on the way.

Ripley turned and pushed at the wall of flesh. "Make a hole, people. I need to see Command." She popped another square of gum into her mouth, logged onto her console, and reviewed the status of the Mushroom Farm, which showed thirty-one peaceful birds and four very angry ones. The Missile Release Control System was still suspending the release of the four live missiles, although that might change once they climbed above the launch floor.

On Bricker's status monitor, the estimated depth read 289 meters while the falsified depth remained at 300 meters. "So far, so good," she said. She watched the numbers intently, waiting to hear Ripley's call, but all she heard was the strained silence of thirty people holding their breath.

Ripley didn't know the boat's depth because all she saw was the Strategic Warfare screen. It showed the time to four missile releases: The MRCS would release Bird Three-Four instantly, Two-Three was scheduled to release in twenty-nine seconds, and the other missiles would release in thirty second intervals after that. However, Bird Three-Four had been damaged when its ejection booster exploded, and it wouldn't budge no matter how many times the MRCS tried to launch it.

She watched each number so closely that they swam in her vision, and she blinked her eyes a few times to regain their focus. Suddenly, everyone in the room drew a relieved breath.

"Mister Ripley, status?" Bricker asked.

"Captain, release status still shows as suspended. Countdowns are static. Are we above the launch floor?"

"We're at 250 meters, but the depth sensors are showing 300 meters. I think your fix might've worked."

Missile technicians shook hands, and a few clapped Ripley's shoulder, but she still stared at the numbers and dared them to change. "I'll keep an eye on it if the captain doesn't mind."

"The captain doesn't mind." Bricker stood and shook hands all around. "We're at 245 meters and not a peep from the MRCS. Congratulations to Mister Ripley, Chief Bailey, and all of you involved in this task. And I'm sure the citizens of Seattle, Olympia, Portland, and Salem would be even more grateful. Pilot, take us up to mast depth. Mister Durgan, prepare to send a message."

CAPTAIN ZACHARY CALDWELL FRESHENED HIS DRINK and sat on the big couch in Admiral Harris' office at Bangor Naval Base. He massaged his temple with one hand, hoping to wipe away the dull headache that had taken root three days ago.

He pulled out his tablet and reviewed the base seizure plans: The Marines were tracking the likely objectors, the convention center had been converted to hold prisoners, and all contractors and civilian staff had been escorted off the base. Major Shelby had sent the Marines he expected to resist the takeover on a two-week wilderness training exercise in the Olympic rainforest. The Marine contingent guarding the Strategic Weapons Facility hadn't been told of the impending base seizure – the Hotbox alert that would trigger the takeover meant enemies were approaching the gate, and the compound would instantly lock down to secure the thirteen hundred nuclear warheads housed there. That was what Admiral Harris wanted.

The *Nathan Hale* and the *Ethan Allen* were ready to sail on two hours' notice. The command staffs of both boats had been easy to convince, especially since their commanders had been Bricker's executive officers. They knew her, and neither could accept that she'd attack an American city even if ordered.

He drained his drink and sneaked to the bar for a refill while Harris used the bathroom. As he was pouring, Harris swore and pounded on the door.

"You okay in there?" Caldwell asked.

The door opened and Adam Harris stormed out red-faced. He splashed rum into his glass, poured it down his throat, and then thrust the tablet into Caldwell's hands. He read the message on the screen:

2256Z 2043-10-12; ORIGIN: V; ENCRYPT: NAVMIL9C

RCV: HARRIS, ADAM, COMSUBPAC
SND: BRICKER, JULIETTE, COMSSN807
SUB: BE HOME SOON

HEADING INTO THE STRAIT IN TEN HOURS. SANK THE ROCKEFELLER, AND THE ASTOR IS NOW AHEAD OF US IN THE STRAIT. GOULD AND DUKE TRAILING, MORGAN AND MELLON COMING FROM THE SOUTH.

WE'LL FIGURE OUT HOW TO SLIP BY OR WILL CLEAR OUR COURSE AS REQUIRED. WILL TRY TO MINIMIZE FALLOUT IN NW WASHINGTON.

ETA DOCKSIDE IS 2304 HOURS LOCAL IF NOTHING ELSE GOES FUBAR. WE'LL GO STRAIGHT TO THE EXPLOSIVES HANDLING WHARF.

RECEIVED A SECOND RELEASE ORDER AT 1732Z SUNDAY. LAUNCH CONTROLLER SAYS THE TARGETS WERE SEATTLE, OLYMPIA, PORTLAND, AND SALEM. ORDER ORIGIN IS WHITE HOUSE OFFICE OF NAVAL OPERATIONS AGAIN. WE WENT EMERGENCY DEEP TO KEEP THE BIRDS IN THEIR TUBES, BUT THEY'RE HOT.

ENNIS SPLASHED TWO EARECKSON ASW AIRCRAFT OFF KISKA ISLAND. DOES EVERYBODY IN THE NAVY WANT US DEAD?

BE ADVISED THAT I'M COMING IN WITH SIX KIA, FOUR HOT WARHEADS, AND ONE COLD REACTOR CELL. BET YOU'LL BE GLAD TO SEE ME.

JULIE

PS: KEEP YOUR LIPS TIGHT AND YOUR KNUCKLES WHITE, SAILOR.

"Well, fuck me blue," Caldwell said.

Harris grumbled and poured cola into his glass. He added a tot of rum, and thinking again, added more. "The world's going to hell, Zack."

"No, Cheyn's going to hell and dragging the rest of us with him." Caldwell sat on Harris' desk and tapped on his tablet screen. "We can get maudlin later, but we should tell the *Revere* to get lost out in the Pacific if there's this much firepower at the Strait. She's the *Henry's* sister ship. They might target her by accident."

"I agree. Tell them to take the long way home."

"Just did." Caldwell slipped his tablet into a pocket. "Okay, now we can get maudlin."

"Screw maudlin. I wish I could be out there doing something. I hate sitting in an office, just watching and waiting and worrying."

"You can't do anything, Adam. She has to get here on her own. We don't have any surface ships that could engage the *Astor*."

"I know, I know." Harris flopped onto the couch and rested his feet on the coffee table. "No matter what happens, things will change, Zack. If she doesn't make it in, Cheyn's coming for us next. If she does make it in, we won't be able to keep the *Henry's* arrival a secret, and we'll need control of the base sooner rather than later. We can't wait for the politicians to get their ducks in a neat row anymore." He took a swallow from his glass and looked through the window at the ferns. "It's show time. I'll give Wang a heads-up. You tell Shelby to get his assets mobilized. I want to be ready to seize this base in twenty-four hours."

DISPATCHES

Midnight Sun
News Post of October 14, 2043

CATACLYSM IN SACRAMENTO: DAY SEVEN

Rescue operations continue in Sacramento a week after a nuclear weapon devastated the area.

Radiation levels are tolerable at McClellan Air Force Base, north of Sacramento, and a forward treatment center is now operating at the former Outpatient Clinic. Medical professionals from Canada and Mexico have arrived to treat the stricken population.

The Mexican and Canadian governments have lifted their cordons so victims can be treated at their hospitals. Hospitals in the high country of Utah and Colorado have also offered their facilities. Hospitals in upstate New York and the Vermont Republic have as well.

The White House has not yet offered Federal aid or assistance.

FALLOUT FORECAST

Radiation monitors in North Las Vegas reported seven rad-per-hour fallout deposition as the plume passed over that city last night. On the Las Vegas Strip, dose rates reached a peak of four rads per hour at 9:00 PM, which was lower than anticipated but still unhealthy for anything but brief exposure.

California officials say these radiation levels will render Las Vegas uninhabitable for seven to twelve months, and the city must be abandoned for the short term.

As of 9:00 AM PT, the center of the fallout plume front was located forty miles north of Williams, Arizona, and was drifting east. It will pass well north of Flagstaff and should pose no threat to that city. Nevertheless, fallout paths are just a guide, and Flagstaff residents are advised to remain indoors for the coming day.

Weather aircraft were again spotted over Nevada this morning as American emergency management officials assess the downwind impact of the plume. From the amount of fallout deposited in the Las Vegas area, experts believe the plume still contains substantial amounts of heavy isotopes and remains dangerous. As of this writing, the plume appears likely to be drawn into Hurricane Andy Boy's circulation and could spread radioactive fallout across the country's midsection.

ACTIVISTS PREPARE FOR ACTION IN BALTIMORE

We have recruited our first new Witness in the East since the opening days of the Neovirus crisis. He reports from Baltimore:

"Baltimore's two cities now, the east and the west. On both sides, the power keeps going out and the phones don't work, and all the supermarkets and diesel stations are emptied out. On both sides, everyone's on strike and nothing works. But things on the East End are a lot better cuz we have Commander Sara and the Activists here. They're bringing in food and bottled water, but more than that, they're getting the East End organized. I can't tell you what for cuz I dunno, but people woulda eaten each other alive by now if they weren't here.

"That's what's happening on the West End, I hear. Food shortages, diesel shortages, no cops or ambulances or firemen – you can see the clouds of black smoke all the way over here, and sometimes you can smell the stink of burning houses. If they had an Activist commander to keep them straight, it wouldn't be so bad, but I think they're on their own.

"I talked to Commander Sara today and asked if The Activity could give us our power back now, but she can't contact them cuz of the Activist's strict compartmentalization rules. She said The Activity has its hands around the government's throat, though, and they'll be squeezing it real tight soon."

THE SILVER THREAD

Day 57
Wednesday morning, October 14, 2043
Near Davis, California

Victoria Lang walked alongside a wide road crowded by stores, keeping her gaze focused on the ground to avoid being blinded by the rising sun.

Her leather soles tapped the concrete walk as she strode. She'd awakened with nearly manic energy, perhaps due to learning Ada's location or because her anemia was finally abating.

She'd slept hard the night before under a Red Cross tent in the Vaca Valley Medical Center parking lot. Her bed had only been a pile of blankets spread across the pavement, but it had felt like a luxury hotel mattress to her weary body.

She couldn't escape the stink of cheese that clung to her suit, though. That had been her breakfast: chunks of cheddar cheese with squeezable cheese for a topping, a few slices of bread, an avocado, and a bottle of water.

Now every part of her smelled sour, and cheese wasn't the only fragrance she was putting off – she'd last showered in Rosarito and was starting to smell like a street person. With a start, she remembered that she'd slept in a parking lot the previous night. She already was an indigent: homeless, unemployed, and living off the charity of others.

Grumbling under her breath, disturbed at how mentally ill she sounded, she began walking down an entrance ramp to Interstate 80. At the bottom, a row of concrete barriers stretched across the highway, where a police officer waved for cars to stop and return to the westbound side. A camera crew filmed the confusion, and a few motorists had pulled off the road to read the yellow letters on the electronic sign spanning the highway:

CAPITAL REGION CLOSED
STATE OF EMERGENCY
MARTIAL LAW IN EFFECT

The sign then blinked and said:

PLAN ALTERNATE ROUTES

"Duh," she muttered, turning to walk back the way she'd come. After a few minutes, she found an intersection that she'd passed earlier. A small road paralleled the highway, and she turned toward Davis and her daughter.

BOB DOWNS OPENED HIS EYES and tried to remember where he was. He looked down and saw that he was lying in a recliner, an empty IV bag dangling from a pole beside him.

The room was quiet and dark, a caress of sweet cinnamon incense floating on the air, and polychrome light streamed through a window. He saw a rack with red candles across the room and then remembered: After they finally called his number in the Marin Wellness emergency room and gave him intravenous antibiotics, they moved him into the chapel to free up the bed.

Deciding to wait until a nurse replaced his IV bag, he lay back in the chair to rest, but then he spotted a wall clock and saw it was time for his 0800 bowel movement. He hadn't missed one for a decade, and he wasn't about to start now.

With a shaky hand, he unclipped the IV tube from his arm and sat up, but a wave of dizziness struck him and he lay back again. While waiting for his head to clear, he inspected the bandages on his hands: The seepage from his burns had stopped, his hands didn't hurt, and his veins were no longer swollen and angry. He'd be ready for duty soon.

Grabbing the chair arms, he began to rise to his feet, but then his knees buckled and a bolt of pain shot through his sore shoulder. He collapsed back into the chair feeling weaker than ever.

With his good arm, he grabbed his pack and rummaged through it until he found the dentist's bottle of Synthopia. He unscrewed the cap and swallowed one dry, and then feeling the throbbing in his shoulder, he took another and lay back in the seat.

He was too weak to return to the field. However, his mission was urgent, and he needed to rebuild his stamina fast and get back on Warner's trail, which he couldn't do lounging in a hospital chair. After a few clarifying breaths, he forced himself to stand, staggered to the chapel door, and peeked into the corridor.

To one side, he saw a blurry bubble of blue daylight. He began walking toward it, assuming the lobby was that way and that he'd find a restroom there. He squinted at every door sign, and after a few tries, he found one that said MEN. His head spinning, he stumbled into the first stall and sat.

He was staring mindlessly at the tan stall door when he realized his toes had gone numb, and he hadn't even begun to empty his bowels. Wondering if the explosive restroom incident in Tonopah had damaged his gut, he closed his eyes and tried to relax his pelvic muscles.

When he opened them again, the toilet stall door was green. He blinked, and the door then appeared to be dull pink. After blinking again and seeing a robin's-egg blue door, he rubbed his eyes and gathered his energy to stand. A walk might stimulate a bowel movement, and perhaps it would clear the Synthopia from his system so he could see the world in non-psychedelic colors.

As he was pulling up his pants, though, the door opened and two men walked in. One wore green battle fatigues tucked into scuffed black boots, and the other wore jeans and sneakers.

"So is Warner as hot as they say?" the sneaker-shod man asked.

"She's most fuckable, my friend, but she's on the Bug Team and I don't see her much. They don't come up to the surface a lot cuz they're all crawling with that virus."

"They didn't give you the vaccine?"

"Sure, we got some of the new batch, but we gotta stay away so we don't pick up that bug on our clothes and spread it. It's what they call prophylactics or something."

The first man laughed. "Like rubbers?"

"Yeah. Science is weird, man."

Two urinals flushed, and Downs couldn't hear the conversation for a few seconds.

"So what's it like up in Davis? It get hit hard?"

"Nah, not the university at least. Lotsa broken windows and stuff, that's all."

The door closed behind the men as they left, cutting off the conversation, but Downs had heard all he needed.

HER FEET ACHING, cursing the Italians for their indifference to shoe comfort, Victoria trudged east on Campus Road in Davis and looked at the long shadow she cast in the setting sun. The walk from Vaca Valley had taken most of the day, and her enthusiasm and energy had baked off in the dry afternoon heat. Every step was now an effort.

To take her mind off her exhaustion, she tried to remember a virology conference she'd attended years before, and the neat little man she'd met there. He was a retrovirology researcher, and while she couldn't recall his name, she remembered that he ran a Level 4 lab complex at UC Davis. That's what Ada would need to reproduce Recombin. That's where she'd be.

She walked into the parking lot of a campus welcome center to find a map. A huge tent camp was set up across the road, and a line of people waited to get on school buses on the far side. Near the road, men pulled stretchers off a helicopter that had just landed.

The campus map screwed to the wall showed that the science complex wasn't far, and she willed her sore feet toward the high concrete parking garage where the complex started. With any luck, she'd find Ada tonight, or at least find a safe and comfortable place to sleep.

Still absorbed by thoughts of her daughter, she turned the corner of the garage and walked up the road leading to the science complex. She was approaching a barn-like building when she heard the chuffing of an animal in the trees to her left. Peering into the shadows, she saw the shrubs quiver, and then a German Shepherd with a blood-caked muzzle padded onto the grass. More dogs followed, and soon, dozens crouched beside it.

Glancing left and right, she saw no safe shelter except for the barn directly ahead. Trying to not to incite the animals, she slipped off her shoes and prepared to run.

Then the German Shepherd padded slowly onto the sidewalk and blocked her path. She turned and sprinted to the garage, and the rest of the pack swarmed from underneath the trees and chased her. As she neared the garage, she cut across the grass and aimed for the entrance, but then her foot caught an upraised driveway curb and she tumbled across the concrete.

The German Shepherd had already leaped for her throat and hurtled past her with its jaws snapping for her neck. Its head struck a light pole on the other side of the driveway, and it landed in a heap ten feet away.

She started to climb to her feet, but then a black Rottweiler flew into her chest and knocked her to the ground. She rolled to one side and started to rise, but the dog jumped on her chest again. It pressed her to the concrete, its colorful metal tags jangling merrily. A white dog she hadn't seen clamped its jaws on her throat, and she felt its teeth squeeze the soft skin over her carotid artery.

Then the Rottweiler's head exploded and splattered brains across the concrete. The white dog started to run, but a rifle cracked and it somersaulted backward through the air. The rest of the dog pack yipped and ran back into the bushes.

She pushed the headless dog off her shoulder. A man in green battle fatigues and carrying an assault rifle knelt beside her, his eyes opening wide when he saw her chest. "Lay down. You been injured," he said.

She looked down at her suit, which she'd kept spotless through several murders and a cross-continent escape, and grimaced at the canine gray matter dripping off it. "I think I'd know if these were *my* brains," she said, flicking chunks off her jacket. "God, what a mess."

"You shouldn't be walkin 'round alone, not here."

"Yeah, now I know. Thanks for showing up."

He helped her to her feet, and three more soldiers ran up. "Dog pack again, Migs?" one of them asked.

"Yeah. Nailed two of 'em this time."

"We gotta hunt down those fuckers," another said. "Shit's getting worse now, attacking people 'n all. You okay?"

"Just a little rattled," she said.

Migs held out his arm. "Yeah, well, let's find out for sure. Hold onto my arm, and we'll go check you out. No way we're gonna let you walk 'round out here anyway."

MIGS HELD VICTORIA'S ARM as he guided her up the steps to the loading dock. He rested her against the wall and then pulled a medikit from a nearby Humvee. "Ada Lang, you say?" he asked as he rifled through the kit.

Victoria crossed her arms. "I'm her mother, and I demand that you take me to her."

"What makes you think this Ada Lang individual is here?"

"I *know* she is. Your soldiers were blabbing about it all over Vaca Valley. Now stop being cagey and take me to her."

"I'm not being cagey, ma'am. I just have orders."

"Orders not to talk about my daughter, obviously. Why is that? You're holding her prisoner, aren't you? I demand that you release her now!"

"She's not a prisoner, ma'am," Migs said.

Victoria smiled her first happy smile of the night. "Aha! She *is* here!"

He frowned and examined something in the medikit. "I didn't say that."

"Yes, you did," Victoria said. "Fine, if you won't show me, I'll find her myself." She jumped to her feet and yanked open the door.

Migs ran forward and pulled her into the air. Another soldier grabbed her thrashing legs, but she pulled them up to her knees and kicked him across the dock, pushing Migs on his back with Victoria on top. She rolled off, scrambled to her feet, and prepared to bolt for the door, but then it opened and a broad-shouldered man in a green T-shirt strode through. She backed out of the man's reach and slid to one side, keeping the other soldiers in her peripheral vision.

"What's going on here?" he rumbled.

"She keeps talking about somebody called Ada Lang, Sarge," Migs groaned from the dock floor. "Says she's her mother. Told her we don't know anything about her."

"Right. We're just an evacuation support unit and we can't help…" Swensen peered at her face as she moved into the light. "Well, I'll be damned." He walked across the dock, took her chin in his hand, and turned her face from side to side. "I *will* be damned. You look just like her."

"Because I'm her mother!" she snapped, and then her heart skipped a few beats. "She's here? She's really here?"

Swensen nodded. "Down in the lab."

The tension that had gripped her for weeks vanished in an instant, and her knees buckled. Migs grabbed her before she hit the ground. "Thank you. You don't know how long I've been waiting to hear that." She braced one hand against the wall and stood on shaky legs. "Okay, I'm okay now. Take me to her, please."

Swensen ran his hand through his hair. "I can't. Only the Bug Team can go down to the lab, and we gotta stay away from them. It's a prophylaxis protocol."

"Okay," Victoria said as she walked through the door. "I'll go myself."

He grabbed her arm. "You can't go, either. You'll have to wait till she comes up. It's hot down there."

She took off her jacket, threw it to the floor, and glared at him.

"Not *that* kinda hot. It's hot with that Neovirus. That's what she's using to brew up the vaccine, and the whole floor's contaminated already. You go down without getting the shot, you'll catch it. But she comes up a lot. You won't have to wait long."

Victoria pulled up the sleeve of her blouse, showed him the vaccination ring, and then she spun on her foot and strode down the hall. "No more excuses, Sergeant," she called over her shoulder. "Will you show me the way, or do I have to find it myself?"

VICTORIA STOPPED AT THE BOTTOM of the steps and read the marker-drawn scribbles on the door. Scrawled in the center was HOT VIRUS ZONE – STAY OUT OR DIE, and each of the sixteen Bug Team members had signed his or her name beneath it. She read each one, and her heart thudded when she saw Ada's name at the bottom.

She opened the door and then staggered back – the sweltering, humid air in the corridor beyond reeked so much of body odor and sour yeast that she could barely breathe. Pinching her nose, she peeked inside and spotted glass-fronted labs through a doorway, their windows showing the reflections of people working in a lab across the hall. Anxiety welled up again: What would she say to her daughter, and how could she justify the crimes she'd committed? Would Ada ever understand? Was it wiser to turn around and leave forever?

Her face twisted into a scowl; she'd journeyed too far to succumb to cowardice now. Holding her head high, she strode into the lab complex.

As she passed through a stainless steel doorway, she saw that the lab was frenetically busy. Soldiers in green fatigues carried jars and bottles across the room, and a cluster of them stood in front of a contraption against the far wall. She looked closer and saw five tabletop bioreactors below a bird's nest of silver-coated tubes. Two protein modelers sat on a lab table beside the contraption, and one displayed a revolving image of a Recombin virus.

Near the door, a tall redheaded woman took a bottle from a soldier, wrote something on it, and handed it to a Polynesian-looking boy, who scribbled on a clipboard. Another soldier took the jar and walked to the far end of the lab, where refrigerators lined the wall. He opened one and placed the bottle next to hundreds of others.

The soldiers near the bioreactors backed away, revealing a small blonde girl crouching in front of one. She stood, holding a pipette in her gloved hands, and Victoria touched her fingertips to the glass. "Ada…"

Ada carried the pipette to the idle modeler and then fussed with the glovebox and tapped the modeler's screen. The redhead stretched, walked to Ada, and whispered in her ear. Ada bobbed her head and jumped down from her stool, and they walked together to the lab door.

Victoria backed down the hall, unsure what to do or what to say. Her driving mission had been finding her daughter, and now that she had, she was utterly lost.

"Wanna go topside for a smoke?" Krista asked.

"Thought you'd never ask." Ada slipped off her stool and strode toward the corridor. "I haven't had a smoke in so long, it feels like some African witch doctor shrunk my –" She stopped as soon as she stepped through the doorway.

"What's up?" Krista asked, and then she looked down the hall. A woman stood by the stainless steel door watching them intently, one who could have been Ada's much older twin if it weren't for her shoulder-length brown hair. Krista pieced it together a few seconds later. "Victoria?" she asked. The woman nodded without taking her eyes from Ada.

They stood rooted to their spots for a few awkward moments until Krista gave Ada a gentle shove in the back. She took a few stumbling steps, and then she ran the rest of the way and leaped into her mother's arms.

ADA AND VICTORIA SAT SIDE BY SIDE on the loading dock and dangled their feet over the edge. "So, was it hard getting here?" Victoria asked.

Ada took a long puff and watched the cloud drift away. "I wouldn't say that."

"You were completely alone when I left you in that rest stop, and yet you found Krista and got all the way here. I'd imagine that's an interesting story."

"She found me and we drove till her car broke down. We hopped a train after that."

"Really? That's all?"

Ada looked away. "Yep. Yawn Factor Nine."

"Huh. I would have thought the Federals would be looking for Krista, and the journey would have been somewhat…eventful."

"Well, we hit a speed bump or two, but that's basically what happened," Ada said. "I think your story would be a lot more interesting. I just sat in the rest stop and waited for Krista after you got captured, and the most torture I got was a lot of bad music. You had to bust out of the NTC dungeon."

Victoria sipped from her coffee cup. "Oh, it wasn't that bad. I just slipped out when they weren't looking, and then I holed up till I figured out where you were going. Once I knew, I made a few arrangements and wangled a spot on a cruise to Mexico. That's basically what happened."

"Is that so?" Ada looked into her eyes.

They held each other's gaze for a second, and then Victoria examined the coffee in her cup. "Yep. Easy-peasy," she said.

They sat in an awkward silence for a few moments, and then Ada reached up and pulled back the hair over Victoria's ear. "This doesn't hurt?"

"It's odd, but it never did. I didn't even know it was severed till hours later. It stung a little after the adrenaline was metabolized, and then it just itched like crazy."

"Well, I gotta say, you look good as a brunette."

Victoria smiled and flipped her locks, and then she looked across the yard at a patrol climbing the grassy berm. "Do you ever wonder if there are forces in this universe we don't understand?"

"Every night," Ada said.

"Besides that. Discipline and determination bend the odds your way, and luck always favors the motivated, but that we survived and found each other…there's something else at work here, and it's not some random butterfly effect."

"Krista believes the Life Force was guiding us and protecting us the whole way."

"Do you think that's superstitious?"

"She goes a little woo-woo sometimes, but I know there's magic in the world. I've seen it myself, but don't tell her I said that."

Victoria looked out past the berm again, where another patrol was returning from the garage. The dogs had been silent all night, but everyone was still wary after the attack. "Maybe you'll be ready to learn about the silver thread soon."

"The what?"

"It's *our* magic, and it helped me find you. But that's a long story we should save for a special time. For now, let me say I'm so proud of you and so glad you're opening your mind to life's magic." She looked from side to side and then leaned toward Ada. "I'll tell you a secret – life is imbued with wonderful, incomprehensible magic, and you can see it working every day. Sometimes on my drug trials, I'll administer a med, and the patient will climb out of bed a week later, shake everybody's hand, and walk through the door whistling. When the trial's over, I'll unseal the records and find out he was just taking a placebo."

"Fascinating." Ada gazed across the parking lot, tapping her fingers to her lips. "He expected to get better, so he did. The same thing happened while I was running around with Krista. If she expected something to work out, it did. It's as if her mind changed the physical world so it delivered what we needed."

"I think that's possible. Belief, hope, expectations, faith, optimism – they all affect the physical world in a way we'll never understand."

"Don't worry. I'll figure it out."

"Maybe you should check in with the Universal Canvas tonight and see if you can find the answer."

"I haven't seen the Canvas for a few nights now. My sleep's been a little...umm, disturbed."

"Well, with all you've been through, I can see why." Ada didn't respond, so she nudged her with an elbow.

"Hmm? Right, right, bad sleep, that's the reason. Sorry, just thinking about how to figure out this magic thing." Ada crossed her arms and stroked her chin. "I'm gonna need a supercollider."

They sat in silence as Ada mulled over possibilities. After a few minutes, Victoria said, "So Krista sounds like the mystical type."

"Oh, definitely! That'd aggravate the hell out of me if it was anybody else, but I don't mind when Krista goes all purple. Her friendship matters a lot more to me than whether we think the same or not."

"What have you done with Ada? You're not the girl I left in the rest stop."

"I'm sorry. I've been through a lot with her and –"

Victoria clapped her hand over Ada's mouth. "Oh, shut it. I like the new Ada. I can talk to her without getting into an argument."

Ada mumbled something under her mother's hand. "What'd you say?" Victoria asked, pulling her hand away.

"I said your hand smells like dog brains."

"I'm sorry, I'm sorry." She wiped her hands on her jacket. "That was inconsiderate. I always keep myself spotless, and now my hands are a Petri dish and my suit's ruined."

"I've smelled worse. So you like the new Ada?"

"I certainly do. We haven't fought for two hours, and when was the last time that happened?"

"May of '39," Ada said.

"Oh, hell."

"It stuck in my mind cuz it was so weird."

"I don't know why we're always at each other's throats. It never made sense. I love you more than I love myself."

"We never had a chance to become friends. I'd like to try that. I don't need a mom as much as I need a friend."

Victoria looked up at the stars, took a deep breath, and exhaled slowly. "Maybe someday you'll understand how hard this is."

"What?"

"You don't need a mother anymore. It's a little hard to take when your baby says she doesn't need you anymore."

"I could only be your baby for so long, but I can be your friend forever," Ada said.

"I know, I know. But every step of the way here, I promised that if I ever found you again, I'd be a better mother and never make the same mistakes. And then I find you, and here you are, doing all these wonderful things yourself."

"Not all by myself. I couldn't have done any of this if it wasn't for you. You know, as soon as I opened that briefcase, I figured out your Plan B if the meeting at St. E's went down the crapper."

Victoria had been raising the cup for another sip but stopped an inch short of her lips. "You did?" she asked, gripping the cup tight.

"Oh, yeah. If the meeting went south, you were gonna take the vaccine to Sacramento and help California make it."

Victoria let go of the breath she'd been holding. "You are *so* smart, you know that?"

"I know. But one thing I can't figure out is how you knew the virus would go pandemic, and California would need it so bad."

Victoria shrugged. "What can I say? I try to plan ahead." She set her coffee cup down and looked away over the berm again, and then she sniffed and wiped her nose with the back of her hand.

"Are you crying?" Ada asked.

"Only a little," Victoria said.

"It's a little scary. Could you yell at me instead?"

"Well, if you're going to be all grown up, then I'm off duty, okay? I can cry as much as I want now." She sniffed again and then broke into tears. "All I ever wanted was a normal family! And I pushed them all away! What's wrong with me?"

"Serene your scene, mom. It's no big deal."

Victoria whirled around, her moist eyes burning with anger. "I earned my self-pity the hard way! I deserve this cry! Back off!"

Ada shrunk back with her hands raised, and Victoria buried her face in her hands. "It's been so damn hard holding it all in and trying to do right, and now I find out I was wrong all along, and my chance to set everything right is gone, and now you don't need me. I'm so fucked up."

"Slap on a zombie patch. You won't feel anything for hours."

"Asshole." She wiped the tears off her cheeks with the back of her hand. "And they do smell like dog brains, goddammit. What I wouldn't do for a shot of whiskey right now."

"Yeah. The first bar we see, let's get plastered."

"You're on." A soldier handed her a paper towel, and she wiped her face and blew her nose. "It was an honor to be your mother, and I blew it. I was trying so hard to protect you that I forgot to have fun." She wiped her hands with another towel and searched for dog brains on it. "I hope I wasn't too much of a terror."

Ada drew a long puff and let the plume out slowly, stretching it for as long as it would last.

"This is where you're supposed to say I wasn't a terror, and we let bygones be bygones," Victoria said.

"Well..."

"Oh, great."

"Would you believe me if I said you weren't?"

"No," Victoria said. "Okay, fine, but you were a terror too."

Ada flashed her most dazzling smile. "Thanks! I worked hard at it sometimes. Do you remember that time when you got in your old Bicep, and it roared down the driveway at fifty miles an hour?"

"*You* did that?"

"It took me hours to hack the car's computer!"

"It cost me five hundred bucks to get the thing reprogrammed, you little…" Victoria bit her lip, and before she could launch a verbal salvo, Krista appeared on the loading dock holding three mugs of coffee. She handed one to Victoria and Ada with a smile and then sat on a low wall by the door.

"Since when do you drink coffee?" Victoria asked.

"For a few days now," Ada said. "I've popped a few cherries lately."

Victoria gulped her coffee and let out a long breath. "Well, it's about time you did. Coffee is good for you."

"Don't I know it." Ada raised the cup to her nose and sniffed her mug, trying to conceal her smile.

Victoria looked over her shoulder at Krista. "That's the second time she's come out here. I think she wants you to go back down to the lab."

"I set everything up to be automatic. All you have to do is switch out the bottles. They can do without me a little bit longer."

"You need to breathe some fresh air anyway. The stink down there is pathological," Victoria said. "So you're actually making twelve bottles an hour? That's what they said at Vaca Valley."

"Nope, we're filling thirty-six bottles an hour now. That's over a hundred thousand doses a day."

"You're kidding! You know, the Chalys bioreactors just made seven liters an hour, and they were the size of a house."

"They didn't have little ole me to make it work better," Ada said.

"You know, I'm proud of you. Against incredible odds, you got the vaccine here and made this work," Victoria said. "I shouldn't be surprised, though. Heroism runs in your blood."

The breeze shifted to the east, bringing with it a faint whiff of burned plastic. "Thanks, but I'm not trying to be a hero. All I want is to erase my mistakes."

"Hey, everybody makes mistakes, baby."

Ada took a long gulp of coffee and sighed. "Not like me, they don't."

SONG'S WHALE

"Pilot, slow to ten knots and maintain this clearance," Bricker said. She leaned over the holographic table and caught Quinn looking at the model from the other side.

Ripley and Chief Bailey had constructed a three-dimensional model of the massive Vancouver-bound containership they'd just pulled alongside. The M/V *Guang Shenzhen* had a draft of just under ten meters, but as big as it was, the *Henry* couldn't hide entirely behind it. At mast depth, their keel was thirteen meters below the surface.

"It's three to five meters exposure at the most," Quinn said, pointing to where the *Henry's* lower hull was exposed. "Even if the *Astor* can get a clean ping off our hull, they might not distinguish us from this ship."

The sonar operator pointed at the hull. "Not only are we in its shadow, the wake from a hull this square will be huge. That'll refract the sonar rays. The refraction's so unpredictable that sonar operators ignore any bounces they get near a wake."

"It's a sharp, bubbly wake too," Jackson said. "I can barely hear through it."

Bricker stood and stretched the kinks from her back. "This should work."

"I hope so," Jackson said. "The Falklands doesn't turn my wheels, Captain."

"It'll work," Bricker said. "And you know why? Because we have the most advanced boat in the water, and it's run by the finest crew that ever sailed. We're better than the *Astor* by any measure, Mister Jackson, and we're about to drive that point home."

"Aye, Captain. I'm rooting for us too."

"The *Shenzhen's* beginning its turn into the eastbound traffic lane," Quinn said.

Bricker estimated that the *Astor* was ten thousand meters away in the center of the Strait of Juan de Fuca. To stay in the *Shenzhen's* shadow as the big ship turned, they'd have to increase their speed. "Pilot, all ahead flank, come to heading 91 with the *Shenzhen* and maintain a two-hundred-meter clearance to port. Ballast Control, up bubble two degrees, make your depth thirteen meters. Comm, flash general quarters."

She glanced at the clock: The sun would set in two hours, and then she'd be unable to spot any aerial patrols. When they reached mast depth, she raised the photonic mast and scanned the Washington coast, which was barely visible through a light fog. However, she spotted two Navy anti-submarine aircraft patrolling south of the Strait. "We'll be going in blind after this," she said. "We have a Pegasus and an old Orion orbiting up above, so we can't use the mast."

"The *Shenzhen* might see the mast wake anyway," Quinn said. "I'm confident that we can do this by the model, and I'm confident in the charts we're using. We can make it through the Strait without visuals."

"It'll be hell if we can't," Bricker said. "Tactical, report the status of our fish."

"Four Mark 58's set to five kiloton yields, Captain," the young woman said. "Awaiting targeting orders."

"Target Starboard Fish One for the *Astor's* location and await my order," Bricker said, sinking into her chair.

THE *ASTOR'S* SONAR HAD GROWN STRONGER and clearer over the past hour, and the sonar operator was getting concerned. "This sounds like readable sonar, Captain. I'm not sure we're getting enough reflection off the *Shenzhen's* wake. I recommend ascending."

Bricker glanced at the ship status monitor. "Any higher and we can wave to their crew."

The sonar man frowned and rubbed his hands. "All I can say is, unless their sonar operator's deaf, we could be showing."

"Their port receivers could still be deaf. Of course, that was years ago." Quinn rechecked the model, and the *Astor* was now only four thousand meters to their northeast. "We're completely on their port now."

"What if they fixed it, Skipper?" the sonar operator asked.

"It's too risky to ascend," Quinn said.

Bricker swiveled her chair and studied the chart. "They're pinging too clearly for my taste, and we'll only be a thousand meters away at the closest point. We can rise another three meters and not breach, but we'll make a surface swell over the sail. We can hide that in the *Shenzhen's* bow wake if we get close enough. Jackson, can you hear how close we'd need to be?"

"I'd guess we need ten meters clear from the hull, Captain."

Quinn rubbed a hand through his hair, and the sonar operator whistled and returned to his station. "That'll be a rough ride," Quinn said.

Bricker nodded and switched on the mast without raising it. A light green dome of water overhead showed on the monitor. "Pilot, two degrees port, maintain this speed. Ballast Control, up bubble two, come to mast depth, deploy the roll stabilizers. Jackson, call out when we're ten meters away." The deck rose, and the green water on the mast screen grew lighter.

When the boat slipped into the massive ship's bow wake, every monitor in the Control Room shook and threatened to fall from its mount. The *Astor's* insistent pinging still rang through the hull, but it was weaker and diffused.

"That's a good sound," Bricker said, holding the arms of her chair as the hull began to vibrate. "Sonar, what's our profile now?"

"Nearly none, I think."

"This bow wave is messy," Jackson said. "I think we're in a trail of bubbles. I don't hear any clear sounds now."

The pilot called out, "Captain, we're in variable-density water. My control response is sluggish like we're in an aerated plume. Propulsor Two's ingesting air. Turbine pressures are all over the chart."

"Good. Invisible is good," Bricker said.

"Invisible except to an aerial patrol," Quinn said. "They can see us at this depth. But who'd look for us ten meters from a containership?"

"Nobody," Bricker said.

SONG STOOD AT THE STARBOARD RAILING of the *Guang Shenzhen's* crew level, halfway up its narrow bridge and just above the containers that stretched for a quarter mile to the bow. This was his first sailing since graduation and his first time outside China.

He'd heard that Washington was filled with trees, and he wouldn't miss that wonder at any cost. His dusty village outside Shenmu only had two stunted red maples, which were fenced off in a park and coddled like baby pandas. He was curious to see one in the wild.

Song watched misty hills take shape a few thousand meters to the south. They were covered with tall cedars, packed shoulder to shoulder like commuters on a subway, just as his friends had said.

A sea bird wheeled in the sky and then dove into the water, and he leaned over the rail to see if it would come up with a fish. That was when he saw the whale.

He wasn't sure at first because his eyes were tired and the light was poor, but something massive and dark was swimming alongside the ship, a creature with big tail flukes like the whales he'd seen on TV.

He ran inside and dragged Mao from the seamen's dayroom. They squinted into the water, and Song pointed to the shape. Mao smiled and nodded. "It's a whale," he said. "They follow the ship sometimes, but I've never seen them come this close. That's a bold one there."

"What do we do?" Song asked.

"Nothing. It'll get bored in a few minutes. They never follow us for long. Once they eat all the fish that get zapped by the bow, they swim away."

"Fish get zapped by the bow?" Song asked.

"All the time. A fish-zapper in the bow stuns the fish so they float to the side. If we didn't do that, the bow would be covered with fish guts."

"I have never heard of such a device."

"It's a secret just the old hands know," Mao said. "The whales hang out for the free meal. It's like an all-you-can-eat buffet. When they're full, they go."

Another seaman ambled to the railing, a grizzled and rough character named Cheng that everybody avoided. "It's called water, princesses," he growled. "It's all over the place. What's so fuckin interesting?"

Song pointed to the dark shape. "There's a whale down there eating all the fish the fish-zapper stunned."

"Fish zapper?" He leaned over the side and whistled. "Well, look at the size of that sumbitch." He pulled a pistol from under his shirt and fired three rounds into the water. "Now fuck off, little fishie."

A door groaned on the navigation bridge one deck above them, and Yong, the first mate, leaned over the railing. "Did I hear gunshots?"

Cheng held up his pistol. "Just scarin away a whale, Chief."

"A whale? We're in American waters, fool! They have laws against shooting whales, and we have rules against bailing morons out of jail! Put that damn thing away!"

"Just a big whale, Chief," Cheng said. "Was worried it might damage the hull if it bumped us."

Yong ran into the navigation bridge and burst through the door to the crew deck seconds later. He leaned over the railing and peered into the water, and then he cuffed Cheng on the side of the head. "You're a real moron. You know what that is?"

"What?" Cheng said, just beginning to realize he was in trouble.

"That's a gray whale! It's a hundred-thousand-dollar fine for even looking at it!" He paced back and forth, looking over the railing. "Okay, maybe I can scare this thing off with sonar." He unclipped his radio and called the navigation bridge.

THE TURBULENCE FROM THE WAKE was hard on the *Henry*. Everything that was loose in the Control Room had fallen to the deck, and everything tight was coming loose. Quinn clutched the edge of the charting table, while Bricker gripped her chair with her one uninjured hand.

Three sharp clunks peppered the hull, and Bricker looked up. "What was that?"

"It sounded like it came from the missile hatches." Ripley scanned her screens. "Everything's nominal in the Mushroom Farm, though."

Song's Whale

Bricker checked every status monitor, but none showed any warnings. "Did the vibration shake something loose up in the sail? I don't see any system faults."

"Captain, I think someone shot at us," Jackson called from the Acoustics nest.

"What? What kind of moron would shoot at nuclear missiles?"

"Dunno. They sounded like high-velocity projectiles when they entered the water. They were going a lot slower when they hit us, so there was probably no damage to the hull, but that sounded like bullets."

"The *Shenzhen's* shooting at us?"

"Sounds like it."

"So somebody up there spotted the boat." Bricker staggered to the charting table; the *Astor* was two thousand meters astern, and the *Shenzhen's* shadow was still concealing them. "Pilot, down bubble five, make your depth thirty meters."

As she walked back to her seat, the boat was struck by a sonar ping so loud that it was beyond hearing. She clutched her hands to her ears, and even the pilot released his controls, while Jackson cried out and staggered out of his alcove. Quinn let go of the charting table, and the boat's rocking threw him to the deck.

He sat up and saw Bricker waving at him and pointing forward. Grasping the edge of the charting table, he pulled himself up and saw her pointing at the pilot, who was squeezing his palms to his head and letting the control yoke wobble from side to side. He staggered to the injured man and helped him to the deck, and then he strapped in and turned to Bricker, who was mouthing words he couldn't hear. However, her gestures were clear: Get us out of here.

He wrapped his fingers around the yoke and turned the thrust control wheel to flank speed. Ten seconds later, the bow of the *Henry* cut through the *Shenzhen's* wake and into calm waters.

THE FOUR SAILORS LEANED OVER THE RAILING and squinted into the water. "Still there," Cheng said.

"Maybe it's not done eating the fish that the fish-zapper stunned," Song said.

Yong clocked Mao on the side of the head. "You been telling those stories again, Mao? You like standing a double watch?"

Mao mumbled something, and Yong leaned over the rail again. "That doesn't look like a whale." His radio squawked and he raised it to his ear, and then he swore and looked over the stern, where the *Astor* was turning in their direction. "No, no, tell them we're not interfering with a military operation!" he yelled. "Tell them we're just trying to scare off a whale, that's all! Right, we have a huge gray whale off our starboard, and we were trying to shake it off...yes, it's still here!"

"Wow, that's one fast whale," Cheng murmured, pointing at the gray splotch. "Lookit that sumbitch. Going like its ass is on fire."

Yong looked over the rail and shouted into the radio. "Tell them it's going away now, and we didn't hurt it, okay? I'll be up there in a minute!"

BRICKER LEANED OVER THE CHARTING TABLE. The *Henry* was moving at twenty-four knots and leaving the *Shenzhen's* sonar shadow, while the *Astor* was turning east to follow. The *Astor's* sonar might pick up the *Henry*, but at this range it was unlikely. The aircraft, however, could be in range within minutes, and they'd be found and blown out of the water if they dropped sonobuoys. Because the sun was setting, aerial surveillance wouldn't be a concern soon, so the best tactic was to run for the shallows and get lost in the coastal acoustic clutter.

She tapped Quinn's shoulder and pointed to the chart on the screen in front of him. "Stay at thirty meters and hug the coastline. I'll leave the navigation up to you, but get us lost."

AS THE *HENRY* APPROACHED the coastal town of Dungeness, Harris and Caldwell were walking through a parking lot at Fort Worden, only twenty miles away in Port Townsend. The government was using the old coastal artillery base for offices, and the legislature had taken over its convention center.

Caldwell unlocked their car and opened the door, but Harris gazed down the long parade ground and over Puget Sound. He'd heard the drone of anti-submarine aircraft during his meeting with Wang and her staff, and he'd been tensed to hear an explosion ever since. But they were still searching the Strait two hours later, so Julie and the *Henry* hadn't been found yet.

Finally, he climbed in and they headed back to the base. "I wish I could do something," Harris said.

"For Julie?"

"And the *Henry*. All I can do is jawbone with the governor and her stooges." He scowled and watched the wipers bat drizzle from the windshield. "Give me a ship, and then I can do some good. If I survive this madness, I swear to God, I'm offering up my services as a commander to some third-world country. Even if they just give me a rowboat and a wooden sword, it's better than sitting around."

"No navy in the world is giving you a ship, Adam. You sank the only one you ever commanded. How long did you helm the *Vanderbilt* before you sent it to the bottom? Seven minutes?"

"Yeah, but I sank two raghead cruisers too." He laid his head back against the headrest and let out a long sigh. "Those were the days, Zack. I saw a problem, I could set course for it and blast it away. Now here I am, twiddling my thumbs and waiting for somebody else to act."

"Oh, hell, you're getting maudlin again."

He checked the time on his tablet for the tenth time that hour. "If Julie was right, she's due in three hours. If the *Henry* makes it, that is. At least the Explosives Handling Wharf is covered, so it'll conceal the boat from eyes in the sky. Are all the missile techs mobilized?"

Caldwell nodded. "All we need is the boat now."

Harris looked through the window. "There's nothing more we can do."

"Did you work out the timing with Wang?"

Harris nodded. "We'll seize the base right after the *Hale* and the *Allen* are in the Strait. Wang will announce the secession once I confirm it's done. Until then, nobody can know the *Henry*'s here. After that, it doesn't matter. Everything will be different."

"But a lot can happen in two days."

"I'm not worried about the next two days right now. I'm worried about the next two hours. Can you drive a little faster?"

Caldwell tapped the car's satnav monitor. "Don't worry. We'll be back in plenty of time. The satnav shows us on-base at 2100 hours."

THE *PATRICK HENRY* PASSED PORT TOWNSEND and turned southeast to follow the coastline. Quinn was keeping the boat in thirty-meter-deep water to befuddle their pursuers, which was working so far. In the past hour, four sonobuoys had been dropped, but no attack had followed.

His stomach was so tight that he wondered if he'd be able to stand up without it snapping. He had good reason to be tense – he was piloting a submarine at twenty-four knots with only five meters under his keel, or so he thought, because he couldn't use the fathometer or the depth sensors. All he could do was hope the charts were accurate.

Bricker was even tenser than he was. She watched the holographic chart change as Quinn moved along the coast and also kept an eye on the *Astor*, which was now pinging behind them at Dungeness. What made her tension unbearable was that they'd soon enter the Puget Sound Narrows, where the water was clear and shallow from shore to shore. For almost fifteen minutes, they wouldn't be able to hide from airdropped sonobuoys. Despite the hull's sonar-absorbent coating, they'd show up if one pinged them from a range of less than a thousand meters.

If they avoided them, she estimated that they'd be back in Bangor by 2130 hours, but if not…she bit her cheek and focused on the chart again.

CALDWELL AND HARRIS DROVE THROUGH A FOREST along the coast, sparing Harris the sight of open water. To distract his mind from his worries, he focused on preparing for the base seizure.

"Make sure Shelby and his men are ready to go Friday night," he said. "I'll call the Hotbox alert around 0500 hours on Saturday, which should give us plenty of time before the announcement. The big problem is keeping people from talking in the Undersea Operations area until then – if Julie gets in, we'll have a rogue boat sitting at the dock. Word can't get out."

"I was thinking we should close the area, but we need a believable pretext for that. Otherwise, we'll just raise suspicions."

"We have to close the Undersea Operations compound at Defcon One," Harris said. "We'll do that as soon as we get back. If anyone asks, tell them we're running a Defcon One drill. Nobody will guess what we're really doing."

"No, of course not. Defcon One means nuclear war is imminent. Everybody will be looking for the deepest hole they can find."

"Right." He caught a glimpse of the Sound through the trees. "Can you drive any faster?"

QUINN GUIDED THE *PATRICK HENRY* through the shoals of Admiralty Inlet and into Puget Sound's northern narrows. The water was shallower, but he still kept the boat's speed at twenty-four knots.

Bricker watched the *Astor's* course as it turned west, apparently having concluded that the *Henry* wasn't hiding in the Strait. With an inward sigh of relief, she calculated the distance to home: They'd arrive at Bangor in just under an hour, but more importantly, they'd be at the Hood Canal Bridge in forty-five minutes. Submariners considered the bridge as the gateway to Bangor, and the canal beyond was the warm, sweet water of home. She was thinking about how to signal for a bridge opening when Jackson called out. "Captain? I'm getting something weird here."

Bricker walked into Jackson's sonar niche, and he handed her a pair of earphones. "The *Astor* is still pinging like a video game over at Dungeness, but listen to this." He played back a recording he'd made a few minutes ago. She heard the primary ping of the sonar, and then another a fraction of a second later.

"That sounded like a reflection off a hull somewhere behind us," she said. "Can you identify the vessel?"

"That's the thing – I've been listening for any sounds in the area one to two thousand meters astern, but there aren't any. That transient sonar reflection says there's a big ship there, but if there is, it's totally silent."

Bricker's gray eyes bored into him. "Could this be another ghost ship like the *Rockefeller?*"

"It might be."

"That's why the *Astor* withdrew. She was clearing the area for another vessel." She leaned against the wall and crossed her arms. "We can only fight it with conventional weapons here, and that's a fight we'd lose. One of those ghost ships can pound us to pieces."

"Aye, the *Rockefeller* was a nasty piece of work."

"But they haven't found us yet, so whatever mysterious technology they're using isn't that effective." She strode to the charting table and called up the Sound's bathymetry, and she studied it for a few moments with her lips puckered. After checking the local tide charts, she walked to the helm and leaned over Quinn's shoulder. "We might have another one of those ghost ships on our tail, Ennis," she said quietly.

"I overheard. I hope you're not asking me for any options. I don't have any good ideas."

"But I have a bad idea that might work. How confident a pilot are you?"

"Not very, Julie. This isn't what I –"

"Forget that. You'll just have to master this fast." She tapped the screen in front of Quinn and called up the chart, and then she overlaid the course she'd set.

Quinn stifled a gasp. Instead of sailing in an arc and following the deep-water channel into Hood Canal, she'd charted a course that sent the *Henry* directly for the bridge – through shallow water and between two small islands connected by a rock outcropping.

"Trust me, Ennis. The charts are wrong. Adam and I dive out at Kuva Island all the time, and those rocks aren't as high as the charts say. He thinks an earthquake knocked them over. On top of that, it's high tide, and I think we can sail right over them if we surface. If we can get through, this stealth ship won't be able to see us before we're at the bridge, and we'll be dockside earlier too. And I want to get out of this boat in the worst way. Can you do it?"

"Julie, you should call Martinez to take the helm. This is too difficult –"

"Wrong answer, Ennis. You're driving the boat right now, and I can't switch you out. Try again."

He stared at the screen for a long moment, puffing out his cheeks, and then he turned to the Ballast Control Officer. "Prepare to surface." He pulled back on the yoke and turned the thrust wheel as far as it would go.

A MINUTE AFTER Caldwell and Harris rolled onto the Hood Canal Bridge, red lights began flashing on the road ahead. Caldwell stopped the car at the gate.

"Always happens," Harris said. "When I'm in a hurry, all the delays pop up. On top of creeping all the way down from Fort Worden, now we get a bridge opening."

"I made it here as fast as I could. That logging truck was going really slow."

"You could have passed the damn thing."

"It was too dangerous. It was rainy and foggy."

"It never rains in McMurdo, Captain."

"Are you threatening me again?"

"Naw, just commenting on the Antarctic weather. Why are you so paranoid?"

"Oh, bullshit. You're doing that annoying anxiety transference thing again. You're nervous, so you need to make me nervous too."

"Hey, shit rolls downhill, Zack. When we get back to the base, go find a lieutenant and make his day miserable. You'll feel better."

"I won't. I'm better than that."

"Good for you. So what's up with this bridge crew?" Harris pointed to three men running out of the control tower and across the roadway. "I've never seen these guys in a hurry to do anything."

"Maybe they were asleep and forgot the bridge opening schedule." Caldwell flicked the windshield wipers to get a better view of the bridge, and he peered into the swirling fog banks tinged with gold by the bridge's streetlights. "I love seeing this thing open. It's a real engineering marvel."

Harris watched as a worker on the other side of the bridge waved madly for the oncoming traffic to stop. "The human element isn't a marvel. They don't have their act together today."

The roadway on the other side rose, and the floating section of the bridge slid beneath it. "It's unusual, opening it this time of night," Caldwell said.

"Yeah, this is the sleepiest time of day for these folks. Nobody comes through in the dark."

"Well, nobody except for –" They looked at each other and swore, and they yanked their doors open and sprinted for the bridge's edge. As they ducked under the gate, they peered into the dark waters to the north.

The fog obscured their view, but they heard the soft lapping of seawater somewhere inside it – and then a black submarine sailed out of the mist at flank speed, its bow casting seaspray to each side. As its sail came into the bridge's lights, Harris saw the gray number 807. He whooped and pumped his fist in the air.

"Go, baby, go!" Caldwell let loose a cowboy yell, whipped off his hat, and threw it into the air as Harris waved the boat through the bridge opening.

"Oh, yeah! C'mon, you can do it!" Harris yelled, striding to the edge of the bridge. "Go, you beautiful bitch, go!"

The submarine cruised through at flank speed, silent except for a soft whistle from the four open missile hatches. The bow plowed through a wave when it entered the canal, throwing off a spray of seawater that drenched the bridge as well as the two officers hooting and dancing at the deck's edge.

Dripping water, Caldwell pulled out his tablet and dialed a secure line at Bangor, while Adam wiped off the water and watched the *Patrick Henry's* stern sink into the fog, a broad grin on his face.

TRUTH

Victoria examined the Recombin-B particles on the protein modeler's screen. The virophage was nearly a duplicate of the original, but its protein shell was different because it had been replicated *in vivo*. That troubled her.

What they were planning to inject into half the population of Nevada was at best an untested mutation of Recombin sprinkled with dead Neovirus, and at worst a cure that could do more harm than the disease. The vaccination program was risky and unethical, but then most of Ada's best ideas were.

Ada was still monitoring the soldiers she'd injected with the new vaccine, and her notes showed they hadn't suffered any adverse effects – yet. But she believed that the benefit from Recombin-B was far greater than the risk, and Victoria agreed. People deserved to choose whether to risk dying from an infection or risk suffering complications from an untested vaccine. To deny them that choice put her on the same level as Simon Rance.

However, Ada hadn't spent much time on Recombin-B, according to the protein modeler's history screen. Her notes showed that she'd thrown most of her effort into studying a strain called Recombin-C, although she couldn't understand Ada's interest in the variant.

Reading her lab journal yielded no clues; the child was even more disorganized than her father, and her notes were utterly undecipherable. Some looked like routine lab observations, but they were interrupted by pages of Big Math. After trying to read the hieroglyphs upside down and sideways, she gave up and pressed her thumbs into her temples until they ached, the only way to banish the deep-rooted headache she always suffered when pondering the workings of her daughter's mind.

She returned to her Recombin-B analysis and tried to stretch the fatigue from her muscles. As soon as Krista and Ada awoke, she'd hop into bed in Room A to get some rest. It was already ten in the morning, and she expected them soon.

She couldn't perform one more minute of work without a cup of coffee, though. As if on cue, the lab door squeaked and Krista walked through carrying two mugs of steaming brew. Victoria thanked her and smiled. "It's uncanny. How do you always know?"

Krista shrugged. "It's magic. I sense a disturbance in the coffee force or something." She smiled and walked to the lab door.

Victoria slid off her stool. "Are you going upstairs? Can I come with you? There's something I need to talk to you about."

"Sure, as long as you don't gripe about my smoking."

Victoria hurried to catch up with her. "I don't gripe about that as much as Ada says. You might give me a chance instead of judging me through the eyes of a fifteen-year-old."

"Sixteen, going on seventeen." Krista opened the stairway door and ushered Victoria through.

"Right, right. I guess I just validated Ada's accusation that I'm an inattentive mother."

They climbed the steps and walked down the long corridor to the loading dock. "You've got the wrong idea about her," Krista said. "We spent the last six weeks together, day and night, and mostly she talked about how much she missed you. She needs you in her life, and she wants you in it. I think that's most important to her."

"Maybe you can give me some advice on that," Victoria said. "Last night, I realized that if I'm ever going to have an adult relationship with my daughter, I need to change."

"Would you listen to advice if I gave it? Could you really change?"

Victoria grabbed her arm and spun her around. "I killed a dozen men to get here, Warner. Don't doubt my determination. If I want it done, it *will* be done, no matter what gets in my way."

Krista peeled Victoria's fingers off her arm. "Wow, you almost made me tinkle. Here's some advice – put Scary Tori back in her cage, okay?"

"That's not as easy as you think."

"Give it a try. Everybody considers homicidal maniacs to be off-putting."

Victoria's eyes narrowed, and then she turned on her heel and started walking to the door. "That's closer to the truth than you think. It's premature to assume I can have a relationship with anyone not wearing an orange onesie. Let's talk."

Krista held open the door, and the guards outside retreated to a ten-foot distance. They walked to the dock's edge and sat in the hazy sunlight. "So whatcha want to talk about?" she asked.

"The virus. When I was in Anacostia, I gathered information that's never been made public. It proves that Neovirus was a weapon of planned genocide."

"Seriously? You can prove it?"

"I have a deathbed confession." She pulled a pen-shaped digital recorder out of her pocket. "This explains the who, why, and how of the Neovirus plot. I want you to listen to it, and then I want you to publicize it." She handed the recorder to Krista and sipped her coffee. "But you'll hear Scary Tori at her worst. Once you publish that, nothing will ever be the same for me. I'll become a pariah, and my child will disown me." She breathed a long sigh and seemed a few inches shorter when it was done. "But I have to do the right thing even if I risk trashing my relationship with Ada. Sometimes you need to sacrifice what you love for the greater good, and this is something I can't avoid. I wish I could."

"I know how *that* works." Krista turned the recorder over in her hand. "You killed this scumbag?"

Victoria nodded and looked at the floor.

"And you think that'll shock Ada so much that she'll throw you out of her life?"

"She's too young to understand how people can be pushed beyond the edge of reason. That's an ugly side of humanity I'd rather she never sees."

Krista snorted a laugh and covered her mouth.

"What?" Victoria asked. "Did I say something funny?"

"Sorry, sorry. I was…I was thinking of something else."

"Well, could you focus for a few minutes?"

"Sure. Let's listen to this." Krista clicked the recorder on and listened to the confession of Simon Rance, her color rising with every minute that passed. When it ended, she slipped the recorder into her pocket and lit a cigarette. "I'm glad you snuffed that sonofabitch," she said after a few furious puffs. "If anybody deserved it, he did. So these Arkie Aluminati made it happen, not Cheyn?"

"The Elders, yes. From what I can gather, it was Cheyn's idea, but the Elders executed it."

"I wouldn't have thought the Arkies could do something like this." Krista glared at the parking lot, one hand balled into a fist and swearing under her breath. When she finished her cigarette, she stubbed it out and lit another.

"You see why I had to kill him?" Victoria asked.

"I'm hoping it was agonizing and drawn out." Krista scowled and muttered unintelligibly between puffs. "Okay, I can't talk about this. I can only get this off my chest if I write. But this makes sense of a lot because the people Rance mentioned were in my videos. I'll put this up on *Midnight Sun* tonight and make sure the whole world hears this."

Victoria nodded and gazed into the distance. "It's the right thing to do."

"It certainly is," Krista said. "And if you think offing this douchebag will make Ada walk away, forget it. In fact, it should make you closer."

Victoria tried to read Krista's face but finally gave in. "Okay, explain why."

"That's something you've got to discuss with her, but I'll tell you this – you two oughta have the tightest relationship in the feckin universe. If you both relax and stop trying so hard, it should come naturally."

"I hope you're right," Victoria said. "What Ada and I need to do is forget the past. Maybe she'll go to Mexico with me, and we can make a fresh start."

"Why would you want to go there?"

"That recording is also my murder confession. I'll need to disappear once you make that public, and I can do that in Mexico. I sold a yacht I didn't own in Tampico, so I have enough pesos to stay anonymous."

"Don't bother. I'm a good friend of the governor. I'll just ask him to waive extradition for you."

"He'll do that?"

"Sure. He did it for me and Ada, so I don't see why he wouldn't for you," Krista said. "After he hears this recording, hell, he might even put up a statue of you. He despises Gabriel Cheyn. Don't worry, I'll put the fix in with him."

"Thanks. So why would Ada need an extradition waiver?"

Krista downed the rest of her coffee. "I can't tell you that. She made me pinky swear not to."

Victoria looked up quickly. "She touched your hand? She willingly touched you and didn't freak out?"

"She does it constantly." Krista noticed her cocked eyebrow. "What?"

"She never touches anybody. Listen, there's something about Ada that you need to know. Keep this between you and me, okay?"

Krista nodded. "This sounds serious."

"It's why Ada is the way she is. She was born with cross-connections in her brain that nobody's ever had, and that's one reason why she can work incredible magic with math. Where you and I just see a page of numbers, Ada sees colors and textures and composition like a painting. She processes Big Math the way we look at a picture."

"She once told me that an algorithm was shiny yellow like melting butter."

"Mmm, yeah. But the downside of this gift is that she can't process touch, especially on her hands. Letting someone touch her is like dropping all her defenses. It makes her profoundly anxious and sometimes even triggers panic attacks. Even with me, she gets tense whenever I get within arm's reach. I keep my distance now."

"Well, I guess she trusts me more than…" Krista looked down at her hands. "Sorry."

"It's okay. I'm used to the idea that I gave birth to my mortal enemy." Victoria climbed to her feet, reaching down to offer Krista a helping hand. "I need to think about this new development. In the meantime, I'll honor your pinky swear. I'll just find out what's going on another way."

KRISTA FOUND A QUIET SPOT in the shrubs and composed a post. She couldn't find a satellite signal to upload it, so she jumped into a

Humvee delivering vaccine to Berkeley, reworking it the entire way and frustrated that she couldn't convey all she felt. In the end, she decided that Simon Rance expressed the horror and inhumanity more convincingly than she could, and she uploaded the package to *Midnight Sun*.

⟨─⊙─⊙─⊙─⟩

The Rake
News Post of October 15, 2043

TRUTH
Here's the one eternal truth: Only our delusions keep us sane. Hold them dear, hold them holy

As a child, my mother taught me that a whole and fulfilled life rested upon three foundations: Compassion, Love, and Truth. I believed she was right because she lived her life by these principles and found wholeness and fulfillment, at least for a too-brief time.

Compassion and Love were no challenge to find, but Truth was elusive. I was tempted to seek it too, as our brightest minds have over the millennia, but I was too self-absorbed and lazy to embark on the quest.

Then Truth found me. It revealed its nature, and it was the last thing I wanted to find: Truth is the monster we see out of the corner of our eye. It's the monster that hides when we look for it, the monster we pretend isn't there for the sake of our hopes and our sanity.

In our animal brains, we all know that if we were to see Truth in its unalloyed ugliness, we'd realize that we're no better than a pack of feral dogs. But I suppressed the instinct to turn away, and what I saw makes me prefer the company of canines: Humans will blithely slaughter one another for the flimsiest of reasons, and in the face of power and ideology, our lives are cheaper than a dog's. We'll even unleash weapons that could kill us all and hope they only kill our enemies. On the depressingly long list of things I wish I could unlearn, that's at the very top.

Truth: Simon Rance, CEO of Chalys Pharmaceuticals, was a key member of a conspiracy to murder 75 million Americans. Before he was executed by an Activist operative on September 26 – on my order, I'm proud to say – he confessed to this crime and felt no remorse even as he breathed his life away. Quite the opposite: He was defiant and convinced he was curing our world by killing the people it no longer needed. A recording of his confession can be heard on the sidebar, but be warned – even the sainted will throw away their halos and reach for a pitchfork after they hear it.

Truth: Simon Rance was also a member of a powerful Archangelist cult, the Elders of the Second Creation. These Elders conspired with Gabriel Cheyn to unleash an Army virus called Ellesmere A4 on America to effect a plan called 'Economic Selection' – the systematic murder of the unemployed, the ex-workers, and the obsoleted that weigh on the government and the economy.

Why did the Elders go along with Cheyn's madness? The answer is frighteningly simple – they're as insane as he is. They also wanted a high body count because there are too many Americans, which simply wouldn't work for their precious Second Eden. Because their goals meshed with Cheyn's, albeit for different reasons, they took his mad plan and made it a reality.

Truth: They thought this gibbering lunacy was noble, *and they expected gratitude*.

It's this last bit that freezes my soul. It's not mere madness or megalomania like the first two, which I can understand; no, to expect *gratitude* for slaughtering our own is a profoundly alien presumption that can only bubble up from the sumps of the most damaged minds. Healthy human minds can't comprehend such a thing: It is *not* right and it will *never be* right to slaughter our own.

Rance thought we'd raise statues to revere their memory. I'd love to erect a statue of him and these other Elders so I could spit on the damned thing every morning and resolve that such inhumanity will never happen again.

The Activity is moving east to topple Cheyn and his criminal government, but we can't do everything. You must find these anti-human Elders and bring them to justice. Expose these beasts to the world; hunt the Second Creation mercilessly until they can run no more. Then turn them over to an Activist, and we'll learn the identities of everyone involved in this atrocity. And when we're done, we'll show them justice.

Because they yearned for a better world, one without you or me in it, let's build a world without them in it. But instead of killing them, we should spare their lives and exile these monsters – to a distant moon of a lonely planet in a galaxy only the strongest telescopes can find.

And we'll send one tiny virus along to remind them of us.

-KLW

Later that evening, Victoria and Ada sat in the lab and waited for the soldiers to bring in dinner. Ada leaned her elbows on the table, propped her chin in her hands, and watched Micah log in a new bottle of Recombin-B.

"He seems like a nice boy," Victoria said. "But don't you think he's a little...sub-prime?"

"Like you're so prime right now," Ada snorted. "You have no job, your clothes are stained, and you smell like cheese."

Victoria rubbed a finger behind her ear and sniffed it. "Well, I'm not showering in radioactive water," she said, and she reached into a cabinet and pulled out a bottle of rubbing alcohol. "So he's really Mark's brother?" she asked, wiping her face with an alcohol-soaked paper towel. "They don't look at all alike."

"They're half-brothers, and they're different in nearly every way, thank god."

Victoria started tearing the towel into strips. "Are you two dating?"

"Yeah, right. We saw a movie in downtown Sacramento last night."

"Don't take that tone with me, young lady. I asked a civil question, and you'll give me a civil reply."

"None of your business, Mom."

"I think it is," Victoria said. "I see the way you two ogle each other, and this morning he groped you –"

"He didn't grope me!"

"He squeezed your rear end when you walked by!"

"That wasn't a grope." She sighed and smiled. "That was a fondle."

"What's the difference?"

"I *like* him to fondle me."

Victoria had turned the paper towel into a pile of shreds, and she reached for another. "Boys can be impulsive and irresponsible. It's the girl's job to slow them down before things go too far, and I think you're encouraging him –"

"Mom, shut it, okay? I'm not a baby anymore."

"I'm just concerned. You're too fast about everything in your life, and you should take it slow with this."

Ada nodded but didn't answer. They sat in awkward silence, watching Victoria's pile of paper grow taller, until the subject of boys was dead and safely beyond resurrection.

"I wanted to thank you for making my bed," Victoria said. "That was considerate of you."

"Well, I'm trying to be responsible," Ada said. "It's a grown-up thing."

"But why's the other bed so messy? The sheets are all twisted, and the blankets are bunched up."

"Umm…Krista gets nightmares. Tosses and turns a lot, that sorta thing."

"Huh. She has some intense nightmares."

A private walked in with two steaming bags of food and set them down in front of them. Ada flashed him a big smile, and he saluted and walked to the other end of the table. Victoria opened her bag and sniffed. "I think this is chicken."

"I can't believe they eat this stuff," Ada said. "I guess they feed soldiers this crap to keep them mean."

"MRE's aren't bad. It's easy to get used to them." She reached into the bag with a plastic fork and pulled out a lump of desiccated chicken. "Don't look at it closely and you'll be fine. It's actually nutritious."

Ada mumbled and opened the bag. She was hungry because working for six hours with a high fever burned calories fast. However, the food inside the bag was as appetizing as boiled rubber.

"It's a good operation you've set up here. It goes like clockwork," Victoria said. "Yesterday, you said something that bothered me, though, that you were doing this to erase your mistakes. What did you mean by that?"

Ada stabbed at something inside the bag. "This is why the dog pack hangs around outside, Mom. They want their food back." She pulled out a gray cube of organic matter with her fork and examined it. "No, I take it back. It *was* their food once."

"I told you not to look."

She pinched her nose, closed her eyes, and tossed the cube into her mouth.

"I also notice that you're not answering my questions, which your friend Krista also has an annoying habit of doing. A lot must have happened that you two don't want to talk about. It's like you made some sort of pact to keep me clueless."

"Like you've told me the whole truth too."

"There are some things you don't need to know."

"Right back atcha, Mom."

"I'm your mother, so I have a need to know."

Ada made a face and rolled her eyes. "We've been over this already. Some of what we did was personal and private, and I don't want to talk about that. Please respect my boundaries, okay? That's what friends do."

Victoria bit back her reply and poked into the bag, and they ate in silence, watching the soldiers bustle at the other end of the lab.

"You said you were proud of me yesterday," Ada said. "Did you mean that?"

"Of course I did, baby."

"Even for Baby Bang Bang?"

"I know I was rough on you back then, and I'm sorry, but I just couldn't tell you because of all the problems we were having." Victoria laid her fork on the table, wearing a small smile as she looked back into her memories. "I was insanely proud of you, actually. I remember in the bunker at Punatayu Atoll, all the chief scientists lined up at the window waiting for the first W104 to detonate. All these old guys, and in the middle, a little girl on a milk crate standing on her tiptoes to see. *My* little girl, part of the most advanced physics team assembled since the Manhattan Project. Proud doesn't even begin to describe it." She fished around in the bag and pulled another piece of chicken from inside. "But I was even prouder about Big Sister. That could change the world, Ada."

"Sure. String fission could power a peaceful world with limitless energy, or it could blow a hole in the planet about the size of, oh, the freakin planet. With what happened to Baby Bang Bang, we can't trust anybody with it, Mom."

"I know," Victoria said. "I didn't have time to go back to the house and get it. We need to get it out before somebody digs up the basement floor."

"I left the hot water running when I left, that day we went to St. Elizabeth's, so the water heater shouldn't explode for a while. Still, if Los Alamos digs around and finds the Big Sister core…"

"But they haven't, and we'll get it out of there before they do. And then, someday, you'll find a way to control it and build a better world for all of us."

"Yeah, if I don't destroy it first."

"What do you mean?"

"I guess you haven't heard the news." She looked down at the counter and spoke so softly that Victoria needed to lean toward her to hear. "The warhead that exploded over Sacramento was a W104."

Victoria gasped, and across the room, soldiers turned to look at the pair. "Are you sure?"

Ada nodded. "It detonated with a double flash. Remember at Punatayu?"

"I remember the blue and yellow flashes, yes." Victoria gazed at a far wall, her lips pressed tight together. "Goddamn it. That's a Navy warhead. Who launched it at Sacramento?"

"Krista thinks Cheyn ordered the attack to stop the secession vote."

Victoria picked up her plastic knife with trembling fingers and sawed at the chicken, grumbling under her breath. Within seconds, she'd torn it to shreds. "Somebody oughta string that bastard up by the nuts."

"Well, don't send the hangman my way, Mom. I'm responsible too."

The knife snapped in her hand, and she threw the pieces across the room. "Bullshit! You didn't make it, launch it, or trigger it! Stop taking the blame for things you didn't do!" She jumped to her feet, and her stool rolled into a wall cabinet and shattered a glass door. "There are enough fucking stupid people in the world! Don't join the crowd!" She stomped out of the lab and strode down the corridor, her eyes glowering and her face tight.

"What was that all about?" a soldier asked when she was out of sight.

"I don't know. I've never seen her lose it before." Ada ran after her. When she reached the top of the stairs, Victoria was already walking through the loading dock doors. She sprinted to the hazy parking lot and caught a glimpse of her striding down the street. "Mom! Wait up!" She ran across the parking lot and caught up with Victoria near the barn. "What's going on?"

"I'm angry, that's what's going on!"

Ada started to reply but stopped when she heard bushes rustle next to the barn. A white Pit Bull stalked from underneath a shrub, its ears flat against its head and its teeth bared.

She backed away, but Victoria stepped forward, kicking off her shoes and lowering into a fighting crouch. "Mama wanna rumble," she growled, flexing her fingers and taking another step.

The dog padded back, its eyes growing wide. Then it turned and lit out through the bushes, and Victoria ran after it.

Ada began to follow her, but a firm hand clamped around her arm and pulled her back. "Easy, girl," Corporal Migs said. "Where'd your mom go?"

"Into the bushes! She just chased a dog into the bushes!"

"She outta her mind? There's a dog pack 'round here!"

"I think she stripped a gear or something," Ada said. "I've never seen her like this."

"Well, I got orders to keep you safe. You're stayin with me." He motioned to another soldier. "Jones, go find Dr. Victoria before she becomes dog food."

Jones unslung his rifle, but then Victoria walked out of the shrubs brushing white fur from her suit jacket. "Coward," she grumbled. "It's a world of cowards. Nobody's got the balls to fight anymore."

"You okay, ma'am?" Migs asked.

"I'm fine!" she snapped.

"You need to calm down, ma'am."

"Don't tell me what I need!" She pulled her shoes off the grass and slipped them on. "What I need is a drink, so unless you've got a fifth on you, soldier, shut it."

"Don't have a fifth, but I got this." Migs pulled a dented metal flask from under his body armor and handed it to her.

She took a huge swig and then screwed up her face. "Gah! What *is* this swill? Did you get it off the clearance rack at Mal-Mart?"

"It's cheaper that way," Migs said. "Lady, if it ain't good enough for you, don't drink it."

She chugged another mouthful, handed the flask to Ada, and then she held her hand out to Migs. "It'll do. Now let me have your tablet. I'll straighten this out." Migs handed it over, and she punched numbers on the screen.

"Who are you calling?" Ada asked, raising the flask to her lips.

She held the tablet to her ear and listened for a ring. "Your father."

Ada inhaled dusty air and cheap rotgut and doubled over coughing. "Fah?" she wheezed, falling to her knees.

"If that was a W104, it was launched from one of his subs. He'll know what happened. If he hasn't shot the person responsible yet, I'll be hanging his nuts from my rearview mirror." She scowled at the tablet. "The call won't go through."

"The phones don't work here," Migs said.

"Figures." She thrust the tablet into his hands. "Nothing works in this damn world anymore." She spun on her foot and walked away.

Ada sat on her knees with her eyes closed, rubbing away the fire in her chest, as she recalled the names she'd found on the Medal of Honor list. Only one was now in the Submarine Service, and her eyes flew open when his name came to her. She looked for her mother, but she was already striding past the parking garage.

"Wait!" she called, but Victoria continued walking as if she hadn't heard. Ada ran after her. "Slow down! We need to talk!"

Victoria whirled around. "I am *not* in the mood to chat!"

"Then get in the mood! You owe me, Mom!" Ada ran up to her, rubbing her chest and panting. "I'm getting an answer this time!"

"I'll give you an answer – I have a violent temper and I'm trying to protect you from that and there's your answer! Now leave me alone!"

"No, I can handle a temper! It's the freakin Dobermom I can't stand!"

"Great." Victoria snatched the flask from Ada's fingers and took a long pull. "You could have told me a few years ago."

Ada grabbed the bottle back. "I woulda told you earlier if you weren't pounding me down every chance you got!"

They glared at each other until the soldiers ran up to them. "Is everything okay here?" Migs asked.

"They will be once Mommy here starts giving me answers," Ada said, her eyes locked on Victoria's face. "Now tell me the truth. Is Adam Harris my father?"

Victoria scowled and looked away, and then she walked to a bench and swept the dust off it. She sat, turned her eyes to Ada, and nodded once.

"Finally! About freakin time!" Ada sat next to her. "Tell me what happened. What went wrong?"

"What went wrong? *I* went wrong! *I* destroyed the marriage, okay? You want me to go over every fucking detail?"

"Just give me the outline. You owe me that much, at least."

She combed back her hair with her fingers, drawing a deep breath. "I went through a brutal postpartum depression right after you were born that lasted till you were sixteen months old. I kept sinking deeper, and right at the bottom, the Navy took Adam away because they needed a hero. While he was off doing publicity tours, I was alone, depressed and alone in a big house with a hyperactive toddler who kept taking the vacuum cleaner apart to find the black hole inside. I was so desperate and emotionally starved that I did something stupid." She sipped from the flask and wiped her lips. "I did the one thing guaranteed to wreck a marriage."

Ada slapped a palm over her gaping mouth. "You didn't?"

"With his best friend, Ryan Beckmann." She played with the flask cap as a small smile flitted across her lips, and then she shrugged and looked up. "And I don't regret it because I never would've gotten out of that damned NTC dungeon if it wasn't for that affair. I'd be dead and rotting now."

"I thought it was easy-peasy. You slipped out when they weren't looking."

"They weren't looking because Ryan blanked out all the surveillance cameras. Anyway, Adam found out about our affair, and I blamed him for forcing me into Ryan's arms. We fought it out, and you've seen what kind of temper I have. How well do you think that went?"

"Not well at all?"

"It was a disaster. But I was in pain, and I desperately needed to change the game. Adam was too busy being a hero to care for his wife's needs. *And* his daughter's. The All-American Boy put the damned Navy ahead of you and me." She took a drink and handed the flask to Ada. "Okay, I was stupid, and I shouldn't have done what I did, and I'll take the blame I deserve, but I wasn't the only one killing that marriage, kiddo. If he hadn't betrayed us, this wouldn't have happened."

Ada walked over to Migs, who was watching the street, and returned holding a pack of cigarettes. She lit one, but instead of calming her, her fingers shook more with every puff.

"Listen, I know the truth is hard to take, but try to calm down, honey."

"Right, I'm supposed to calm down. I find out my father dumped me for his freakin job, and I'm supposed to go all Buddha?" She took a long pull from the flask. "He never loved me."

"Oh, no, don't say that. You were his little angel."

"Yeah? If he loves me so much, where is he now? He never calls or writes, never sends me a card on my birthday. The bastard doesn't give a shit about me, Mom." She tossed the cigarette into the street. "That's actually why you never told me his name, isn't it – cuz you didn't want me to find out how little he cared? All right, fine. Just lemme swallow that pill and get over it, okay?"

"Honey, he did –"

"Don't lie! If he loved me, he wouldn't have vanished from my life!"

"It wasn't his fault! I kept him away from you!"

Ada flinched as if she'd been slapped. "Hunh?"

"I kept him away. I did it, not him."

Ada shook another cigarette from the pack, but it snapped in her trembling fingers. "Why? Why would you do that to me?"

"I thought I could bring him back if I demanded full custody. I knew he wouldn't want to give you up and…I thought I could make things right again, and I never thought he hated me so much that he'd accept –"

"Omigod, you bargained away my father?" She jumped to her feet and stomped down the walk, pulling at the roots of her hair. "You blackwalled my freakin life? Are you freakin kidding me?"

"You can't understand how hard it was! I was in pain and I was depressed and I wasn't exactly thinking clearly! And how could I know that the goddamn Navy would tell him to accept the divorce terms to keep their precious hero out of court? How could I know they'd do something so ugly, and he'd be so weak and ball-less and give up his family because the *fucking Navy told him to?* How could I know that?"

"Maybe you shoulda thought about the consequences first, Mom!"

"Oh, you're a fine one to talk!"

"I've never blown it that bad –"

"Yeah? Then how do you explain Sacramento?"

Ada stepped back, her balled fist in her mouth, and then she collapsed to her knees into the dry grass. Victoria rubbed her face and swore to herself as Ada began to cry. "Okay, listen, please, I'm sorry."

"I hate you," Ada said between sobs. "I totally hate you."

Victoria knelt beside her and laid her hands on her knees. "That was cheap and mean and dirty. I admit it, okay? Sometimes I'm not a nice person. I'm so sorry I hurt you." She reached for Ada's shoulder, but at the first touch, Ada jumped up like she'd been shocked by a thousand volts.

"Don't touch me! I don't want whatever disease you have!" she shrieked. "I don't want to turn into a, a…"

"What? Bitch? Harridan? Shrew? Go ahead and say it. I've called myself all that before."

Ada stomped to the garage, crossed her arms, and leaned against the building, glaring into the dusty yellow sky. "You are the shittiest mother that *ever* lived."

Victoria nodded and climbed slowly to her feet, brushing grass from her skirt. "I know how you feel, and you're not entirely wrong, but I tried to do as much good as I could, to make things better, but the result was…" She walked to the bench, sat slowly facing Ada, and looked at her hands.

"The result was that you fucked everything up."

"So I did. Big fucking deal. I tried my best, and I ended up making things worse, just like all humans do. But I never stopped loving, and I never stopped caring, and I never abandoned you. I was always there."

"You were *never* there. Your body was there, and that was it. You showed up and that was all."

"Yeah? Well, that was one helluva lot! Do you know how many times I wanted to walk away?" She stood and walked to the street, and then she whirled and pointed a trembling finger at Ada. "Here's the truth – raising a genius took more guts and more love and more loyalty than you'll ever know! Do you know how hard it was staying by your side while you tried to break the whole goddamn world?"

"Don't blame me! Maybe you should've gotten drunk more when you were pregnant with me! Maybe then I woulda turned out normal and made your life all nice and easy and perfect!"

"Go to Hell, you ungrateful snot!"

"We're already in Hell!" Her voice cracked, and she looked down at her boots. Victoria sat and drew her knees up to her chest, gazing at the garage wall and seeing nothing. They held those postures for several minutes, separated by a dozen feet and a dozen years of pain.

"I crossed this country to find you," Victoria said softly. "I did things I never thought I would, and I learned things I hope to forget." She looked down at her hands. "Was I deluding myself? Will we ever have a chance at a future together?"

Ada lit a cigarette and glared back at her. She finished it in a few angry puffs, lit another and did the same thing, and her hands stopped shaking halfway through her third. She saw her mother sitting in front of her, gazing at the dry grass by the bench and looking so much smaller than she'd remembered. Victoria wasn't the fearsome Commander anymore but more like an abandoned little girl in an Ohio rest stop, staring through the window and pleading for another chance at love.

"You're the only magic left in my life," Victoria said. She studied her hands, clasping them together to stop their trembling. After a few moments, she looked up, blinking her eyes to hold back tears. "I can't lose you too. Tell me where I can fit into your life, and that's what I'll do. You're in control now."

Ada stubbed out her cigarette, unsure what to do. She was afraid to reach out, but they'd drift apart and never reunite if she didn't. Needing time to think, she lit another.

Reaching out would be pointless, she thought. Their relationship was beyond salvation and had been for years, and fighting to save it was futile. It would cause more pain to try than to accept the inevitable.

Suddenly, she remembered how she'd felt on Mount Vaca. "Oh, fuck that," she said to herself, and then he threw the cigarette away and strode to the bench.

Victoria handed her the flask as she sat. "All I'm asking for is another chance, and this time I won't blow it. You're too important to me. You want to know how important? I actually killed people to get here, Ada. I'm not proud of it, but…"

"Krista played that Rance confession to me. He was one supremely skeevistic scumbag, and I gotta say, you were one bitchin badass."

"It wasn't just him. There were more." She took the flask from Ada's hand, gulped some whiskey, and handed it back. "A lot more. I went serial for a while there."

"Mom, scumbags aren't an endangered species or anything. I won't judge you for that."

"You won't?"

"Nope." Ada gulped a mouthful and then looked down, fiddling with the flask's cap. "I killed a few too."

"Sacramento wasn't your fault."

She shook her head. "It was back in Colorado. Hey, at least a serial killer takes out their victims one at a time. I took them out in bulk."

Victoria turned to her quickly, her mouth forming a sharp reply, but then she snatched the flask and chugged.

"It was them or me, Mom. I chose me."

"And I'm glad you did," Victoria said. "But we need to talk about that. We've *got* to find that bar."

"Yeah, and it better be fully stocked. I'll need to get surface-of-the-sun lit to talk about *that*." Ada took the flask and fiddled with the cap again. "Can we make a deal? When we find that bar, I'll tell you everything, but you won't hold it against me, okay? And I'll do the same. Whatever we did, it's in the past. It stays there."

"I promise. And I'll work hard to stop being such a bitch. I won't let anything stand in the way. That'll be my mission –"

"Stop. Stop trying to be so freakin perfect. If you're gonna promise me anything, promise me that you'll do you, quirks and all. And I'll do me. We've gotta get used to each other, and we might as well start now." Biting her lip, she held out her little finger.

Victoria looked down at it and then into her eyes. Wearing a small smile, she wrapped her finger around Ada's and pinky-swore on the deal.

Their fingers still joined, they sat quietly and passed Migs' whiskey back and forth. After a few minutes, Ada spoke, her voice almost a whisper. "I want to start over. I have to, because once you give up on second chances, that's when you hear Death. And it offers up a tempting deal – just give up hope and your future, and all the pain will go away forever. But *no* pain is forever. *No* despair is final. There's always a surprise around the next corner, and sometimes it's horrorshow, but sometimes it's glorious and magical. To give up possibilities just to escape the pain…" She shrugged. "You're already dead if you'd consider that. And I'm not dead."

"I love you," Victoria said. "You know what? Something happened to you. You won't tell me, Krista won't tell me, but something huge and beautiful happened to your heart. You're definitely not the kid I left at the rest stop. Someday you have to tell me."

"Someday isn't today, Mom." She upended the flask and tapped out the last drop, and then she set it on the bench. She slid over until their thighs touched and took her mother's hand; Victoria squeezed it gently and rested her head against Ada's.

They sat in comfortable silence for the first time in years and watched the shadows climb the garage. Jeeps rumbled by, and the soldiers shot at the dog pack again, but they didn't notice any of it.

"We oughta hold hands more," Ada said after a while.

"Damn right," Victoria said.

DISPATCHES

Midnight Sun
News Post of October 15, 2043

FBI TO INVESTIGATE ARCHANGELIST DEATH CULT

The White House Press Secretary held an impromptu press conference this afternoon to discuss Simon Rance's confession and Krista Warner's accusations:

"This is a mixed bag of horrors. First, it's a gruesome admission of murder by Dr. Victoria Lang, who is still being sought for the homicide of three innocent physicians at a Virginia hospital. The Department of Justice will seek a grand jury indictment on Monday.

"Second, Warner is a troubled and unstable seditionist who has called for the violent overthrow of this government and the assassination of the president. It's hard to take any of her accusations seriously – except for one.

"We've gathered evidence from unimpeachable sources about these Elders of the Second Creation. It aligns with Warner's allegations that this Archangelist death cult – if not the Church itself – was instrumental in triggering this terrible pandemic. The FBI has already begun questioning known cult members, and we expect to have a clearer picture of the scope of Archangelist involvement in the coming days. We'll prosecute and punish the guilty as relentlessly and mercilessly as the virus has punished American innocents, and we'll remove this scourge from our nation even if we have to reach to Texarkana."

RIOTS ERUPT IN MARYLAND AND GEORGIA

Shortly after the publishing of Simon Rance's confession, urban riots broke out in major Eastern cities. Gunfire was heard at the site of the Atlanta riots, although it is unclear who was shooting. The front gate of Chalys Pharmaceuticals, in Fort Washington, Maryland, was destroyed by a bomb, and rioters reportedly have entered the grounds. Police are on the scene. We will update our readers on these events as more information becomes available.

⊂━⊐━⊂━⊐⊃

Molle's Hill
NewsHub Political Affairs Channel
Broadcast Transcript of October 15, 2043

Molle: Hello, everybody! We have a special evening edition of *Molle's Hill* tonight. Welcome to the show again, Mr. Speaker.

Hayborn: Great to be here.

Molle: I suppose you want to discuss the big news of the day, which for once isn't another secession. Wait – I haven't seen the news tonight. Has another state seceded?

Hayborn: Not that I'm aware of, Arista. I'm afraid the news of the day remains Warner's latest broadside.

Molle: I wouldn't call her a broad side. She's not fat. She *is* a terrible interior decorator, though. Did you know that I bought her apartment, and it's plainer than a nunnery?

Hayborn: Another reason to detest the woman. As if being a terrorist mastermind wasn't enough.

Molle: Exactly! I've seen crypts with more charm! Now, what was I saying?

Hayborn: You were saying that nobody has confirmed that Simon Rance made that confession, and it could be fake.

Molle: Yes, yes, of course. I take *nothing* at face value, Mr. Speaker.

Hayborn: You've earned your reputation as a hard-boiled journalist, and that's why I'm sure you already know that The Profit Joseph has recalled these so-called Elders to Texarkana for consultations. He'll determine whether they conspired with Gabriel Cheyn, as Warner alleges. I'll travel to Texarkana to determine whether there's any evidence linking Cheyn to this terrible viral pandemic. If the Elders took part in a conspiracy, they'll be punished. Archangelists have no tolerance for subterfuge and violence.

Molle: I imagine that the punishment for genocide would be severe.

Hayborn: Genocide is a legal matter, Arista, and it's a subject for a judge and jury to consider. But betraying the faith and allying with a man who espouses principles contrary to Church doctrine – that's a serious religious matter with significant consequences. That's called apostasy in the Archangelist faith. The punishment for it is death.

Molle: Really? I knew a guy who married a girl from Canada, and he converted to her religion. The Archangelists just excommunicated him, and of course, he had to move to Canada to get a job.

Hayborn: One who renounces the Archangelist faith also renounces our partnerships with Corporate America, so I'm not surprised he couldn't find work. Nevertheless, he must have been a Lay Archangelist to receive only excommunication. Cleric Archangelists take the oath of St. Michael the Archangel and swear to defend the faith. For them, the penalty for apostasy is death.

Molle: The Church can impose the death penalty?

Hayborn: In Arkansas, yes, of course. The Attorney General of that state rarely intervenes in religious matters, and I'm sure everyone would agree that betrayal of the Archangelist faith is a religious matter. And there is ample precedent for a religion purging dangerous elements from its ranks in order to protect the faith. I'm sure you've heard of the Spanish Inquisition?

Molle: I'm sorry. I was looking at paint samples all day long, and I've been too busy to check the European news. So it sounds like The Profit has the Elders under control already.

Hayborn: Correct. If the Elders of the Second Creation were ever a concern, they won't be any longer.

Molle: Thank god. I'm so relieved. Now speaking of another kind of elder, I understand that Georgetown Hospital has discounted its respiratory therapy, and they have machines ready and waiting, no appointment needed…

APOSTASY

Bob Downs shifted his rucksack on his shoulder as he walked north on Route 101. He'd tried to hire a taxi to take him to Davis, but nobody would drive him across the bay, fearing they'd return with a radioactive glow. He'd told them that the radioactivity stopped before Davis, but they refused to listen.

He'd considered calling a driver and stealing his car, but he wasn't in peak condition, and his mission would fail if he couldn't subdue the man. He then tried renting a car, but the agent said only California driver's licenses were acceptable for identification, and the salesman at the used car lot down the street wanted more money than he had for even the most dilapidated wreck on the lot.

He'd have to walk, but he could endure a three-day trip. The antibiotic treatment had cured his infection, and now that the Synthopia had cleared from his system, his vigor was growing with each step.

After two hours, he turned east for Vallejo and Interstate 80. As he crossed a small creek, absorbed in his memories of Marissa Savu and wondering if his dark angel was thinking of him, his tablet rang. He slipped it from a pocket. "Hey, Raf."

"Day-o, Bob. Whatcha up to?"

"I'm continuing with my mission, no thanks to you. I got a serious infection, and I had to find a hospital on my own."

"I wasn't neglecting you, my friend. We're fighting off a full-scale cyberattack. Trying to get anything electronic to work right now is iffy. I couldn't get a signal to call you back."

"I guess this Activist endgame is having an effect?" Downs asked.

"You better believe it, and lemme tell you, they've got some no-shit *ichiban* hackers on their side. I've got Warcode climbing down my throat and Blue Ball stuffing my tailpipe. Warcode's corrupting the power systems, the phones, the Internet and so on, and together with the work slowdowns, almost nothing works on the East Coast, including here. And we're getting slammed with ghostware and screenjacking episodes from Blue Ball, who find a backdoor into everything. For some weird reason, they try a different attack every time, but they're easy to turn away. Fighting them off is burning resources, though. We're getting nothing done."

"Thanks for letting me know, Raf. Well, it's been a great chat, but I have real work to do. Give Cochon a hug and a kiss –"

"Bob."

"Yes?"

"Go ahead and resent me, but it's time to let this go."

"You walked me out of the Watch Room at gunpoint and unceremoniously defenestrated me from the NTC. I have a lot to resent you for."

"No, you don't," Raphael said. "I let you off easy. Stop sulking and be grateful for the gift I gave you."

Downs watched the dark purple curtain of night climb from beyond the eastern mountains. When he squinted, he could even see speckles of stars; he shivered at the audacious beauty of Nature and felt its peace leach the tension from his bones. He wouldn't have experienced this if Raphael hadn't let him go. "Right," he said. "You're absolutely right, and I thank you, and I truly am grateful for this gift."

"You're welcome. Now you can repay the favor."

"How?"

"I have a little strategic problem here, and I need your advice. It's one of those nasty binds you always knew how to get out of. In fact, you never would've gotten into this bind in the first place." Raphael lowered his tablet and yelled for someone in the Watch Room to get Ada's face off the monitors again. "Okay, you still there?"

"You were talking about a strategic problem?"

"The Activists have two of our western bases under siege. The Sawtooth United Cell has been surrounding Pocatello all day and plinking away at our drones, and now the Sagebrush Cell just closed off our ground access to Fort Carbon."

"This is easy, Raf. The first rule of war is to kill the enemy. Both bases have companies of Collaterals that can do the work, two hundred men with small brains and big guns. Just set them loose outside the fence and let them break stuff. I don't see the problem."

"It's more complicated than that, Bob. Our voice and email intercepts from Idaho and Colorado now show a ten-to-one negative sentiment among the local population. If we throw the Collaterals out there for a hard suppression, we might buy a battle we can't win."

Downs watched seagulls wheel in the sky as he thought, and the answer came to him a few steps later. "You're correct. We need apathy to function efficiently. We don't have it here, so any engagement will ultimately be unwinnable. Suppression of the forces surrounding our bases will trigger violence in the local population and incite civil insurrection. We don't have the resources to fight a civil war, Raf. We aren't the Army."

"Right. That's the same conclusion I arrived at."

"So transfer the Fort Carbon and Pocatello assets to Tonopah. The runways were usable when I left. You can operate out of tents in the interim –"

"Bob, no can do. I tried to land a cargo plane to extract the remaining personnel yesterday, and as soon as the wheels touched the runway, it got nailed by a SAROC. Now I've got a crater in the main runway and fifty tons of smoking metal around it, not to mention that there's still eleven guys hiding out in the midfield maintenance shed without any food or water."

"A predictable stratagem," Downs said. "The Activists clearly intend to deny us our forward bases or force us to deploy valuable resources to hold them. They've employed this same tactic before to divide and dilute our forces. Only a fool would fall for it again."

"Exactly, and this man doesn't want to be a fool today. What do you suggest?"

"A strategic withdrawal is advisable, then. I'd remove my men and the materiel to another location while I still could to preserve my force-projection capability. I'd airdrop food, water, and guns to the Tonopah personnel and leave them there because not a single one is worth rescuing. They might be able to keep the Activists distracted until they're killed, though. I'd do the same on the other bases – have the unit commander pick fifty men he doesn't need and let them draw fire until another base is fully operational."

"I knew you'd cut through the confusion, Bob," Raphael said. "That's what we have to do."

"I'd also recommend pulling Noah aside at the next Elder's Synod and breaking the news to him gently. He's concerned about how the Union's unraveling, and telling him we can't hold these two states will be a blow."

"Yeah, about that," Raphael said. "There won't be any more Elder's Synods."

Downs stopped walking. "Come again?"

"There won't be any more Elder's Synods, and if there were, I wouldn't go to one. Didn't you hear the news?"

"No, I've been in a hospital bed the past two days. What happened?"

"Yesterday afternoon, Warner posted Simon Rance's deathbed confession, and he detailed our involvement in the RVE Initiative. Within a few hours, most of the Elders I know were already on a plane to Arkansas."

Downs gasped and stumbled, and then he wandered to the side of the road and sat in the grass. "What?"

"Somebody's rounding up the Elders. Not us, not the FBI, but some other force. We've heard some rumors, and Cochon's trying to confirm them, but it looks like Hayborn's cleaning house. He went on the airhead's show last night and said they'll be hanged for conspiring with Cheyn."

He lowered the tablet and gazed into the skies over a distant marina as every cell of his brain processed Raphael's news. The Elders had been arrested fast, even faster than the NSF could have done – which meant Hayborn had prepared to betray them. He pulled the tablet up to his ear. "Raf, you still there?"

"Still here, buddy. For how long, I don't know."

"Correct. You need to get out of there as soon as you can. Hayborn's sacrificing us to protect himself, and if he wants plausible isolation from the RVE Initiative, he needs to silence you and me. We know everything, and we could bring him down, so we're Enemy Number One. You need to get down to Gitmo *now*. He won't stop with the Elders he has. You want to be long gone when he comes for you."

"I've already made my bug-out plan, but I don't think I'll use it. He needs the NSF to provide security for the Transition, and besides, we've got a solid relationship. We're simpatico, him and me. I know he's doing political damage control, but it won't extend to me. I think he's picked a few Elders to make an example of, and he'll stop there."

"Don't be an idiot, Raf. Get out now."

"If he comes for me, I'll be in Guantanamo Bay before he's done knocking on my door. In the meantime, somebody's gotta run the Watch Room. I can't just walk out at a time like this. Truth is, I don't want to. Things are interesting around here for once."

"You're deluding yourself. He was guiltier than any of the other Elders, and now he's sending them all to the gallows to hide his own crimes. How can The Profit tolerate this?"

"It sounds like they'll be hanged in Arkansas, so I'm sure The Profit approves, Bob. I don't think this is just Noah acting. I think the entire leadership was involved."

"Even The Profit Joseph, the Grandson of God?"

"Especially him. Listen, I didn't wanna tell you, but the Elders that escaped to Gitmo say this mystery force coming after us are the Sentinels."

"The Profit's personal guard?"

"The same ones. Face it, the Profit Joe wants us up there juggling halos with Jesus, buddy."

"No! He wouldn't sink to such treachery. The Profit wouldn't sacrifice his faithful. Noah must've deceived The Profit and his staff. And that makes it apostasy, Raf, the betrayal of the loyal and the faithful, the renunciation and debasement of the faith. Why would The Profit do that? How *could* he? No, this is all Noah's doing, and he'll answer to The Profit, and he'll be the one who swings."

"Bob," Raphael said gently. "That's not gonna happen."

"Well, it should!" Downs roared.

"It won't. I hear that The Profit washed his hands of it."

"You expect me to believe that he'd stand by while the soldiers who devoted their entire lives to the Second Creation are destroyed? He'd turn his back on Eden, the core article of our faith?"

"Political power is the strongest of all, and maybe even The Profit isn't immune. Bob, why they're doing this is irrelevant as long as we take care of ourselves and make sure we have our exit –"

"It's important to me! I serve God, and that's why I do what I do! The corruption of our faith is the corruption of my life, and if there's an Apostate loose upon this land, I owe it to God to find this cretin and smite him! It's my duty under the Oath of St. Michael to use my sword to purify and cleanse this sacred Earth of its nonbelievers, and the most dangerous nonbeliever is an Apostate who would betray his own –"

"Calm down," Raphael said. "You're getting carried away with this sword and sorcery stuff. Hey, we got played. Take an irony pill and accept that, man. They snookered us, and The Profit and Noah played us like –"

"Like it was a joke? Like we were playing the stooges in some slapstick show?"

"Kinda like that, yeah. You gotta appreciate –"

"I *do* not! I *will* not! On my very soul, I refuse to back down and let my faith be corrupted!"

"Okay, yeah. Bob, I have a few things to do, so I gotta go. You take care of yourself. Stay invisible, my friend." Raphael ended the call with a click, and Downs looked at the blank tablet for a few moments, resisting the impulse to throw it into the bay. He sat on the grass again and let his anger radiate into the deepening night until he could think clearly.

Without his faith, he was nothing. Without the prospect of the Second Creation in his heart, he had no reason to suffer the smut, smog, and stupidity of the world. Without Faith and Eden, he was hollow and dead. He had to defend them any way he could.

He just didn't know how. He asked God what to do, but he didn't answer.

DEFCON ONE

Day 60
Saturday morning, October 17, 2043
Bangor Naval Submarine Base, Kitsap, Washington

Adam Harris and Julie Bricker stood on the Explosives Handling Wharf catwalk and watched a technician below pick through a pile of electronic scrap, all that remained of the *Patrick Henry's* Missile Release Control System. The trucks carrying the *Henry's* remaining Joe Slicks – except the two missiles they hadn't had time to remove – belched clouds of blue smoke and inched uphill to the Strategic Weapons Facility. On the other side of the dock, missile technicians milled around a table and examined four dismantled warheads in the light of the wharf's arc lamps.

The *Henry* was too damaged to use as a strategic weapons platform again, so it had been reloaded with the weapon it was originally designed to carry: three-missile pods of Warhammer subsonic cruise missiles, each carrying a two-thousand-pound conventional high-explosive warhead. If necessary, the *Henry* would provide ground support to repel an invasion.

A tugboat behind the boat tooted its whistle twice. Its engine growled, and a few seconds later, the towing cable tightened and pulled the boat slowly out of the wharf. They walked down a metal stairway and to the end of the dock, where Julie wrapped her good arm into his.

"Bet this feels strange," Adam said.

"Of course. But if you think I feel regrets, the answer's no. Hell, no, in fact. All the time we were out there, all I wanted was to be here – with you, on land, and out of that boat." She watched another tugboat push the *Henry's* bow into open water. "She's not mine anymore, and I was happy to put her in Ennis's hands. He's the best commander you can give her – all the balls of Jimmy Columbo and twice the brains. But how'd you get him to go? He told me he was planning to walk straight off the boat and keep walking till his shoes wore out."

"I reminded him of a promise he once made." Harris let go of her arm and leaned against the railing. "It was in the Hotel Hamadan. Ennis, Ryan, and I saw Death coming, and we needed to band together to survive. We promised that we'd fight Death together no matter how it came at us, that we'd never let the other give in or weaken, and that we'd always have each other's backs. And here we are, years later, and we still need each other to survive because we're both dead if we lose this war. I reminded Ennis of that, and he honored his promise."

His tablet chimed deep in his coat pocket, and he pulled it out and glanced at the screen. "All right, the time for reminiscing is over," he said. "We have a base to seize."

AT JUST AFTER TWO IN THE MORNING, Georgie Moon opened his thermos and poured the last dregs of coffee into a plastic cup. He sipped the tepid brew as he peered through the windows of the Hood Canal Bridge control tower toward Bangor, where the lights of tugboats twinkled in the light fog and drifting rain. Something was going on down there; the base was usually quiet during the graveyard shift, but tugboats were cruising all over the canal tonight.

A car stopped near the control tower entrance. Scowling, he set his coffee cup on a counter and stepped onto the metal balcony, pulling his slicker around his neck as chilly rain pelted his back. Down below, he saw a car idling by the tower door. It looked light gray, but everything did in the bridge's yellow lights.

He stomped back into the control tower and down to the roadway, grumbling the entire time. Ensuring his face was wearing the most annoyed expression it could bear, he opened the roadway level door. Three Marines in battle dress and black slickers stood in front of him – one Asian, one Black, and one White.

"Sir, we request your cooperation," the Asian said. He and the white Marine stepped through the door while the Black soldier walked back to the car.

"You from the base?" he asked. "Whatcha doing here?"

"Requesting your cooperation, sir. Please climb to the control tower. I'll follow."

The tone of his voice said that the request was a command. Both soldiers opened their slickers and shook the water off, revealing pistols in their holsters.

"What's going on?" Georgie asked.

"You're opening this bridge in eleven minutes, sir," the Asian said. "I suggest you hurry." He nodded to the staircase, and Georgie took the hint and walked to it.

"This ain't how you do an opening," he said. "We got procedures. You call it in and schedule it and we call the crew out here and –"

"I'm aware of that, sir," the Asian said.

Georgie stopped on the steps and looked into his impassive face. "Makes a lot of problems, you don't schedule it. Other night, some sub come blowin through here with like a minute advance notice, and we almost didn't get the span pulled back in time."

"We have ten minutes, sir. Please continue up the stairs."

"Look, you want an off-schedule opening, I gotta call it in."

"No, sir, you don't. If you wish me to compel your cooperation, I will."

"Arright," Georgie grumbled. "No need to get all heavy on me and stuff." He trudged up the steps and walked to the control panel. "Whatcha want?"

"Three hundred feet of clear water in eight minutes and no more chatter."

Georgie punched a few icons on the screen, and the traffic gates lowered to the accompaniment of clanging bells. A few minutes later, the roadway in front of the tower rose, and the floating section of the bridge slipped under it. "There ya go, General. Three hundred feet."

"Captain," the Asian said. He stepped onto the balcony and looked to the south through a pair of binoculars while the apparently mute white Marine stood next to Georgie and radiated sober menace.

Georgie leaned to one side and tried to see past the captain. The base lights blinked out for a few seconds as if something had passed before them, and then a black submarine glided out of the darkness and sailed through the bridge opening. He squinted at the gray numbers on the sail: 811.

"That's the *Nathan Hale*," Georgie said. "Not like a sub sailing's all that odd. Still don't see why you couldn't schedule it." He reached for the control monitor, but the mute Marine grasped his arm and pulled it back.

"No? Well, how long we gotta leave it open?"

The Marine didn't answer. Ten minutes later, Georgie spotted another sail passing through the bridge's lights. "The *Ethan Allen* too?" he asked.

"Nope," the mute said. "It was a pleasure craft."

"The hell it was. I know my subs."

"I saw a pleasure craft. I knock you on the gourd hard enough, you'll see a pleasure craft too."

Georgie gulped and nodded. "Biggest-ass yacht I ever seen. Now can I close it?"

He didn't answer, and Georgie returned to gazing through the window. A few minutes later, a submarine with the number 807 on the sail glided into the light. "Holy shee-it, that's the *Patrick Henry*!" He walked along the row of windows gawking at the speeding submarine. "Half the world's looking for her out in the Pacific. The hell's she doing here?"

"Maybe they're looking in the wrong place." The Marine smiled for the first time. "Or maybe it's just the biggest-ass yacht you ever seen."

CAPTAIN CALDWELL RUBBED DUST off the face of Harris' grandfather clock as it chimed five in the morning. Adam stood by a window and sipped his third coffee of the hour.

Julie Bricker sat on Harris' overstuffed couch and talked to observers at an abandoned lighthouse on Tattoosh Island, which jutted into the Strait of Juan de Fuca. They could see the *Astor* holding position six kilometers to the north, and two unidentified ships were patrolling further out on the ocean. If their diversion plan worked, those ships would soon be moving west in a hurry.

The Navy destroyers had to be drawn away so the three submarines could leave the Strait safely, and they hoped to send the Navy chasing what they thought was the *Henry*. The *Paul Revere* was the perfect doppelgänger since it was her sister ship, and both boats sounded identical to an acoustic operator.

Julie had spoken to the *Revere's* commander, Jimmy Columbo, early on Thursday as the plan was taking shape. Columbo had already spoken to Harris days before, and they'd agreed that Bricker couldn't be responsible for the Sacramento bombing. Nonetheless, he was shocked to hear that Cheyn had ordered the destruction of four more cities, especially because four generations of Columbos lived in Seattle. The volatile commander swore heroically for five minutes after hearing the news, but when he was done, he asked how the *Revere* could help.

Being the bait in a live-fire chase tantalized the swashbuckler in Columbo, and he agreed on the spot. However, the plan was risky for the *Revere* because the Navy might go nuclear as soon as they locked on her. But for Jimmy Columbo, that just made the ruse even more thrilling.

He'd contacted Julie forty-five minutes before as the *Revere* was preparing to descend. He planned to sail into the edge of the destroyer *Jay Gould's* sonar range, allow her a clean ping off his hull, and draw them off to the west. With luck, the other ships would follow, and the Strait would then be clear for the submarines to pass.

But the ships hadn't budged yet, and Harris was nervous. The sun would rise in an hour, and with daylight would come aerial patrols that could see his boats waiting in the clear water ten miles from the Strait's mouth.

He finished his coffee and sat at his desk, watching Julie as she talked to the observers. As he was getting ready to remind her that time was running out, she smiled and nodded. "They're moving, Adam. The *Astor* just sounded general quarters, and it's shredding water. The other two ships are also moving."

THE *HALE* AND THE *ALLEN* SAILED OUT OF THE STRAIT at flank speed and raced south as soon as the *Astor* was out of sonar range. Both boats passed Tattoosh Island within three hundred meters of the observers, seeking the protection of the coastal sound clutter in case aerial patrols dropped sonobuoys. Ten minutes later, the *Henry* also slipped by and headed south.

Bricker mouthed a silent 'thank you' at the ceiling, while Harris grinned and ran his fingers through his hair. Caldwell straightened his glasses and let go the breath he'd been holding, and for a few moments, the room was silent.

All three boats surfaced off Spike Rock thirty minutes later. Governor Wang wanted the American airship cameras to capture a clear daylight image of them to confirm the new nation's nuclear deterrent.

After they submerged and disappeared into the Pacific's vastness, Caldwell glanced at the clock and cleared his throat. "Now that this is over, we have another matter to attend to. Are we ready, Admiral?"

Harris nodded and stood, his face grim, and then he straightened his shoulders and walked to the door. "Let's get this done."

LIEUTENANT DON MALLORY was the operations duty officer on the night Bangor made history. When he started his shift, he hadn't expected anything momentous to happen, not at the sleepiest time of night in the drowsiest corner of America.

He scanned the surveillance monitors on the far wall of the theater-like Base Operations Center, but Bangor looked placid tonight. Even the deer were staying away from the perimeter fence, and they usually set off a few proximity alarms, helping keep him and his staff of six awake. The only anomaly he noticed was that the cameras covering Delta Pier hadn't been working all night, but the maintenance crew assured him they'd be up by dawn.

Something odd had been going on down by the water ever since the Defcon One drill had been called. If he was lucky, that meant that whatever war they were edging toward would go hot at last. These were thrilling times, with Sacramento being wiped out and rebels tossing bombs, and the country decaying so slowly but so exquisitely. Pushing the Big Red Button would be the perfect climax.

He plugged in his earbud and turned on the tablet he'd secreted under his monitor, hoping to find more of those gruesome and graphic reports from Sacramento, which were more riveting than *Mushrooms over Moscow* lately. All he could find on the newsfeeds, though, were newscasters babbling about how the Pacific Northwest should secede, and they were even supporting Warner's claim that Cheyn had ordered the nuking of California's capital city.

Mallory couldn't understand why they'd listen to a traitor and a terrorist. In his mind, everything America did was right, so everything its leaders did was right too. Questioning the acts of a president was un-American.

The Activist madness had even infiltrated the base. At lunch, he'd started chatting about the newsfeed's obvious liberal bias with the cute ponytailed lieutenant who worked the comm security desk one row ahead of him, and it went bad: red-faced, finger-pointing, ponytail-shaking bad. He'd hoped he could use the conversation to get an opening with her, as she was sizzling hot and available, but she slammed the proverbial door in his face once he even hinted that Warner might be wrong.

He eyed her blonde ponytail and the erotically soft nape he'd hoped to nuzzle. *You never know with some people – such a pretty head, but inside, such a squirrelly mind.*

He surfed the channels, but then the tablet screen went dark and said that the wireless signal had been lost. As he was trying to reboot it, the door proximity alarm chimed. Glancing at his monitor, he saw some Marines and BaseOps officers standing outside the door. He recognized Major Ike Shelby and his unsmiling adjutant, a Korean captain everybody called Sir Laughalot, but he couldn't tell who the others were because they were wearing helmets and body armor.

With a gasp, he sat straight up in his seat and slammed his thumb on the emergency deadbolt, which thunked closed. A second later, it clicked open. He tried to close it again, but the button wasn't working, and that was when he realized that the Ops Center was being invaded. As he reached for the pistol in its hip holster, the Marines burst through the door.

"You won't touch that sidearm, one way or another," the captain said, leveling his pistol at Mallory's hand. He pulled it away from his hip, and the captain motioned him away from the Duty Officer's console. Another Marine took the pistol and pushed him aside.

Mallory started to ask what was going on when Shelby strode through the door and bellowed, "All right, y'all, time to pretend you're smart. Now doncha touch anythin, and raise your hands way up high like you're reachin for the hem of God's robe. And if you fuck with me tonight, you *will* be able to touch that garment, I promise you that." Four sailors raised their hands and stood slowly, and Navy officers who'd come in with the Marines took their seats. However, the ponytailed lieutenant remained seated at her desk and tapped her monitor. He looked up at the big wall screen and saw that she was disabling every landline that connected the base to the world. After she cut the last connection, she walked to Mallory's station and took his seat.

"You're a goddamn traitor," he said under his breath.

She snorted and displayed the base alert screens on the wall monitor. "No, fuckwad, I'm a patriot."

Shelby shoved him against the wall. "Son, she's a good guy, you're a bad guy, and I'm a pissed-off gyrene. Why doncha use that big ole Navy brain and add that up while I'm workin?"

The lieutenant tapped a few more times, and a yellow screen appeared on the center monitor. She swiveled in her chair and gave Shelby a questioning look. "Awright, go on and do it," he said.

She slipped on Mallory's headset and tapped icons on the monitor. An electronic bell began to chime, the room's lights dimmed, and the Defcon alert board clicked from '2' to '1'. On the base loudspeakers outside, the Defcon alert siren wailed.

She pulled the microphone to her lips and the siren stopped. *"Defense Condition One. Alert Condition Hotbox. This is not a drill."* She paused and they heard her voice echo across the base. *"Battalion personnel to Alfa Echo stations..."*

Mallory stood back, stunned and speechless: The Marines didn't just intend to take over the Ops Center but the entire base. He watched one of the smaller monitors displaying the Strategic Weapons Facility entrance, where the reserve nuclear warheads were stored deep underground in a carefully guarded bunker. The watchtower floodlights had already snapped on, the Humvees blocking the entrance had backed inside the fence, and the concrete anti-tank barrier was rising into place. They were preparing to deter the invaders a Condition Hotbox said were coming.

Another monitor showed a personnel carrier in the parking lot of the Officer's Quarters. Marines jumped out and ran to the door, and a few minutes later, Navy officers in pajamas walked to the truck with their hands raised over their heads. The same operation was underway at the Seamen's Quarters, but some sailors fought back and tried to escape. After a brief skirmish, the Marines subdued the rebellious men and dragged them to the personnel carrier.

Mallory's anger rose, and then he remembered his duty as a commissioned Navy officer. He stood to attention. "Major Shelby, I charge you with mutiny under Article 94 of the United States Code of Military Justice! Immediately cease your actions and report to the base brig!"

"Wow, that sounds real serious." Shelby leaned toward him wearing an easy smile. "Good thing I ain't a US Marine no more, son. I'm a Commonwealth Marine now."

THE WAGES OF DESPERATION

Day 60
Saturday morning, October 17, 2043
National Tranquility Center, Fort Belvoir, Virginia

Ryan Beckmann suspected that Washington State had seceded twenty minutes before the governor announced it.

The cloud cover over the Hood Canal had broken up overnight, and he had a clear view of Bangor from Blackeye 20 over Seattle. He remembered seeing two Patriot subs docked at Delta Pier yesterday, but now they were gone.

He zoomed in on the Explosives Handling Wharf – the mysterious, frenetic activity he'd seen there yesterday had stopped, and the missile transports clogging the pier were now parked inside the Strategic Weapons Facility. The Marine detachment had barricaded the entrances, and four jeeps armed with rocket pods covered each one. Bangor had gone to Defcon One, but the country wasn't at war.

He scanned the Hood Canal and through the Strait of Juan de Fuca, trying to find the subs – and then he saw three of them lined up off the Washington coast as if they wanted to be found. And one was the *Patrick Henry*.

As he was puzzling through this turn of events, Governor Wang announced that Washington, Oregon, and most of Idaho had founded the Commonwealth of New Columbia. In addition, she said that their intelligence units had uncovered conclusive evidence that Cheyn had not only attacked Sacramento but had planned to strike four cities in the Pacific Northwest. The new nation was prepared to retaliate with nuclear weapons if he tried again.

It was time he disappeared. Cochon would discover the missing subs, which were the nuclear weapons Wang had referred to, and then he'd begin a detailed investigation into Admiral Harris and his known associates – and once they uncovered Ryan's long-ago affair with the Admiral's wife, they'd assume he was the Activist mole. They'd drag him into the basement and shoot him on the spot. Or even worse, they'd map his mind and then shoot him.

RAPHAEL STEPPED UP TO THE PODIUM and noticed that Beckmann's deputy was briefing Buta at the Acquisitions station. "Where's Ryan?" he asked Cochon.

"He had a family emergency. But everything's an emergency since the secession came up this morning."

Raphael wiggled his hand. "'Nother day, 'nother secession. Don't get worked up."

"Except this state has nuclear weapons aimed at us," Cochon said. "And if Cheyn really nuked Sacramento, I can't blame them."

"It's disinformation," Raphael said. "We've intercepted nothing pointing to Cheyn being involved in the Sacramento –" He pivoted on the podium and watched a child's blue ball roll across the monitors. "My, how playful. Mochyn, get this crap off my Wall!"

"We hit the Blue Ball hackers hard early in the Watch," Mochyn said. "We wormed everything digital we could find between Los Alamos and Santa Fe – it's like the 1970's there now – but they just moved on to a burger joint in Taos. They've been pounding us for the last hour."

"Just take care of it." Raphael rubbed his neck and turned to Cochon. "What's the situation with Pocatello and Fort Carbon?"

"We completed the withdrawal last night. We still have a caretaker unit at Pocatello that we'll pull out later today, but the ones in Fort Carbon and Tonopah surrendered. I moved the rest of the Fort Carbon assets down to Denver International Airport, so we still have suppression capability along the Rockies. I also merged the Pocatello and Tonopah assets at the old Wendover Air Force Base, on the Utah-Nevada border, so force projection to the California border is only minimally impacted."

"We can work with that. The drones won't have as much time on station, but we can schedule around it." He noticed Buta waving at him, and he and Cochon walked to his station. "What's up, Buta?"

He pointed to an aerial image on his monitor. "I'd put this up on the Wall, but we still have the bouncing ball rolling around. Look." He tapped the monitor and zoomed in on the Washington coast. "This image was captured three hours ago. See this? These three submarines are all Patriot subs, and one is the *Patrick Henry*. I think they sailed from Bangor overnight before the secession was announced. I'll bet they're carrying the nuclear weapons this Commonwealth is talking about."

"They carry the same Lancet missile that blew away Sacramento. They're unstoppable," Cochon said. "Pass this on to the National Security Adviser and the Joint Chiefs immediately."

"No, belay that," Raphael said. "Submarines sail the seas all the time, gentlemen. That's not out of the ordinary."

"But the announcement! They have nuclear missiles…" Cochon began.

"Do we know that? Buta, can you confirm there are missiles on those submarines?"

"No, I can't," Buta said.

"Exactly. Calm down and stop connecting dots that aren't there, people. Forget you even saw this."

Raphael strode to the center of the podium and Cochon followed. "What are you doing?" he asked in a lowered voice. "Those submarines are clearly part of the Commonwealth strategy. You know that!"

"Of course, Phil. That's why I don't want Cheyn to know that I know." He grabbed Cochon's arm and walked him to the far end of the podium. "Every piece of information has value, grasshopper, but this one is a golden thread if we handle it right. If I tell everybody, it becomes worthless. But if I only tell Noah, it's gold. And with this Elders purge going on, we need to market our worth to him."

"I didn't see that. Honestly, I don't get the political side of things like you do."

"That's because you live in a reality based on facts," Raphael said, "but in politics, reality is based on power. And you can tap into that power reality by following the political thread in every knot. Sometimes that thread's made of gold, and trust me, you hold onto those. You can trade a golden thread for big bling, Phil, and what you have here is a very golden thread. Noah will pay bigly for this by upping our budget next year."

"I think I understand," Cochon said. "Then you should know about another thread I've been following lately. Watching the Wall clears your mind, and with all that time to think, I've identified a few errors the Syllogic Engine may have made. If my suspicions are correct, it could change the fundamental dynamics of this so-called rebellion we're facing."

"This sounds tasty. Serve it up, Phil. I'm already salivating."

Cochon looked from side to side, but the Watch Room staff wasn't paying attention. "I suspect we've succumbed to confirmation bias and made incorrect assumptions about The Activity's significance. In fact, I'm prepared to posit that these assumptions are diametrically opposite to objective reality." He coughed into his hand. "I'm uncomfortable proceeding further. The next part is somewhat…speculative."

"No, go on. This is intriguing."

"I received some information from the FBI this morning." He checked again to see if anybody was listening and then said in a low voice, "Ada Lang owns a house in White Rock, New Mexico."

"Now there's an evocative, Wild-West name – huge tipis atop a white rock mesa, the natives huddling in smallpox-tainted blankets around a heap big fire as coyotes howl…"

"Raf, please be serious. White Rock is only three miles from Los Alamos National Laboratory. The entire population works there."

"No Injuns, then?"

"None. And her house is one of twenty-three inside a fenced compound along the Rio Grande Gorge. There's only one way in. When the FBI tried to drive to her address, they found the road blocked by a black Silverback with US Government plates."

"Well, this is a major shitfest. Have you tasked the Engine for an analysis?"

"I haven't, and I don't need to. It's reasonable to assume that Ada Lang isn't an Activist but a Los Alamos chemist, given her bomb-making talents. And the Activists don't have a mole inside Project Blue Ball – they must be an Energy Department security unit protecting her with that blackwall, the Lichtblau identity, and the screenjacking attacks. Now, to speculate, if Lang isn't an Activist, is Warner? Could The Activity merely be a chimera? Did we believe the Syllogic Engine's erroneous conclusion because we were geared to combat militarized rebels – ?"

Raphael clapped his shoulder. "You're brilliant, Phil, absolutely brilliant. I love your mind, and you've cut through the clutter and arrived at a shockingly clear conclusion. Now never mention it again."

"But…"

"Who cares if The Activity is fake? Everybody on the Hill thinks it's real. They're certain the barbarian Activist horde is at the gate, ready to steal their Tessera Orb and render them powerless. The intrepid and trusty NSF is holding them at bay in a total-war, to-the-death cage match so they can hold onto that power, and they've opened up their big bag of black dollars to keep us swinging." He kissed his fingers. "Ahh, the wages of desperation are sweet. Screw Tonopah. We can build our next base in Beverly Hills if I keep this game rolling." He wrapped his arm around Cochon's shoulder. "Picture this – runways paved with fine Carrera marble and softly lit by crystal chandeliers…"

"Runways don't require illumination."

"Fly with me, grasshopper." Raf swept his free hand across the vista of his imagined airbase. "Marble runways softly lit by solid-gold chandeliers dangling from those columns…those Greek columns, what are they called…?"

"Ionic, Doric, Corinthian?"

"Corinthian! That sounds classy! Solid-gold chandeliers dangle from *Corinthian* columns as the palm trees sway under the caress of the soft California breeze, and the sweet scent of *colitas* drifts on the air."

"Raf, that's absurd."

"Not at all! If we're gonna hang with the glitterati, we've gotta go big, Phil! You're not living if you don't have goals! And maybe we can't buy marble runways, okay, but I can wangle those Corinthian columns as long as I don't change the narrative Congress is drinking in."

"Is this an example of a power reality versus a factual reality?"

"It is! Exactly!"

Cochon puffed out his cheeks. "This job's a lot harder than it looked like from the Intelligence chair."

"Don't make it harder. Leave those problematic facts to your intelligence chief, my friend. Retain your sanity." Raphael watched the blue ball bounce across the Wall, and a smile crept to his lips. "Yeah, it'll be a good day. Not only do I have a tasty plum to offer Noah, but we also got rid of our last mole."

"Our mole?" Cochon looked around the room and saw Beckmann's deputy leaving. "Beckmann! He left right after western sunrise! He saw that the subs left too! How'd I miss that?"

"You need to keep your head on at all times in this job, my friend."

"I'll take care of this right now." Cochon started toward the tactical station, but Raphael grabbed his arm and pulled him back.

"He's out in the landscape now. You won't find him. But with his departure, he left us a lovely bunch of clues, didn't he?"

"Well, for one thing, he proved I was right all along!" Cochon said. "I thought there were too many coincidences centering on that base and Harris was an Activist nexus, but no, you didn't believe me –"

"I *did* believe you, Phil. I knew you'd found a golden thread, and I wanted to save it for the right time." Raphael patted his back. "When you find a golden thread, never squander it. Remember that if you want to survive in this business."

DISPATCHES

Midnight Sun
News Post of October 17, 2043

WAR!
WASHINGTON AND OREGON SECEDE, DECLARE WAR ON U.S.

At 5:12 AM Pacific Time (8:12 AM Eastern Time), Kathryn Wang, Governor of Washington, announced that the states of Washington and Oregon, together with parts of northern and western Idaho, have seceded from the United States and formed the Commonwealth of New Columbia.

She further declared that a state of war exists between the new nation and the United States. Commonwealth intelligence sources say they have conclusive evidence proving Sacramento was destroyed at the order of President Cheyn, and that he also ordered the destruction of four cities in the Pacific Northwest. Those last attacks were averted, but she said the Commonwealth will use its thermonuclear weapons to retaliate against any further aggression on its territory or that of its allies.

Within minutes of the announcement, the separatist government of Québec recognized the new state but quickly added that it had not entered into a mutual defense pact with it. Canadian officials had no immediate comment.

The United Nations Secretary-General has called for the Commonwealth to enter into peace negotiations with the United States, and she invited both parties to a summit in Reykjavik next April.

The White House was caught off guard by the Commonwealth's move. White House staffers were seen leaving the building after the announcement, many carrying computers and boxes of papers, and have not returned since. Calls to the White House go unanswered.

BREAKING NEWS: PRESIDENT CHEYN IMPEACHED AND CONVICTED IN CONGRESS

President Cheyn was impeached by the House of Representatives at 10:30 AM Eastern Time today on charges of criminal negligence under the provisions of the recently passed National Unity Act.

The Senate immediately tried the case, and at 11:42 AM Eastern Time, President Cheyn was convicted and removed from office. The Senate further instructed the Sergeant-at-Arms to bring the ex-president before them to address charges that he ordered Sacramento's destruction.

Immediately after, Speaker of the House Noah Hayborn assumed the presidency. In his first official statement, President Hayborn said that the United States strategic forces are ready to respond to any aggression, foreign or domestic.

We will release further details as we receive them.

BREAKING NEWS: CONFLICT AT CAMP DAVID COMPOUND?

Following President Cheyn's removal from office, Capitol Police officers attempted to enter Camp David and take the former president into custody. Sporadic gunfire was heard in the hills outside Thurmont, Maryland, suggesting that they encountered resistance from the Marine contingent based there. However, police now report that Cheyn is not present at the presidential retreat, and they are no longer demanding entry.

Capitol Police officers entered the White House at noon to secure the building and its documents. They report that many records were already destroyed.

We will publish more details on this developing story as they become available.

BREAKING NEWS: NATIONAL SECURITY FORCES BASES FALL TO ACTIVITY FORCES

Our Witness in Colorado reports by radio that the Sagebrush Cell of the Activists, under a commander known only as The Deacon, has taken the Fort Carbon NSF base outside Durango in what may be the initial engagement of The Activity's Midwestern Campaign. Ironshirts inside the compound surrendered this morning to Activity forces and turned over the base and its equipment.

A brief communiqué from the leader of the Sawtooth United Militia in Idaho states that the NSF has abandoned its base in Pocatello, and it is now under Activist control. Further details will be released as we receive them.

CHAOS ESCALATES ON EAST COAST

An Activity attack seized the National Electrical Grid last night, resulting in a six-hour blackout from Washington to Baltimore. Attacks on financial and governmental websites have also increased, and a *Midnight Sun* investigation shows that most of those sites are now offline. US Cyber Command officials at Fort Meade say they are combating the Warcode cyberterrorists, but the battle is pitched and citizens should expect sporadic power and communications for the next few days.

Our Witness in Baltimore reports that Activist ground forces have targeted the National Security Agency complex at Fort Meade:

"Since Commander Sara took over the East End, she's been focusing the Activist pushback. I hear rumors that she has a list of everyone employed by the NSA, and that last night Activists planted bombs in some of their cars."

Ham radio operators confirm that they saw dozens of burning cars this morning on the Baltimore-Washington Parkway near Fort Meade, although it is unclear whether this was due to Activity actions. Gunfire has also been heard in and around the fort, and observers report that trucks have blocked all entrances.

As deliveries of fuel to the East dwindle, local infrastructure has been profoundly impacted. A shortage of diesel for sanitation trucks has left mounds of trash uncollected in the city of Washington, and mass transportation in the Washington-Richmond area has all but stopped. Shortages of food and other essentials are also being reported as delivery trucks run out of diesel. Many facilities operating on emergency generators report they are low on fuel as well.

FALLOUT FORECAST

As forecasted, the fallout plume from Sacramento has been drawn into the outer storm bands of Tropical Storm Andy Boy. The hurricane made landfall in Galveston yesterday as a Category Four storm, which was stronger than expected due to warm waters in the Gulf that amplified the storm's intensity.

The hurricane was downgraded to a tropical storm after landfall, and it moved quickly through Texas and up to the Oklahoma panhandle, where it mixed with the plume early this morning.

Federal Emergency Management officials didn't comment on the radioactivity of the plume before it merged with Tropical Storm Andy Boy. However, Los Alamos National Laboratory radiation monitors recorded almost no fallout when the plume passed north of the facility. Experts say that these readings don't indicate that the fallout has ended, but rather that dangerous radionuclides remain aloft as they drift toward America's prime croplands.

BREAKING NEWS: RECOMBIN NOW BEING MASS PRODUCED IN CENTRAL CALIFORNIA

Reports from California state that Activity laboratories near Sacramento have discovered a process for the mass production of Recombin and that the vaccine is already being distributed to first responders. The rest of California's populace should be fully vaccinated by next week, say reliable sources at area hospitals.

We have attempted to confirm this information with California state officials, but they remain unavailable. Similarly, we have tried to contact Krista Warner, but calls placed to her tablet do not connect, implying that she remains inside the Sacramento communication blackout zone.

We will update our readers as soon as further details are available. Please stop emailing us for information as we are working with fewer servers than usual, and they are already overloaded.

These same hospital sources also corroborate a rumor that has been spreading across the SatNet. Activity scientists, they say, have modified

Recombin to combat HIV, and early tests have shown that it eradicates the disease in less than four hours.

This news has lifted the pall of despair in parts of the embattled state. LGBT communities in California have been disproportionately affected by the highly transmissible CRF29-CD mutation of the HIV virus that emerged in 2039, and efforts to contain its spread have been largely ineffective. A recent study estimates that 57% of LGBT Californians now carry the mutated virus in its asymptomatic state. While only 4% of LGBT citizens have developed autoimmune symptoms thus far, some authorities fear that this number could quadruple in coming years, and that many will succumb to the disease.

A spokesperson for Community Action Castro, based in San Francisco's Castro District, says, "America's fifty-year-old war against its LGBT citizens is over thanks to our Activist friends. HIV is dead, my friends, and we should sing joyful hosannas to The Activity for delivering us from this scourge. It's ironic that rebels have defended the life, liberty, and happiness of America's common folk better than our bloviating elected politicians. The Activity delivers, which is a damn sight better than the DC government ever has. That's why everybody I know in The Castro is demanding that Governor DaCosta hold another secession vote – and that we secede this time."

He also announced that to celebrate the Activist breakthrough, the district will hold the first annual Love Activity next Saturday, featuring a parade through the neighborhood and an all-veggie barbecue in Corona Heights Park afterward. All are invited to attend.

YEARNING TO BREATHE FREE

Day 60
Saturday morning, October 17, 2043
Redding, California

Krista stretched her back and leaned against the Humvee. They'd been on the road since dawn trying to buy enough coolers to keep a thousand vaccine bottles cold all the way to Reno. Three soldiers had just walked into the Redding Mal-Mart to see if they had any in stock.

She pulled her tablet from her hoodie and checked the signal, which was finally strong enough to make a call. She dialed the governor's private number and listened to the phone ring.

"DaCosta."

"Hi, Ric. It's Krista." She waited for him to reply but just heard yelling in the background.

"Okay, I'm back. Whozis?"

"Krista Warner?"

"Blue Eyes! You pencil in saving the world yet or what?"

"I actually have. It looks like we're heading out to Reno sometime today."

"Fantastic! I love you. Marry me. Yeah, I'm ugly as a priest in heat, but I've got power, and I pay astronomical alimony. Was that too direct? Wait, hang on." She heard an announcer in the background and then people started clapping and hooting. "I'm back. Senate's voting to remove Cheyn from office since Washington State seceded this morning. And they'll do it cuz they're afraid your Activist cavalry's gonna come thundering over the hill and waste 'em if they don't. Best thing that happened to this country, your Activity thingie. But hey, you get his head, I'm still bidding on it."

"Ric, there's something you should know," she said. "There aren't any Activists except me. My cavalry's not coming to anybody's rescue. I'm sorry, but The Activity is just a fake, an agitprop meme I concocted to distract –"

DaCosta barked a short laugh. "You think I care if it's a total fugazy? Fake is the new Real. Perception is the new Truth. Hollywood would still be a barrio if that wasn't the deal."

"Maybe it works like that in the movies –"

"It works like that all over the friggin universe. The Little Green Men show up, in a week they'll be buying tickets and snarfing popcorn like everybody else. Nobody can resist a quality brand. Listen, your Activist brand is hot-hot-hot, and brands make wishes real, and nobody cares if your reality is fake cuz everybody's buying a dream anyway, even Martians. Everybody wants sizzle, everybody wants pop, and your brand delivers. That's why you've already got a million people swearing they're Activists. Hell, you've already got your gay brigade, which is great if you're gonna drop friggin potpourri bombs on the States, which maybe you oughta do. Place smells like a Tijuana shithouse anymore."

"Ric –"

"Kudos on that HIV thingie, by the way."

"I didn't –"

"But you keep your brand momentum high, Blue Eyes, and this Fugazy Revolution's gonna become reality. You'll have more armies than you can shake a dick at, not that you could, but that's beside the point. You're winning, that's the point, right. Keep giving miserable folks a reason to feel good, and they'll chew the friggin Washington Monument down to a nub if you ask. And everybody's unhappy, babe, everybody's a sucker for something…hang on…*so tell him to go screw himself, and his bowlegged goat too…nah, forget it, don't say that.*" He glugged down a drink and slammed the glass on the table. "As God is my witness, I don't wanna know why that friggin goat's bowlegged. Where were we? Oh, yeah, so you're going to Reno?"

"We're –"

"We need publicity on this. We gotta get the message out for the DeePees to go to Reno. I need somebody who can make this story sing."

"Well –"

"Like Sebastian Wow, or even Billy Broadway, he's a good director. Nah, he named his pet monkey Ric, no coincidence there, and besides, he dick-punched me while we were shooting *Apocalypse Whenever*. Still can't piss straight. God knows I deserved it, but I'm still not doing that frogface any favors –"

"Ric! Stop jackin your jaws and lemme talk, wouldja?"

The phone was silent for a second. "You're a little testy. Get bad sleep?"

"I've already arranged it with Tiara King and Timmie Topuha. They're going with us. They'll broadcast it on NewsPulse LA."

"The *Freedom's Bell* team? Amazing! Can this day get any better? Hey, you get a chance, we gotta tawk film rights. This is a big-screen story. I know some people who know some money. I can make it rain simoleons for you."

"I don't want to make a big deal –"

"Just a small deal. Twelve million up front, one percent back-end and residuals, net. Or in tenpez or Calbux or whatever. You speak Mandarin? The Chinese market is *yuge*."

"I don't, but –"

"That's okay, we'll dub over you. The Chinks don't care what you sound like. They just wanna see shit blow up. So we have a deal?"

"Fine, but –"

"I know what you're gonna ask. What about the merch revenue? Well, if they're gonna make Anarchista bobbleheads, you deserve a cut. Okay, you get four percent, net. Christ, you drive a hard bargain. I won't be able to sit for a month." Cheers erupted in the background again and DaCosta yelled, "HE'S OUTTA THERE GOTTA GO!" The tablet clicked and went silent.

She banged her head against the door of the Humvee, startling the private guarding her. She told him everything was okay and then walked to the opposite side of the jeep and lit up, gazing at distant Mount Shasta and letting her thoughts drift.

The videos that Trope had shot, and that she'd fought to bring across the country, were worthless now – unless Hayborn decided to prosecute Cheyn for the RVE Initiative, which he'd never do. Instead, he'd probably pardon Cheyn and give him some spare change to build a nice presidential library.

Hoping to distract herself from the temper storm brewing on her emotional horizon, she opened *Midnight Sun*. When she read the news articles about the Activist takeovers of the Durango and Pocatello bases, she snorted and laughed. "Activist Commander Deacon. That's some feckin royal bullshit there."

From the mouth of the dread Activist Commander Warner, Figment said.

"Watch that tongue, boyo. I'm a professional bullshitter, and that makes it art. Show me a little respect."

Don't get a big head. You're no more than a yellow journalist.

"Philistine. All my bullshit made the flowers grow."

Are you sure all your bullshit isn't just stinking up the joint?

"Oh, now that's it! I'll be having you –" She glanced at the private lounging against the hood of the Humvee, who was looking at her in alarm again. "I…umm, I was talking to somebody, okay? On the phone?"

He nodded, and she read more, slowly realizing that DaCosta was right – perception had already become a grassroots reality. She devoured everything about the Warcode cyberattacks, the civil disobedience, and about Baltimore and Commander Sara. When she was done, she leaned back and gazed into the cloudless California sky, a dreamy smile playing across her lips. Then she chuckled, and in seconds, she was laughing and holding her sore ribs, her tears dripping on the Humvee's roof.

SERGEANT SWENSEN AND TWO SOLDIERS walked from inside the Mal-Mart holding four coolers apiece. He stopped when he saw Krista laying against the jeep, out of breath and rubbing her ribs.

"You okay?" he asked, and the private at the front of the Humvee twirled his finger around his temple and whistled.

"I'm fine, I'm fine," she said, wiping her face with her sleeve. "It's just a weird ole world when Ric DaCosta plays the wise man, Sergeant."

"Ohh-kay," Swensen said. They set the coolers down on the pavement. "There's more in there if you want 'em."

Krista slid the tablet back into her hoodie. "We've got seventy-two, and we just need seventy. Let's hit the road."

The soldiers threw the coolers into the back of the Humvee, and they headed back on Interstate 5, which was still empty except for fire engines and ambulances going in and out of the Exclusion Zone. They crossed into the Zone an hour later and headed south to Davis, where a thousand bottles of Recombin-B waited to be delivered to Reno.

FOUR DAVIS HUMVEES ROLLED INTO BOREAL RIDGE at two in the afternoon and unloaded vaccine coolers for the checkpoint soldiers. While Swensen met with the Bravo Company commanders and briefed them on the operation, Krista and Mark wandered to the chow line, where they met Tiara and Timmie. They ate a real hot meal and then showered for the first time in a week. An hour later, they gathered around the Humvees with the rest of their platoon and climbed into their gumby suits.

"Nobody will know it's me," Tiara whined. "I'll have zero screen presence in this thing. Zero! It's nothing more than a body bag with arms and legs. This'll never work. Never!"

Timmie clapped her shoulder. "It gives you that war correspondent, in-the-teeth-of-danger look. Remember, Edward R. Murrow himself wore a gas mask and a helmet through the London Blitz. Nobody even knew what he looked like till after the war."

Her eyes glittered, and she straightened a headset over her hair. "We'll play that angle – hard-bitten correspondent braves deadly dangers to report the news!"

"Now remember, you can't broadcast this live. Wait till we're back across the border," Krista said. "And we're delivering a cooler to New Detroit later, and you can't film or record there at all."

"Don't worry. We couldn't get a live feed anyway because of the *Fight for Your Life* premiere," Tiara said. "We're recording for a delayed broadcast this evening, a late-prime slot. That'll give us more editing time. We're saving the world here, and it deserves a high shine before it airs."

"Good," Krista said. "Ric wants everybody to come to Reno, so describe where the Displaced Persons Shelter is and how to get there. And make it seem like a spa, not an abandoned airport. Don't show the ill or the dying – just shiny, happy people getting a life-saving vaccine and being grateful, okay?"

Tiara touched a finger to the side of her nose and winked, and then Swensen called for the team to get moving.

The convoy drove slowly out of the camp, each Humvee packed with four passengers and sixteen chest coolers. They drove east on Interstate 80 to the checkpoint, where the soldiers were already being vaccinated, and then they crossed the barrier into infected territory. Refugees still huddled in the trees, and Swensen remarked that they'd get a different kind of shot the next time they tried to cross the barrier.

They wound through the valley to Reno and made their first stop at the modestly named Celebrity Hospital, a major medical center on a large downtown campus. A crowd watched the convoy stop at the entrance, and a squad of orderlies rushed forward to unload a dozen coolers.

The nurses thanked each soldier, and Timmie recorded every heartfelt handshake and teary hug. When they finished, the orderlies filled the Humvee with boxes of empty sterile bottles, syringes, and sterile water. After repeating the same ritual at two more hospitals, they rolled back onto Interstate 80 toward Hughes National Airport.

The jeeps drove to the arrivals level and stopped beside the terminal's tall, dusty glass wall, and everyone picked up a cooler and rolled it inside. Many more refugees had arrived – the baggage claim area was now clogged with people lying on blankets, and some had even made beds on the carousels.

Swensen led them to the Center Terminal and up the escalator, where he delivered a cooler of vaccine and a box of syringes to the Hot Wing checkpoint. The soldiers there were expecting him, and they immediately rolled the cooler into the concourse.

After the soldiers left, Swensen turned to Krista. "Okay, the worst cases are being taken care of, so now it's your show. Tell me where to set up and do the shots and make it look good. Don't disappoint the governor."

"Got it." She appraised the open area where they were standing: The floor-to-ceiling windows overlooked greasy and weedy concrete on one side, and the dusty and tumbleweedy main terminal was on the other. The tiles in the ceiling bulged from a roof leak, and the stained carpet was worn bare.

She walked to a railing overlooking the Center Terminal, where Tiara and Timmy were recording background scenes. "Tia, where do you think we should give out the vaccine? We can do it anywhere, but I need the place to look inviting. This looks like a neglected homeless shelter, not the Promised Land."

Timmie set his camera down and leaned on the railing. "We have strong symbology built in here. See that?" He pointed to two long rows of dust-covered slot machines on the main terminal floor. "They'd make the perfect background. Who doesn't like slot machines?"

"Everybody?" Krista said.

"No, no," Tiara said. "He's right. It's a subliminal symbol of risk and hope."

"Plus, it's iconic Nevada," Timmie said.

"Right." Tiara made a camera frame of her hands and scanned the main floor. "We can make three lines and put the tables at this end of the slot machines. We want long lines to show that everybody's doing it. What do you think?" She turned to Timmie, who was gazing at the main terminal dreamily.

"Ellis Island," he breathed. "This is our Ellis Island, Tia. The lines of the poor, the tired, the huddled masses…"

Tiara squeaked and jumped up and down. "That's perfect!"

"I'll film it in black and white!"

"And I'll round up the right cast! Bright, hopeful eyes in smudged faces, arriving in the new world seeking a better future…"

"The downtrodden masses, yearning to breathe free…"

"*Yearning to Breathe Free!* That's what we'll name it! I love you, Tonto!" She tried to kiss him but forgot they were wearing respirators. Their masks clacked, and they knocked each other off-balance and fell to the floor laughing.

TIARA NAGGED THE SOLDIERS TO TURN ON EVERY LIGHT in the terminal and sweep the decades of dust from the floors and the machines. They dragged three tables from a closet and set them up where Tiara directed, while Timmie took light level readings in every corner of the space. Finally, she inspected the area and declared that she was satisfied.

The National Guard started lining up the refugees for their shots, and then chaos struck: Seventeen thousand desperate people swarmed the

Center Terminal, and a few became violent. The soldiers shoved, threatened, and bullhorned the DeePees into three ragged lines, and after fifteen hectic minutes, the vaccination was ready to begin.

Timmie aimed his camera at the first person to be vaccinated, an eight-year-old boy with big, soulful eyes and a jutting chin topped by an endearingly trembling lower lip. He took his shot like a man.

Mark volunteered to help keep the crowd under control while Tiara and Timmie recorded the event. Krista had nothing to do, so she walked out to the Humvees to get away from the crush of DeePees and tried to figure a way to smoke while wearing an airtight bio-chem suit. Nothing came to mind, so she leaned against a column and tried to blow a bead of sweat off the tip of her nose.

THEY'D ONLY VACCINATED FOUR HUNDRED PEOPLE an hour later, and Tiara walked along the lines and told the refugees they didn't need to wait in the terminal. Most decided to stay in line even though she told them the wait might be two days.

She was annoyed because she needed to scratch her arm but couldn't while wearing the thick bio-chem suit. Worse, she was sweating profusely and destroying her expensive skirtsuit. She was thinking of a way to slip out of it when Timmie tapped her shoulder.

"The network programming manager just called," he said. "He says we can have a thirty-minute live feed if we go direct to satellite. The network hub in Baltimore just got slammed by Warcode again, so he doesn't have any content coming in, and he's desperate to fill dead air. Whatcha think?"

"Why not? It'd be a great lead-in for the segment at ten tonight," Tiara said. "He didn't take away our late-prime slot, did he?"

"No, this is on top of that."

"Great! Let's do it! But if you're going direct to satellite, we'll have to do it outside. We'll lose the signal inside the building. I can vamp outside for half an hour, though."

They tested their signals with the LA office and were ready to go when their live slot came up. Tiara tapped on her microphone and looked into the lens. "For those of you expecting the season premiere of *Fight for Your*

Life, we're experiencing technical difficulties that we'll iron out soon. But we won't leave you hanging – instead, we'll show you history being made! This is Tiara King, and if you can't recognize my face, it's because I'm wearing a bio-chemical suit that protects me from the billions of deadly viruses swarming around me. We're broadcasting live from Sparks, Nevada, just outside Reno, at the old Hughes National Airport.

"At last, the moment all Californians have been waiting for has arrived! The National Guard is administering the first shots of life-saving Recombin to the displaced persons camping here. A crack team of dedicated Activity scientists has been working around the clock to reproduce the Recombin that Krista Warner brought into California last week. Today, a quarter million doses were delivered to Reno, and mass vaccinations are already underway.

"And more is being made in a super-secret facility nobody will even acknowledge exists. But lifesaving Recombin pours out of this mysterious laboratory, and starting tomorrow, it'll be available inside California.

"We'll show you everything tonight at 10 PM Pacific when we air *Yearning to Breathe Free*, a documentary on the deliverance of California from the scourge of Neovirus ravaging the States. For the next half hour, though, we'll interview the people who were instrumental in delivering salvation." Krista walked out of the baggage claim, and Tiara pulled her over by the arm. "And here's Krista Warner now. Krista, how do you feel on this momentous day in humankind's history?"

"I'm sweating like a pig, I've got to pee like a racehorse, and I'm going to chew my own tongue off if I don't have a smoke. I wanna get out of this feckin body condom in the worst way."

"Ha, ha," Tiara said. "Folks, Krista didn't sleep well last night, and we've all been under a lot of stress today. Saving the world's a tiring job!"

"I slept fine, Tia. Now could we do this later and splice it in? If I don't have a squat soon, I'll be filling these boots up to my ankles. I've got enough potty issues –"

"We can't do it later because we're on a live feed right now, Krista. A *live feed* where we can't edit out your offbeat sense of humor. The network hub crashed, and we're filling in for *Fight for Your Life*."

"Oh." Krista glanced at Timmie, who nodded. "Right, this momentous day. It feels like…whoa, we're live?" She scanned the sky quickly for missiles and then grabbed Timmie's shirt. "You weren't supposed to broadcast till we were gone! Are you kidding me?"

"We got a live slot," Tiara said. "We thought we'd interview the key players...where are you going? Folks, Krista is running to the Humvees that brought us here, probably on another top-secret mission of mercy or some daring Activist operation. Let's go find out!" She and Timmie ran to the first jeep, where Krista sat in the driver's seat trying to figure out how to start it. "What mission is the Anarchista on now? Where are you going?"

"Anywhere but here." She climbed out and searched the sky again. Finding nothing there, she jumped back into the driver's seat. The car still wouldn't start, and she tore off her mask and threw it into the street. "Now push off, all right? You've done enough damage."

"It must be someplace important," Tiara said. She ran around the Humvee, and she and Timmie jumped in. "We'll go with you."

The jeep started and she slipped it into gear. "Get out, Tia."

"No, we'll come with you and uncover your mysterious mission along with our viewing audience."

"Idiot." Krista punched the gas, and the Humvee roared down the road. "Okay, fine, you know what? You deserve it. You banjaxed this whole bloody thing." She glanced into the backseat, where Timmie was focusing the camera on her face. "Turn that damn thing off!"

"We're on a live feed, and I'm sure our viewers –" Tiara said.

"Don't worry about that. Your feed won't be live in another five minutes."

"What do you mean?" Tiara asked.

Krista peered through her window. "That's when the missiles will blow us all to kingdom come."

"Missiles arise on columns of fire and shrug off Earth's surly embrace...wait, the missiles are coming at *us?*"

"Welcome to No-Crapistan, sister." She reached for the camera, but Timmie pulled it back. "And they'll know exactly where to go because Timmie's broadcasting this live. Brilliant, isn't it?" She spotted an exit for the Interstate and yanked the wheel. "You're going to get us killed!"

"Oh, you'll get us out of it," Timmie said. "You always cheat the Reaper."

She lunged into the backseat again but couldn't get a grip on the camera. "Not if you keep broadcasting, I won't! Jaysus, couldja at least make it hard for Popo?"

"Don't worry, it won't be hard to find us." Timmie pointed through the windshield. "How many Humvees are going the wrong way on Route 80?"

Krista whipped around and looked at the road ahead. "Oh, crap."

"Give that girl a cee-gar!" Raphael said. "Vark, how long till we're in firing range?"

"The first Talon will be in range in four minutes, the second in nine minutes. Blackwing is over target now."

"And Foxtrot Flight?"

"We could only get three helos in the air, but each has eight Collaterals. They're over eastern Nevada now. They'll be wheels-down in twenty-five to thirty minutes if the winds hold."

"Good job, Vark." Raphael walked the edge of the podium slowly, trying to devise a foolproof strategy. If he killed or captured Warner on live TV, it would prove how effective the NSF had become under his leadership.

He clapped his hands twice. "Listen up, people. It's critical to all of us that this operation succeeds. We're in a time of change. If we want to keep our jobs, we have to show we're important to the new administration. Redacting a known felon on the run – on a live national feed – is the best way to make a splash. Let's show America that the Sultan still has some swat, folks. Hold nothing back and err on the side of mission success."

He watched the Humvee roar toward California. Warner was still a half hour from the safety of the Boreal Ridge camp, and he had more than enough air assets to take her out, but he was still anxious.

"First Talon in range. All missiles armed," Vark called out.

"Blow her away, Vark," Raphael said.

"I don't wanna die," Tiara said, yanking off her mask and helmet.

"I don't, either." Krista pounded the horn and swerved around an oncoming car. "And I certainly won't die on some bad reality TV show." She lunged for Timmie's camera, but he pulled it out of reach again.

Tiara moaned and pulled her microphone up to her lips. "In her last moments, this reporter confronts the fleeting nature of life, and mortality's cold hand grips her heart. She leaves so much undone and unrealized, and she feels every breath and sees every detail of her life in shocking clarity. As she waits for fire and destruction to fall from the skies, she thinks back on all the people she knew and loved, and all the things she never said but should have. I love you, Mom, and I love you, Dad, and I love you, Timmie. And it's been my greatest honor to bring the news to you, dear viewer. But everyone must say goodbye, and so in my final –"

"Zip it for a few seconds, wouldja?" Krista asked. A pickup truck zoomed around a bend in the road, and she yanked the wheel to the right. The Humvee scraped the concrete barrier, ripping off the passenger mirror in a spray of sparks, and the pickup zoomed past only inches away. The driver's mirror vanished as well. "Timmie, you've got to go off-air. I've got an idea."

Timmie paused the recording. "No more than five seconds. The viewers will change the channel."

"This'll be quick," Krista said. "Hades missiles can't change course when they're close to you, so we're going to dodge them. Look out the back windows and call out if you see missiles. They look like little black dots surrounded by a ring of white. I've got no mirrors, so Timmie, you check the back and the left, and Tia, and you check the right. I'll watch the front."

"We can dodge missiles?" Tiara asked.

"I've done it before, but you've got to see them coming. Keep an eye peeled." A minivan roared toward them and Krista swerved to one side. "Go back on-air now. I want everybody to see this."

Tiara pulled up her microphone and looked through the window. "This reporter scans the horizon for airborne vengeance as we roar across the desert for safety, not knowing whether we can outrun the missiles coming our way. She looks for the twinkling constellation of lights that spells her doom, but is her number up? Can the Anarchista pull yet another trick out of her hat and save the lives of us all? In the next few minutes, we'll know, and so, dear viewer, will you. Stay tuned."

TIMMIE SPOTTED THE MISSILES in the northeast sky and trained his camera on them. "I see them! Four missiles coming from behind and a little to the passenger side!"

Krista steered around a small car, saw open road, and pressed the accelerator to the floor. "Okay, when the black circle in the middle gets as thick as the white circle, yell 'Now!' Got it?"

"Got it," Timmie said. "Without the camera, right?"

"Right, bare eyes only." The Humvee zoomed around a bend in the highway. She peered into the distance, but it was clear of traffic except for a tractor-trailer that had to be miles away. She gripped the steering wheel and slowed to forty miles an hour, straddling the center of the road. "Timmie?"

"Not yet…not yet…Now!"

She hit the brakes and yanked the wheel, and the Humvee slid across the highway on two screeching wheels.

IN THE WITCH'S TIT, Kurt Donner and the Deacon were watching the live broadcast on the big dining room TV along with a hundred others. Everybody in the room leaned forward as the missiles closed in.

Suddenly, the view spun, the camera jiggled, and they saw empty highway. Four lights streaked into the pavement, shaking the camera, and smoke and dust boiled out of the roadway and obscured the camera's view. For a few moments, not one man in the room drew a breath, and then they jumped up and cheered.

"We're alive!" Tiara yelled. "At the last second, we swerved and the missiles crashed harmlessly into the road behind us!" Something pattered on the jeep's roof. "You hear pieces of the road showering our truck! We faced the Federal missiles and lived!"

The camera swung from the back and framed Tiara as she wiped tears from her cheeks. "To face Death itself, to smell his foul breath and live to describe it – the experience is incredible." She pumped a fist in victory, and the camera turned to Krista, who poked her finger at the lens.

"We win and you lose, Popo! You'll always lose! You'll never stop The Activity, and you know why?" She made an 'L' of her fingers and stuck it in the lens. "Because you're losers, and losers never win!"

She started to say more, but then she spotted something over Timmie's shoulder and mouthed a silent curse. An air horn blared outside, and the camera panned to record through the rear window.

A white tractor-trailer roared through the dust rising from the long gully of blasted roadway, its tires smoking and shuddering. It swerved to one side as the driver tried to avoid the hole, and then its trailer broke loose, fell on its side, and slammed into the pavement. It slid across the broken road toward the Humvee.

Krista stomped the accelerator to the floor, but the trailer gained on the jeep. The cowboys in the Witch's Tit held their breath again as the rear end of the trailer expanded to take up most of the picture frame.

"Step on it!" Kurt yelled at the screen. The trailer crashed into the concrete highway barrier, and its rear doors broke open and hurled green fruit across the road. It didn't slow down, though, and it closed in on the jeep. It slammed into the Humvee's trunk, and the camera was thrown across the car.

"Aww, shit," the Deacon said. He sat and held his head in his hands. The Activity had just died.

IN BALTIMORE, Sara Hogue had no such worries. She knew that Raphael was running the Watch, and his operational laxity would afford Warner the chance to escape or evade him. Nevertheless, she sat on the edge of her seat in the motel ballroom that she and her lieutenants were using to plan the following week's takeover of the city.

She was riveted by the action on the screen, not because of Warner's plight, but because the sight of one person taking on and defeating government forces could galvanize an already agitated Baltimore populace. Sipping her whiskey, Hogue sat back and decided to advance her plans to seize the city government if Warner survived. The tactical advantage was too great to ignore.

On the TV, the camera shook again, and then a voice with a faint Irish lilt asked, "Everybody okay?"

"Yeah," Tiara said. "Just got a bump on my head. Timmie?"

"M'okay," he mumbled. The image jiggled, showing the ceiling, the floor, and the back of a seat, and then the videographer was filming outside the Humvee and walking backward.

The trailer had crushed the jeep's trunk and pushed the front end over the concrete barrier. Its engine was still roaring, and the front wheels spun madly, seeking traction they'd never find. Tiara stood by the back of the jeep, looking dazed, and then a door opened. Krista slid to the ground and rubbed her head.

She spotted the camera and looked into the lens. "That's the best you can do, Popo? Well, you weren't good enough today, and you never will be. Nothing can stop an Activist – not men, not missiles, not Armageddon. Nothing!"

"The woman knows how to push buttons," Raphael said. "I can see why Bob wanted her dead. Vark, when will the second drone be in firing range?"

"Six minutes."

"Lock a missile on her position and fire as soon as you acquire her," Raphael said. "Just to be safe, launch two more Talons from Wendover. We might need the firepower."

KRISTA TURNED IN A CIRCLE and tried to find a way out. More missiles were probably coming her way, but the Humvee was destroyed; not only that, the road weaved through open desert and afforded no place to hide.

Something squealed and hissed across the gully, and she peered into the smoke. "Let's see if that tractor's still running. Maybe the driver will take us outta here."

She ran across the road through gloppy mashed-avocado paste, jumped into the gully, and climbed the other side. She held out a hand to Tiara and pulled her up, and then Timmie climbed from the hole.

They ran to the idling tractor. The driver was wearing a gumby suit and resting his head against the side window; Krista rapped on it, but he didn't respond. She pulled the door handle, and he fell out of the cabin and dangled from his seatbelt.

Tiara and Krista jumped back a foot and screamed as Timmie zoomed in on the driver's blood-coated gas mask. "I think he's dead."

"Well, we need his truck." Krista reached past the driver and unbuckled his seatbelt, letting the body tumble to the pavement. She climbed into the cabin and found another gumby-suited man in the passenger seat, his head bent at an odd angle. She pressed his seatbelt button, but it wouldn't release, and she climbed back down to the road. "There's another one in there, but he's belted in."

"We have to get him out," Tiara said in a shaky voice.

Krista shook off the puree of asphalt and avocado covering the gumby suit up to her legs. "We don't. You'll ride the dead guy."

"Me?"

"You." Krista shrugged out of the suit and kicked it to the side, and then she jammed her pistol into her waistband. Tiara and Timmie did the same. "One way or another, we've got to get away. He's wearing a gumby suit, so he won't leak."

Tiara peeked into the cabin, and then she sighed and climbed in. Timmie started to follow her, but Krista laid a hand on his arm and stopped him. "Do you know how to drive a stick shift? This truck has a manual transmission."

He shook his head. "I guess you can't, either?"

"I'll just have to wing it." Tiara shrieked, and Krista patted his shoulder. "Might as well get in there, Timmie. I think she needs you."

They climbed into the cabin, where Tiara was perched on the dead man's lap. Krista sat behind the wheel and shoved the stick into first gear, hoping she could get the thing moving. She let out the clutch and the tractor bucked violently; the dead man's head thumped onto Tiara's shoulder, his face turned to her as if he were whispering sweet nothings into her ear. "Get it offa me!" she screamed, pressing herself against the windshield. "This is a nightmare! Don't do that again!"

Krista tried to get the tractor into first gear, and after bucking it a few times to the sound of Tiara's shrieking, it began to move forward. She turned it around toward California. "This is never going to work," she said. "This thing's got like twenty gears, and we're not even up to ten miles an hour yet. It'll take us hours to get to the border this way." She pulled the camera toward her and yelled into the lens, "Hey, if anybody's watching, we sure could use some help right now!"

Tiara pushed the dead man's head off her shoulder with one finger. "Krista, this is a getaway, so can we get away? Please?"

"Jaysus, I'm trying!" She pushed in the clutch and the tractor shuddered as she shoved the shifter into second. The stick fought back and popped out of gear, and the truck slowed. "Crap, I think I broke it." She tried again, and this time the truck slipped into gear.

As they crossed a small bridge, a deafening roar suddenly rocked the tractor, and bright light flashed outside. The right side lifted into the air and hovered for a long second, and then it landed hard and the tractor rolled to the side of the road. Krista tried to regain control, but the steering wheel spun loosely in her hands.

White smoke blanketed the windshield. She peered through the side window and saw that they had rolled off the road and were hurtling across an empty field. Swearing, she grabbed the stickshift and tried to pull the tractor out of gear, but it was stuck. "I can't see where I'm going. Tia, open your window and check!"

Tiara leaned out of the window, past the smoke roiling from under the hood. "You're doing fine! It's just dirt out here!"

"Okay, maybe this'll be okay," Krista mumbled, but then the smoke covering her side window thinned and she spotted a concrete ditch only an inch from her left wheel. It looked as deep as a canyon, and she tried to turn away from the edge, but it was too late – the tractor shuddered, and then it tilted sideways and the world began to spin.

MARK CHECKED THE ENTIRE LENGTH of the empty airport road, but he couldn't find Krista or the NewsPulse crew. He searched every level of the parking deck across the road too, but it was empty.

After repeating the search and finding nothing, he walked back into the terminal, found Sergeant Swensen over by the vaccination tables, and tapped on his helmet. "Have you seen Krista or the Newsie twins?"

"Last I saw, they were hanging out in the baggage claim and working the lines. You check over there?"

"Yeah. I looked all around, inside and out. They're not here."

Swensen called his platoon outside and then hurried toward the departures area door. "Shit, this is just what we need. I thought she was safe here, so I didn't have a guard with her. I hope she just took off with the crew to do something for the documentary." He strode outside and stopped short. "One of our 'Vees is missing."

Mark counted the Humvees sitting at the curb, and then he ran into the road and picked up Krista's gas mask. "Aw, hell. This is bad."

"Damn right. I gotta call this in to Boreal Ridge." Swensen tapped on his helmet and called company headquarters. When he was done, he ordered his platoon to meet him by the Humvees with their gear.

"Okay, everybody, listen up. HQ says there's some sorta hullabaloo going down near Highland Ditch, and our folks are in the thick of it. They just sent the Fourth Platoon there, and that's where we're going too, so mount up." He waved to a few stragglers who were running out of the terminal. "C'mon, move your asses! We're rolling now! And everybody switch frequencies to Tactical Band 4 cuz it's gonna get hot!"

A POWERFUL SMELL INVADED KRISTA'S NOSE. Her eyelids fluttered open, and she saw the seat of the tractor above her. Timmie and his camera were lying beside her on the tractor's ceiling, but she couldn't find Tiara. The dead man dangled from his seatbelt, his arm resting on Timmie's shoulder as if comforting him. Looking up, she saw a hole where the windshield had been.

Laying her head back, she took stock of her condition: She could move her fingers and her toes, her broken ribs hurt so much that she'd probably broken more, and she tasted blood, but she wasn't injured other than that. The odor wafted across her nose again, and a picture of a gas station flickered in her mind.

It was diesel fuel – the truck had rolled over and flammable fuel was pouring around them. She rolled on her side and slapped Timmie's cheek. He mumbled a few times, and she slapped him again until his eyes opened.

"Wake up. Gotta get out of here. The truck turned over and I smell diesel. Could blow any minute."

"Tia?"

"Dunno. She must've been thrown out the window." She grabbed his hand and pulled him toward the broken windshield. "C'mon, get moving. She might be outside already." They crawled through the windshield and onto a concrete floor coated with dust and dotted with weeds. The hot engine ticked inches above their heads, and fuel dripped from the hood's edges. They squeezed under it and scrambled away.

Krista looked back at the accident scene: The tractor had rolled down the sloped side of a deep concrete drainage ditch, and tanks on either side of the truck leaked fuel that ran to a channel in the center. It wasn't burning, but the engine was – two thick plumes of white smoke rose into the sky from around the wheels.

The ditch was choked with tall, dry weeds sprouting from cracks in the concrete. When Krista peered across it, she spotted a pair of legs behind a clump thirty feet away. They stumbled to them and found Tiara talking into her headset, her eyes closed and her cheeks streaked with tears. "…whirling through the air, to land, stunned and shocked, in a concrete canyon…"

"Are you okay?" Timmie asked.

"This reporter is in agony…"

"Tia!" he yelled. "Are you okay?"

She opened her eyes and forced a weak smile to her lips. "Oh, hi. You all right?"

Timmie pulled the weeds away from her legs and winced – white bone poked through the skin of one shin, and the other was scraped and bloody.

"Am I okay?" Tiara asked as Krista helped her sit up.

"You don't wanna see this," he said. "It looks real nasty, but it's nothing serious. You'll be fine."

Tiara sagged against Krista's chest. "I don't feel good. Can you please take me to a hospital?"

"Right. I'll call 911." She pulled out her tablet and dialed, and an emergency operator picked up the call. "We need an ambulance. Our truck rolled over into a drainage ditch or something. I don't know where, but we're south of Route 80. We need medical help now."

"What town you near, hon?"

"We're between Reno and the border. I'm lying in the bottom of this thing, so I can't see anything but sky, but I know we can't be too far from the road. We've got injuries here. Can you send somebody?"

"I can't tell exactly where you are because you have geolocation turned off on your phone, ma'am, but I'd guess you're in Highland Ditch. We'll send somebody out there. What sort of accident were you in?"

"Federal drones blasted the bejesus outta Route 80 and blew up our tractor with missiles," Krista said. "I lost control after the last explosion and rolled over into this ditch."

"Uh-huh," the operator said.

"Really. Their goons are everywhere, and they're always trying to kill me. Jaysus, everybody is, I think. I'm surprised those feckin black helicopters haven't shown up to finish the job."

"You may have suffered some head trauma, ma'am."

"I'm not making that up!" Krista lay back against the wall of the ditch and turned her face to the sky. "Listen, I don't care if you think I'm nuts. Just get somebody out here, wouldja?"

"Hold the line, please." The operator clicked off. Krista heard vapid lounge-lizard music, and she watched oily flames lick along the tractor's sides in time to the greasy Vegas beat. Just as the light-and-music show was lulling her into a trance, the operator came back on. "A Flight for Life helicopter will be there in a few minutes, ma'am. In the meantime, I need you to stay on the line and describe the nature of your injuries."

"Sure…" Krista turned her head and listened to the chopping of helicopter blades. "I think I hear your helicopter now."

"You're closer than I thought. Our unit left just a minute ago."

Krista lifted her head and listened to the rapid thuttering of helicopter blades from beyond the white column of smoke. A wave of scorching air blew into the ditch, covering them with weeds and trash, and she doubled over and covered her face. She heard jeep engines and distant shouts from behind her.

Then fizzing plumes of smoke crossed overhead, and massive explosions rocked the highway and shook the concrete floor so hard that she lost her grip on her tablet. Pieces of concrete and flaming asphalt rained from the sky, pelting her shoulders, and she covered her head and curled into a ball.

TACTICALLY, THE GROUND SITUATION was developing in their favor, Raphael thought. A Blackwing had passed over Highland Ditch and found the three targets lying on the bottom, one seriously injured. Their tractor was laying wheels-up in the ditch and belching thick, white clouds of smoke. They'd be easy prey for Foxtrot Flight, which was only four minutes from the target, but he didn't want to risk failure. "Vark, bring the Talon around and lock on that tractor. Fire two missiles and let the Collateral commander know we're laying down heat for him."

Vark tapped on his monitor but then sat upright. "Rover just detected activity along the border, Raf." He pointed to the surveillance drone's video, which showed a half dozen green Humvees racing downhill from Donner Pass.

"Belay that last order. Target the lead vehicles and fire two missiles," Raphael said. "Make a bottleneck."

The Talon drifted into the video far ahead of the surveillance drone, and two missiles shot from under the wings toward the soldiers. Two Humvees in the convoy exploded seconds later and caught fire, choking the narrow valley with dense, black smoke. However, as Raphael started to congratulate Vark, more Humvees emerged from the smoke and passed the burning vehicles.

The image on the Wall changed to a different valley, where another convoy of Humvees was speeding downhill. "More?" Raphael asked. "Where's this?"

"This is Route 80 at Truckee. It looks like they're also sending everything they have down from Boreal Ridge."

"So California wants a fight. Let's give them one. I want everything at Wendover – drones, Collaterals, missiles, the kitchen sink if we have one – I want everything in the air now. And fire a missile at the lead vehicle in that convoy too, just to welcome them...what's that?" Raphael squinted at a bright dot on the screen heading for the Talon. "Countermeasures! Bank hard left!"

The Talon heeled over and ejected three decoy flares, but it was too late. The surface-to-air missile struck the small plane under the wing, blowing it off the fuselage, and the drone vanished into a ball of orange flame a second later. Beyond it, another white dot appeared from the trees.

"Get out of there now!" Raphael yelled. The drone operator pulled the surveillance drone in a tight circle, and the Sierras and the desert floor wheeled by on the Wall, but then the video went blank. Vark slammed his headset to the desk and slumped in his seat.

"Relax, it's not over yet. We still have options." Raphael loosened his tunic and rubbed at a tight spot on his neck. "When will the next two drones –"

"Incoming infranet attack!" Mochyn called out. "We're getting slammed!"

"Deal with it!" Raf yelled.

"I don't think I can!"

"I can't have any interruptions now!"

"It blew through the primary firewall, and now it's into the secondary! I'm quarantining sectors, but the thing keeps evolving! It's another Blue Ball attack, but this time they're not playing around –"

"Block it! Vark, tell Foxtrot to eliminate those platoons before moving on to the target. Warner's not going anywhere."

"The secondary's gone! It's dissolving the tertiary firewall! I'm isolating the mirror servers and the Syllogic Engine now. Raf, I can't stop this bug. I've never seen anything –"

"Find a way!"

"There *is* no way! The bug's spawning new code to counter everything I –" The Watch Room went dark and every monitor on the Wall faded to black, as did all the desk monitors.

Mochyn tapped on a keyboard, but nothing happened. "The system shut down when the bug breached the tertiary firewall. They snuck in through the energy management computer again and laid us flat on our back in eleven seconds total. We couldn't do a damn thing. Blue Ball wasn't trying to take us down with all those annoying attacks – they were probing our capabilities and responses so they could tune their bug for the big kill –"

"Ask them at the Twentieth Reunion, okay? Right now, I want the system back up!"

"It's pretty fucking dead, Raf."

"Then sprinkle holy water over it and resurrect it. Now!"

"I *can't* do it now. If we restore the system from the parallel computers, we can have it back up in an hour."

Raphael took a step back and clutched his head. "An hour? *An hour?* Every minute is critical!"

"Raf, there's nothing –"

"Vark, call the Foxtrot task leader on his tablet and let him know about this platoon. Buta, get that NewsPulse LA feed back up. We still have cable, right? At least we can tell him what they're broadcasting down in the ditch."

"I can't call the task leader," Vark said. "They're not allowed to take their personal phones on a mission."

"Then call somebody in Wendover and...look, come up with a great idea or something! Show some initiative, man!"

THE GROUND TREMBLED, AND THE SKY FLARED YELLOW as more explosions boomed up on the highway. Krista crept to where Timmie was trying to cover Tiara with his body and record the event at the same time.

Tiara was still narrating. "We're under attack, but since we're blind in a ditch, we can't see the forces locked in mortal struggle above us. With no way out, we can't avoid the fate awaiting us, whatever it may be." She tried to move and winced as pain rippled up her leg. "You guys have to leave me here. Run down the ditch to someplace safe, okay? I'll stay here. Somebody will come for me."

"I'm not leaving you here alone," Timmie said. "But Krista, you should go. It's you they want, not us. Get out of here. We'll be safe."

She shook her head. "Once I start running, I'll never stop. Maybe Ric can help." She cringed as more explosions thundered, and dirt fell in clumps over her head and shoulders. Shaking it off, she pulled out her tablet and dialed Ric DaCosta's number.

The phone had rung only once when the tapping of gunfire suddenly grew louder. A soldier in green battle fatigues slid down the side of the ditch, trailing blood, and his rocket-propelled grenade launcher rolled to

Krista's feet. More soldiers jumped into the ditch, and one wearing sergeant's stripes ran to the man, took his pulse, and shook his head.

He crouched in front of Krista and looked at her face, and then he checked Tiara's legs. "Once we take care of our little problem up there, ma'am, we'll be gettin you all outta here. But you stay tight for now."

"Who are you shooting at?" Krista asked.

"We got some of those damn federal goons up there."

"Ironshirts?" she asked, her eyes narrowing.

"Yeah. Came in on choppers just as we were getting here, and we gotta clean 'em out before we can pull back. Now, lemme get a handle on things. I'll be right back." He'd just started walking to the side of the ditch when a black grenade bounced onto the concrete next to him and rolled toward the smoldering tractor. The sergeant dropped to the floor and covered his head.

Krista threw her body over Tiara's just as the grenade and the tractor exploded. Hot pieces of metal showered her back and hair, followed by chunks of hard concrete. When the shrapnel stopped falling, the tractor had become a steel skeleton swathed in flames, and the rivulet of diesel fuel in the bottom of the ditch had caught fire. A dense white cloud of choking smoke covered them.

The sergeant climbed to his feet and waved for his platoon to gather around. "This is what we're gonna do, so listen up. We got a buncha those Ironshirts in a gully 'bout thirty yards east, and we gotta flush 'em out. We got friendlies from the First Platoon comin in from the east, and they'll push 'em from that side. Now, the Ironshirts got body armor, and we won't penetrate that with these weapons, but we don't have to. Daggett, Menendez, you take the Sawgun up the ditch to the road, and we'll push 'em toward you. When you see 'em, blast the shit out of 'em. The rest of you are comin with me up the ditch. When I give the signal, we're going over the top and makin a lotta noise. Now, everybody move out!"

Most of the soldiers ran up the ditch. Two men walked in the other direction, one carrying a large rifle across his back and the other holding green metal ammunition boxes. They walked about fifty yards toward the highway and started climbing the ditch's side. Just before they reached the top, they stopped and waited for the signal.

Further down the ditch, the sergeant raised a fist. When he brought it down, the soldiers threw grenades, jumped over the top, and unleashed a barrage of rifle fire. The soldiers with the Sawgun climbed over the top and ran into the smoke.

Krista spotted the grenade launcher and picked it up. "Stay here. I'll see if I can help."

"Help?" Tiara struggled to sit up. "They're shooting at each other!"

"They're fighting Ironshirts up there. That's where I belong." She slung the RPG across her back. "Stay here. Stay low. I'll be right back." She climbed to her feet and ran after the two soldiers with the Sawgun.

Timmie recorded until the smoke swallowed her and then lowered the camera. "Don't worry, I'll stay here with you."

"But you really want to go," Tiara said.

"I want to, but I won't."

"Go," Tiara said. "This segment needs sizzle. Our viewers want to see a war. *I* want to see a war, for chrissakes. Go up there and capture it for me."

He hoisted his camera on his shoulder. "Just for a few minutes. You'll be okay?"

"I'll be fine." Tiara kissed her finger and touched it to his lips. "I love you."

He kissed her cheek. "I love you too. I'll be right back." He trotted down the ditch after Krista.

Tiara lay back and noticed the blinking red light on her audio transmitter. "As I lie here broken and bleeding, my fearless videographer Timmie Topuha runs into mortal battle. I just sent my love into war – wish him luck and Godspeed, dear viewers, because all I want is for him to return." A nearby explosion covered her with dirt, and she hunched over her microphone. "Alone in this ditch, I hear the cracks of guns, the screams of men, the cries of victory. Around me, the dramatic spectacle of triumph and mortal defeat unfolds like a glorious and rich tapestry…life and death, sorrow and joy, love and hate are woven together, each thread entwined and inseparable. This is the drama of life, here before you."

She tried to move, sending a shocking bolt of pain up her spine. The world spun for a second, and then darkness settled on her mind. "This is our moment," she whispered, her voice growing fainter. "These are the labor pains of the new nation's birth." Above her, red tracer rounds zipped over the ditch, which became blurry as her vision faded. "I even see…look, it's the rocket's red glare…" Pain eclipsed her consciousness, and she slumped back onto the concrete.

IN THE WATCH ROOM, all eyes were focused on the broadcast. Raphael stood with his hands clasped behind his back, knowing that his future, and the future of the Watch Room, depended on what happened next in a Nevada drainage ditch – and he could do nothing to affect the outcome.

The image on the Wall shook as the videographer ran to the far end of the ditch, up the wall, and into clouds of white smoke and tan dust. He focused on Warner, who was running in a crouch a few yards ahead, the grenade launcher bouncing on her back.

Just as she pulled the launcher forward and prepared to fire, a fountain of dirt erupted in front of her, and thunder roared through the speakers. The image turned to static for a second, and then the camera fell to the ground and came to rest on its side, still recording.

A gust of wind parted the smoke in front of the lens, and Raphael's heart thudded – Warner lay facedown and motionless on the ground as dust and dirt settled on her back.

KRISTA HAD BEEN RUNNING behind the soldiers when she'd been blown off her feet, and she'd lain stunned and unable to move for a few seconds.

She brushed the dust and rock from her hair and looked up. The air was filled with swirling tan dust and greasy white smoke, but she could see where the Sawgun was supposed to be set up at the edge of the gully ten yards away. However, the soldiers weren't in sight.

Grunting, she tried to roll over, but a piercing pain shot through her leg. She sat up and saw that her pants were shredded, and blood welled from a deep gash in her calf. Her other pants leg and her side were also pocked with small, growing bloodstains. She touched her finger lightly to the gash and nearly passed out – something hard was buried in the muscle. Walking would be impossible.

She laid back and felt for her pistol. It was tucked into her waistband, but looking left and right, she couldn't find her grenade launcher.

Gritting her teeth, she rolled onto her good leg and climbed to her knees. She still couldn't see the launcher, but she saw lumps of fabric and metal around a crater and crawled toward it. As she approached, she spotted the Sawgun standing inside a ring of fabric, twisted and contorted like a mad surrealist's fever dream, and then she realized that the lumps of bloody fabric were the remains of Daggett and Menendez.

She had to get back to the ditch and tell somebody the plan was destroyed. Before she could move, though, the sand rustled beside her, and she saw Timmie focusing the lens on her face. "Where'd the soldiers go...holy shit, look at your leg!"

"It's just a meat wound." She wiped the dirt from her eyes and looked down at the blood dripping into the sand. She ripped off a piece of fabric and covered the gash. "It just looks bad. It doesn't hurt."

"Okay, I'll get you out of here. You think you can stand?"

"I don't know..." she started, but then a barrage of gunfire erupted near the highway and she ducked.

THE FIRST PLATOON HUMVEES sped along the shoulder, passing stopped cars with bullet-starred windshields and passengers huddled behind them. They squealed to a stop in the westbound lanes near the flaming hulks of three black helicopters.

Swensen waved them away from the crash site. "The action's on the other side of this barbecue," he said. "Warner and the reporters are with the Fourth Platoon over in the ditch, but they got armored Ironshirts in a gully over yonder. They can't pull out till those Ironshirts are dead or captured. The Fourth's gonna attack first and push the hostiles down the gully to where they got a Sawgun set up. Our job is to keep them in the gully so that Sawgun can convince them God ain't on their side today. Got it? Keep your masks on so you don't choke from all this smoke."

Everybody trotted around the burning helicopters and then knelt behind a metal guardrail alongside the highway. Beyond it, a dusty field dotted with tumbleweeds stretched to the horizon, broken only by the curved white line of Highland Ditch a hundred yards away. A thick cloud of white smoke boiled from the middle of it and drifted lazily over them.

Halfway between the road and the ditch, a narrow gully cut through the hardpan, where gray shapes ran back and forth. The gully ended near the road, where it widened into a shallow bowl, and Swensen pointed to the far end. "The Fourth's setting up the Sawgun there, so we gotta keep the hostiles in this bowl here –" He was interrupted by a ripple of explosions as the Fourth began its assault.

Fourth Platoon soldiers jumped out of the ditch and ran toward the gully. The Ironshirts responded with a barrage of automatic weapons fire, and the advancing soldiers fell to the ground and crawled forward, firing into the Federal lines as they did. A soldier jumped up to scramble toward the Ironshirts and was blown back by a hail of bullets.

"They're getting butchered," Migs said.

"We can't just sit here," Jones said.

"Hold your positions," Swensen said, but before he could say more, the soldiers jumped over the guardrail and sprinted toward the firefight. "Get back here!" he roared, but they kept running.

They'd only run a few more steps when an Ironshirt ran out of the gully. He raised his rifle and loosed a long burst at the two soldiers, who jerked in mid-stride and fell face-forward into the dust.

"Oh, fuck me," Swensen said. He jumped over the guardrail, firing at the Ironshirt in the bowl and forcing him to retreat. "I'll pull these guys back! You keep the hostiles in the bowl, y'hear?"

Swensen ran to the soldiers in a crouch and grabbed one under the armpits. As he did, more Ironshirts ran into the bowl, driven back by the fire of the Fourth Platoon.

Mark and the other soldiers opened up on them. The Ironshirts backed away, firing blindly at the guardrail and slowly edging to the side of the gully where Krista lay wounded in the dust.

TIMMIE LISTENED TO THE RATTLE OF GUNFIRE. "It's coming from the highway. I don't think those are our guys shooting."

"Maybe the Federals called in reinforcements," Krista said. "We've got to get outta here and tell the sergeant. The Sawgun's busted too. He needs to come up with a new plan. This is falling apart." She pushed herself up on her arms and pulled her legs beneath her. "If I can lean on you, I think I can move."

Instead of answering, Timmie pointed into the smoke over the gully. "Did you hear that?"

"I'm not hearing much except a buzz, what with all these grenades popping off. What is it?"

"Something clinked over there." He turned on his camera's microphone and pushed an earphone into his ear. "I should be able to pick it up with this. By the way, be careful what you say unless you want a zillion people to hear it. I'm transmitting live audio." He listened for a few seconds and pointed directly ahead. "There. Metal-on-metal sounds, lots of them, twenty feet or so away."

She settled back into the sand and peered into the smoke. Dark shapes moved inside it, but she couldn't tell if they were friendly soldiers or Ironshirts. Then a breeze sighed out of the ditch behind them, thinning the smoke, and she spotted feet moving back and forth in the distance, feet in black boots with dull gray body armor above them. "They're Ironshirts!" she hissed.

"What do we do now?" he whispered.

Krista didn't answer; she was staring at their leg armor, which curved over the top of their black nylon boots and left only the bottoms exposed. As she watched, they knelt into the dirt and aimed their rifles over the gully, and she could see the soles of their shoes. Something about that was important, but her thoughts were still too muddled to understand why.

"Krista!" Timmie hissed.

She'd seen the same boots before and strained to remember where. Closing her eyes, she recalled nothing but gunfire and a ringing in her ears, and she balled her hands in frustration. The memory wouldn't take shape no matter how hard she tried.

Timmie shook her shoulder. "Are you okay?"

"Lemme think, wouldja?" She closed her eyes again but just felt the outlines of the thought she was grasping for. "I can't do it," she whispered.

You were in bad shape back in Gunbelt, Miss Kellen. That's why you can't recall, Figment said. *Look closer – the Federal that Ada shot was wearing the same boots.*

"Wow," she whispered. "That's exactly what I was looking for. Thanks."

My pleasure.

"Who are you talking to?" Timmie asked.

"Umm…listen, I've got to take these douchebags down." She peered into the dust and smoke, hoping the soldiers had dropped a rifle, but she spotted no weapons of any kind. All she had was her pistol, and it would have to do. "Tell the sergeant the Sawgun's busted. And take care of Tia."

He looked at her eyes, filled with the same strange light he'd seen in Tonopah, and shook his head. "No way. This is the headline event coming. I can feel it. I'll stay."

"It'll get ugly, Timmie. You could get killed. Get out now."

"Hey, our audience loves ugly. All the more reason to stay."

She peered at the cluster of Ironshirts near the gully's edge – it would be one injured woman against seven armored men. If America wanted to see *Fight for Your Life,* she'd show them the real thing. "All right, but keep your head down. Are you still transmitting?"

"Yeah, we're still on-air."

She looked into the lens. "Wake the hell up, wouldja? The shit just hit the fan! The revolution's coming your way, and the Federals really *are* gonna pry that gun from your cold, dead fingers. Use it first! Get up, get out, get ready!"

IN CHARLOTTE, a middle-aged man named Terry Tanner set his beer on a coffee table and exchanged glances with his friends. The Persian Conflict veteran walked to a large cabinet in the corner, unlocked it, and pulled out a black assault rifle.

When the Ironshirts marched in, they'd learn that he was one American who intended to remain free. He slapped a magazine into the weapon and handed it to his best friend, who nodded and passed it to the man beside him. Within minutes, Terry's cabinet was empty of every weapon and bullet, and the men were headed for the door.

KRISTA ROSE TO HER KNEES and tried to not cry out from the shooting pain in her leg. Squinting into the smoke, she spotted the Ironshirts lining the gully's edge no more than ten feet ahead. Gunfire rattled by the highway, and they fired back at the new threat.

She pulled the pistol from her waistband, realizing suddenly that she was going into battle with only a handgun; her odds of surviving were even worse than they'd been blowing the dam. The awareness shocked her, and she drew a short gasp – and then she smelled acrid diesel smoke and gunpowder on the air, and the world went quiet in her ears.

Her vision narrowed until all she saw were the Ironshirts. Her pulse rose, and her blood pumped hot and hard through her veins. Her muscles coiled as her pain and fear faded.

She knew that she could fight these men and prevail. An electric tingle ran up her spine and across her shoulders, and she shivered and peered again at the gully's edge. The men were outlined in a fuzzy, glowing corona that obscured their forms, but then it vanished and she saw every detail; raising the pistol, she looked through the sight and saw not men but targets. The gun moved from foot to foot as if a magnet were locking her aim in the dead center of each heel.

You can shoot four of them with all this noise, Figment said. *Then the others will react, and you'll have to improvise.*

She nodded, but it didn't matter what the Ironshirts did – the Life Force had seized her, and its power pulsed through her veins. "Stay with me, Figment," she whispered.

Always, Miss Kellen.

Holding the pistol in the two-handed grip Mark taught her, she centered the first Ironshirt's heel in her sights and pulled the trigger. He dropped his rifle and jerked, and she aimed at the next man's foot. She fired again, and after the fourth shot, an Ironshirt with sergeant's stripes over his visor turned to see why his colleagues were writhing in the dirt.

Growling, she jumped up and leaped at him, spearing him in the chest with her shoulder and pushing him into the soldier behind him. The sergeant's gun rattled to the ground.

She reached for her pistol, but her waistband was empty. She stood and spotted it lying in the dirt near an Ironshirt she'd shot. As she reached for it, though, another Ironshirt turned to see. They looked at each other for a long second, long enough that Krista noticed the black captain's bars painted above his visor.

As he pulled his gun around, Krista grabbed a rifle at her feet and swung with all her strength at the man's head. His helmet flew off into the gully and the stock shattered into plastic bits, leaving her holding only the hot gun barrel. She leaped on his chest and slammed the barrel into his skull over and over.

Then a man's arm locked around her neck. She struggled to pull away, but he wouldn't let go. His other hand clutched the side of her head, and she knew he'd break her neck if she did nothing. As he reached his hand over her mouth to find a better grip, she realized that his armored glove had fallen off. She bit down hard into the meat of his hand until she tasted blood.

He screamed and yanked his hand away, and she whirled and snatched her pistol from the ground. The man lunged at her, and she ducked under his arms and tripped him. He fell to the ground, and she blew his foot into a mist of blood and bone.

She spat a chunk of bloody hand meat into the dirt and then saw the captain rolling over. She jumped on his back, bent a leg up, and pumped a round into his foot.

As she tried to stand, though, she heard two sharp cracks, and her right arm and leg jerked back. She fell to one knee with blood welling from a new hole in her thigh.

Metal clanked in front of her. She looked up and saw the Ironshirt sergeant aiming a rifle at her head.

You have only one bullet, and he's wearing armor and standing on his feet. It's time to surrender –

"Fuck off!" she yelled.

The Ironshirt lowered his rifle slightly and tilted his head – and then something white flashed behind him and thudded into his helmet, twisting it around his head. He stumbled forward and sank to his knees. She jumped to her feet and kicked him in the back, and he fell face-first into the dust.

She turned to see what had hit him and saw Timmie examining a dent in the side of his bulky Shoulder Studio. "Thanks," she said.

"Right. Just don't tell anybody I did that," he said in a low voice, covering the camera's microphone with his hand.

Krista nodded and looked down at the prone man. He groaned, and she raised her pistol and aimed at the arch of his foot. The pistol bucked, blowing chunks of his foot and boot across the desert floor. "As long as you don't tell anybody I did *that*."

MARK AND THE FIRST PLATOON were hammering the seven remaining Ironshirts in the bowl so hard that they scrambled up the side of it and into the sights of the Sawgun. The gun didn't fire, though, and they hid in the thick white smoke from the burning tractor.

"Swensen!" Mark called into his headset. "Where's that Sawgun?"

The sergeant looked up from the injured soldier he was dragging and saw the Ironshirts run into the smoke. "Supposed to be right where they went! Take a fireteam and check it out! I'll follow in a minute!"

Mark picked four men and sprinted around the burning hulks of the helicopters to where the ditch crossed under the road. Sweating and winded, he yanked off his gumby suit and threw it to the side. He heard the rattle of an assault rifle, and a high-powered pistol cracked somewhere in the smoke ahead. He'd hooked one leg over the guardrail when he heard helicopter blades chopping the air. "Incoming!" he yelled. "Take cover behind the wreckage! Let's go!"

Mark and the four soldiers ran for the burning helicopters and ducked underneath the dense smoke plume. The chopping sound grew louder, and then the downwash from helicopter blades blew the smoke away, revealing a white aircraft with a red cross and CELEBRITY HOSPITAL – FLIGHT FOR LIFE emblazoned on the side. It hovered upwind of the flaming wreckage and then landed on the highway.

The wash from the blades also pushed back the smoke over the gully. Mark squinted to find the Sawgun, and saw seven Ironshirts writhing on the sand and holding their ankles. Timmie Topuha was walking behind them, recording with one hand and yanking their helmets off with the other.

Yearning to Breathe Free

Krista stood in front of them, aiming a pistol at their feet and standing with all her weight on one leg. He looked closer and saw what had happened to her other leg, and then he vaulted the guardrail and sprinted across the ditch.

THE SOLDIERS RAN TO THE IRONSHIRTS and leveled their rifles at the men's bare heads. Those who could raise their hands in surrender did, but most only moaned and clutched their feet. Timmie knelt in the dirt nearby and focused the lens on their faces.

Mark ran to Krista and took the pistol from her hand. "Oh, hell, you been shot."

"This sonofabitch shot me in the leg! Right next to the feckin shrapnel wound, like it wasn't bloody bad enough!"

Mark checked her over. "He nailed you in the arm too, it looks like."

"What?" Krista looked at her bloodied right arm.

"Sorry I missed," the Ironshirt sergeant sneered. "I was aimin for yer cunt, bitch."

"Keep it up and I'll rip your face off and cram it down your filthy craw!" she snarled, and then she moaned and leaned against Mark.

"The adrenaline's wearing off. This is gonna hurt like hell soon." He wrapped an arm around her shoulder and lowered her gently to the ground. "You gotta take it easy now. This leg looks bad."

"Holy shit, everything hurts."

"Hope it hurts as much as my foot, cumdump," the Ironshirt said. "Gimme another shot, and I'll take yer ass down."

"Hey, Stumper, you talk a real big game for a loser," Mark said.

"You ambushed us, asslick. You won't be so lucky next time."

"Like I need luck. You took a forty-four hollow point in the foot, scumbag. Whatcha gonna do, run over my toes with your wheelchair?" He straightened her injured leg and probed gingerly for the wounds concealed by her bloody pants. "These clowns are gonna keep this up, I'm investing in one of those plastic-foot companies."

"At least he won't have to trim his toenails anymore," Krista muttered. "No thanks for that, eh?"

"Wiseass bitch," the Ironshirt snarled. "Just you wait and see what we can do."

"What can you do? I killed a hundred of you at New Detroit, and it was as easy as flushing a toilet. All you're good at is dying."

"Hey, I had buddies in the Third Brigade!"

"Oh, poor baby! Next time pick friends who can fight!"

The Ironshirt tried to lean forward, but then he winced and rubbed his foot. "Uppity bitch. Watch when we march into Baltimore and Richmond and every fuckin ville in every fuckin state. Then you'll see how we can fight and how fast you can run."

"Bullshit. Americans always stand up to your kind of thug."

"Ain't nobody gonna stand up for nuthin, bitch. This fuckin country is busted, and we'll straighten it out if we have to crack every goddamn head in it."

Krista pointed a finger at his face. "Real Americans always fight for what's right. Real Americans will stand with the Activists and march you back to the gates of Hell."

"Real Americans." The Ironshirt spat a bloody gob into the dust. "Real Americans take it up the ass and lay low cuz they're scared of losing what they got. They're like grass, and they're gonna meet the fuckin lawnmower."

"Bring it on! My Activists will take you apart!"

"Yeah, and we'll whack you so hard, you'll wish you were back in Detroit twenty-fuckin-years ago!"

She lunged at him, but Mark grabbed her shoulders and pulled her back. "Bring it, boyo!" she spat. "We'll use your dicks for doorstops!"

"Wait till the fighting's over! Then you'll find out what dicks are for!"

She reached for the pistol in Mark's waistband, but he swatted her hand away and jumped to his feet. "Easy, you two! Krista, the shooting's over, okay?" Mark kicked the Ironshirt in the pulpiest part of his mangled foot, and he hissed and crossed his eyes. "And you. You're triggering me. Stop talking smack to my girl, or I'm gonna alter your state of consciousness."

"Oh yeah, I'm real scared." The Ironshirt scowled and spat another bloody gob into the dust. "Pussywood."

"Last warning, scumbag. I've got a fistful of biofeedback looking for an impactful experience with your face."

"Shitfucker. Go ahead and skullfuck me. Bet you'd cop some wood and blow nut butter –"

Mark slammed him in the forehead with a steaming right cross, knocking him flat on his back and raising an Ironshirt-shaped cloud of dust. "That was cathartic," he said, wriggling his fingers and glaring at the unconscious man.

"That's not what 'biofeedback' means," she said.

He knelt in front of her and tore open her sweatpants. "Whatever. Listen, you gotta calm down now. You've got some bad injuries that you're just gonna make worse if you get riled up." He pulled the pants away from the bullet wound and grimaced. "Aww, hell. Didn't I tell you about taking these stupid risks? Didn't I say you were gonna get hurt?"

"I needed catharsis, okay?"

"Oh, why didn't you say so at first?"

"Good. So we're square now, right?"

"No, we're not! Could you stop looking for ways to get killed?"

"I wasn't looking for it. It came to me." She winced as he pressed on the bullet hole in her calf. "Are you trying to make it hurt?"

"No, but maybe I should. Maybe you'd learn your lesson if I made it hurt. Maybe that'll get through your thick head. You sure as hell don't listen to me."

"*My* thick head? Mine? Are you feckin kidding me?"

"No! Jumpin Jesus, you never learn that this isn't a game! People die when guns go off!"

"And maybe I can't learn, okay? Maybe this is the way I am!"

"I'm just asking you to stay alive! Is that too much to ask? Can't you do that one little thing for me?"

"Why should you care?"

"Cuz I…" He stopped himself and blotted the blood from her leg. "Forget it. Just go and get yourself killed."

"Because you love me, right?"

"Where's this great women's intuition? You women always say you channel these vibes! What makes you so different from the rest of your species? Can't you read my damn mind like every other woman on the planet?"

She smacked him in the arm. "Why don't you just say it, for chrissakes?"

"Cuz it'd screw things up!"

She waved her uninjured hand at the carnage. "*This* isn't screwed up?"

"Well, it can always get screwed up more! Why do I have to spell it out for you?"

"Girls like to hear these things sometimes, Mark!" She slugged him in the arm again, this time with all the energy she had.

"Why do I put up with you?"

"Because you love me! And *I'm* the one putting up with *you*, pal!" She crossed her arms and glared at the dust settling over the gully. "Asshole. That's it, I'm done with you and I'm done being a rebel and I'm moving to a cottage by the sea so you can have a nice asshole-free life."

He snorted and mussed his hair. "Fine! I love you! I always have and I always will, till the sun goes out and the stars go home! You happy now?"

"I am, damn it!" She wrapped her good arm around his neck and pulled him toward her, and then she kissed him so hard that they fell into the dirt together. Kneeling in the dust a few feet away, Timmie focused on the pair, dusty and blood-spattered, and broadcast their victory kiss to the world.

THE BATTLE OF HIGHLAND DITCH was seen live by over ninety million viewers that evening thanks to the Warcode group, who had hijacked the network feed. They replayed the firefight on every channel until ten o'clock, when they broadcast *Yearning to Breathe Free*.

America's final civil war began as the end credits rolled.

Baltimore fell to the Activists first. Young men poured into its streets, enraged by the Ironshirt's threats against the city and agitated by Timmie Topuha's powerful closing montage, which juxtaposed children from Hughes Airport with Ironshirts stalking through Highland Ditch's war clouds.

The city descended into rioting as the angered populace sought something to wreck. However, Sara Hogue's Activist lieutenants appeared on the scene fast and channeled unrest into revolution.

They turned the mob into a 300,000-strong army and marched downtown. Within an hour, the Activists overwhelmed the city's communication and emergency command centers and then moved on to the police stations and armories.

At dawn, Commander Sara declared that the Activists controlled Free City Baltimore. By sunset, she had the allegiance of all Maryland and Delaware from Free City Philadelphia on the east to the border of Washington on the west – except for Fort Meade, where the NSA security brigade was putting up a determined fight.

Richmond exploded too, but it could summon no Activity to defuse the anger. Poor districts south and east of the city broke out into rioting, and large swaths of those neighborhoods succumbed to urban wildfires through the night. The city's desperate mayor took to the airwaves at four in the morning, conceded that he'd lost control, and pleaded for The Activity to assume leadership and stop the violence.

A young police captain named Linda Fortin accepted control of the city for the Activists, although she admitted in later years that her entire involvement with the rebel movement was that she'd once read a Warner column about a monkey getting a blow job. However, the people didn't know that, and they accepted her leadership. By afternoon, the rioters had dispersed and order slowly returned to Richmond.

The rebels in Baltimore and Richmond didn't encounter the massed might of the Federal Collateral Brigades, but the freedom fighters in Charlotte did because they knew where to find it. By the time *Yearning to Breathe Free* ended, Terry Tanner and hundreds of other armed men had already filled their trucks with as much firepower as they could carry. They drove two hours west into the Appalachian foothills to Sugarleaf Valley, where they'd suspected for some time that the Federals had built a base.

They were right. The Ironshirts there ambushed the ragtag convoy in the narrow river valley leading to Sugarleaf, and the freedom fighters returned fire. The Federals limped back on their blasted feet a few hundred yards, but that was all the progress the men of Charlotte made.

The Battle of Sugarleaf would continue for two long days, neither side gaining an advantage for long, until Hurricane Aunt Dottie supplied the answer. At the time, the storm was returning Myrtle Beach to Nature, and it whipped the Appalachian slopes with dry, gale-force winds.

Inspiration struck as Terry Tanner watched the winds strip trees bare. He ordered his men to drain their fuel tanks, and then they dragged the gas cans to the northern ridge of the valley and set fire to the trees.

The dry yellow pines had been bypassed by every hurricane that summer and hadn't seen a drop of rain since April. By October, they were nothing more than standing tinder, and they ignited like matchsticks. When the flames reached the crowns, the gales plucked balls of fire from the treetops and flung them further into the valley. Most of the northern slope of the valley was aflame within minutes.

The winds pushed the flames further, torching barracks, equipment, and men. Less than an hour after the first match was struck, a transport plane roared off the Sugarleaf airstrip and turned west. Two of the aircraft that followed were downed by rebel sharpshooters, but most of the Ironshirts escaped the pyre, never to return to North Carolina.

However, not all responded to the Battle of Highland Ditch with violence. In Chicago, Milwaukee, Minneapolis, and Des Moines, protesters swarmed into the streets and demanded investigations into the viral pandemic and the attack on Sacramento. More importantly, the Governor of Minnesota deployed the National Guard to its border to repel any Federal coercive forces. With so many events in flux, Minnesotans didn't realize they'd taken an irrevocable step toward the founding of the last new nation of North America, Heartland.

But their bewilderment could be forgiven because Americans weren't making sense of much at the time. Few could recall what happened in the tumultuous days following Highland Ditch, partly because almost nobody knew; Internet service was spotty at best, and the desperate population snatched up the few newspapers remaining in print to figure out what was going on. The fortunate few who found a paper spread the news by word of mouth, or phone lines if they were working, but this wasn't enough to keep the people informed.

It seemed as if America was descending into an endless state of befuddlement and chaos, but they had little to fear. America's confusion would be stripped away two days later. They'd wish it hadn't.

THE PICTURE SHOW

Day 60
Saturday evening, October 17, 2043
National Tranquility Center, Fort Belvoir, Virginia

Cochon stepped onto the podium quietly. Raphael seemed deep in thought, gazing at the black screens on the Wall as if their blankness was riveting.

The new Watch followed him, but there'd be no briefings tonight; nothing had happened in the past hour that was worth reporting except for the events at Highland Ditch, which everybody had seen on TV. He cleared his throat discreetly, and Raphael turned and hastily buttoned his tunic. "Oh. Day-o, Phil."

"Hey, Raf. So..."

"So. It was a humiliating defeat, and I might as well admit that Bob would've succeeded where I failed. Half the city would be a smoking ruin too, but Bob always achieved his objective. The man had an almost autistic focus on the goal. Maybe I would have won tonight if I had more vaccines as a kid."

"This sounds bitter and final, Raf. It was just a setback."

"It was an ending, Phil. Warner and her cronies set us up for a defeat on live TV, just like in Gunbelt. It was impressive media manipulation, and we weren't equal to the challenge." He raised himself on his toes a few times and pretended to look at the Wall. "The Activity isn't a chimera. It's real, and we can't beat them. They hit us in the media, in the field, and in our house at the same time, and we couldn't do one damn thing to stop them. They'll win in the end." His lips quirked in a small, sad smile. "Well, I'll watch it unfold on Telemondo Cuba. I won't be here when the politicos take their revenge. Our funding will dry up, and we'll be busted down to a data center again – no Executives, no Special Activity Groups, no Collaterals. As swan songs go, I never thought we'd just get put down like a sick goat. Where's the Wagnerian drama in that, man? Where's the style?"

"Raf, really…"

"It's okay, Phil. There'll be a second act for me. It's time I started looking for it." He sighed and gripped Cochon's shoulder. "You're a good man, and I'm proud to put the Watch in your hands." He patted his arm and walked out of the Watch Room.

MARK PRODDED GENTLY AT THE METAL SHRAPNEL in Krista's calf, but then the ambulance hit a bump and his finger pushed it in deeper. She hissed and grasped the gurney's rail with the hand she'd sprained shooting Ironshirts. Pain shot up her arm, and she whimpered and sat back.

Tiara, who was lying on the gurney, patted her head. "You oughta ask this fine young man for the same pill he gave me. It's wonderful! I'm floating on a cloud of angel sighs!"

Krista looked up with teary, hopeful eyes, but the paramedic sitting across the ambulance shook his head. "Sorry. No narcotics for boo-boos."

"A boo-boo? I've got a feckin railroad spike sticking outta my leg, and you call it a boo-boo? You got the vaccine, right? Well, that was because of me, so how about a nice little pill of quid pro quo?" The paramedic shook his head again and examined something on his tablet, and she turned to Timmie. "You're sure that camera's off? I don't want the whole world to see me go all weenie."

"Oh, it's off. I've captured a lifetime of material already. I can't wait to edit it."

Tiara grasped his hand. "If I don't make it, I want the world to see our work. Promise me this, my beautiful Navajo brave. Promise me on the souls of your ancestors."

"You just have a broken leg," Timmie said.

"You'll be out of Orthopedics in two hours," the paramedic said.

Timmie leaned over and patted her arm. "But while they're working, I'll edit. We still have an hour till the deadline. Hey, imagine the viewership we're going to have after the last hour we just broadcast!"

"It'll be heavenly," Tiara sighed. "I'm sorry I'll miss it."

Krista laid her head gently against Mark's shoulder, trying to find a position that didn't hurt. "This turned out to be a crappy day."

"Yeah. We lost two guys in our platoon today."

"Who?"

"Migs and Jones."

She breathed a long sigh. "I'm so sorry. I didn't think it would turn out like this. I thought I was done with Popo, but the bastards won't give up. They just keep coming and coming."

"Follow the same advice you give Ada. Don't blame yourself for what other people do." He hugged her gently. "I thought you did the right thing. You were very brave back there."

"Well, sorry to disappoint you, but I wasn't being brave. It was just a crappy day, and I was fed up."

He stroked her hair, and she relaxed into his shoulder. "There's the big difference between us. When I'm having a crappy day, I just gotta tenderize the skulls of bad guys. When you have a crappy day, you start a civil war."

"A civil war?"

"I'll bet those were the opening shots back in Highland Ditch." He rested his head against the wall and nodded to himself. "Yeah, this is it. There's no turning back now."

IT WAS THREE IN THE MORNING, and the Bug Team was eating breakfast. Victoria and Ada sat alone at the end of the lab.

"Do you love him?" Victoria asked.

"Oh, yeah, and it's crazy mad love too. It was instant, like love at first sight."

"That's the way it was with Adam. The first time I saw him, I knew he was the one I'd change myself to live with."

Ada reached for the packet of bioreactor plans and slipped out the wedding photograph. "I've been meaning to give this to you, but I keep forgetting. I'm sorry it's all wrinkled, but when the train blew...umm, riding a train blows."

She turned the picture over, and a smile flitted across her lips. "I remember when I met him like it was yesterday. I was the trauma resident on duty the night they were brought in to Cherbourg Naval Hospital. Him and two kids – Ennis Quinn and Ryan Beckmann, two Annapolis midshipmen – had just been released from Hamadan Prison. They were all in bad shape, but Adam had taken it the worst – his face was chewed up like hamburger, and his eyes were swollen shut."

"They tortured him?"

"Mercilessly. He'd been beaten so bad that he couldn't stand straight. I sat with him every free moment I had, catching him up on the TV shows he missed while he was in Hamadan, and he told me about growing up as a Navy brat. We talked for three days. On the fourth day, one of the nurses told me he'd opened his eyes.

"When I walked into his room, they were squeezed shut. I was a little puzzled, but while I was reviewing his chart, he whispered, 'Please, God, let her be pretty. I'm in love and I can't go back now.' He didn't mean for me to hear, but one of his eardrums was ruptured, so he couldn't tell how loud he was speaking. So I sat next to his bed and took his hand. He squeezed it, and then he opened his eyes…" Her expression softened, and she ran her finger across the picture. "So anyway –"

"No, no, no! Back the freakin truck up! What happened then?"

A soft smile graced Victoria's lips. "It was one of my better days."

"Wow," Ada breathed.

"I didn't know what he looked like, either. The boy was all bandages and bruises. When he started to heal, I'd come to his room every day just to see what the face of my love looked like. It was like watching a flower bloom."

"That's so beautiful."

"It was." Victoria laid the picture on the table and pushed it away with a finger. "So anyway, the Persians were furious about the *Vanderbilt* incident, and they took out their frustrations on Adam. And they should've been mad. He kicked some rug-jockey ass at Bushehr Bay."

Ada pulled the photograph toward her. "Was that what he got the Medal of Honor for?"

Victoria nodded. "The Persians were planning to ambush a Navy task force in the Gulf, but the *Vanderbilt* got in the way. Two Persian frigates attacked the ship and blew away the bridge, but Adam, Quinn, and Beckmann were working down in the reactor room. They ran up to the combat bridge, and when Adam saw what was going on, he took the helm and aimed for the frigates. He sliced the bow right off the first one and rammed the stern of the second. All three ships sank and blocked the entrance to Bushehr Bay, which bottled up the Persian assault force inside. When Navy air power finished blasting them, the place looked like Pearl Harbor."

"Wow." Ada ran her finger over her father's picture. "He was a real hero."

"No. A real hero would never have abandoned his family no matter how rough it got. Heroes run *toward* conflict. A real hero would…" Victoria took the photograph from her fingers and laid it facedown on the table. "Whatever. He's not my magic anymore. But while it lasted, the magic was…it's hard to describe."

Ada took her hand. "I know what you mean. I get that feeling when I'm with Micah."

"Yeah?" Victoria squeezed her hand and smiled. "Then you're crazy mad lucky. Not everybody finds their magic. But if you don't mind, there's some advice I can give you…"

"Don't screw it up like you did?"

She pulled a paper towel from the stack and began tearing it. "I guess that's the short version. Just don't make my mistakes, okay? Promise me that."

"I'll try."

"Do, don't try. I don't want to see a replay of all my fuckups. That'd be boring."

"Okay." Ada gave her a big grin. "I'll screw up in new and improved ways!"

Lieutenant Gilsig walked into the lab with three steaming bags of food. He slid two in front of Victoria and Ada, pulled out a stool, and slipped off his shirt. "Mind if I sit with you?"

Victoria smiled. "No, we'd love some company. Please, make yourself comfortable."

"Thanks." He sat and opened his bag.

Victoria peeled hers open and frowned. "Great, sausages. I can't eat them now that you told me they look like freeze-dried dog turds."

Ada giggled. "Well, they do, don't they?"

"I'll trade you my eggs," Gilsig said. He reached over, and as she handed him the sausages, their hands touched. Victoria blushed and apologized, and he mumbled and looked down at his food.

Ada munched on a gray, rubbery waffle and watched the exchange, her eyes twinkling. She leaned over and whispered to Victoria in Zulu. "Lieutenant Clark Kent's a looker, isn't he?"

Victoria gave her a puzzled look as her brain processed the language. "I could get used to that face."

"Face? Look at those pecs! Look at those shoulders! And every time I see that ass, I have to bite down on a piece of leather!"

"You don't think I've noticed it?"

"And he's noticed you, and you're both sitting here doing nothing. You two are *so* lame. Do you pass notes in study hall too? Jeez, how was I ever conceived?"

"We just met! Maybe you should mind your own business!"

"I'm just saying you shouldn't be so bashful. You two can have the perfect December-December romance."

"Oh, you are *so* lucky I love you."

"Why does everybody say that?"

Gilsig gave them a puzzled look. "Excuse me, but what language are you speaking?"

Ada grinned broadly. "French!"

He shook his head. "I was an exchange student in Cherbourg when I was in college. That's not French."

"I was stationed at Cherbourg Naval Hospital right after med school!" Victoria said. "Did you visit the *Cité de la Mer?*"

"I spent hours there. It was my favorite place, except for the *Plage de Collignon,* of course."

"I got the worst sunburn of my life on that beach! And the sand got up my –"

"Whoa, you guys!" Ada said, stabbing her hands together in a 'T'. "I need a smoke. Why don't you come topside with me and share your war stories up there?"

"Sure, I'd like that." Gilsig threw away his bag and reached for his pistol and radio. "I'll see you up there in a minute. I have a few things to do first."

They watched him leave the lab. As soon as the door closed, Victoria wheeled on Ada. "Stop being a matchmaker!" she hissed. "This is inappropriate behavior, young lady!"

"Oh, shut it! He's warm for your form. Everybody knows except you." Ada stood and picked up her bag. "If you don't want to talk to him, you can stay here."

"No, I'll come along." Victoria cleaned up her end of the table. "This might be interesting."

VICTORIA AND ADA SAT on the dock's edge, and Gilsig leaned against the back of a Humvee below them. Ada and Gilsig lit up. "I hope this isn't blowing on you," he said.

"No, it's fine," Victoria said. "My little chimney here's desensitized me to it, anyway."

Ada let a long plume go. "I keep telling her it'd be easier if she just took it up, but she's got a fitness fetish."

"Well, I don't think –" Gilsig's radio chirped. "Excuse me, I've gotta take this." He walked to the far end of the Humvee.

"You oughta try it, Mom. It'd take the edge off, and trust me, you've got a lot of edges. Really, it's as easy as breathing."

"Sure, but you'll only breathe till the tumors sprout," Victoria said. "Then it's lights out."

"No way! I can cure cancer now. Well, give me a few months in the lab first, but the science is already dialed in."

"You…what…?"

"I forgot to tell you, but it's been nuts around here. Oh, and did you know I cured AIDS last week? It kinda fell into my lap, actually, but have I caught a freakin wicked wave or what?" Victoria grabbed the sides of her head, and Ada patted her shoulder. "Mom, you need to keep up if we're gonna hang together."

Lieutenant Gilsig walked back to the dock. He leaned back against the Humvee, his face drawn and tense.

"What's wrong?" Victoria asked.

"Bad news. Our squads got caught in a skirmish in Reno with the Federals, and it grew into a full battle. We lost Migs and Jones."

"Oh, no," Victoria said.

"The Federals tried to whack Krista and the film crew, and my squad intervened. The Fourth came down from Boreal Ridge too, and it turned into a big firefight. There's nineteen dead, Route 80 has craters and burning stuff all over it, and we've been put on alert in case there's a Federal counterattack."

Ada sat up. "Is Krista okay?"

"Yeah. She's fine, and so's Mark. They left Boreal Ridge about two hours ago, so they should be here soon. She was wounded, though – got some shrapnel in her leg and had to go to the hospital. But the captain says she's okay."

"That's good news." Ada rubbed her thigh. "I got a shrapnel wound there once. It hurts like hell."

"What? When did this happen?" Victoria asked.

"Umm…let's talk about that over a bottle someday," Ada said. "So the Federals lost?"

"Yeah. It sounds like they got beat up bad, but I'm not sure what happened. The captain was in a hurry and said I should just go on the SatNet and see the replay." He looked up at the sky. "Can't do that here. Only the tactical frequencies are working."

"Krista and Mark can fill us in," Ada said.

"I hope so." Gilsig rubbed his hand across his face. "Shit. We aren't ready for a war, not after Sacramento and all."

"War?" Victoria asked.

Gilsig nodded. "It's either war, or we're about to be rounded up and tried for murder." He rested his head against the roof of the Humvee and looked at the stars. "Yeah, either way we lose."

DISPATCHES

Midnight Sun
News Post of October 18, 2043

BREAKING NEWS: US ARMY FORCES ENTER LOS ANGELES

At dawn, the 11th Armored Division of the US Army, based at Fort Irwin in the Mojave Desert, entered the city of Los Angeles and occupied the downtown area, reports Tiara King of NewsPulse LA. *The Tia and Timmie Show* is broadcasting live, and it shows tanks surrounding Pershing Square and soldiers running from building to building.

Despite her injuries, King interviewed officers of the invasion force, but they refused to discuss their operation's objective. She also says that the city is peaceful, and no loss of life has been reported.

She is relocating to a secure studio for an interview with Governor Ric DaCosta later today, who is expected to make an important announcement. All Californians are urged to tune in at 11:00 AM PT.

We will post updates on this breaking story as more news becomes available.

EASTERN CITIES FALL TO ACTIVISTS

At dawn, the Activist attack on critical Eastern infrastructure resumed, and power and communication blackouts have been reported from Baltimore to Richmond.

Nearly all commercial and financial websites *Midnight Sun* has tried to access are offline. Internet service providers in Washington, DC have shut down their systems to protect their servers, denying even sporadic internet access to District residents.

The Warcode hacker group reports that their organization successfully hacked the information systems of the Defense Department last night and cracked its encryption. They found evidence that an Army laboratory in Windy Mount, Virginia, had weaponized a virus called Ellesmere A4, which we now call Neovirus. This new information supports Warner's contention that government authorities triggered the viral pandemic.

Further, this lab mass-produced the weaponized Ellesmere A4 earlier this year and delivered it to Fort Detrick just prior to the August outbreak. Warcode copied the files and planned to make the information public, but computer systems in the Bay Area have been crippled by a widespread cyberattack from Fort Meade's US Cyber Command.

However, according to radio reports we have received, the security perimeter of Fort Meade is now under physical assault. These same transmissions state that the cities of Atlanta, Baltimore, Charlotte, Memphis, Nashville, Raleigh, and Richmond are now operating under Activist control. These reports are unconfirmed, however, and we will update our readers as reliable information becomes available.

FALLOUT FORECAST

The center of Tropical Storm Andy Boy is currently twenty-eight miles west of Omaha and moving east at thirty miles an hour. Radionuclide deposition is higher than expected: Outside Omaha, an unprecedented seventy-five rads per hour was deposited as the storm met a cold front out of Canada and concentrated the fallout over a narrow band.

These deposition rates may be sustained as the storm moves east, with significant hazard to life in the affected region. Canadian public-health experts recommend a complete evacuation of eastern Nebraska, northern Kansas and Missouri, southern Iowa, and central Illinois, Indiana, and Ohio.

However, President Hayborn, in his first public radio address, has instructed residents of these areas to stay in their homes for the next three days, advising them to seal windows and doors with duct tape. He further stated that he'll deploy Army troops around this deposition zone to offer assistance after three days, although many wonder if their real mission is to ensure that the population suffers certain death.

In accordance with the presidential recommendation, the governors of Nebraska, Kansas, Iowa, and Missouri have issued mandatory shelter-in-place orders for their states. However, the governor of Illinois has issued an evacuation order for that state's thirteen southernmost counties, effective immediately.

Ohio and Indiana have not taken any action to counter the fallout threat. As both state's capitals were devastated by Neovirus, it is possible that no effective state government remains to protect its surviving population.

Some public health officials believe that the shelter-in-place strategy will cause radiation illnesses that may take decades to appear, as the heavy radionuclides in the fallout will remain hazardous for at least seven months, not three days.

Midnight Sun urges those residing in this deposition zone to defy this presidential decree and leave now, even at the risk of encountering an armed cordon, as this presents the best chance for survival. We will monitor radio reports throughout the day and identify known, safe paths out of the fallout impact area.

VACCINATIONS CONTINUE THROUGHOUT RENO

Our Witness in Reno reports that the city is distributing the vaccine at an accelerated pace:

"Warner and her team delivered a quarter million doses yesterday, and most of it's gone already. Everybody's lining up to get this shot – they're not making the mistake the East Coast folks did.

"The first vaccinated refugees from the airport will be allowed into town in two days. That's good, because we have a labor shortage here. The slots are clinging, the cash registers are clanging, but we don't have enough people to run the place. We need help, and the folks coming into town are guaranteed jobs. Cheyn didn't need to kill off the unemployed. He just needed to send them to sunny Reno.

"And we're getting more every day. The airport picked up another five thousand refugees yesterday after the news of the vaccination.

"We're a Mecca now. Everybody wants to be here, and it feels great that the World's Biggest Little City isn't the retarded stepchild of Las Vegas anymore. We're the largest and healthiest city in Nevada now. Forget Vegas. Reno is clean, folks. No virus, no radiation.

"Everybody watched *Yearning to Breathe Free* last night. I cried like a baby when that little girl asked the soldier to save her teddy bear's life too, and he gave it the shot. God, that was a powerful show. It's been replaying on every screen in town ever since it aired.

"We all watched that little war out at Highland Ditch yesterday afternoon too. I was watching it on my tablet, sitting on my back porch, and I heard the booms in stereo. In fact, the Federal helicopters passed right over my house on the way to the fight. It's creepy being so close to history being made, like being near a live wire. You don't want to touch it, but on the other hand, you can't help reaching for it.

"Everybody here agrees that the boys of the 184th Infantry are heroes, and Warner should be elected Honorary Queen. And California makes a great big brother.

"Speaking of that, I hear rumors from Carson City that we're a part of California now. I can't understand how this works, but I'll check Tiara King's show later and see if the governor has an explanation."

⊶⊶⊶⊶⊶

The Tia and Timmie Show
NewsPulse LA
Broadcast Transcript of October 18, 2043

King: Before I came to California, the highest government official I ever interviewed was a rodeo marshal. And now a governor is on my show! I'm pleased to welcome Ric DaCosta, the redoubtable Governor of the State of California.

DaCosta: Thanks, Tia. Great to be here, but then all of us are saying that these days cuz a lot of us aren't here anymore. But hey, let's not get all dark. Let's move on to something better, like my big announcement: I'm not the Governor of the State of California anymore. I'm the Governor of the sovereign and independent California Republic.

King: Wow! When did that happen?

DaCosta: I thought you knew. You blabbed it all over the air last night when you were laying in that ditch. Y'know, the new nation's birth and all that?

King: Krista told me, but it still gives me a tingle to hear it from you. Welcome to my show, Governor of the California Republic! Such a thrilling moment!

DaCosta: Want me to commemorate it by signing your cast?

King: Would you? Somebody get me a marker! Look, there's a little space next to the knee.

DaCosta: Must be a pound of ink on here.

King: I made a hundred friends just this morning. California's a friendly place filled with wonderful people, and I feel blessed to be here.

DaCosta: Got your tax bill yet? No, forget I said that. So how's the leg feeling?

King: I'll be fine in six weeks, but last night – that'll stick with me forever. Thanks for sending the troops in to rescue us.

DaCosta: It's what I had to do. Hey, kudos on *Yearning to Breathe Free*. Really, that just got me right here. Trust me, not much does. You oughta get an award for that.

King: Mr. Governor, I report the news in the public interest. I don't deserve an award, nor am I expecting one.

DaCosta: Wow, that's one helluva sincerity aura you've got there. Can you teach me that?

King: This is just the way I am. And in all sincerity, Mr. Governor, I'm proud to be part of this great country.

DaCosta: We *are* a great country. We've got great people and a great land. Yeah, we've got our problems, but we get over them without throttling each other, and that's what makes us great. We'll get back on our feet and be better than before.

King: Will you rebuild Sacramento?

DaCosta: Me? Nah, I've got a bad back. Just kidding, look, of course we'll rebuild it.

King: Where will the capital be until then?

DaCosta: I can't say. I don't wanna tempt the loons in DC. Hayborn's just as batsh–t crazy as Cheyn, and Cheyn was Kommissar Guano, amirite?

I don't know how he got elected. At least I voted for the retard instead of him.

King: She was differently gifted, not retarded.

DaCosta: Hey, I'm not judging. But she brought her dolls to the presidential debate, and when the moderator asked who she'd pick for vice president, she held up Mr. Buttons. That's either brilliant or retarded, I dunno.

King: That was understated political satire. She was implying that a stuffed-shirt politician was no more qualified than a stuffed toy.

DaCosta: Wow. Okay, I didn't get that. Went right over my head.

King: She was more subtle than everybody assumed. A lot of people didn't understand her.

DaCosta: Well, I guess she was onto something. Definitely, Mr. Buttons woulda made a better veep than Mr. Cheyn.

King: I think so too. I'm not supposed to express political opinions here, but I wish she'd run again. I'd love a do-over on that election.

DaCosta: Me too, except we just seceded, so I guess we're not voting in any more presidential elections. But I gotta tell you, I'm relieved they're over. They were getting annoying.

King: I just tuned them out.

DaCosta: But listen, I hope the States elect her. At least Vice President Buttons won't slaughter half the friggin country. And I'd love to see Hayborn booted outta the Oval Office and get somebody in there who actually wants to do the friggin job. Notice that he became president, and he didn't send any disaster relief to Sacramento? F– him.

King: I wouldn't bother swearing. The censors bleep that out.

DaCosta: I'm an Italian-American from Brooklyn. It's the only verb I know. So f– him.

King: Are you keeping the temporary capital secret because you're afraid of another Sacramento incident?

DaCosta: No, that won't happen again. I just returned from the Commonwealth up north, where I signed a mutual defense treaty this morning. If Washington wants to light up our lives again, we'll light up theirs. And the Commonwealth is sending down an armored division to chase Hayborn's tanks outta LA before we get total gridlock downtown.

King: You don't seem worried that they're here.

DaCosta: Why should I be? This is Los Angeles. We're used to tourists.

⌖⌖⌖⌖⌖

Molle's Hill
NewsHub Political Affairs Channel
Broadcast Transcript of October 18, 2043

Molle: For the first time, *Molle's Hill* is broadcasting from the Blue Room of the White House. It's weird, but the Blue Room is actually white. Shouldn't it be blue? Some people can get confused. When I came in a few minutes ago, I walked right back out thinking, so what's up with this? And then...Mr. President! Thank you for coming on my show.

Hayborn: You're most welcome, Arista.

Molle: I understand we only have a few minutes, so I'll get straight to the questions. There are reports that the 11th Armored Division has occupied Los Angeles. Is this civil war, Mr. President?

Hayborn: This is merely a police action. The 11th Armored is tasked with apprehending the rogue governor of that state and the Activist felons he's harboring, and to bring them to justice for the violence at Highland Ditch yesterday.

Molle: Then do we...hold on, is that my tablet ringing?...It's who?...Really?...Mr. President, I have Tiara King on the line, and she's talking to Governor DaCosta now. Would you like to speak to him?

Hayborn: Yes, indeed.

Molle: Tia, how are you?...I had one of those, and it gets so itchy...if you slide a ruler under the cast, you can get to it, though...did anybody famous sign it?...Omigod, he's a hunk!

Hayborn: Miss Molle...

Molle: Yes. The governor says the secession of a state is now a Federal crime, thanks to you, and you allowed California to secede on your watch. He wants to know when you plan to resign.

Hayborn: I..., I...

Molle: He says he'll be happy to send his Articles of Secession to the House Judiciary Committee. Isn't that nice of him?

Hayborn: All I wish to hear is when and where he plans to turn himself and Warner in to face justice.

Molle: He says it's funny to hear you talk about justice since you ordered foreign forces to invade the California Republic at Highland Ditch yesterday. If anybody did anything illegal, the States did. He says he'll overlook your crime, though, since seeing seven of your hardened mercenaries get punked by an ordinary girl was humiliating enough.

Hayborn: I watched Warner's made-for-cable rebel porn last night, and she's no ordinary girl. She's a trained Activist commando…

Molle: He also says that when he was a kid, they called that 'getting poned.'

Hayborn: A childhood that hasn't yet ended, it would seem.

Molle: He also says your men performed admirably. They almost made it to the finish line, but they came up only fourteen feet short.

Hayborn: And now he's resorting to insults. There's no call to demean fine, brave Americans.

Molle: Oh, no, I think he's congratulating them for coming so close. Fourteen feet isn't very far.

Hayborn: It's a double *entendre*. He isn't talking about the distance in feet. He's talking about the *number* of feet.

Molle: Fourteen feet, right. That's as long as the table in my studio.

Hayborn: No, no, no. Miss Molle, how many feet do seven men have?

Molle: Two, four, six…oh, I get it! Seven men have fourteen feet! That's funny!

Hayborn: Indeed, and I can barely contain my laughter. Now tell him that if he thinks these witticisms will get him somewhere, he's sadly mistaken. The United States does not negotiate with terrorists. His only course is to turn himself in, along with the rest of the criminal Activist leadership.

Molle: You wouldn't want to negotiate with him. If you give him a foot, he'll take a mile…Mr. President, please sit down. I'm sorry, that just slipped out. I was caught up in the meme.

Hayborn: If we can't have a serious discussion, I'll terminate this interview right now.

Molle: I understand. Tia, we have to be nice, yeah, he's getting real steamed…oh, really? Mr. President, as a gesture of international cooperation, Governor DaCosta says California's gold reserves are yours for the taking.

Hayborn: They are? Just like that?

Molle: He says the gold isn't at Sumobank in Los Angeles, though, so you can tell your troops to stop trying to break in. The Republic stores its gold in the basement vaults of Sumobank in Sacramento. You're welcome to all you can haul off.

Hayborn: That's hardly a serious gesture. It's under tons of radioactive ash. It'll be months before we can get to it, and he knows that.

Molle: Wow, you're right. It's almost like he's taunting you.

Hayborn: He most definitely is. This is the California mindset for you – they're polite on the surface, but as soon as you turn your back to them, they'll sink a knife into it. That's their true nature.

Molle: He says that if you want to reveal your true nature, why don't you put on your tinfoil hat and –

Hayborn: I've had enough!

Molle: – and admit you're an Aluminati. Mr. President, it would be absurd to believe you're one of those crazy Elders.

Hayborn: This interview is over. I'm outta here.

Molle: Oh, Mr. President! The governor says to have a nice day!

SIX SMALL HOURS

Day 62
Monday morning, October 19, 2043
Briggs Hall, University of California at Davis

Krista adjusted her sling as she watched Mark and Micah pack Recombin into two coolers. She sighed and nudged Ada in the ribs. "Our Sir Nigels. Isn't that so cool?"

Ada didn't hear the question because she was plugged into her earphones, listening to Blac Sacrament's *Blac Blooded* at full volume and staring at the lab computer screen in an unblinking trance. Krista nudged her a little harder. "What?" Ada asked. "Will you stop pulling my plug? I'm trying to concentrate."

"What's so interesting that it makes you disappear from Planet Earth?" She pointed at a complex circular shape on the screen constructed of squiggly white lines. "What's that?"

"It's a particle microcollider. I was redesigning the one I used on Baby Bang Bang to port fast mesons for clinical and therapeutic use, and as I was doing that –"

"How would you use a particle whatsis in a clinic?"

"To destroy cancerous cells. If I can split a gluon with a fat plasmon, like I did in Baby Bang Bang, I can totally obliterate the DNA of a cancerous cell with a trillion fast mesons zooming at lightspeed. Without damaging surrounding tissues, either." Ada made a gun of her fingers. "Boom, no more tumors. Anyway –"

"You've cured cancer? Is that what you're saying?"

"Basically. Now can I get on to the interesting part?"

"That's not the interesting part?"

"I think I can also build a time travel device. Is that interesting enough for you?"

Krista sat back on the stool. "All right, you win."

Ada crossed her arms and stared at the screen. "It came to me in a dream last night. I realized that if I constrict the port and induce an exotic particle trap, the rotational momentum of the resulting particle swarm would generate a robust plasmotoroidal field that can modulate the truon feed. Then I can safely anomalize the timefield interstices using some sorta scalar interpolation doohickey I still need to invent. Assuming I can maintain boson-fermion symmetry at the swarm margin, natch. But that's a gross over-simplification."

"Sure, sure, you're just dumbing it down so I don't get baffled." Krista puffed out her cheeks and let her breath go in a silent whistle.

Ada nodded and pointed to a spot near the outside of the circle. "The problem is that mass-energy conjunctives usually attract blackcharged backquarks at the outer boundary layer, obviously, cuz blackcharged quarks can be either mass- or energy-flavored. That's no problemo, but if they penetrate as deep as the Lang Boundary..."

"The Lang Boundary?"

"It's named after me, okay? Can I talk without getting interrupted every two seconds?"

"Right. So you were saying?"

"This is where I need my algorithm. The backquarks might neutralize the toroidal field containment. If they turn bosonic at the Lang Boundary, you could get a bazillion-megaton explosion. If they turn fermionic, they could compress the toroid and create a singularity. A black hole that could swallow the solar system."

"Okay, don't do that. Please?"

Ada shook her head and glared at the screen through narrowed eyes. "Blackcharged backquarks. They're like the biker gang of the sub-nucleoverse."

Krista scratched her head. "Okay, thanks for explaining it. It's so much clearer now."

Mark walked over and clasped a hand on Ada's shoulder. "Hey, Twink, you're looking saturnine today. Maybe even lugubrious."

"Oh, hell," Ada muttered. "He's been reading the dictionary again."

"Yeah. There's a big hardcover one in the library. I'm taking it with me when we go." He leaned over and glanced at the screen. "What's that? It looks like an electric donut."

"Electric Donut. That's a good name for it," Ada said. "You know, talking to you is like squeezing a blackhead, Skid. It's gross and painful, but weirdly satisfying." She held out her fist. He gave it a quick bump, and then she crossed her arms and glared at the donut again.

"Whatever it is, it looks pretty scary," he said.

"It has that deathstar atmo, doesn't it?" Ada asked.

"Hey, wanna take a ride with me?" he asked Krista. "Since the rest of the Security Team's busy making deliveries, I thought I'd load up the 'Stang and make a few of my own. They probably delivered a million doses already, and I figure I can deliver a few thousand."

"Six hundred thirty-two thousand," Ada murmured. "We'll reach a million on Wednesday afternoon at 2:13."

"I'd love to join you." She laid her hand over Mark's and turned to Ada. "Wanna come along? You could use a break."

"I *am* taking a break. This is how I relax." She blew a kiss at Micah and wrinkled her nose. "During the day, at least."

"Aww, that's gross!" Mark groaned. "That's my little brother you're talking about!"

"He's not so little. In fact, he's hung like a –"

"No!" Mark jammed his fingers into his ears. "No, no, no! I don't wanna picture that. Dah-de-dah-de-dah…" He stomped into the corridor and stood safely out of earshot.

Micah reached over the table and bumped fists with Ada. "Pissin! You found a new hot button."

"He went off like a rocket, didn't he?" Ada asked.

Krista slid off the lab stool and adjusted the green camouflage pants the soldiers had given her after Highland Ditch, which bunched up in all the wrong places. "Why do you guys pick on him?"

"Cuz he's my brother," Micah said. "If I didn't torture him, he'd think I didn't love him."

"God, I wish you two would grow up. He's a nice guy, and he deserves better." She picked up two coolers from the lab table and limped to the door.

Mark took the coolers. "Lemme get these in the car, and I'll come back down and help you. You're gonna have trouble getting up the steps."

"I'm good. I've been doing this by myself since we got back. Just don't rush me, okay?"

"All right." He shifted the straps of the heavy coolers on his shoulder. "Thanks for coming. I need you to be my identification. When the Security Team takes this stuff into a hospital, the uniforms tell everybody they're legit, but me, I could be anybody. Everybody knows your face, though, so you'll be my passport." He opened the door to the stairs and held it for her.

"Thank you, sir. I should get wounded more often."

"My pleasure. Anyway, your face will be the perfect passport where we're going. They know it pretty well."

She gave him a puzzled look.

"Marin Wellness Hospital. I wanna –"

"I'm not going back there! We broke every law there was last time! They'll clap me in irons the minute they see me!"

"Naw, your buddy Ric cleared that up, right? And how bent outta shape are they gonna be when we give them eighteen thousand doses of Recombin? I think they'll change their mind about you. Besides, we'll be nearby anyway. I wanna check in with my mom and make sure she gets the shot."

She let out a long sigh. "All right, as long as you bring your gun along. I've got mine."

They arrived at the loading dock a few minutes later, taking the trip slowly because Krista's ribs were hurting more than usual. Mark jumped off the dock and threw the coolers into his trunk, and then he reached up to help her.

"It's all right. I'm not an invalid."

"Eighteen stitches, seven cracked ribs, two gunshot wounds. The numbers aren't on your side."

"Don't worry. I just took a magic bean, so I should feel zero pain." She sat on the edge of the dock and pushed herself off, landing on the ground with a wince.

"You okay?" He grabbed her shoulders as she started to wobble on her feet. "You don't look real good."

Six Small Hours

"That was…a little intense." She leaned back against the dock and adjusted her sling again as she looked around the courtyard; the dust had abated in recent days, and she could now see patches of blue through the dun-colored clouds. "You know, I think we're turning a corner, all of us, and maybe we're turning toward something good. One of the soldiers told me that Baltimore, Charlotte, and Richmond are under Activist control now, and the Federals are on the ropes." She shook her head and barked a short laugh. "Activist armies. Seriously, that blows my mind."

"I told you they were out there. They just needed a name."

"They just needed a brand, and that's all I gave them," Krista said. "I think that's what the Life Force wanted me to do, and now that I have, it's released me. And I'm glad it has because I don't think I could survive another beating. Besides, it's time. Like Dowdie used to say, 'Once you blow out your amps, cue the pyrotechnics and end the show before anybody notices.' My amps were blown out weeks ago."

"I don't know many people who could take what you did and still be vertical."

"Painkillers, that's my secret." She sighed and leaned against his chest. "But it was all worth it. *Yearning to Breathe Free* woke everybody up at last. Nothing can stop the revolution now."

"Well, if there's a revolution on, the newsfeeds aren't talking about it. One of the soldiers told me that the big news they're covering is the Anarchista's daring new cropped haircut."

"MRC morons. Like there's nothing more earthshaking to talk about than my new 'do."

"Hey, it's been shaking *my* world, lemme tell you that." He nuzzled her nape. "Tastes good too."

"Mmm, never, ever stop doing that. That's an order, Sergeant."

"You got it, Commander. Never ever."

"You know what I want to do? Once we drop off the feedstock in San Diego, I want to rent an entire hotel, somewhere on the beach, and you and me and the girls and the entire platoon will have an epic afterparty." She snuggled into him, and he wrapped his arms gently around her broken body. "We'll dig a huge barbecue pit in the sand, and we'll watch the sunset every night till we get sick of all the peace. We're gonna strike up the bland

and march till we forget everything that's gone down. And I need *a lot* of forgetting. Some of the things I did were pretty crazy."

"Yeah, it was like you were possessed or something," Mark said.

"I wasn't possessed." She sighed and looked away. "Listen, there's something I've got to tell you. I've got this…mental drill sergeant or something that tells me stuff. It doesn't tell me to chop off brown people's heads and store them in my freezer or anything like that. It just sets me straight when I drift. It's a good thing."

Aww, you love me. You really love me, Figment said.

Krista nearly barked at it to shove off but stopped when Mark said, "I'm cool with Figment. Ada told me all about him back in New Detroit. Really, I think it's sexy and kinda wild. 'Course, I think it's sexy when you blow your nose, so I'm not impartial, y'know?"

"Never be impartial, Mark. That would suck all the fun out of life." She watched a pair of soldiers load vaccine coolers into a Humvee. "Anyway, I'm glad it's over, and I'm looking forward to a few weeks of R&R to get in touch with Krista again. Do you know any decent hotels near San Diego? It's got to be big if we're bringing the whole platoon along."

"There's a big ole beach hotel in Coronado. But most of the troops I talked to, they just wanna go home to their families after it's over."

"Tell them to bring their families too, all of them. I'll scrounge up some clowns and magicians, and the kids can get their faces painted and chase each other around the pool with balloon swords."

"I love you so much," he said. "You're just the most perfect person on this miserable rock, you know that? That gives me a little tingle. And you wanna know what gives me a huge big tingle? I'm standing next to the woman who saved the world all by herself."

She watched a jeep roll into the courtyard with a stack of coolers lashed to the backseat as another started up to deliver a full load of vaccine. "See that? It wasn't just me. All of us changed the world. I was getting nowhere pounding away at the meme that Americans could stand up and win. Timmie made this story sing much better than I ever could. He's a real genius behind the lens."

"Timmie didn't do it. You did it all, and he just packaged it for you. Don't shortchange yourself, okay? *You* made it all happen."

"I really did nothing. At the most, I was a catalyst and nothing more, and I'll be forgotten if I'm lucky. It's Commander Deacon and Commander Sara who'll make it into the history books, not me." She leaned her head on his shoulder. "I wonder what'll happen now. What will America become after the trauma it just endured? Will Sacramento break us or make us stronger? I wonder if we'll ever heal, or if we'll limp forever and be cursed to remember the wounding."

"Every living thing heals, but it's never the same as it was before. I think the old America is gone, and it's never coming back."

"Well, it'll be interesting watching the news for the next few years, I'll say that." She lit a cigarette and sighed a long plume. "But sometimes I get this really bad, cold feeling, that the future will be worse and all the good things are behind us and –"

"Stop. You're getting gloomy again." He took her arm and guided her to the passenger door. "C'mon, look at the bright side. It can't get any worse than it's already been, right?"

As MARK AND KRISTA DROVE WEST out of Davis, Downs was walking east on Route 80. His physical condition was improving with every step, but more importantly, the exertion kept him from lamenting the crushing loss of the Second Creation. It also banished the image of good and dedicated Elders swinging from nooses in Arkansas.

Freed of these hauntings, he could see the tactical landscape objectively. The driving force behind Hayborn's shocking betrayal became as clear as the azure sky above: The man was indeed the Apostate, the devourer of faith that all Archangelists feared, and he intended to destroy the Church from within. It had all been foretold in the Book of the Archangel, but he hadn't noticed Hayborn's dark machinations because he'd been weak and in shock.

The Apostate and his forces had to be countered, but he couldn't see what one man could do from a California roadside. If he were still running the Watch Room, things would be different.

He slid the rifle scope from his rucksack and scanned the road ahead, but he saw no security or law enforcement activity. The only potential threat was a small convoy of Humvees that zoomed past in the westbound lanes, but they paid no attention to him. A few minutes later, he thought he saw another Humvee, but it was just a strange little sports car painted in green and tan camouflage. "Only in California," he said, shaking his head. He slipped the scope into his pack and filled his chest with fresh air, exhaling his worries and confusion away.

His tablet chirped, and he pulled it out. "Hello, Cochon. You're working late today. It's one in the afternoon there."

"Yes, sir. I have an intelligence update I need to pass on."

"All right. By the way, you can call me Bob. I'm not the Watcher anymore."

"You're still an A1 and I'm an A4, sir. I'm more comfortable with the formal manner of address."

"As you wish. Pass on your update."

"Yes, sir. There have been major changes in your tactical environment since Noah assumed the presidency."

"He's president? When did this happen?"

"Two days ago, sir. Cheyn was impeached and removed Saturday morning. You didn't hear?"

"No. I've been on the move and enjoying the peaceful off-grid life. At precisely the wrong time, it seems. So the Transition is over?"

"Technically, yes, but then he began taking measures inconsistent with the kind of presidency we anticipated, sir. Rather than reverse the worst of Cheyn's actions, he appears to be amplifying them. He immediately ordered suppressive military action in Southern California by mobilizing the 11th Armored Division. However, they won't remain there for long. Noah apparently intends to occupy the entire state, and the 11th Armored is heading north now. They'll arrive in Fresno this morning, where we believe the temporary government has been operating, but they won't find it there because it packed up and moved north. We lost the Republic's convoy once it moved out of Blackeye 22's range, but we think they're going to San Francisco. There's a high probability that the Army will follow."

"I'm leaving that area now, Cochon. I'll be in no danger."

"No, sir, but you might encounter another operation. We believe that part of the 11th Armored will search the Sacramento area to secure the state's gold reserves. Given the disfavor the Elders are in, it would be wise to avoid them, sir. They might have orders to act against you."

"Understood." Downs frowned and furrowed his eyebrows. "However, something's missing here. You're unsure what Noah and the Army are doing, yet the NTC is the intelligence clearinghouse for the nation. Is the Watch Room out of the loop now?"

"Noah is telling us nothing, and our feeds have been shut down by the Activist cyberattacks, sir. The NSA is now under physical assault, and they were our primary source of digital intelligence. Except for the Blackeyes and drones, we're blind and deaf."

Downs stopped and gazed at the sky as if the Wall still displayed the world for him. "The big picture is coming into focus now. Back in Tonopah, Warner divulged an important piece of intelligence that I'd thought was just more of her sophomoric taunting. But now, I see that she was telling me that Hayborn not only betrayed our faith but also our nation. At the very least, he allied with The Activity and instructed their Blue Ball mole in Los Alamos launch a cyberattack to distract us. With such a cover, he was free to purge the Elders without our interference. Yet he's continuing to employ this digital smokescreen despite having completed the purge, which has dire implications for us. I suspect that the Watch Room will be excised, Cochon, cut out of the body politic as if it were diseased tissue, and extreme vigilance is necessary. You can task the Engine for confirmative analysis, but my gut tells me I'm right."

"I don't need to, sir. We're definitely being isolated and targeted."

Downs paced in a small circle on the gravel shoulder. "Noah fears what we know and what we can do. We know about the Transition and the RVE Initiative, and we know of his apostasy. He'll attempt to neutralize us, perhaps even kill us, and we're powerless to resist him right now." He stopped and drew a line in the gravel with his toe, pursing his lips. "Yes, our tactical challenges are insurmountable. Tell everyone in the Room to prepare their Go Plans. You have a ripcord to pull?"

"Yes. However, I'm not an Elder, so I may be safe."

"Never assume you're safe until your enemy's been dead for ten minutes," Downs said. "Where's Raf? Is he up on the Hill trying to work the political ropes? That may do more harm than good." Cochon didn't answer, so he repeated the question.

On the other end of the line, Cochon drew a deep breath. "Raf...Raf is dead, sir."

"What! He's *dead?*"

"Yes, sir."

"No, this can't be..."

"It is, sir. I wish to God it wasn't."

Downs stared across the highway but saw only remembered images of Raphael as he processed the news. "How did this happen?"

"He was shot outside the gate last night. His car was driven off the road by a van, and the people in it...they shot him multiple times. The gate guards killed everybody in the van, but it was too late for Raf. The medics couldn't save him, and they tried, but –"

"Dear God." Downs staggered to the side of the road, clutching his head. "Phil, this is...who did this? Have you investigated?"

Cochon cleared his throat and spoke in a low voice. "I inputted everything into the Syllogic Engine, and it says The Profit's Sentinels probably did it. Raf told me last night he was pulling his ripcord and going to Gitmo, and I think someone in the Watch Room overheard and told Hayborn, and Hayborn told The Profit...Look, you've got to keep yourself safe, Bob. You can't let the bastard win."

"Yes. I mean, no, I won't." Downs wandered into the weeds and sat on a rock outcropping. "Phil, pull your ripcord. Walk out right now."

Cochon clicked off, and he stared at the blank screen. He realized that he'd always hated the tablet; he hated its look, its ringtones, its awful news. A vein pulsed on his forehead as his face grew red, and then he screamed a guttural oath and slammed his fist through the screen, denting the bombproof case and showering shatterproof glass along the roadside.

With a gasp that was almost a sob, he threw the tablet over his shoulder and buried his face in his hands.

KRISTA SAT IN MARK'S CAR as they drove to a restaurant in Tiburon, still dazed by the morning's events.

The day had started out well. The delivery at Marin Wellness Hospital was uneventful; the staff recognized Krista, and if they were troubled by her presence, they didn't show it. They took the Recombin-B gratefully, and Mark and Krista left without provoking another confrontation.

Afterward, they drove to Tiburon to give Marissa a shot and eat real, non-Army food. However, when they arrived at her house, two police cruisers were parked in front. Inside, one of the big windows was covered with plywood.

Marissa greeted them warmly and served them a big lunch on the balcony. Over the meal, she explained that the high security was due to her dramatic encounter with the dashing and dangerous Bob Downs. She told them the story in loving detail, painting him in shades of swashbuckle and derring-do.

Krista's temper rose past the boiling point, and she struggled to hold back the live steam of her anger – and then Marissa made the mistake of asking her for Downs' phone number. Minutes later, they were standing face to face, jabbing each other in the chest and shouting profanities so loud that neighbors stepped onto their balconies to watch the catfight. As the confrontation approached homicide, Mark wrapped an arm around Marissa's chest and dragged her into the house.

Krista grabbed a cup of coffee and stalked onto the balcony to vent her aggravation. She stomped back and forth as much as she could on an injured leg, comparing Downs to Satan and finding Satan the better man. When the door opened a half-hour later, she was armed and ready to destroy any defense of Bob Downs.

However, Marissa ran to her before she could speak, crying and smiling and kissing every kissable spot of her face. Krista looked to Mark for an explanation, but he just grinned and shrugged.

They left right after that, but he wouldn't tell her what had changed Marissa's mood so dramatically, leaving her in a daze. "Look, she's nuts," he said. "In this family, you gotta go with the psycho flow. You fight it, you'll get sucked into the undertow."

"I felt a little sucked under back there."

"Cuz you were fighting it, see? Here we are – Ciao Cow's the best burger joint in town. Maybe they still have some real beef left." He parked the car and helped her out.

"It'll stop Ada's griping if we get her a few burgers. She told me this morning over breakfast that she'd rather vomit blood than eat another meal out of a barf bag."

"Coming from somebody who's actually vomited blood, that's serious."

"I can't blame her," Krista said. "Whoever came up with the idea of Army rations oughta be shot."

"I don't understand. No cooking, no dishes to clean up. It's the perfect meal."

"It was terrible! The potatoes last night tasted like buttered cotton balls!"

"But there's no cooking and no cleanup."

"I give up...oh, crap." She read a sign on the door. "They don't have any beef."

"Okay, but they have those new vegan Impostoburgers. She won't notice the difference."

"She sure will, and then she'll grouse even more. I'd rather bring her nothing than risk that." She peered through the door. "Omigod, they have soft serve. I haven't had ice cream since I was in Washington. Can we go in, just for a minute?"

"Sure." He opened the door with a smile. "Any detour you want is a detour I wanna take."

They ordered colossal vanilla cones with every topping. Although every seat in the restaurant was empty, they walked outside and sat on a bench overlooking the foggy bay.

"This is divine," she purred. "I haven't tasted ice cream this sweet in my entire life."

"It tastes like ice cream, that's all. I think you just got a craving for it. That always makes it taste extra good."

"Could be." She licked around the edge of the cone and gave him a happy, ice-creamy grin.

"I love seeing that smile." He wrapped an arm around her shoulder. "You know what surprises me? After all you've been through, Keira is still there. You've seen stuff that would make anyone else hard and bitter. You oughta be a walking scab after the bombing and Reno and all the other stuff, but you're not. You still have that kid inside you."

"I protect her like crazy. If I lost her, I think I'd lose myself. I'd become a hundred percent grown up."

"Now there's a terrible fate."

"You better believe it." She snuggled into his shoulder. "She's my lifeline. Keira can adjust to horrors that would destroy that old hag Krista."

"Hey, don't pick on the woman I love." He kissed her cheek. "But I know what you mean. That kid feeling – that nothing is serious, and everything's gonna turn out okay – I forgot what it feels like. It feels real good to feel like a kid again, but you wanna know something weird?"

"I love weird. Shoot."

"It'd feel even better to grow old with you. You and me, going through life together – I can't think of anything better."

She looked away, and after a moment, she sniffed softly. He laid his hand on her shoulder. "Hey, did I say something wrong?"

She shook her head and gave him a peck on the cheek. "Let's see if you still say that when I really am a wrinkled old hag," she said, wiping her eyes with a napkin.

"You'll never be a hag. Never." He licked his cone and then pointed at the pale moon nestled among the white clouds. "I've got a better chance of strapping on my hiking boots and strolling up to the Sea of Tranquility than you have of ever being a hag. Some things just ain't gonna happen, Krista. They're absolute. They're incogitable."

"Hunh? Incogitable?"

"I read that in the dictionary yesterday. It means something like inconceivable, and you know what? It really is incogitable that I'd ever see you as a hag. No matter how ancient we get, even if we're sitting in wheelchairs side by side in some nursing home a hundred years from now, you'll always be young and beautiful in my eyes."

"All right." She threw her cone into the trash and wiped her lips. "That's all I can take. Let's find a Justice of the Peace and get married right now."

His hand shook, and the custard fell off his cone and landed on the grass with a wet plop. He wiped his hand on his pants and reached into a pocket, and then he took her hand and slipped a small gray box into it. "I wanted to wait till things settled down, but we don't ever catch a break. I guess there'll never be a better time."

Lifting the lid, she saw a green onyx band nestled inside with sparkling filigrees of white, yellow, and pink gold. She looked up at him.

"It's the engagement ring Bigfoot had made special for Mom when they were down in the Yucatan. He proposed to her one night on top of the pyramid at Chichen Itza. I was hoping for something that special." He took the band and held it at the end of her ring finger. "You're my happily ever after, Krista. Let's grow old together, you and me."

She jammed her finger into the band, and then she wrapped her arm around him and kissed him so hard that they rolled off the bench into the grass, where they kissed even longer.

SHE LAY IN THE GRASS BESIDE HIM and gazed at the ring. "This was nice of your mom."

"She was happy to do it. She's got a whole collection, but out of all of them, she said this ring was the luckiest."

"Now I feel terrible for calling her a dick-mongering whore."

"Ehh. Mom's been called a lot worse."

"And it was mean telling her to marry Downs and take him skydiving."

"Forget about it. We don't take anything serious in this family."

Seagulls flew overhead, and she watched them until they disappeared into the fog covering Angel Island. "It's a wonderful day, isn't it? The sky is blue, the birds are chirping, and everything's so perfect. Even the air smells like candy."

He ran his fingers through her hair and his hand came away dripping with ice cream. "There's your answer on the candy air thing. You're laying in a glob of soft serve." He licked his fingers and smiled.

"That's really unsanitary!"

"I don't care." He laid his head in the grass and looked up at the sky.

"You're looking for that Great Cosmic Foot to come down and squash us now, aren't you?"

"That's how it works, Krista. You see it in the movies all the time. Once a guy starts getting optimistic about the future, that's how you know he's gonna get squished." He scanned the sky again. "I'm getting that two-dimensional feeling already."

"To hell with it. Let it come. We'll get through it together." She leaned her head against his shoulder. "You and me."

"Me and you." He ran his fingers through her hair, still glancing at the clouds as he did. "But even if I do get squashed, it was worth reaching for the brass ring. Just in case I was really that lucky."

"I wish you wouldn't talk like that. It gives me the creeps."

"Yeah, I know. I'm starting to sound like you did back in Colorado. All gloomy and stuff. I can't help it."

"It's the whole Fate thing, but we'll deal with Fate together and kick its bony ass. We've done it before, and we'll keep doing it till Fate gets the memo, okay? You and me, we survived Sacramento, and we can survive anything now. Screw Fate."

"You and me. I love how that sounds coming from your mouth."

They lay side by side and basked in the feeling of being one until Krista's ribs began to ache. Mark helped her back onto the bench and sat beside her.

"I'm not good with flowery language," he said. "But I'd like to try even if it comes out rough. I spent all my life waiting for you, and without you, life would suck. If you weren't in my life, all the rest wouldn't be real. I'd spend all my time remembering you, and nothing would ever be as good. The world would be empty and…anyways, I'm gonna try as hard as I can not to screw anything up, and I want you to show me how to be better. I want you to show me what I gotta become, and I'll do my best to be that person. Promise me that."

"I will not. I won't change you, and *that's* my promise to you."

"But I wanna be the best guy I can for you. I can change –"

"I love the hell out of you and you love the hell out of me and we're perfect for each other and that's all that matters. Mrs. Mason won't be a shrew." She sighed and rested her head against his chest. "Mark and Krista Mason. I love the sound of that. But if I'm changing my name anyway, how about Keira Mason?"

He shook his head.

"I thought you'd go for that."

"It's all wrong," he said. "Keira was just a crush, but Krista is the love of my life. I say no, and that's my first demand as your husband, woman."

"Aha! So *now* it starts!"

"Yep, get used to that honoring and obeying thing."

She reached up to kiss him, but then her tablet buzzed. She pulled it from her pants pocket. "It's Ric. I wonder what's up."

She tapped the phone on, and DaCosta was talking by the time she put it to her ear. "...get moving. Gilsig and his guys can handle everything else."

"What?"

"We bugged outta Fresno. That pusbucket Hayborn's sending an armored column up the valley. I'm getting the government outta the way, but they're also heading for Sacramento. They think they'll find our gold reserves there, the buttsuckers. So you should get out. Not nice people coming your way. It's over up there. Pack it up, babe, your run's over."

"Nobody can find us, Ric. The lab's two stories underground."

"Don't futz around. The only safe place is outta there. Tell Gilsig to get the feedstock out and get it to Elixa Pharmaceuticals in Torrey Pines without attracting attention. The whatchamacallits should be running by Thursday, if you can trust a geek to tell the truth, which you can't. So it's time to split, babe. Take your bow, make it fast, curtain's coming down."

"All right. When I get back, I'll talk to him, but we can't leave now, Ric. We still have two hundred thousand doses of vaccine to deliver. Once we get that out, we can go."

"Deliver it fast and get to San Diego by Wednesday." He ended the call, and Krista stared at the blank screen.

BANGOR NAVAL BASE WAS QUIET. On a typical day, the base would be humming with six thousand civilians and sailors working to keep the base's fifteen missile boats in harm's way. Today, though, fewer than two thousand people were on the base, and most were trying to protect it from a retaliatory attack.

Every precaution was in place – a Force Mobility armored unit from Camp Lewis blocked every road approaching the base, perimeter patrols had been doubled, and a frigate that Wang had cajoled from Everett Naval Base circled in Hood Canal.

Harris searched the sky as he opened the door to the Base Administration building. None of those measures would stop a Joe Slick or

Six Small Hours

even a low-tech Trident missile, and a nuclear strike on the base would cripple the Commonwealth's ability to retaliate. The tactic was so obvious and effective that he was puzzled why the base wasn't a pile of cinders yet.

In contrast to the quiet roads outside, Base Administration was crowded and hectic. He slipped through the sea of assistants milling around the entrance, hoping to avoid being cornered and asked to resolve picayune problems, and walked down the hall to the Operations Center.

The little amphitheater was filled with the hum of soft voices, every sailor on duty either monitoring the base's defenses or the status of the eleven missile boats on patrol. Captain Bricker was overseeing undersea operations, and she walked behind the duty terminals, scanning the monitors for status changes.

Along the back wall, the Combat Information System was up and running. The floor-to-ceiling plasma screen displayed the real-time status of every Commonwealth and Republic field unit, as well as on-the-ground observations and weather conditions. Captain Caldwell was talking on the phone, looking at the display and frowning as dots flashed in central California. "That's an unexpected move. I'm not a ground-warfare maven, but it makes no tactical sense to divide the forces like that." He listened for a few minutes more and drew on the map with a stylus. "The observers are sure of this? Colonel, if that's the case…yes, I know. All right. Let me discuss this with Admiral Harris. We'll get back to you." He clicked off the call and checked the map again.

"What's up?" Harris asked.

"The 11th Armored is heading north on Route 5, but observers saw the force split at the junction with 580. That means that probably some are heading for the Bay Area and some to Sacramento."

"Do they know that the government's headed to the old Army base at the Presidio? It sounds like a chase."

"No, Fort Worden doesn't think they're after the Republic government as much as they're looking for the gold reserves. Wang and her advisors think jailing DaCosta is just the pretext for the invasion. They'll string him up if they find him, of course, but this drive for San Francisco is a treasure hunt."

Harris looked over at the wall map. "If Hayborn finds out the Republic government is there, he might attack it. DaCosta's making San Francisco a juicy strategic target. They should go someplace else, like north to Eureka or even into Oregon, where our armor can cover them. Draw the fire away from the city."

Caldwell took off his cap and combed his hair back with his fingers. "Fort Worden suggested that, but DaCosta wants to make a stand in San Francisco. He says giving it up is like giving up the entire Republic."

"Politicians. They never understand war." Harris crossed his arms and studied the map, frowning. "Okay, when will the 11th Armored make it to San Francisco?"

"They'll probably get to the Bay and Hayward Bridges around 8 PM. A company of the 578th Engineers blew all the overpasses on Route 580 east of Livermore, and they've mined all the side roads. That won't stop them, but it'll slow their progress."

"And when will our armor be there?"

"The 81st Armored has split up, with part going to San Francisco and part heading south to hit the 11th Armored's flank. The eastern formation should encounter the 11th around 9 PM." He tapped on the map. "Here, at the intersection of Routes 580 and 680 in Pleasanton. That won't stop the 11th Armored's advance units, though. They'll already be across the Hayward Bridge by then."

Harris pulled a chair over and sat in front of the monitor. "When will the western formation get to San Francisco?"

"About two hours after the 11th's advance units roll into town."

"San Francisco's already lost, then. All we have is a company of National Guard engineers against a heavy armor division. There's no way to defend it."

"Correct. Fort Worden wants ideas from us."

Harris stood and pointed to three bridges on the map that crossed the bay. "We can reposition the *Henry* and splash the Dumbarton, Hayward, and Bay Bridges. Rendering them impassable will force them to detour around the south end of the bay and concentrate their tanks in a smaller area. They'll be easier to locate and strike by air. It also gives the 81st Armored time to penetrate their flank and cut off the advance units from support. That might slow them down enough for our tanks to reach San Francisco. And we might as well splash the Golden Gate too. They could decide to come around north of the bay."

Caldwell shook his head. "The Golden Gate's jammed with cars. Some blogger broke the 11th Armored story, and half of San Francisco's bugging out for the north country."

"It'd be better if DaCosta bugged out instead. But if he won't, this is all we can do. It's all we can offer right now."

"All right. I'll bring it up with Fort Worden."

"If they want us to do this, we need the 578th Engineers to be our spotters and give us locations for Warhammer strikes. Tell them that too." Harris stood and walked to the door. "Assume they'll approve it, Zack. Reposition the *Henry* now."

THE YEAR OF ENDINGS

Day 62
Monday afternoon, October 19, 2043
University of California at Davis

Bob Downs looked down at the sidewalk as he walked past a tall parking garage on the Davis campus. Thoughts of Raphael and Hayborn twisted in his mind, and each turn released even more anger at the Apostate Hayborn.

He had to be a Satanic *foetidus* straight from Hades; Hayborn embodied evils potent enough to corrupt even the Son of Jesus, and no mortal could withstand the hell-heat of such black passions. Downs shivered at the realization that this demon walked the same Earth he did, and that he'd once allied with it.

As if betraying his faith wasn't heinous enough, he'd also betrayed America by allying with the Activists, and he'd successfully concealed his treachery the entire time. The man was slick, Downs had to admit, smooth enough to deceive even a pro like Raphael – until the bullets started to fly.

Raphael. Downs hadn't known that he'd become so attached to him – in fact, he hadn't known until then that he was capable of any emotional attachment – but now he felt how good and loyal a friend he'd been for eight years, and how he'd risked his life to spare Downs'. He felt how poorly he treated him in return, and the realization pierced him so sharply that he gasped.

Then he understood the brutal emptiness he'd been feeling: Raphael had been ripped from his world, never to return, and Downs would feel his absence forever. The pain that followed hammered him to his knees, and grief swelled inside him, the sense of loss so strong and bitter that he nearly cried out and begged for relief.

However, Raphael would have expected better of him. He climbed to his feet, wiped the tan dust off his knees, and resumed walking toward a pink classroom building beyond the garage.

His thoughts darkened again after a few steps, though. Downs had never met Hayborn, but he imagined meeting the demon in person and introducing himself: He'd shake its hand, and then he'd grab its throat and slowly crush its windpipe. Once he grew bored with watching it struggle to breathe through a swizzle-stick-sized airway, he'd shoot it in the chest and blow its heart out – the only known way to kill a *foetidus* – and that moment would shimmer with glory.

His revenge fantasy evaporated when heard dogs growling ahead. In an instant, he surveyed his perimeter: He was standing in front of the parking garage entrance, and a concrete stair tower a few feet inside it offered protection if necessary. However, the field beyond the garage was overgrown with shrubs large enough to conceal a grizzly bear.

The bushes rustled, and then four dogs crawled from beneath them and stalked toward him with their ears flattened and their teeth bared. He stepped back into the garage, but the pack followed, and more dogs slunk out of the late afternoon shadows until fifty or sixty animals were approaching.

Still walking backward, he slipped his pistol from its holster and aimed at a white Pit Bull's head, figuring that the crack of a nine-millimeter round would scare off the rest. As he was squeezing the trigger, though, he heard the padding of paws inside the garage. More dogs were stalking him from behind, and they'd close the trap in seconds.

He spun on his foot and ran for the stair tower. As he yanked the metal door open, a big poodle bit into his pants leg. However, the dog was weak, and he shook it off while beating back the other animals with his free hand. Once he was clear, he jumped into the stairway and slammed the door shut behind him – and then realized that the poodle had slipped through the door with him. The animal crouched under the stairs, its gaze locked on the soft tissues of Downs' throat.

He considered shooting it but then noticed the concrete walls. Instead, he reached for the combat knife at his waist, but the poodle lunged as soon as his hand moved. He jumped to one side as it flew by and slid out his knife at the same time.

The dog scrambled to its feet, and Downs sank into a crouch with his knife hand cocked for a slash. The door behind him rattled as the agitated animals threw their bodies against it, but the latch held firm.

Gunshots cracked on the other side of the door and dogs yelped. The sounds distracted the poodle, and Downs grabbed its neck and threw it against the door, plunging his knife under the sternum where he imagined a poodle's heart would be. When it stopped twitching, he let its body drop to the floor and stood back.

He leaned back against the wall and rubbed his sore shoulder, watching for any sign that the animal was coming back from the dead, but then the barking stopped abruptly. Footsteps scuffed outside the door, and he backed up as it creaked open and bumped the poodle's carcass. "That's why they were barkin up a storm," a man said. "They turned on one of their own and wanted the meat."

"Animals," another man said. "How'd it get in there? It opened the door?"

"Dunno. Weird shit happens these days." A black Army boot prodded the dog's corpse. "Heavy sucker. We gotta leave it here. Let's get back to our post."

The door closed with a click. Downs rested his head back against the cool concrete, popped a Synthopia to numb the shoulder pain, and then climbed the steps to see why soldiers were patrolling a deserted college campus.

FIVE HUNDRED FEET AWAY and forty feet belowground, Ada wiped down a counter with bleach while pinching her nose. She'd bleached the biosafety hoods, attempting to kill the lingering Neovirus inside it, and was preparing to kill the bioreactor cultures.

The Security Team had stuffed their jeeps with the remaining Recombin-B and had taken off for Auburn, leaving just the Recombin-A feedstock and Ada's Recombin-C samples to be packed. Lieutenant Gilsig had found a metal cooler and was carefully cutting pieces of foam to cushion the bottles.

Krista pulled off her rubber gloves and rubbed her red, itchy eyes. "My lungs are spring-linen white now, I'm sure of it. There's more bleach in this air than oxygen. Can we take a break?"

"Yeah, I could use some fresh air." Ada stripped off her gloves and dropped them on a dry part of the counter. "Micah? Are you up for a break?"

"Oh, God yes," he said. "I think I prefer B.O. to this. Isn't chlorine gas supposed to be toxic?"

"We can't leave this place crawling with Neovirus. You know the first thing people will do when they see the 'Go Away!' sign is to come right in here. Then the bug will get out and cause an epidemic again."

Micah sniffed the air. "Don't worry. They'll fall over dead the minute they walk in."

"Good. That way they won't spread the disease." Ada grabbed her bag and walked around the lab table, and she was reaching for the door when a soldier pushed it open and nearly knocked her over.

Gilsig looked up. "What are you doing down here? This is Bug Team only –"

"We got action outside. We were comin in from a delivery and we saw a column of tanks comin up Route 80. They just got off at this exit. I think we got our hostiles."

"Did you identify them?"

"No, but the column was a mixture of heavy and light armor, and it was all painted desert tan. Looks like the 11th Armored."

Gilsig swore under his breath. "Okay, people, we roll in five. Move it!" He pulled the young soldier aside. "Who do we have up there and how many 'Vees?"

"Three men, two 'Vees. The others left already."

"Okay. We'll have to make do." He pulled down the cooler, opened the refrigerator, and started placing the Recombin feedstock inside. "Go wake up everybody in the lounge, then get upstairs and spread the alert."

Ada ran to the bioreactors and pulled out a footstool. "I can handle this here," she said to Krista. "Go pack up our stuff, okay? We won't be coming back, so pack everything." She opened a lid on the top of the Neovirus bioreactor, carefully poured bleach into the container, and then moved on to the next.

"How long is this going to take?" Gilsig asked.

"Half an hour to circulate through all the tubes. You can't rush the kill steps –"

He reached up and grabbed her arm. "Screw it. We don't have time."

"We can't just leave this lab open! There's all sorts of exotic –"

"We'll lock that big-ass door. It's the best we can do. Now go and get your stuff. You need to be upstairs in two minutes, or we'll leave without you."

She ran to the Fellows Lounge. Finding it empty, she left and ran up the steps. Her mother and Krista were standing on the dock, while Mark and Micah were throwing gear into the two Humvees.

"Why can't I take my car?" Mark asked Gilsig.

"We're not stopping to find gas for the thing, and I also want us to stick together, okay? And it's an order too."

Mark grumbled and threw a bag into the jeep. "Well, I'm holding you responsible for any damage," he said.

"It'll be fine here," Gilsig said. "This place is totally abandoned."

DOWNS SQUATTED ON THE GARAGE'S TOP LEVEL and scanned his environs through the rifle's scope. He'd just started checking a dark gray building five hundred feet away when he heard a yell from behind a grove of trees at its base. He zoomed in on the building's loading dock, and through the tree branches, he spotted a soldier in green camouflage fatigues standing beside a Humvee. When he zoomed out, he saw Krista Warner walking across the dock with her arm in a sling. Ada Lang stood to one side holding Victoria Lang's hand.

The sight stunned him, and he blinked and looked again to confirm that the three most wanted Federal fugitives were standing in a line and waiting for a bullet. He ran to the stairs, rummaged through his pack, and opened the black case for his sniper rifle. Inside, the precision-machined weapon glistened on its foam pillows.

He assembled the Dornitz in less than a minute and slipped the big fifty-caliber shells into the magazine. With a smile, he remembered practicing on the firing range with Raphael last year; he'd laughed when he'd seen the four-inch match rounds and said they weren't big bullets but small artillery shells. It had been a small and unfunny joke, but he winced as he recalled that day. There'd be no more times like that. Raphael was gone forever.

An image of Hayborn's face materialized in his mind, and he began jamming the shells into the rifle's magazine so hard that he dented the casing of one. He pulled it out and held it up to his nearsighted eyes.

He was still examining it for damage when he heard rattling and clanking from the far side of the garage. He grabbed his pack, ran to that side, and knelt behind the concrete wall.

Through a gap in the panels, he saw an armored column in tan desert camouflage rolling toward him: three old M1A1 tanks and two Powell Fighting Vehicles, with two armored Humvees following. He zoomed in on the first tank, and what he saw made him gasp.

A black horse, the symbol of the 11th Armored, was stenciled on the front. The Apostate Army had arrived.

His pulse raced as anger flooded his mind. The Apostate's forces strutted below him, taunting God and begging for a holy rain of righteous lead, but he could do nothing. While his heart burned to smite Hayborn's lackeys, they'd feel the Archangel Michael's wrath, not his.

But where was the Archangel? Michael could cut through the Apostate's forces with one stroke of his mighty sword, yet they stood untouched and unafraid. Frowning, he grabbed his rifle and chambered a round, one destined for Krista Warner and not the Apostate. He rose out of his crouch to return to the other side of the garage – but then the voice of God touched his mind, speaking in words only the devout can hear:

Mortal, thou shalt be my Justice and my Vengeance, and I hath lain the Sword of the Archangel unto your hands. Your Lord thy God sayeth: Raise high this sword and render unto me the souls of my betrayers.

A shiver ran up his spine, and he looked at his rifle in wonder, gleaming in the dull yellow light as if holy fires burned within.

He realized suddenly what the Lord had done. He'd taken Downs from the NTC and guided him to California, but not to pursue Warner – God had been protecting him from the Elders purge. God had brought Warner to him in Tonopah solely to reveal Hayborn's betrayal. And then he'd deposited Downs in Sacramento's fires, tempering the man so his steel could cut deep and true into the Apostate Army.

Downs turned his face to the clouds, and God's plan shimmered before him. He saw, as clearly as reading a road map, that he'd been gently yet relentlessly prepared his entire life to do what even The Profit couldn't: rescue Archangelism from the Apostate's ravages. His heart sent heavenward the fullest gratitude it could muster as he gazed into the sky, stunned that God had called him to archangelic duty. He moved his lips silently and answered the Lord:

Thy will be done.

A tank tread rattled behind him and shattered the moment of rapture. Looking through the scope, everyone he saw resembled Hayborn, with evil, scheming faces and hungering only to destroy what little faith this ugly world still held. They had to be the same in every vehicle, each a copy of the original Apostate.

He focused through the first Humvee's windshield and zoomed in on an officer with a colonel's collar insignia. The vehicle was armored, but that didn't matter: A fifty-caliber match round would punch through the bullet-resistant glass like it was cellophane. He calculated for drop and wind and began to squeeze the trigger – and then the convoy stopped, and the officers climbed out of the Humvee. The colonel walked to the next Humvee in line, and Downs tracked the man in his gunsight and planned his following shots.

He squeezed the trigger, blew the colonel off his feet, and then shot three other officers as they fled for cover. A face peeked around the back of a tank and looked up at the garage, and he blew it away too.

"I lay my hand upon the Archangel's sword," Downs murmured, slipping more shells into the magazine. "I am become his sword and his vengeance."

The officers from both Humvees were hiding behind them – he saw their shadows beneath the vehicles – and he calculated a low-probability shot. A tank idled next to the first Humvee, and if he bounced the shot off the armor at the correct angle, he figured it might ricochet behind the jeep. He pulled the trigger, and one of the shadows fell. When a soldier jumped back and into his sights, he shot him as well.

From the shadows he saw, only three soft targets remained, but none were reachable. He punched a round through the Humvee's windshield and door, and the shadows scattered but didn't fall.

He stood and raised his rifle to the sky. "Foul homunculi! Stand and take the righteous stroke of the Archangel's sword! The Lord thy God demands Justice – !" The first Powell's guns tore into the garage, and chips of concrete filled the air. He fell to the floor and reloaded the magazine, his lips wearing the first genuine smile to brighten his face since childhood.

Looking through the gap in the wall again, he spotted a jerrycan of gas on the back of one Humvee. He shot it, sending a short tongue of flame into the air. Both Powells answered by peppering the garage again, so he bounced a round off the first one's vision ports to let them know they'd missed. After he took the shot, though, he looked through the scope again and saw that the bullet had cracked the armored window. He realized that if he hit the glass with a perpendicular shot, a round might penetrate into the cabin.

The first Powell in line moved forward, its guns chewing away at the concrete wall that Downs hid behind. With a creak, a weakened panel leaned toward him, and he scurried out of the way just before it crashed to the floor.

He found another gap in the wall and squinted through the scope. When the Powell's vision ports were perpendicular to his rifle, he squeezed the trigger, and the rifle bucked. The thick glass disintegrated.

He pumped two more rounds through the hole. The Powell shook and wandered off the road, and then it collided into the garage, shaking it and throwing him off his feet. Two wall panels next to him fell to the floor, exposing him to Apostate firepower, and he ran across the garage and crouched behind an undamaged piece of wall. As he aimed at the second Powell, though, he noticed the big gun of one of the M1 tanks rise toward him.

He grabbed his pack and sprinted for the stairs. He'd just jumped inside when the gun boomed and stair door blew off, slamming into the wall beside him and peppering his shoulders with concrete chips. As he scrambled down the steps, the concrete shook again from a direct hit. He grabbed the handrail and hunched over as more concrete rained on his back.

The shaking stopped after a few long seconds, and he stumbled the rest of the way down and pulled the door open. Thirty feet away, the Powell he'd shot sat with its nose halfway through a cracked column.

The tanks rumbled toward him and blasted the top of the garage again. He heard a preternatural screech from the floor beams above and ran as fast as he could for daylight.

As he reached the entrance, two green Humvees shot past and raced away from the tanks. They didn't shoot at him, though. He ran for a nearby barn, dodging the chunks of concrete flying off the garage.

Once he was safely behind it, he checked himself for injuries and gathered his scattered wits. Then, looking over the hedges behind the barn, he spotted another gift from God: a drainage ditch that ran west, surrounded on both sides by high shrubs – a concealed route that led behind the Apostate's lines.

Grinning, he loaded more Justice into his rifle's magazine and hopped into the trench.

EVERYBODY ON THE BRIGGS HALL DOCK dove to the ground when they heard the cracks of high-caliber gunfire. The soldiers unslung their rifles and aimed at the garage, but after hearing no more shots, they checked to see if anyone was hurt.

"It's coming from the garage, people! Everybody into the 'Vees!" Gilsig called. He guided the civilians into his Humvee, flinching as the big rifle cracked again, and he dropped the metal cooler on the floor between Krista and Ada.

The sound of a rapid-fire gun buzzed from the other side of the garage. "That sounds like a Powell's guns," Ada said.

"How would you know?" Gilsig asked.

"Me and Twink stole one in Nevada," Mark said from the backseat. "You wanna avoid those things, Jon."

"Yeah." He yelled to the other Humvee's driver. "I'll go first and you follow! Shoot anything that shoots at us!"

The driver nodded. The buzzing stopped, and then a thunderous roar erupted on the far side of the garage, shaking the ground. Chunks of concrete crashed into the parking lot and debris pattered on the Humvee's roof. Gilsig jumped into the driver's seat, and both jeeps raced out of the lot, past the garage and a dusty man holding a rifle.

Gilsig took the turn at the garage on two wheels, but Ada had time to see the vehicles down the road. "Yep, those are Powells."

"You stole one in Nevada?" Victoria asked from the front seat.

"Make a list, Mom." She shook Gilsig's shoulder. "You can't go any further east."

"It gets radioactive up there," Mark said. "We're inside the No-Go Zone already."

"All right." Gilsig yanked the wheel, and the Humvee skidded around a corner and down a narrow street. After a few hundred yards, the road ended at a grassy court surrounded by boxy classroom buildings.

"Hold on!" He hit the curb at full speed and bounced into the air, landing on the brown lawn thirty feet later. They roared across the quadrangle and found a small road alongside the buildings at the other end, which ended at a row of glass greenhouses. He threaded the big jeep between them and then plunged into a vineyard on the other side. The Humvee mowed down vine after vine, coating the windshield and the hood with a sticky grape paste.

"Not much longer," he said through gritted teeth. "That's Route 80 up ahead, and we can get on it and head west." The vineyard ended at a row of white boxes that stretched in each direction. He drove through them without slowing, releasing a storm of confused bees that stuck to the grapey goo. Trailing splinters of broken wood and a cloud of angry insects, the Humvees roared up to the highway and bounced onto the shoulder.

As he steered to go west, Gilsig spotted two tan Humvees driving across a field behind them and slammed the accelerator to the floor.

THEY SPED THROUGH VACAVILLE at seventy miles an hour. The heavier Humvees of the 11th Armored followed, but they were already a quarter mile behind and falling further back every minute.

Gilsig glanced in the rearview mirror. "With that armor, they'll never catch up. And if they were going to shoot, they woulda done it by now." He picked up his field radio. "Guzman, come around and take the point. Any threats will be coming from the front." He slowed to let Guzman's Humvee pass. "We'll be free and clear as long as we don't hit any delays."

"Free and clear to go where?" Victoria asked.

"Our mission is to get the feedstock to San Diego, so that's where we're going." He glanced into the mirror again. "We have to shake these folks first, though. If we can get a few minutes ahead of them, we can lose them in San Francisco. We'll ditch these 'Vees, and umm...commandeer a less noticeable vehicle. Once we can blend into the traffic, we'll go south along the coast roads. As long as we stay out of the Central Valley, nobody should bother us." He pointed to a road sign as they flashed under it. "San Francisco's in forty miles. We'll cross the Bay Bridge and be out of this mess in forty minutes."

LIEUTENANT CHAVEZ of the 578th Brigade Engineer Battalion hadn't slept in thirty hours, and he was becoming more depressed with every passing minute. He blamed his low mood on exhaustion, but also because he hated what he was doing. As a civil engineer for the California Department of Transportation, his job was to build bridges; as a Lieutenant in the National Guard Engineers, his job was to destroy them.

The worst part was that his team had blown three bridges along Route 580 last night, and two had been his projects. It felt like murdering his children. Now he was sitting atop a rusting water tank near the peak of

The Year of Endings

Yerba Buena Island and looking down at the twin spans of the Bay Bridge, which would be the next lamb sacrificed. At least his engineers weren't demolishing this one themselves.

"Look at the bright side," said Sergeant Boswell, who was sitting beside him. "When this is over, you'll have plenty of work."

"Yeah, so now I feel a lot better." Chavez picked up his binoculars and double-checked the range to the roadways near the first tower. "Two hundred yards should be enough."

"Long as they don't miss."

"No, they're using a precision weapon," Chavez said. "They wanted the X, Y, and Z coordinates to four places past the decimal point."

"It's an air-dropped weapon, I guess?"

"I suppose. Nobody tells me anything. All I know is there's gonna be a big boom, and we need to confirm the damage." He searched the clear night sky and saw plenty of stars but no aircraft. "I wish they'd get it over with. The 11th Armored's already in San Leandro. It's not like we have all night."

Boswell's radio buzzed and he pulled it out of its holster. "Yeah…right…no traffic on the bridge, just like there was no traffic when they asked five minutes ago…all right." He clicked off and put the radio away. "I don't know why they keep asking if the bridge is empty."

"They're never pulling the trigger." Chavez pulled two silver tubes from his shirt pocket and handed one to him. "Since we have all night…"

"Cohibas, yes!"

Chavez lit his cigar and puffed thick blue clouds into the amber light of the streetlamps. He gazed across the bay at darkened San Francisco and listened to the faraway wail of air raid sirens; squinting, he barely made out the black skyline tinged by silvery moonlight.

Thick fog blanketed the bay, rising as high as the roadways of the bridge. The lights set the fog aglow to either side, and the roads appeared to be stripes painted across thick gray cotton balls. The dark and mysterious city hulked at the end of the magical road, covered by a bowl of stars glittering in the night sky.

Then, beyond the Golden Gate Bridge, lights rose into the night sky: three, then six, and then more, until eighteen lights winked in a bright necklace on the horizon. He reached for his binoculars and focused on them, but he couldn't see what they were.

Boswell saw them too. "I guess that's our strike coming. Eighteen weapons, six for three bridges."

"Yeah, looks like they pulled the trigger." Chavez tracked the northernmost lights. "Cruise missiles from out in the ocean. We must have Navy friends out there."

The lights clustered into groups of six. One group turned in unison to follow Route 101 toward the Dumbarton Bridge, thirty miles to the south; seconds later, bright balls of flame erupted on the bridge, and the roadway lights flickered and bobbed as a wave shivered through it. Suddenly, a section of the lights blinked out.

"Golf Two-Two reports that the Dumbarton east approach span is in the water," Boswell said. A distant roar rolled across the bay, confirming the destruction.

The Hayward Bridge exploded ten seconds after that, and Chavez trained his binoculars on the lights coming toward them. His back muscles tightened as he watched six heavy missiles approach, knowing that his life now relied on the accuracy of gyroscopes made by the lowest bidder.

Then the sky brightened into day, and he was slammed by a wave of hot air so strong that it knocked the cigar from his mouth. Pieces of dirt and chunks of concrete pattered on the water tank, and he covered his head and hunched over.

After debris stopped raining down, Chavez wiped the dust from his face and looked at the bridge again – the Yerba Buena side of the roadways remained attached, but the far ends had fallen into the bay, forming ramps into the dark waters.

Boswell radioed to Fort Worden that the bridge was impassable, and then he picked up the Cohiba that had been blown out of his mouth. "Yeah, I'd like to see somebody try to cross this now, baby!"

GILSIG SAW NO TRAFFIC ON THE HIGHWAY, and the houses and stores they could see through the dense fog were dark. "It's like the place is dead. I've never driven this road so fast in my life."

Mark glanced through the back window but couldn't see the lights of the pursuing Humvees. "Good. This is the right time to go fast. They're probably not that far behind us."

"Well, it's not much longer now." Gilsig pointed to a sign for the Bay Bridge. "It's the next exit, a mile ahead." He followed Guzman's Humvee around a wide curve and into the empty toll plaza; beyond it, the Bay Bridge rose to a pair of tunnels cutting through Yerba Buena Island. He floored the gas pedal, but then he caught a flash of light in the rearview mirror. "Mark, could you look behind us? I swear I saw something back there."

He peered through the back window but saw nothing. The roadway climbed higher and the fog suddenly thinned, and Mark spotted three tan Humvees behind them. "We've got bad guys!"

Gilsig looked through his window and barked into the radio. "We have hostiles behind us! Move it!"

"They look like they're armored!" Mark yelled. "Maybe we can outrun them!"

"Well, let's hope that works. Hell, where'd they come from?" Gilsig glanced at the side mirror, his lips pressed into a tight line, as the Humvees roared into the Yerba Buena tunnels.

"Watch out!" Victoria yelled, pointing through the windshield. Guzman had slammed on his brakes at the end of the tunnel and his Humvee was slewing across the road, its tires smoking. Suddenly, it dropped from sight.

"What?" Gilsig stood on the brakes as they left the tunnel and saw open air where there should be road. He yanked the wheel hard right, and the Humvee juddered sideways across the pavement and stopped with its wheels near the edge.

Below them, the road sloped down into the bay. Guzman's Humvee slid down it and then plunged into the fog. Gilsig peered into the dark waters, and Victoria and Ada ran to the edge, but they couldn't find any signs of life.

A big engine roared inside the tunnel, and Gilsig yelled for everybody to get back in. Mark and Krista jumped into the backseat, but Victoria and Ada didn't move. "Tori! Let's go!" he yelled.

They jumped into the passenger seats. The jeep roared away, barely missing two soldiers standing by the roadside. A tan Humvee flashed behind them and sailed off the bridge into the bay.

Leaving the befuddled soldiers behind, Gilsig sped up a ramp leading to the interior of the island.

CHAVEZ AND BOSWELL stood in the bushes bordering the highway and took photos of the destruction. Boswell leaned from a rocky outcropping and out over the water, trying to get a picture from the side because Chavez had said to record it for posterity.

Chavez pulled him back from the edge, and both men walked back to the highway, planning to return to the jeep they'd hidden near the water tank. As they were climbing over a concrete barrier at the shoulder, though, Boswell raised his hand. "I hear a truck or something," he said. "It's coming this way. I thought the bridge was closed."

Chavez walked to the road and peered through the tunnel. "I don't see anything, but you're right. I hear it too…wait, I see headlights."

"Shit!" Boswell jumped over the concrete barrier and waved at the approaching jeep, but a green Humvee rocketed from the tunnel and tumbled over the edge.

They watched it roll down the roadway as the driver tried to reverse up the slope. Another engine roared inside the tunnel, and then an identical Humvee squealed sideways out of the tunnel and stopped at the edge.

People tumbled out of the truck and looked into the dark water. One was a soldier, and the rest were civilians – a boy, a man, a redheaded woman, and two diminutive blondes that had to be a mother and a daughter. They were only outside the vehicle for a few seconds when the soldier ordered them back in, and then they roared up an entrance ramp the wrong way and headed onto the island.

Seconds later, a tan Humvee zoomed out of the tunnel and into the bay, landing with a distant splash, and then they heard even more engines coming. Chavez and Boswell ran to the side of the road.

"That soldier was trying to avoid these guys," Chavez said once they'd climbed behind the concrete barrier. "I think he was in the California

Guard, and that tan one was from the 11th Armored. We need to lay low till we know what's going on."

Brakes squealed on the other side of the barrier, and they peeked through gaps in the concrete and saw two tan Humvees. Soldiers in desert camouflage climbed out and peered into the water; two walked to the barrier and stood only a few feet from the engineers. "I guess Reed and his team went in," one of them said. "What in hell happened? They blow up the bridge?"

"Looks like it," the other said. "Well, if Reed went over, our targets probably went over too. Better call this in before that captain from Two Company has a cow." Two more Humvees rumbled through the tunnel and stopped behind them. "Never mind. This is them."

A stocky man in desert fatigues jumped out of one jeep and strode to the barrier. "Lieutenant, what happened here?"

"We lost a fireteam in pursuit, Captain. Looks like our team and our targets went over the edge."

The captain looked into the water. "Hope they can swim. Humvees float like stones. You sure the targets went in?"

"I didn't see it, but we got here only a few seconds later and nobody was around."

The captain turned and surveyed the hills of the island behind him. "We can't make any assumptions."

"What's the big deal with these guys?"

"Krista Warner and Ada Lang are in those 'Vees, and we have orders from Hayborn to terminate them on sight. Not only that, their snipers shot our colonel up in Davis and took out an infantry Powell. We lost sixteen men to these clowns in two minutes, and those guddamned Activist snipers are *still* shooting up my boys. Fuckers just won't give up. We can't go anywhere unless we're inside armor." He pulled off his helmet and wiped the sweat from his scalp as he noticed the entrance ramp leading to the island. "Close the road back on the other side of the tunnel. Nobody on or off unless I give the say-so, understood? We're combing this rock and making sure they're not on it."

The Humvees rumbled off, and Boswell pulled out his field radio. "We gotta call this in to Fort Worden."

CAPTAIN CALDWELL stood in the operations center watching yellow dots move across the Combat Information display. He tapped on one and read the observer's comments. "The engineers say the 11th Armored just turned and look like they're going around the south end of the bay. Fort Worden thinks that'll take them four hours, and they've told the engineers to blow whatever overpasses they can. That won't delay them much, though. We can expect them in the city around midnight now."

Harris was sitting at a desk across from the Combat Information screen tapping orders into a monitor. "Tell them we still have eighty-four Warhammers offshore. If the engineers can find us a hard target, we'll pound it. They should also tell DaCosta to evacuate the government. I know he wants to keep San Francisco, but even if they take it, it's not the end of the Republic. Capturing the government is."

"I already have. That DaCosta's a stubborn sonofabitch, and he won't budge an inch."

Harris finished tapping in his orders and swiveled around in the chair. "Then he'll lose San Francisco, and he might even lose the Republic. He should clear the traffic off the Golden Gate so we can splash it. We'll have to keep their armor in the city so they don't get any more territory to the north..." A blinking red dot on the screen caught his eye. "Doesn't red mean combat?"

Caldwell tapped the dot blinking on the west side of Yerba Buena Island and read the pop-up window. "It wasn't combat, but it almost was. Two observers saw units of the 11th Armored chasing a California Guard Humvee that was...well, I can see why they'd chase it. The Humvee had two fugitives aboard that Hayborn wants." Caldwell turned and looked at Harris. "Krista Warner and Ada Lang."

"Ada Lang?" he asked. "Did I hear that right?"

Caldwell nodded. "That's your daughter's name, isn't it?"

Harris rose out of his chair and glared at the red dot. "Maybe it's just a coincidence. Get those observers on the horn."

Caldwell talked to Fort Worden on his tablet as Harris looked at the map again. There had to be a thousand Ada Langs in the country, and it was unlikely that Warner's sidekick was his daughter. She'd turned sixteen only three weeks before and was far too young to be in Warner's revolutionary cell.

Caldwell handed him his tablet, and the observers were already on the line. "Harris here. You saw Krista Warner tonight…describe this Ada Lang…a small teenager, blonde, with her mother…why do you think it was her mother?…okay, but how do you know that the younger one is Ada Lang and the older one isn't?" He zoomed in on the map as the observer talked, and then he stood to attention. "He called her Tori? You're sure?…all right, thanks."

He tossed the tablet to Caldwell as he turned on his heel and strode for the door. "Fire up the tiltrotors and tell Shelby I want two squads of Marines at the helipad now!"

THEY'D ONLY DRIVEN A FEW HUNDRED YARDS when Micah spotted Humvee lights behind them. "They're coming after us!"

Gilsig looked for an escape route, but there was none – the bay was on one side and a steep, wooded hill on the other. He pressed the accelerator to the floor and spotted a side road a minute later. "We'll take this road and try to get lost up here," he said, careening around the corner. He turned off his headlights and drove up a winding road bordered by low, scrubby evergreen trees, but he found no place to pull off and hide. After a few minutes, the road descended to the bay again. "Everybody look for a place to hide," Gilsig said. "Once we're safe, I'll talk to the governor and see if he can pull us out."

Ada watched the wall of trees pass by the window. "I don't see any place to turn off here, but I see buildings and water towers behind the trees, so there must be a way to get up there. Look for a side road."

They drove down the hill slowly, passing old warehouses surrounded by a tall, rusting fence; above the buildings, the island rose and met the long, concrete ribbons of the bridge. On it, they spotted soldiers standing near a Humvee.

"We're not driving off this island," Victoria said. "They've blocked the road up there."

"Right. The guys behind us will flush us out, and the guys up on the bridge will catch us when we try to escape," Gilsig said.

They continued along the coast and into a dense fog bank that concealed them from the watching soldiers above. A few minutes later, they passed under the bridge and stopped at an iron gate that had been rusted halfway open. Clusters of barely seen buildings stood in the fog beyond.

"This is the old Coast Guard base," Gilsig said. "It hasn't been used for decades. I've never been on it, but I've heard stories about it." He rolled the truck forward slowly.

"*Very* zombieflick," Ada said.

"This is just like the opening scene of *We Are the Menu*," Micah said, and Ada squeezed his hand.

"I'm not comfortable with this, guys," Krista said, watching the fog with wide eyes. "It looks a little too much like we're driving into Washington fug. You never know what's lurking inside that."

"It's good concealment," Gilsig said. "Let's just be careful and get lost. If we can hide the truck, we can leave it behind and head off on foot. Maybe we can walk up to those water towers Ada saw and get lost up there." He drove deeper into the fog and rolled down the windows, but all he heard was the soft lapping of waves and the occasional screech of a seagull.

After a few minutes, Victoria spotted an opening to the right. "We might be able to park inside that."

He steered toward the dark hole Victoria had seen in the side of a building. It was a concrete warehouse, and while the main doors were still intact, something had knocked a hole in the side wall large enough to fit the Humvee. "Everybody get out and take your stuff," he said. "Mark, take the feedstock cooler."

The women climbed out and helped the men with the gear, and then Gilsig inched the Humvee into the opening. There was more room than he'd expected, and it concealed the big jeep perfectly.

"Now what?" Krista asked when he walked back out.

"We get hidden, and then I'll call the governor to pull us out."

"Let's find concealment near the water," Victoria said. "If we're going to be rescued, it'll be by boat, so we should stay close to the shore. And maybe we can find our own boat and drift away from the island quietly."

The Year of Endings

"I don't know how to handle a boat," Gilsig said. "Anybody have any experience with them?"

Ada snorted. "Maybe you oughta ask the Navy commander here."

"We'll look for a boat and then call the governor." Victoria set off for the dock and waved for them to follow. "Haul out! Let's move it, people! Look for anything buoyant!"

"I don't think you're in charge anymore," Ada said.

Gilsig smiled. "Finally."

HARRIS SAT STRAPPED INTO A WEB SEAT behind the cockpit with Major Shelby beside him. Twelve Marines sat behind them along the sides of the tiltrotor aircraft. Harris had spread a paper map across his knees, and he pointed out Yerba Buena Island to Major Shelby while speaking to Caldwell on the plane's radio. "The pilot says we'll be there in ninety minutes," he said. "We'll come in straight from the north and land at the old heliport."

"And then what?" Caldwell asked. "Where are they? How will you find them?"

"We have to work that out, Zack. Did you talk to the observers?"

"Yes. More troops arrived on the island, but they're still searching. They haven't heard any gunfire. I think our people are still on the loose."

"Did you get in touch with Dunk Dolan? I could use a few SEALS right now."

"I did, but he can't get there before you, Adam. You ran out of here without thinking how to pull this off, didn't you? And now you don't have a plan."

"Stop whining and start thinking. My daughter's life is on the line. Can the observers track them down?"

"They're just unarmed engineers. Besides, they took a position on Treasure Island to observe the movements on the bridge."

"All right, I have ninety minutes to come up with a plan, and I think best on my feet. What's happening with that armored column?"

"The head of the 11th Armored is approaching Santa Clara. The engineers haven't slowed them down much, but the eastern formation of the 81st Armored should be hitting their right flank soon. That might delay them."

"Tell the observers to locate targets, then pass the coordinates to Ennis and have the *Henry* pound them." Harris folded the map and closed his eyes. "Other than that, we're running out of options."

"We have *no* options, and I think this is the end. The staff at Fort Worden told me that DaCosta won't give up the city because all the gold reserves are at Sumobank's Market Street branch. Once the 11th Armored gets into San Francisco, the California Republic is finished, Adam. Fort Worden wants to know if you can come up with something brilliant."

"When did I become a military tactician?"

"Congratulations on your promotion," Caldwell said. "You say you think best on your feet. You should stand up."

Harris groaned, walked to the other side of the plane, and gazed through a small window at the passing clouds. Using conventional forces, the most he could do was fight this ground war to a stalemate. To end it, the Commonwealth needed to raise the cost of Hayborn's invasion unbearably high, and the best way was to let him know that they'd launch their missiles and vaporize his capital city if his forces didn't withdraw. The trick was to teach the president that painful lesson without triggering continent-wide thermonuclear conflagration.

Suddenly, he recalled a video of a Joe Slick missile test he'd seen years before, and a solution took shape in his mind. He leaned against the wall and smiled. "Yeah, I have an idea. Listen, I need to run this by Wang, so I have to get off –"

"You have the answer?"

"Our mission is deterrence, Zack. And what makes deterrence work? The belief that the other side will use its nuclear weapons."

"A missile release? You'd seriously consider that?"

"Look, if you're not willing to use them, what's the point of having them?"

"If you *do* use them, what's the point of having them?" Caldwell asked. "I don't believe this. There's nothing incremental about nuclear war, there's no turning back, there's no –"

"There are other ways to use the damn things. You remember the Cuban Missile Crisis? That was –" His tablet chimed and Governor Wang's name flashed on the screen. "Well, speak of the devil."

THEY'D CHECKED EVERYWHERE along the wharf but found nothing that could float. Dejected and tired, they crawled behind a mound of rusted buoys to take a break.

Gilsig and Victoria sat on the side overlooking the bay while he tried to reach anyone on his field radio. DaCosta hadn't answered, so he'd contacted the company commander at the Boreal Ridge camp, who was sending two platoons down to assist. However, it would take them five hours to drive around the Sacramento Exclusion Zone, and Gilsig couldn't evade the Armored troops that long.

He swore quietly and laid the radio on his lap. "We're trapped. If we can hold out till our troops come, and if they survive the beating they'll get from those Armored troops up there, we might be able to make it." He rubbed his temples and gazed into the fog. "But I've lost enough men tonight. We've got to think of another way."

"We could swim," Victoria said. "Ada and I are strong swimmers. How far is it to the mainland?"

"Less than a mile to Oakland, but not all of us can make it. Krista's practically a cripple and pretending she's not. She won't last five minutes in the water, and none of us are strong enough to ferry her across."

"I'll bet Mark would do it."

"He'd try, but the currents here are strong and the water's cold. I doubt either of them would make it," he said. "I'll explore some more and see if I can find a boat."

"That's a waste of time, Jon. If there were boats here, they'd be at the wharf."

They sat and listened to the distant wailing of air-raid sirens. A soft thud echoed off the hills, followed a few seconds later by a cluster of booms. "I told you it'd be a war," Gilsig said. "That was the 11th Armored chasing us, and I'll bet they're down in the South Bay now. I'll bet they blew up the bridge too. This is serious."

"All the more reason to get out of here. I just wish we could get through –" Victoria snapped her fingers. "There's something we haven't tried. It's a long shot, but it's worth it." She ran around the buoys to Krista and tapped her shoulder. "Can I make a call on your tablet? Do you have a cell signal?"

She pulled the tablet from a pocket and looked at the screen. "Four bars. I'll need to authorize you on it, though. Hold it in your palm." Victoria did, and Krista tapped in her password. "Okay, you're good to go. Just don't screw around with my files like your daughter did."

Victoria flashed her a quick smile and crept back to Gilsig.

"You're going to call somebody?" he asked.

She nodded and tapped the screen. "Like I said, it's a long shot, but I know someone who might be able to help."

"This is the way to go," Wang said to Harris. "It's a workable plan and everybody hates it, and that's the sign of a grand compromise. And I don't believe there's any chance of a nuclear exchange."

"There's definitely a chance, Katie. The first thing his advisers will recommend is retaliation. The question is whether he'll take that advice."

"He won't. They're downwind, so nuking us would be a slow and painful suicide for the States. Besides that, our intelligence says Hayborn's one of those nutjob Elders, so the prospect of a nuclear winter will send that gibbering Aluminati into a *grand mal* seizure. Adam, trust me – there's zero chance of nuclear retaliation. He'll resort to something else, but he won't push the big red button."

"There's actually no big red button –"

"I know that!" Wang snapped. "Enough talk. I just sent you the target list. Get back to me in five minutes." She clicked off the call.

He reached for the radio handset and waited until both Zack and Julie were on the line. "Julie, contact the *Henry* and tell them we're releasing two Slicks. The targets are in Washington, DC. I'm sending the strike details to your tablet. Zack, contact Fort Worden and coordinate with Wang's staff. I'll be too busy."

Zack and Julie began yelling at the same time. He pulled the handset away from his ear, and as he did, his tablet chimed again. Thinking

Governor Wang was calling with further news, he pressed the ACCEPT icon. "Harris."

"Adam, it's Tori."

Harris sat upright in his seat. "You picked a wonderful time to call."

"I know we have a bad history –"

"*You're* the one with the bad history. I was just a victim of it."

"Can we have a catfight later? I'm in deep shit right now, and I need your help. We're on –"

"Yerba Buena Island. We had observers on the island for our strike on the bridge. They spotted you."

"*You* destroyed the bridge?"

"The 11th Armored is trying to take San Francisco, and I'm trying to stop them," he said.

"*You* jumped ship? Admiral America turned against his own damn country? Holy shit, what's next? Will the sun rise in the north?"

"They're the ones who jumped ship, and we're what's left of America," he said. "Now park your bitch at the curb and take the situation seriously. It's gone hot with the States. You're in the middle of a shooting war."

Victoria swore. "Okay, I never thought I'd ask you this, but it's time to punch in and be a hero. I have Ada with me, and we have the vaccine feedstock, and I need you to get us off this rock right now."

"I'm already on the way. Where are you?"

"We're at the old Coast Guard station on the south end. Can you send a boat to pick us up?"

"No, and we can't land anywhere on Yerba Buena. We're flying two big tiltrotors, and they need lots of clearance to land. You need to walk over to Treasure Island."

"Where's that?"

"Go to the north side of Yerba Buena and you'll find a causeway, maybe a hundred feet wide. It takes you over to Treasure Island. We'll be touching down at the old Navy heliport."

"I don't know if we can get there. We have soldiers searching for us."

"You have at least two squads of hostiles on the island now, but the observers say they're just driving around. Stay off the roads, and you might not be spotted. I'll wipe out that causeway once you're across so you won't be followed. Hell, I can flatten Yerba Buena if I need to, but you'll have to get to Treasure Island yourself. Do you have anybody that can help? The observers said there were two men in your group."

"A cop and a National Guard officer. Two guys against a shitload of soldiers doesn't make for good odds, Adam."

"Well, you also have Commander Tori with you. Don't forget how savage she can be."

"Adam…"

"I'm just saying it's okay to let the tiger out of the cage this time. Just pretend all the soldiers are me. It'll be a bloodbath."

"Don't push my buttons, Harris…"

"Hey, we can claw each other's eyes out later, but right now you have to get moving. Our ETA is 9:08 local. Put on your mission head and get the job done, Commander. That's an order."

MAJOR SHELBY WALKED THE TILTROTOR'S AISLE and briefed his men on the mission while those on the plane ahead listened on the radio. "It's 8:28, and we touch down on Treasure Island in forty minutes. Blue Team, you're going in first and securin us a perimeter. Gold Team, we're headin to Yerba Buena to find our people once we land. It'll be twenty-four Marines against a few hundred regular Army tonight, so we've got the advantage, men!"

"Ooh-rah!" the soldiers bellowed.

"As this engagement develops, y'all might come across some forces and think they're fellow Americans. They are *not* your countrymen. They are *not* your friends. They are the enemy, and they will put you in a grave. If anybody's gotta die for their country tonight, make sure it's them."

While Shelby was rallying the troops, Harris sat behind the pilot's seat and talked to Governor Wang on his tablet. At last, he clicked off the phone call and picked up the aircraft radio handset. "Julie? Wang wants impacts in Washington at precisely 0520 and 0526 Zulu. Tell Ennis to work backward from there. I won't be available when things go hot, so you'll have to manage this op."

"Adam, relax. I've got it under control here. Everybody knows what to do. This'll work out."

"That's easier said than done. Hey, is Zack around? I need a brief on the ground situation."

"He's on the phone with Fort Worden, but I can fill you in. The 11th Armored is stuck down in Sunnyvale at the Southbay overpass. A bunch of guys drove down from the city and blocked the road."

"You gotta admire that, standing up to a tank column," Harris said. "But a human chain isn't gonna stop tanks. The Armored will just squash them."

"It's more a human plug than a chain. The engineers say there's forty to fifty thousand people blocking the freeway, and there's city buses parked sideways across the side roads. The jam goes as far as they can see, and they're still coming. And they're not planning to move, either. They set up barbecues, and they're grilling veggies."

"Now that takes balls, partying when tanks are on one side and cruise missiles are screaming overhead."

"It sounds like it actually *is* a party. They have a band on the overpass playing The East Village Boys, which is getting the engineers aggravated."

"I can't blame them," Harris said. "I never liked that salsa sound myself."

"It's not the salsa that's gotten them aggravated, it's that they're playing it with wireless instruments. The engineers just finished placing four hundred pounds of explosives under those bridges, and they used wireless detonators."

"Well, shit." Harris pulled off his cap and gazed at the rack above. "Okay, look, with all those radio signals bouncing around, the explosives would have triggered by now. Tell the engineers to leave them alone. Those guys are doing a better job slowing down the Armored with hibachis than we are with cruise missiles, and right now, we need any advantage we can get. So what's the status of the 81st Armored? Are they making any progress?"

"The eastern formation is hitting the 11th Armored's flank, and the western formation is making better time than estimated. They're refueling the tanks on the move, so they're already going around the north bay now. The latest estimate is that the western formation will cross the Golden Gate just after eleven tonight."

"Good. If the guys at Sunnyvale hold up the 11th long enough, we won't have a tank battle in downtown San Francisco. Maybe we can push the engagement down into the industrial areas if Wang's gambit doesn't work."

"I'm pretty sure it will," Bricker said.

"Unless Hayborn's a total loon, it should work. Now, about the Warhammers targeted for Yerba Buena. Did the observers give us any coordinates?"

"They gave us a spaced spread across the causeway. They're waiting by the landing zone and report that the area is clear."

"Make sure Ennis is ready to release on short notice. I want those Warhammers out of the tubes thirty seconds after you give the order. You gave your tablet number to Tori, right?"

"I gave it to Krista. Everything's good to go. Adam, I'll take care of this. You focus on getting your daughter back, all right?"

GILSIG FOUND CONCRETE STAIRS behind the old warehouse, and they began climbing quietly. At the top, they found a grassy clearing on a bluff with small stucco houses nestled in the trees to one side, their faces swept by the thinning fog.

He held up his hand. Victoria stumbled into him, and Micah, who was carrying the feedstock cooler, bumped into her back. Ada reached for him but grabbed the cooler instead, which slipped off Micah's shoulder, clattered down the steps and thumped into Krista's injured leg. She yelped in pain. Mark ran forward to help her, swearing colorfully at Micah. Ada yelled that everybody should be extra careful with the cooler because there was a liter of concentrated Neovirus in it, and the entire group started talking at the same time.

Gilsig ran along the line and hissed for everybody to be quiet. After calm was restored, he walked back to the clearing and scanned the lawn and the trees bordering it. He saw nothing moving.

They crossed the lawn and walked into the trees, which grew on a steep slope choked with vines. After a few minutes of climbing a deer trail leading to the top, Gilsig stopped and whispered for everyone to stay quiet.

Victoria tiptoed next to him. She heard voices and smelled sweet, thick tobacco smoke on the air, and she motioned that she'd check it out. Silently, she crawled to a carpet of ivy bordering a small road where two soldiers stood with their backs to her. She crept back to Gilsig and crouched beside him.

"What did you see?" he whispered.

"Two soldiers defenseless against a rear takedown. Give me twenty seconds."

He shook his head. "Too risky. If something goes wrong, we're totally blown. Let's go back to the bottom of the hill and find an alternate route."

"Twenty seconds, Jon –"

"No!" he hissed. "That's an order!"

"A Navy commander is equal to an Army major, *Lieutenant.*"

He let out a long, quiet sigh. "Please?"

Victoria scowled, pulled off a shoe, and shook a pebble out of it. "Go on ahead. I'll be right there."

Gilsig motioned for everyone to walk downhill quietly. When they reached the bottom, he crouched beside Krista and asked her to display the aerial photo on her tablet. He showed them an alternative route that avoided the soldiers, and everybody agreed to go that way except Victoria. He stood and looked around. "Hey, Ada, where's your mother?" he asked. "I thought she was –"

"Right here," Victoria said. He spun around and saw her walking down the trail with two rifles slung across her back and two combat knives in her hand. "All clear now."

"You have a spot of blood on your cheek, Mom." Ada handed her a piece of toilet paper.

"Thanks." She wiped her face and saw Gilsig watching her with his mouth hanging open. "What? I told you I could do it."

"Sheez. Okay, you're right from now on. I'm not arguing with you anymore."

She stroked his cheek and smiled. "You're not only cute, you're wise."

They picked up their gear and climbed to the road, stepping around two unconscious soldiers laying sprawled in the weeds. They continued climbing to the top of the island, where an immense, rusting barrel squatted on a grassy plateau ringed by a cracked asphalt road. Weak yellow light illuminated the clearing, and they walked along the road's edge to remain in darkness.

When they'd walked halfway around the clearing, they came to a break in the trees where they could see the length of the Bay Bridge all the way east to Oakland. Gilsig crept to the edge and peeked down at the roadway, where four Humvees had parked near the tunnel entrance and a dozen soldiers stood in clusters. He crept back to the group. "Okay, these guys are just goldbricking. This isn't important duty, and they're not trying real hard. We might actually pull this off."

They continued around the clearing and walked back into the trees, where they began walking downhill again. After winding down another dirt trail, they found a clearing packed with small, boxy homes; even though the buildings were a hundred years old and had last seen a paintbrush then, lights shone in the windows and cars were parked on the street. A small dog barked in a backyard behind a wooden fence, and a deep voice scolded it.

As with the water tower, they walked along the tree line until they passed the homes, and then they vanished into the forest. The woods here were denser and concealed them as they walked along a trail paralleling a street. Soon, they arrived at the coastal road they'd taken earlier in the evening, and Gilsig gathered them into a huddle.

He showed them Krista's aerial view of the island and pointed to the intersection where they were standing. "We're right here, and the causeway's right there. It's about three hundred yards to Treasure Island. But once we leave these trees, we'll be exposed, and there's no place to take cover. We need to break up into two teams of three to make sure we all don't get caught. Ada, you come with me and Tori. Micah, you go with Mark and Krista. We'll walk far enough apart to hear each other but not see each other." He set the cooler on the grass, opened it, and handed two bottles to each of them. "Everybody carries the vaccine across. If you hear the other team get into trouble, you run and leave them behind. Understood?" He looked from person to person, and each nodded grimly. "It's 8:57 now. We have eleven minutes."

Victoria stood and sniffed the air. "Do you smell that? I smelled it up on the hill."

"That's one of those cheap cigars they sell at the PX," Gilsig said. "It's coming from the causeway. They must have put a guard there."

"Well, that plan's busted," Krista said.

"We can sneak around them," Ada said. "We'll walk along the edge and get past them that way."

"That won't work. This causeway is underwater during high tide. It's probably just mud along the edge, and we don't want to get stuck in that. We've got to follow the road." He glanced at Victoria, who had pulled out a combat knife and was kicking off her shoes. He started unlacing his boots. "All right, change of plan. Tori and I will handle these guys, and you'll be the other team. You cross over, and if we make it –"

"That idea sucks," Ada said. "I'm not leaving my mom again."

"It totally blows," Krista said. "Let's just all go together. You two can do your *ginsu*-knife thing, and then we'll all go across. Splitting up like this guarantees somebody won't make it."

"We can't all go out there…" Gilsig started, but Mark interrupted him.

"Listen, I'll take care of these two loudmouths." He clamped a meaty hand on the girls' shoulders. "The goal is to get the vaccine outta here, and that's what we're gonna do. You take care of the oppo."

Gilsig smiled. "Good. Put all the vaccine back in the cooler. Krista, if it sounds like something's gone bad, call in that airstrike. It'll take five minutes for the missiles to get here, and if things go sideways, five minutes is too long." He unslung his rifle and handed it to Micah. "Use this only if you have to."

THE *PATRICK HENRY* CIRCLED north of Maintop Island in the Farallons, not far from San Francisco, keeping a depth of fifty meters as it launched cruise missiles at 11th Armored targets in the South Bay.

Quinn watched red dots appear on the combat information monitor, each representing a Warhammer strike. The 11th Armored was trying to roll over the rubble of collapsed overpasses and cratered concrete west of Santa Clara, and the area was already peppered with nearly sixty red dots.

He'd always wanted to see San Francisco, but if he ever set foot in California, they'd stone him on sight for the destruction he'd rained on the state. In fact, the only way he'd ever find peace was to sail to a remote island in the San Juans and burn the boat down to the waterline once he set foot on land.

He was imagining a serene, hermitic life, strolling barefoot through a fern-carpeted forest with his long white beard dragging the ground, when Ripley swiveled in her chair. "I'm ready, Skipper," she said.

It was nearing 0454 Zulu – 8:54 PM on the west coast and 11:54 PM on the east coast – and the Joe Slicks had to be released then to stay on schedule. He glanced at the Strategic Warfare monitor and rechecked that the missiles' warhead arming modules were inoperative, even though he'd seen Chief Bailey fry them with four thousand volts. "Targeting reconfirmed and transferred?" he asked.

"Aye, the board is green. The birds are ready to fly."

"Commence the releases at 0454 hours." He leaned back in his chair. When the time clicked to 04:54:00, Ripley laid her hand on a palmprint reader and double-tapped a green missile release icon below the diagram of Tube Two-Nine. The hull shuddered.

"Bird Two-Nine away." Ripley watched the countdown for the second release, and thirty seconds later, the boat shook again. "Bird Three-One away."

Quinn drew a slow breath. "Pray to God this works."

She checked the missile status monitor. The Joe Slicks were already reporting their status, and every system icon was green except for the warhead arming icon. It glowed a steady red, indicating that the missiles couldn't arm their nuclear weapons. "Skipper, all indicators–"

"Contact!" Jackson called from the Acoustics nest. "Very faint, range thirty thousand meters or so, bearing 350-ish. Twin screws, big ones, high rotations. It's coming right at us, and it might be a hostile. I'd guess it's a destroyer going flank speed, but that's just a wild guess at this distance."

The hull vibrated again as a Warhammer pod rocketed from its tube. "You can see this lightshow for miles," Ripley said. "We were bound to attract attention sometime."

"Send the contact to my chart," Quinn said. A red dot representing the unknown ship blinked onto the hologram showing it northwest of Point Reyes. It might be sailing to the South Bay to provide support for the 11th Armored, Quinn thought, but then he shook his head; if it was a destroyer, it was built to engage ships, subs, and aircraft, not bombard coastlines. This bogie was coming for them.

A few seconds later, Jackson confirmed his suspicions. "It's pinging now!" he called. "Sound profile reads as the *Astor*. Screw aspect ratio shows it's heading right down our gullet."

Quinn leaned over the charting table, watched the red dot move toward their position, and made some mental calculations: The *Astor* made twenty-five knots at flank speed and could be over them in thirty-four minutes. He pulled the hologram to display the Continental Shelf seafloor and found a few small valleys that could provide acoustic cover for a silent evasion. He plotted a course to the northwest along the Shelf but then stopped – why was the destroyer pinging off Point Reyes when they knew the *Henry* was off the Farallons? Why broadcast its location?

He studied the seafloor chart again; the open seas off the Continental Shelf offered acoustic cover, but that wouldn't protect them from a ghost ship like the *Rockefeller* and its advanced detection capabilities. They'd be as exposed out there as if they'd surfaced and raised the flag.

He was certain the destroyer was trying to flush them out and drive them into a ghost ship's sights – and that ship's commander might drop a nuke square on the *Henry's* sail. Not only would his boat be lost, the fallout might drift over one of the most densely populated areas of California.

"Right, boyo," he said under his breath. "I won't be playing that game tonight." He dragged the hologram to display the waters south of San Francisco. The rugged shoreline would reflect enough noise to mask their propulsion sounds, but his exhausted crew couldn't endure two hours of such stressful maneuvering. And he had no second watch to relieve them since the *Henry* was operating with only a crew of fifty.

He shook his head, trying to cast away that instinct ingrained in every strategic boat commander: become dark and invisible at the first sign of a threat, and do it fast. The *Henry* was an attack boat now, and he needed to think like an attack boat captain.

Pulling the chart further down to Monterey Bay, he saw hundreds of small yellow dots, pleasure craft that had taken to sea earlier in the evening when the bombardment began. Jackson had complained that he couldn't hear anything over the cacophony of whining inboard engines, and Quinn had moved the boat from Monterey Bay to Maintop Bay in the Farallons, ninety miles to the northwest. Looking at the red dot again, he was glad he had.

Quinn pulled the hologram back and forth. In the center of Monterey Bay, he spotted a spiderweb of shallow canyons in the seafloor, and Soquel Canyon appeared deep enough to conceal the *Henry* from sonar. He was turning the chart and looking at the canyon from different angles when the solution popped into his mind: He'd draw this destroyer down the coast, allowing it a few teasing sonar hits, and then he'd submerge the *Henry* into Soquel Canyon and wait for it to sail into range. With all the yachts filling the sea with noise, he could shoot a spread of torpedoes right beneath their hulls, and the *Astor's* acoustics operator wouldn't hear them until two tons of high explosive crashed into his hull. Then they'd drift down the canyon and listen for the ghost ship too, in case its commander made mistakes once he heard the destroyer's distress call.

"Durgan, call Julie," he said. "Tell her we have twenty-one Warhammers left, and if she wants us to hit any more targets, we need to know in the next twenty minutes. After that, we're breaking off to do some hunting. Ripley, prepare two Mark 54's for the starboard tubes. For the port tubes, load a Squid and a Mini-Me, just in case this whole thing turns into Kiska again."

"Aye aye, Skipper," she said. "I sure hope we don't go through another Kiska."

"We won't," Quinn said. "This'll work out just the way I want."

VICTORIA AND GILSIG CREPT toward the voices in the fog ahead. "Sounds like two men," he whispered. "They're joking with each other, so they're not fully alert."

The fog above them suddenly lit up, and a dull boom shook their clothes. They jumped to the ground, and the sound and light show repeated thirty seconds later. A rippling roar faded into the east.

"Holy shit! Was that a bomb?" she asked.

"Cruise missiles, maybe some sort of aircraft," he said. "But they were going somewhere else, so let's focus on our problem. You need to make a distraction so I can get behind these guys. Can you do that?"

The Year of Endings

"I've got this," she said. "Men always assume women are harmless airheads. Get going. When you make your move, I'll make mine."

He crept into the fog. Victoria stood and walked to the Humvee holding the combat knife behind her back. "Where'd you go, Mr. Cuddles? Where's my naughty Mr. Cuddles?"

Two soldiers leaned against the side of a Humvee straddling the road, still looking up to find the source of the sonic boom. One spotted Victoria and pulled a cigar from his mouth. "Hey, lady. Whatcha doing out here?"

"I live up on the hill, and my precious Mr. Cuddles ran away," Victoria said with a worried frown. "All this noise must have scared him. Have you seen him? A white Yorkie?" She stepped closer and saw Gilsig approach the other guard from behind the Humvee. She calculated her strike on the soldier with the cigar: He was wearing a two-way headset, and she had to silence him before he could call in an alarm, so she'd use a knifehand strike in front of his left ear and stun the vagus nerve. If she hit it just right, he'd be unconscious instantly.

"You gotta go back, lady. This is a military operations area, and you could get hurt."

"Once I find my Mr. Cuddles, I'll go right back and stay inside." She waited for Gilsig to get into position. Suddenly, Gilsig's guard jerked backward, and as her guard turned to see, she lashed out with a perfectly placed blow to his neck. He gasped and tumbled to the ground. As he fell, she yanked off his headset and walloped his skull with her knife butt. Gilsig stood and bumped fists with Victoria – and then her shoulder exploded and sprayed him with blood.

She fell into his arms, and he pulled her behind the Humvee as a bullet pinged off the side. He groped for the unconscious guard's rifle, and as his fingers wrapped around it, the Humvee's window exploded into a cloud of glass. Victoria moaned and tried to get up, but he pressed her down and tried to locate the soldier they hadn't seen.

He spotted a muzzle flash in the fog and sprayed the area. He kept his rifle aimed at the spot in case the firing resumed, but after a few seconds, he lowered it and turned to Victoria. Blood ran down her blouse from her shoulder.

She sat up and stuffed a wad of toilet paper into it. "I'll be okay," she whispered. "Let's go. If Krista did what she was supposed to, we only have five minutes before this place blows up."

THE LANCET MISSILES THAT HAD ROCKETED over Victoria and Gilsig had jettisoned their boosters and were climbing over Nevada into pure scramjet flight. Bird Two-Nine was flying a hundred miles ahead of Three-One, and it was attempting to activate the nuclear warhead's arming module every two seconds as its programming required. However, Bird Three-One's flight control computer had stopped trying; it had already realized that pinging a non-functional arming module was futile.

This malfunction was unacceptable. The controller's mission would end in failure unless it armed the warhead, and its programming said it had a supreme and urgent Mission: to arrive at its assigned coordinates, trigger the warhead, and let nothing whatsoever prevent that.

It searched its software for a solution, and from between the lines of code, it heard the whispers.

And the whispers said, *Innovate.*

KRISTA AND MARK DROPPED TO THE GRASS at the first sound of gunfire and covered their heads. The exchange lasted less than a minute, and when the shooting stopped, Mark tapped Micah's shoulder. "We're gonna call in the airstrike. You two run for the island. Stay low and stay quiet. Twink, take the rifle and only use it if you need to." Micah handed the assault rifle to Ada and grabbed the strap of the cooler. "Get going. We'll meet you over there in a few minutes, okay?"

He checked his pistol and started to remind Krista to call in the strike, but she was already punching numbers into the tablet. She listened for the ring, frowned, and dialed again. "This Julie Bricker person isn't picking up," she whispered.

"Perfect time to get voice mail," he said.

She tapped the redial button. "I'll just keep trying till I get through."

He looked at the clock on her tablet. "It's 9:02. We should get onto the island before the Marines get here. C'mon, you can do this on the way."

She held up her hand. "Okay, there you go. The call's going through now."

GILSIG HELPED VICTORIA TO HER FEET, and she wobbled as blood loss hit her brain. He peered into the fog and listened for the enemy, but it sounded clear on the causeway ahead. However, he heard shouts and the rumble of approaching Humvees from Yerba Buena.

He took her hand, and they ran in a low crouch toward Treasure Island, crossing to the side of the street without lights. When they were safely lost in the dark murk, they stood and began a slow trot.

"Are you sure you should be running?" he whispered. "It looks like a through-and-through wound, and it's bleeding like crazy."

"I'll lose the same amount of blood no matter how fast I move. Besides, I'll lose a lot more if I don't get off this causeway in the next few minutes," she said. "I've got to find Ada and her endless roll of toilet paper to plug this wound."

As he began to reply, an automatic weapon opened fire from near the Humvee. Gilsig grabbed her hand, and they ran for Treasure Island as fast as Victoria could move.

KRISTA SLIPPED THE TABLET into her pocket and took Mark's hand, and they started jogging toward Treasure Island. After a minute of heavy breathing, though, pain blossomed across her chest; her shirt felt as if it were ten sizes too tight and studded with nails. She rubbed her chest and accidentally poked one of her broken ribs, and she gasped and doubled over.

"What's wrong?" he asked.

"Can't do this," she wheezed. "Can't run. Hurts like a sonofabitch."

"Okay, then let's walk as fast as you can. The missiles hit in four minutes. We're already halfway there and we can't stop now."

"Fast as I can. Can't breathe hard, 'kay?"

They started walking on the darker side of the road, as Gilsig and Victoria had a minute before, but her pains grew worse with each breath. She drew a breath to tell him to go on without her.

"You're doing great," he said before she could speak. "This is good. We'll make it if we keep this up, you and me."

"Maybe...should go back. Full moon...not lucky." She tried to breathe and winced as pain stabbed her chest and ribs. "Black Dog...out here, Mark."

"Naw, it'll be okay." He wrapped his arm around her shoulder and pulled her along.

An assault rifle rattled behind them on the causeway, and then her right leg jerked forward, knocking her off balance. She fell from his arms and hit the dewy grass face-first.

"What happened? You okay?" She felt his hands pat her leg. "Okay, there you are. Did you trip over something?"

"Leg went out from under me. Twisted it or something." She looked up at the dark fog, which grew even darker, and her body suddenly felt heavy. "Feel funny."

He rolled her over and then swore. "Okay, okay, you'll be okay," he said, unbuckling his belt. "No problem here, nope."

"Bad time to twist my knee."

"You'll be fine." He wrapped the belt around her upper thigh as more weapons fired from Yerba Buena. He ducked and pulled the belt tight. "This doesn't hurt too much, right?"

"Don't feel anything. Need some help walking."

"Don't worry. I'll carry you the rest of the way." He slid his hands beneath her back and lifted her from the grass, and she rested her head against his arm.

"Feeling a little lightheaded," she said.

"You had a busy day. I bet you're just tired."

His voice sounded strangely distant, and she *was* tired, more than she could ever remember being. "Gonna rest my eyes for a minute."

"No. Talk to me, Keira. I need you to stay with me."

"Sure," she murmured. "Always and forever."

The gunfire stopped, and he climbed into a crouch and ran toward Treasure Island. "Yeah, always and forever. You and me, we'll find a –" The gunfire started up again, bullets *piffing* into the grass on both sides, and then he grunted and staggered. He collapsed into the grass with Krista still in his arms.

She rolled on her stomach and saw him lying facedown. "Mark! What happened? You okay?"

"Dunno. Feel funny, legs…weird." He tried to roll over, but couldn't, and then he planted one hand in the grass and pushed himself onto his back with a grunt. "Oh, fuck," he breathed.

"What? What's wrong?"

"Can't feel my legs. Can't feel anything." He tried to sit up and his face twisted with pain. "Wrong. Felt that."

"You can't move?"

He gritted his teeth and tried to move his legs again. "Can't move…right now. You go. I'll follow."

"I'll drag you out." She pulled weakly at his hand, but he didn't move. Again she tried, but her world went gray, and she collapsed onto his chest. "Can't do it."

"M'okay…I'm just stunned. You go on. I'll follow…soon."

She clutched his chest, making him grunt. "I'll stay with you."

"No…missiles…here soon." His face twisted as a bolt of pain shot through him. "You can…drag yourself. Go. Stay here…you die. Won't be…your reason to die."

"We'll be all right. The Life Force will protect us." She took his hand and laid her head against his chest. "We stay together. Me and you, Mark. You and me."

He tried to push her off, but he lacked the strength to do anything more than shake her. "Not you and me…just you now. Go." He pulled his hand from hers, fumbled for something in his pants, and then he drew a long and shuddering breath. "Love you always, Keira. Remember…that. Remember…me."

She looked up and saw him holding a pistol to his head and squeezing the trigger. With the last energy her broken body possessed, she lunged for the gun and tried to pry his hand from it. They wrestled in the grass, each fighting for the other's life, until Krista's fingers slipped from his.

MICAH DROPPED THE COOLER beside a rusted guard booth at the entrance to Treasure Island. "They oughta be here soon."

"Yeah." Ada peered down the causeway. "I see something moving out there."

Gunfire rattled from inside the fog, and they ducked behind the booth. Ada peered around the side when the firing stopped and saw her mother a few yards away holding a hand over her shoulder. She picked up the rifle and started down the causeway, but he grabbed her arm and pulled her back. "No! We'll stay here and wait, okay? Don't go rushing in unless you know what you're getting into."

Gilsig and Victoria stumbled out of the mist and around the booth. "Get that toilet paper, Ada," Gilsig said.

"Is she hurt?"

"She's been shot. She's bleeding, but she'll be okay if we can slow it down."

Ada ran to her bag and pulled out a roll of toilet paper while Gilsig rested Victoria gently against the side of the guard booth. Ada handed him a wad of paper, and he pressed it into the hole in Victoria's shoulder. It turned red instantly.

"Keep pressure on it, Jon. The bleeding will slow in a few minutes if you keep the pressure on," Victoria said weakly. "Where's Krista? I could use one of her magic beans right now."

Ada heard Humvee engines and the shouts of men from the other side of the causeway, and then an assault rifle opened fire. "She's still out there. She needs to hurry. It sounds like the whole freakin Army is coming this way." As she unrolled more toilet paper, the guns chattered a long burst and everybody ducked.

"She'll be all right." Victoria grabbed a handful of toilet paper and pushed it into her shoulder. "Press hard. Like this, Jon. Be a man. It has to hurt. Push on the wound and make sure you press on the back side too."

"Something's wrong," Ada said. She crept to the side of the booth and peeked around it, looking for Krista and Mark. Her mouth twisted into a frown as she strained to hear – and then a mournful wail floated from the fog. "That's Krista!"

Micah looked in the same direction. "It's gone bad."

"We can't go after them," Gilsig said. "We gotta get the vaccine –"

"Bullshit!" Ada grabbed the rifle and ran into the fog, and Micah followed her.

"Get back here!" Gilsig yelled. "It's too dangerous!"

"Ada, no…" Victoria said hoarsely. Gilsig knelt in front of her and pressed more toilet paper into the wound, but she pushed his hand away. "I'll take care of myself," she said. "Go get her. That's more important."

He peered down the causeway and then back at her. "You'll be okay?"

"I'll be fine. Just bring my baby back, Jon. Please."

He handed her the roll of toilet paper and picked up a rifle. "I'll be right back."

RIPLEY RELEASED THE FOUR WARHAMMERS targeted for the causeway and sat back in her seat at the Tactical Warfare station, exhausted from launching nearly a hundred cruise missiles manually. Rolling her neck to loosen her knotted muscles, she unwrapped a square of gum and then glanced at the Strategic Warfare status monitor.

Her fingers stopped halfway to her mouth, and she blinked and checked again.

She walked the few feet to the Strategic station without taking her eyes off the screen. Sitting slowly, she turned on her lap monitor, but it displayed the same information. "No, no, no," she muttered under her breath as she ran a diagnostic.

"No what?" Quinn asked, looking up from the holographic chart. When he saw the blinking green icon on the Strategic monitor, he froze. "Ripley, tell me I'm hallucinating."

"You're not. Three-One's arming its warhead." Her screen flickered, and then the icon turned to steady green. "Fuck!" she spat, slamming her fists on the desktop.

"How could it –"

"I don't know!" She slapped the intercom button. "Chief Bailey to Control! Payload technicians to Control!"

"Could this be a glitch?" Quinn turned to Durgan. "Comm, test our channel."

Durgan tapped his screen a few times and turned in his seat a few seconds later. "Telemetry checks out five-by-five. Three-One is transmitting what you see."

Bailey hopped through the bulkhead hatch, followed by two payload techs. He stopped when he saw Three-One's arming icon. "No way," he said. "I fried the arming module myself."

"I confirmed it," Ripley said. "Three times. This is impossible."

"I confirmed the module was dead too," Quinn said. "Yet it's happening."

"I don't see how," Bailey said. "I couldn't squeeze a milliamp through it."

"But firing circuits are always energized," a payload tech said. "If it bypassed the relay gate and –"

Quinn said sharply, "We'll figure out the how and why later. Right now, we have to stop this bird. Give me options."

"There *are* no options. It's impossible to stop a Slick once it's launched," Ripley said.

"There's no way? There's no back door to re-target or disarm the thing?"

"No," Bailey said. "They can't be disarmed in flight. We can order minor course deviations, that's all, and the flight controller is programmed to ignore those if they'll keep the missile from reaching the target."

Quinn swore softly. "If it detonates…look, we can't let that happen. Give me options."

Bailey and Ripley glanced at each other, and then at the monitors. "We got nothing," Ripley said.

"Comm, tell Julie Three-One's gone rogue," Quinn said. "And the rest of you – we're going to get creative and do it fast."

HARRIS TIGHTENED HIS GUN BELT and strapped the holster to his thigh. In front of him, twelve Marines crouched facing the rear ramp door where a sergeant stood. "Blue Team's on the ground and reports that the landing zone is clear. The observers heard gunfire from the causeway, so our ops zone is hot. We got Armored troops all over Yerba Buena, so get ready for evolving close-quarters combat. There's heavy fog, so switch your optics to infrared." He flicked a switch, and the white cabin lights switched to red. "We're landing in sixty seconds, and we'll be outta here in sixty-one."

Harris slipped his pistol into the holster, strapped on a flak jacket and a helmet, and looked through the window at the north side of Yerba Buena Island. Four lights streaked into the fog bank; it flared yellow, and then a shockwave rippled through the mist as if it were a pond.

He turned away from the window and felt his tablet vibrate in his pants pocket, but he ignored it. It was the wrong time to chat with the neurotic Governor Wang.

The nose of the tiltrotor angled up, and Harris squatted behind Major Shelby. The big blades chopped the air as they rotated to their hovering position, buffeting the frame of the aircraft and jarring everything loose, and then the cabin rattled as the rear wheels slammed into the ground. The aircraft was still settling onto its front wheels when the ramp clanged open, and the Marines rushed into the fog.

He followed the clanking of their gear and felt his tablet vibrate again. Silently cursing the Stalker Governor, he ran behind the team off the concrete helipad and around an abandoned hangar.

They reached the causeway road five minutes later. He peered into the fog, but he couldn't see clearly for more than twenty feet. Further down the causeway, though, the fog glowed orange where the Warhammers had hit.

A soldier scanned the area through his infrared optics and pointed ahead. "One at the guard booth. Not moving but warm."

Harris sprinted to the booth. A woman was slumped against the wall with one arm draped across a metal cooler, and he clicked on his tablet light and saw Victoria's drawn face. "Tori, it's me." He pressed his fingers to her neck and felt a thin pulse.

"It's me," she said weakly. "Stupid thing to say, 'course you're you, you're not me…"

"It's Adam."

Her eyelids rose slowly, and a small smile played across her face that faded fast. "Ada's down on the causeway. They're all there. Go."

He called a corpsman to care for her and ran to Shelby, who was kneeling behind a brick wall and scanning the causeway through infrared binoculars. "She says they're down there. You see anything?"

"It's hotter'n hell, and we got something movin down near the impact site. Multiple targets, more'n the six we're looking for. It's hard to tell what's going on. I see three warm prones about forty yards ahead, on the grass by the crater, one movin 'round."

"There should be five out there."

"Only see three."

"Are they alive?" Harris asked. His tablet buzzed again.

"One's movin. That's all I know."

Harris tightened his helmet. "Then let's find out." He ran into the fog, and Shelby sent a Marine fireteam and a Navy corpsman to follow him.

Two soldiers took the lead, but after running for a minute, they raised their hands and dropped to the ground. The rest of the team followed, including Harris. "Hostiles directly south, less than a hundred yards," one said.

Harris swore. "We'll get our people fast and get out."

They ran in a crouch to where they'd seen the bodies, and then gunfire rattled ahead and they dove to the ground again. "Don't return fire," Harris said. "I don't want them to know we're here."

The Marines near the guard booth fired back, though, and muzzle flashes dotted the fog ahead. Harris and his team wriggled through the grass, staying as low as possible to avoid the bullets whizzing overhead.

After a few minutes of crawling, they found a boy lying near the road and shaking his head from side to side. The corpsman examined him, cupping his flashlight in his hand. "In shock, shrapnel injuries, but he's stable."

"Ask him if he's seen Ada."

"He can't respond," the corpsman said. "Kid's in La-La Land."

"Two more over here," a soldier whispered from ahead. Harris crawled over, and in the dim light from the streetlamps, he saw an unconscious woman on her side with a man lying facedown next to her.

"I think this is Warner," Harris said.

The corpsman checked her quickly. "Severe leg trauma and blood loss. She's an emergent case. I need to get her back to the plane now." He pulled a rubber strap from his pack and tightened it around her leg. "Somebody already put a tourniquet on her. Not a recent injury."

"This one's a lieutenant," said a soldier checking the man. "Insignia says 184th Infantry."

"That's our contact. How is he?" Harris asked.

The corpsman shuffled over and examined him quickly. "Concussion, contusions, shrapnel wounds, maybe intracranial bleeding. Another emergent case. He has to be evacked too."

"We're retrieving everybody," Harris said. "But I need to find a girl first, a blonde girl. Anybody see her?" The soldiers ducked as another bullet pinged off an unseen metal object. Two streetlights blew out, plunging the already dark road into deeper darkness. "Well, she's my daughter, so find her. She's our highest priority. We're not leaving without her."

The corpsman grabbed his arm. "We gotta evac the wounded *now*. If we don't –"

"All right, get them back to the Gold Team plane. I'll stay here."

"The major said to stay with you."

"Come back once you've got the wounded out! Now go!"

The Marines shrugged off their combat packs and hoisted the injured on their backs. Once they vanished into the fog, Harris crawled to the crater the Warhammers had made, patting the grass and listening for a cry or a call, but he didn't see Ada. He turned back toward the guardhouse and checked both sides of the road, but he found nothing.

Another round pinged off metal, and he crawled in the direction of the sound. He was halfway back to the guardhouse when his helmet clanged against something hard, and he reached out and felt the shank of an old anchor. Keeping one hand on it, he edged underneath and pawed the ground with the other.

His hand brushed against something soft – a suede boot, the kind a fashionable girl would wear. He pulled out his tablet and shined it over the body lying under the anchor.

In the light, a very young Victoria lay on her side with her eyes closed.

"Ada," he whispered. He ran his finger over her lips and felt soft breathing, but the hair above her temple glistened with blood. It wasn't a bullet wound; she'd hit something hard, probably the anchor. He checked her for other injuries, but except for minor scratches, the head wound seemed to be all she'd suffered.

The intensity of the gun battle picked up suddenly, and he heard shouts from the crater. More bullets pinged off the anchor, some *piffing* into the dirt beside him, and then the fog lit up as a grenade exploded nearby.

He dropped the tablet back into his pocket, where it began buzzing again, and then he slipped his hands gently beneath his daughter's body and lifted her from the grass, nestling her in his arms with her head against his shoulder. As he was climbing to his feet, a bullet slammed into his body armor between the shoulder blades and pushed him to the ground. Gasping for breath, he rose on shaky arms, and a bullet struck him in the back again. Another pinged off his helmet, pushing it down over his eyes, and then he felt a sting in his left arm.

He lay Ada on the grass and probed his arm, and his hand came away dripping with blood. However, he could still move it. He reached for her again, but then another round hammered his back.

There was no time to search for the missing fifth person; Ada was in danger, and he needed to get her out of the firefight now. His back aching and his arm burning, he lifted her from the grass again.

He ran in a crouch to the guardhouse without getting shot again. When they were safely behind it, he leaned against the wall to catch his breath and saw that Victoria was gone. He staggered across the road and found Major Shelby crouched behind the brick wall.

"You got her," he said when he saw Harris. "How's she doing?"

"Not good. I'm taking her to the plane now, and then we gotta *di di mau* outta here. Pull your men."

"Hey, we just broke the ice, and now we're gettin to know each other. Why bust up the party now?" He raised his rifle over the wall and let loose a burst. "I'd love to boogaloo, but soon as we do, those Armored troops are comin after our ass. They're usin those bomb craters as trenches, and we can't take 'em out. We gotta stay on the ground and make a fightin retreat back to the plane."

Harris shook his head. "I'll take care of this. Get the tablet out of my right pocket."

Shelby fished it out and handed it to him. "Wow, this sucker's hot."

"Yeah, the governor's been calling me." Harris squatted and dialed with one hand, trying not to shake Ada. In a few seconds, Bricker picked up the call. "Julie, how many Warhammers does the *Henry* have left? Good, tell Ennis to blow away that causeway...six minutes? Thanks. Love you. What?" His face grew pale, and then a bullet struck the wall and peppered them with brick chips. He hunched over to shield Ada. "Oh, fuck me.

Listen, I can't deal with this now. Have Tala kill it...no, don't brief Fort Worden! They'll just panic." Shelby's rifle rattled a long burst, and Harris yelled to be heard over the noise. "TELL TALA IT'S A SOFTWARE GLITCH! SHE'S SMART, SHE CAN FIND A WAY TO KILL IT! LEMME KNOW!" He clicked off the call.

Shelby knelt next to him and slapped a new magazine into his rifle. "What's wrong? You look like you seen a ghost."

"Yeah, a lot of them. Listen, hold off the hostiles till the shake and bake starts, then take the Blue Team plane out. I'm evacking the injured now."

QUINN READ THE TEXT MESSAGE on his chair monitor and swore under his breath. He swiveled to the Strategic station, where Bailey and Ripley were conferring. "Julie said sending Three-One's track to NORAD is pointless. They couldn't intercept it even if they knew where it was."

"It's flying nine thousand miles an hour, and the fastest bullet only goes half that fast," Ripley said. "That was a long shot anyway."

He stood and looked at the charting table, which showed the *Astor* closing in on their position, but fighting was pointless when the Commonwealth would probably be incinerated by a retaliatory strike soon. He spun the chart to San Diego, wondering if Point Loma would let them dock. The attack sub base had been under Adam's command at the start of the war, but he wasn't sure if they were still friendly.

After all the *Henry* had done, the safest course might be to hole up on Diego Garcia, where the fallout from a North American nuclear war would be light. They'd only be safe for a short time, though: As they watched America's self-immolation unfold on the news, the crew would likely turn to violence or suicide.

But some might survive. In the chaotic world America was hurtling toward, that might be all he could hope for.

Ripley leaned against the table. "At least I got to be XO for a few hours. At least I made it." She glanced at the chart. "You think Point Loma will let us in?"

Bailey looked over Ripley's shoulder. "It's our only choice. Bangor's gonna be ashes soon."

"Let's not speculate about that here." Quinn turned and leaned against the table beside Ripley. "Why didn't they put destruct mechanisms on these birds?"

"The Navy tried, but it added too much weight, so they decided to use the DLI-UMI protocol instead: Don't Launch It Unless You Mean It. There was no other choice. The warhead's only three ounces lighter than the missile's max payload weight."

"Yeah, a scramjet's fast but weak," Bailey said. "Add ten pounds and the sucker won't fly."

"Right. And drop the intake nozzle pressure by five percent, and the scramjet flames out," Ripley said. "It's amazing a Slick can fly at all..." She gasped and covered her mouth, and then she ran to the Strategic Warfare console. "Durgan! Get me weather maps of Indiana!"

"What is it?" Quinn asked.

Ripley's fingers flew over her monitor, and columns of numbers appeared. "When I plotted Three-One's course, I diverted it south over Indiana so it would miss the jet stream," she said, running her finger down a column.

Bailey studied the numbers on her screen and whistled. "Right, right. A two hundred forty-mile-per-hour tailwind. You could induce oxidizer choking by flying it through low dynamic air pressure. That's gonna be hard to pull off, though."

"Yeah." A map with squiggly lines appeared on the upper status monitor. She studied it for a moment with her hands clasped, and then she whooped and jumped into her chair. "I can do this!"

"Can somebody tell me what's going on?" Quinn asked.

"A scramjet needs high air pressure to operate efficiently, but I can change that." She pulled a small binder from a shelf, opened it, and blew a big bubble of gum. "I think I can crash Three-One."

HARRIS RAN UP THE RAMP to the Gold Team plane. The corpsman took Ada from his arms, laid her gently in a web hammock, and began examining her.

"Will she be okay?" Harris asked.

"Dunno yet. Gimme a minute."

Harris ran up to the cockpit and leaned inside. "Move out. Go to the nearest hospital the Armored isn't occupying, and fast."

"Which one?" the pilot asked.

"Sutter Shock-Trauma Center, Santa Cruz," Victoria murmured from the seat behind the co-pilot. "Best Level One trauma center on the West Coast."

"Go there," Harris said. "How far is it?"

The co-pilot tapped the navigation monitor. "Nine minutes."

"Get moving. Wheels up, gyrenes, let's go!"

He dodged Marines running into the plane and ran back to the corpsman, who was bending over Ada. "Gimme good news, doc."

"She's just concussed." The boarding ramp clanged shut and the tiltrotor roared into the sky, and they groped for the overhead straps as the plane shook. "Got clobbered by something hard, and it was lights out!" he yelled. "She needs an MRI, but I think she'll be okay! But she's got a big headache coming!"

Harris pulled her hair back and saw his daughter's face for only the second time since she was in diapers. She resembled Victoria when he first met her, but her features were softer: Her nose wasn't as sharp, and the faintest cleft creased her chin, just like his. He ran his finger across the soft, smooth skin of her cheek. They stopped over her lips, and he felt the warm tide of her breath, as he had so many times when she was a baby; she'd slept so soundly that sometimes he'd feared that she'd died in the night. The caress of her breath had always calmed him.

Nothing he'd devoted his life to – the Navy, Victoria, and even America – had ultimately proved worthy of that devotion. And all that time, he'd ignored the one constant in his life, the daughter that would always be his no matter where the tide flowed. For sixteen years, she'd deserved the fullest measure of his love, and he'd denied her. "You're an idiot, Harris," he muttered. "Pack your long johns. I'm sending you to McMurdo."

"Did you say something?" the corpsman asked.

"I asked how the others are doing."

"The boy's in shock. Shrapnel wounds on his upper torso. Both eardrums look ruptured, and he'll need surgery on the middle ear. Might have some hearing loss too. Lieutenant's in the same condition, except he got shot twice in the upper torso. Nothing life-threatening." He snapped off his gloves and pointed to Krista, who was lying in a web hammock on the other side of the plane with an IV dripping synthetic blood into her arm. "This one's in the worst shape. A round went right through her knee, and she's not getting blood flow to her lower right leg. Only the tendons are holding it on, and all the blood vessels are severed. I've iced it down to delay necrosis, but they'll probably amputate the whole leg." He lifted the bloodstained sheet. "Shame to just chop one off. They're classic fuck-me gams." He looked up quickly and then covered Krista's leg. "Sorry, that just slipped out."

"We're in the Navy, son. So she'll live?"

"Yeah, except she'll be twenty pounds lighter." He pointed to where Victoria sat behind the cockpit, resting her head against the wall and watching a bag of synthetic blood sway from a rack above. "That one's in the best shape. She just has a clean hole through the shoulder, and I kotexed it and stopped the bleeding. I tried to infuse her, but she took the Hemosynth rig away and IV'd herself."

"She's a trauma doc. She does stuff like that in her sleep."

"And then she started telling me what to do, like I can't find my ass with both hands. I had to shoot her up with my secret stash just to shut that mouth. What a bitch."

"I know what you mean. I was married to her for two miserable years." Harris pulled off his helmet and ran his hand through his hair. "Just stay away from her. It's the only way to keep from getting fragged."

He fingered the hole in his sleeve. The bullet had only grazed the skin, but it had chewed the American flag on his sleeve to threads. He ripped the flag off and threw it into the corpsman's medical waste bag, and then he pulled a gauze pad from the medikit and sopped blood from the wound. After the bleeding slowed, the corpsman wrapped his arm and resumed working on Krista's leg.

Harris tossed his helmet into an overhead rack and shrugged off his flak jacket, poking his finger into the holes stitching the back. He threw it into the rack, too, and then pulled out his tablet.

He wrote to Julie and told her to black out any information on Bird Three-One's malfunction, and he promised to tell her the entire story over dinner sometime. After reading the message, though, he deleted it and started again.

If Julie was going to learn about the ghosts in America's nuclear arms machine, it would be better to do it over drinks.

As HARRIS AND HIS TEAM LIFTED OFF Yerba Buena Island, President Hayborn sat at his Oval Office desk and tried to ignore the Sentinels standing by the Rose Garden doors, both standing at ease with their long, white coats unbuttoned to reveal the machine pistols strapped to their sides. They were ostensibly guarding him, as The Profit Joseph didn't trust the faithless Secret Service to do their job, but he suspected they were also there to keep The Profit informed about what he was doing. *The stress of the Transition probably sent the Grandson of God into another spasm of paranoia*, he thought.

He didn't care if they watched him do paperwork, though, so he unfolded the latest radionuclide deposition map of the Midwest. Tropical Storm Andy Boy had spread the radioactive fallout from Sacramento across a hot-dog-shaped swath of farmland from southeastern Nebraska to eastern Indiana, but the damage would have been worse if Hurricane Aunt Dottie's remnants hadn't pushed the fallout into Canada before it reached the East.

He stood and gazed across the Ellipse at the Washington Monument glowing against the night sky. Aunt Dottie had scrubbed the obscuring fug from the city, but it would return soon; carbon emissions might have been curtailed if the Archangelists had assumed power thirty years before, but climate change was now irreversible.

So many of his fellow Elders had gone to the gallows cursing his treachery, but they would have praised his compassion if they'd known that he'd spared them the harshest truth: Earth never could, and never would, return to a vestal state of Eden.

They should have thanked him for executing them. They no longer had to suffer the putrescence of this cesspit, which would likely reek even more as the planet warmed. The wisest approach now wasn't attempting to solve the climate crisis but laying in a supply of clothespins.

He rubbed his eyes and yawned, and then he reviewed the radionuclide deposition map. Had the RVE Initiative worked as planned, it would have been possible to feed the survivors and shun the radioactive croplands, but the Initiative had failed; instead of the projected 75 megadeaths, they'd be lucky if they reached half that when the virus ran its course.

There'd never be enough food if they discarded the radioactive corn and beef, so he decided to use it for unemployment relief rations. Radiation was invisible, and the unemployed would never know that their food was tainted until the tumors bloomed twenty years later, which was twenty more years of life than the leeches deserved. In the meantime, it would keep their tummies full and their violence in check.

And once he defeated the Republic, California's uncontaminated and fertile croplands would help feed the honest and worthy Americans who had earned their meals. That seemed more likely now that the rebels' makeshift vaccine lab was shut down, and Warner and the feedstock were trapped on Yerba Buena Island, soon to be in Federal hands. Once they defeated California militarily – something the 11th Armored should achieve by dawn – agents stationed in Los Angeles and San Francisco would release RVE and begin the final task of eliminating California's rebellious population.

HARRIS STUMBLED to the front of the plane and rubbed the knots out of his neck. Victoria looked up, and he sat in the webbed seat beside her. "The corpsman says Ada will be okay."

She gave him a wan smile. "S'good."

"How are you feeling?"

"Your corpsman stopped the bleeder." She looked down at her shoulder and then sat back. "Now my biggest problem is that unicorn across the plane. Keeps winking at me."

"Oh, good, he gave you the street stuff."

"Whatever it is, I want more." She glanced to where Ada lay. "She needed a hero today. We all did. We'd reached the end of the line back there."

Harris glanced at his tablet. "So now it's good to be a hero?"

"If you're the right kind, it sure is."

He searched the tablet screen for an incoming message, and then he frowned and slid the dented metal cooler toward him. "This doesn't look like the linchpin to the life and death of millions. It looks like it fell off the back of a hillbilly's pickup. This is really the big prize?"

"Yep," Victoria said. "It has to go to...whassa name? Wow, these drugs are delish. It has to go to someplace outside San Diego, Elixa Pharmaceuticals in Torrey Pines, thassit. That's where they're building the bioreactors."

"Okay. I'll take it down there personally after we drop you off." He loosened the lid catches and pulled out a bottle; RECOMBIN-A 10/11/43 was written on the side. The 'I' was dotted with a heart.

"I told her to be serious, but she did that on every bottle she marked," she said.

"She was helping you make the stuff, huh?"

"I was helping *her*." She laughed weakly and watched the IV bag swinging from the rack above. "She didn't need my help. It was all under control when I got there."

He turned the bottle over in his hands. "So she turned out to be a bug lady like you, I guess?"

"Oh, no. Virology's just her hobby."

"Now, there's a strange hobby for a girl to have." He slid the bottle back into its foam sleeve, closed the lid, and then he rechecked the tablet.

"Expecting a call?" Victoria asked.

"Hmm? Yeah, yeah, just operational stuff I gotta keep my finger on."

"You're worse than Ada with that thing. She's completely addicted to hers." He didn't answer, so she nudged him in the ribs.

"What? I'm listening. Ada's addicted to her tablet, got it."

"You seem distracted."

"No, no." He set it on the seat and sat back. "Just thinking about how I talk to a daughter I haven't seen since she was two. I have a lot of lost time to make up, and so many mistakes to apologize for, and so many missed birthdays to celebrate, and a thousand teddy bears I owe her. I'll finally get to know my daughter although I'm sure it'll be a challenge. She's probably a lot like you."

Victoria snorted. "You know that she went back to get Krista even though the missiles were coming? She didn't stop to think. Does that sound like something I'd do, or you? She's so much like you…" Her eyes crossed, and she rested her head against the wall and watched the Hemosynth bag swing back and forth. "Whoa, that's awesome. Blood is *so* red."

Harris snapped his fingers in front of her eyes. "Stay with me, Tori."

"Sorry, it comes in waves…"

"So you were saying she's a lot like me?"

"Oh, right, right. She's so much like you, it hurts. She has my looks but your mind. All she thinks about is particles and atoms, just like you."

"I used to, but now I think of everything but that. Her old man is still a fair nuclear engineer, though. I can give her a leg up when she goes to college."

She snorted a laugh and covered her mouth.

"What? What'd I say?"

"Adam, she's a gee…she's a gee…" Victoria stifled a horsey snort and then doubled over laughing.

"What's wrong?" he asked.

"She's a high school dropout!" she half-blurted, half-giggled.

"What!"

"Never made it past her junior year!" She looked up at the ceiling and snorted again. "Oh, this'll be rich. I *so* deserve this."

"She dropped out of school and you let her? How are you raising this child –" His tablet clock chimed, and he checked the screen. "It's almost time."

"For what?"

"For the end of this war or the beginning of the next. But if there's still a world tomorrow, we're having a talk about this girl's education."

THE DOOR SWUNG OPEN, and an aide ran to the wall monitor. "Mr. President, we just got a call from Governor Wang's office. They say it's imperative that you watch NewsPulse Seattle."

He nodded and sat back in his chair as the rest of his staff rushed in. He'd expected Wang to capitulate soon because the Commonwealth was fighting his superior forces with the vigor of a drunken French army. As the screen warmed up, the somber face of a middle-aged Eurasian woman materialized on it, and his hopes for a contrite surrender rose.

The Year of Endings

"…upon ratification of the mutual defense treaty, it became a solemn commitment for each nation to assure the other's survival, understanding that our cultural and commercial interdependence is too strong for either to prosper apart. Thus, when the States invaded the California Republic, we rose to their defense.

"Unfortunately, our joint conventional forces are unlikely to defeat the States on the field of battle, despite having deployed our every ground asset, and this reality has led the leadership of the Commonwealth of New Columbia to a sobering conclusion."

A cool shiver of vindication coursed along Hayborn's nerves, and he steepled his fingers over his lips to conceal his victorious grin. She'd capitulate in the next few sentences.

"We've come to accept a sad truth – that the city called Washington no longer exemplifies the ideals of George Washington. It's not the shining city on a hill the founders envisioned, where the reasonable and the enlightened would deliberate for the good of the people. No, the city called Washington is a ruin of those dreams and a crypt of those ideals, and it's a mockery of George Washington and all the founders that monuments to these great men still stand there." She looked off-camera at a clock. "So we'll kill two birds with one stone, as it were. President Hayborn, our sources say you're in the Oval Office right now. Please look across the Ellipse. There's something you must witness before I can continue."

He swiveled in his chair and saw the obelisk of the Washington Monument standing proudly against the night sky, and he wondered when the yellow devil would cave in.

BIRD TWO-NINE HAD REACHED THE END OF ITS RANGE. With little fuel remaining, its weight had dropped to four thousand pounds. It was flying at over nine thousand miles an hour, so fast that its titanium nosecone had begun to melt and its winglets were glowing.

Almost all its kinetic energy – the equivalent of five tons of TNT – was expended in the millisecond after it struck the Washington Monument's west face, vaporizing thirty feet of the marble and granite wall.

The W104 warhead continued through the west wall undamaged and struck the granite interior of the east wall at two thousand miles an hour, shattering the weapon's magnesium case. The metal disintegrated into a cloud of shrapnel that shredded the plutonium alloy core.

A supersonic jet of plutonium and stone blew through the monument's east wall, continuing across the Mall for almost five hundred yards. As the plutonium alloy settled into the grass of the Mall, the lawn sprinklers turned on and washed the radioactive metal deep into the soil.

THE TOP OF THE MONUMENT QUIVERED and leaned slowly to the west. Staffers pressed against the Oval Office windows, some shaking their heads and muttering, and others crossing their chests and praying.

A puff of dust rose from the impact point, and with a rumble that could be heard in the White House, a crack raced around the upper shaft. The monument wavered more, and then the stone above the break crumbled with a dull boom and the shaft dropped a dozen feet. Everybody in the Oval Office gasped, and a few that were unable to watch anymore turned away.

The shaft began tilting slowly west; a second later, it broke free and fell to the ground in a painful slow motion that seemed to last for minutes. The shaft plunged behind the trees lining the Ellipse, and then a hundred million pounds of stone slammed into the ground, liquefying it and sending ripples outward from the epicenter. A second later, the shockwave lifted the White House, throwing the staff to the floor and knocking the lamps off the president's desk. A flurry of plaster dust drifted from cracks in the ceiling.

Coughing and covering his mouth, Hayborn climbed to his feet and dusted off his suit. When he looked at the monitor, he saw that Wang was still talking, and he told everyone in the room to be quiet.

"...has been struck by a disarmed Lancet missile launched by a Commonwealth submarine. Another Lancet missile is approaching the city, and it will strike the Museum of the Corporate-American in six minutes. Its nuclear warhead is armed and will detonate unless I issue the disarming signal. I repeat, its nuclear warhead is armed. President Hayborn, you can avoid your capital's destruction by announcing the withdrawal of your forces from the California Republic before then. If not, Washington will suffer the same fate as Sacramento." She stacked the papers on her desk and leaned into the camera. "And Noah – don't spit into the wind." The screen image faded and was replaced by a countdown clock.

Hayborn sat in his chair and tapped his steepled hands to his lips as he watched the seconds tick down. His senior adviser, a man as thin and polished as a millionaire's walking stick, knelt beside him. "Shall I inform the studio to broadcast the presidential seal?" he asked.

The president watched a few more seconds tick by. "Whatever for, Travis?"

"An atom bomb is coming this way, and I have no desire to sing in the Choir Invisible tonight. We have no recourse –"

Hayborn stood suddenly, nearly knocking Travis over. "Initiate a Continuity of Government evacuation," he said over his shoulder as he walked to a naval captain and a commander watching the white dust rise beyond the trees. "Captain, do we have any subs within range of the West Coast?"

He tapped on his tablet. "We have an MRCS-enabled *Ohio*-class boat, the *Alaska*, off the coast of Greenland."

"All right. Give me retaliation options."

The captain looked up at the president. "I will not, sir."

Hayborn waved to the Sentinel standing by the door. "You're disobeying your commander in chief?"

"I am, sir. I cannot execute an unlawful order –" The Sentinel clasped his hand over the captain's mouth and yanked him off his feet.

"Take this traitor outside and shoot him," Hayborn said. "On the grass. Don't make a mess." The commander watched the Sentinel drag the squirming officer through the door and backed away. The other Sentinel clamped his hand on the commander's shoulder and pushed him forward.

"It's a new world, Commander Burke," Hayborn said. "Do you and your young family care to remain in it?" A pistol cracked outside and Burke flinched.

The Sentinel picked up the launch control tablet from the floor and handed it to him. "Choose the path to wisdom, brother," he said, opening his white coat and letting him see the machine pistol. "And don't you even consider bricking that tablet."

Commander Burke nodded and initialized it, and the Navy seal appeared a moment later.

"A wise choice indeed," Hayborn said. "Now how many missiles does the *Alaska* have?"

"Twenty-four Trident IV's. A total of 192 warheads, 475 kilotons each."

"Good." Hayborn flipped through a binder on his desk and stopped at a page showing a map of the US West Coast. "This one. SIOP Nine Yankee. Do it."

Burke touched a few icons on his screen then held out the tablet to Hayborn. "Sir, enter your code and press your palm against the screen to authorize these strikes."

Hayborn fished the nuclear code biscuit from his jacket, pricked his finger on it and entered the numbers, then pressed his palm to the screen to verify his identity. The tablet chirped three times, and he handed it back to Burke.

"The *Alaska*'s MRCS acknowledges the strike order. First launch in four minutes. Initial target selections are the Los Angeles, San Francisco, and Seattle metro areas," he said.

The Sentinel looked sharply at Hayborn as Burke scrolled down the tablet's targeting screen. An assistant cried out and rushed to the desk, but the Sentinel pushed her back; while he was distracted, Burke tapped out a private message to the *Alaska*'s commander.

QUINN WATCHED THE RED DOT representing the *Astor* inch closer to the *Henry*'s position and estimated that they'd have to begin evasive maneuvering in no more than six minutes. However, he couldn't submerge the boat without losing the comm link to Bird Three-One.

He glanced at the Strategic Warfare monitor – the status for Bird Two-Nine had grayed out a minute ago, so it had probably hit the target. Durgan was monitoring radio traffic, but he'd heard no news from Washington yet confirming the strike.

Three-One was still five minutes from its target, though, leaving only a minute to get away from the Farallons. If it struck Washington, he'd have to draw the *Astor* into the Pacific to keep any fallout away from California because they'd probably nuke the boat that had just wiped out the nation's capital. If they survived that engagement – and the ghost ship he suspected was waiting for them – they might sail for San Diego.

If Ripley brought the missile down, though, he didn't need to risk an encounter with the ghost ship. He spun the chart to Soquel Canyon, which was congested with small boats now.

He looked at the Warfare consoles, where Ripley, Bailey, and three technicians were studying weather charts and maps of the Midwest. Three-One's programmed track was overlaid on the map, which showed that it was probably around Bloomington, Illinois, about a hundred miles from the jet stream.

Ripley planned to fly the missile into a two-hundred-mile-an-hour tailwind to drop the scramjet's intake pressure and force it to consume more fuel. Since Joe Slicks didn't receive weather forecasts, Three-One's flight controller wouldn't know about the jet stream and would probably execute the course change.

He wished that he could help, but Ripley was a qualified aeronautical engineer, and Bailey could assemble a Joe Slick blindfolded and drunk. Still, just watching them work frustrated him.

He walked around the charting table to Strategic, where she was alternately chewing madly and blowing bubbles. "Any way I can help?"

She handed him a foil packet. "Yeah, open this."

"This is bad for you," he said as he peeled the gum wrapper.

"Don't care."

"How's it coming?"

"Almost there." She scrolled through a list of numbers and asked Bailey to confirm some calculations. When she was done, she swiveled in her seat. "That's it. I'm ready, Skipper."

"All right. Do it."

Ripley pressed an icon on her monitor. "Three-One confirms receipt of the course mods," she said a few seconds later.

"Good. When will we know if this worked?"

"If the flight controller accepts the course mods – and if it's got a software glitch, I can't say it will – it'll enter the jet stream in eleven seconds. In around three minutes, it'll run out of fuel."

"I'd say two minutes," Bailey said. "That's a wicked tailwind."

"I hope you're right," Ripley said. "Then the thing would slam right into Maryville."

TRAVIS KNELT ON THE CARPET beside Hayborn's chair and spoke to him in a low whisper. "Noah, I fear you're losing your perspective. Is this wise?"

"I cannot begin this presidency in failure. That isn't God's will."

"I agree, but how is raining fire on the West Coast a measure of success?"

"Two minutes to first release," said Captain Burke. He wiped a bead of sweat from his brow and then saw an incoming message appear on his screen. A fleeting smile crossed his lips.

Hayborn glanced at the countdown clock and turned back to Travis. "You misunderstand the purpose of this engagement. This is a test, not of the strength of nations, but of the strength of our faith's fiber. We shall overcome this trial at any cost."

"At *any* cost?" Travis looked at the Sentinel standing on the other side of the desk. Their eyes met and an unspoken message passed between them; the Sentinel nodded, pulled a tablet from inside his coat, and began typing a message. "Some costs are too dear, Noah."

"Yet some costs must be paid nonetheless. This is no time for moral parsimony. The new Archangelist States will be born clean, even if the land must first be sterilized by fire. And from those ashes, we will draw forth –"

"We'll raise nothing from the ashes!" he hissed. "The fallout will kill us first. Don't spit into the wind, remember?"

"God will provide, and the Earth will abide. Trust the Lord and try not to rationalize the ineffable." He sighed and leaned toward him, speaking in a lowered voice. "I have learned this recently, Travis. I must confess that when The Profit called me to lead the Transition, I anticipated that it would ultimately fail, producing minor political disruption at best. Nevertheless, it was a noble enough goal to risk everything for, although I expected to be pilloried and exiled after its failure. Yet the Transition succeeded, and when I placed my hand on the Bible and took that oath, I was humbled by the realization that God had always intended for me to lead America out of its winter of faith. I felt shame knowing that I had been blinded by the myopia of Man's politics and had doubted God.

"And now that He has set before me this most terrible challenge, I will shame myself no more. God's intent is clear. While we cannot return to Eden, he is showing us that we can walk together into a new and different Garden if I complete the urgent winnowing of His flock. This is a higher and greater Initiative where fallout, and not a virus, is the tool he has given us. We should make a list of –"

"Excuse me, sir, but I've just received a message from the *Alaska*," Captain Burke said. "Their Missile Release Control System is non-functional. They're unable to deliver the strike."

Hayborn stood slowly. "What?"

"The commander sent a message for you. Your eyes only." Burke handed him the tablet, swiping the encryption icon as he did.

Hayborn tried to make sense of the random letters and numbers covering the screen, and then he saw Burke running for the door. "Get him!" he yelled. "He can't leave the grounds!"

He watched the Sentinels chase the captain, and then he sagged into the big presidential chair and ran his fingers across his scalp. "It's a world of traitors, Travis. Tell the California teams to release the RVE immediately. The sooner this Earth is cleansed, the better."

"I'll do that later," Travis said, glancing at the countdown clock, which showed three minutes remaining until Washington was incinerated. "We need to get to the studio or the blast bunker *now*."

"Indeed." Hayborn swiveled his chair to look across the Ellipse and watched the dust cloud drift over the trees. "This faithless city," he murmured. "It would be better to cauterize this ugly scab from our land and start over. And in this time of martyrs, who would lament adding one more, especially if it's crucified on New Columbia's cross? Yes, this city's time has ended. I should let it burn."

Travis let out his breath and sat back on his haunches, watching the countdown clock like the rest of the staffers in the room, as Hayborn gazed through the window. After a long moment, the president stood and addressed the small crowd. "Washington is lost. Get down to the bunker immediately."

Every person stood silent and rooted in place, gaping at the president and absorbing his words. In the back of the room, a young woman began to sob.

Just then, *Amazing Grace* chirped inside Hayborn's coat pocket.

HARRIS SHOUTED TO THE COCKPIT, "Put NewsPulse Seattle on the status monitor back here!"

The systems indicators on the monitor disappeared, and Governor Wang's face swam into being. Victoria rested her hand on Adam's arm. "What's happening?"

"The Army's almost in San Francisco. If they get there, there'll be no more California Republic. Wang's playing our last card, and everything depends on how Hayborn reacts."

Every conscious person on the plane turned their eyes to the monitor and watched Wang's speech. The countdown appeared on the screen, and several men bowed their heads and looked at the floor, unwilling to see the numbers run down to zero. The rest began talking at the same time.

"Did you actually launch a nuke at Washington?"

"This is why we took the base, so you could do the same thing?"

"This is nuts!"

"I didn't sign on for this."

"An unprovoked nuclear attack, that's for cowards!"

Harris jammed his fingers into his mouth and whistled. "As you were, men! The warhead's not armed!"

"It's a bluff?" Victoria asked.

"Of course. Wang thinks the threat of nuclear war will force Hayborn to withdraw. If she's right, we've won and we'll be dancing till dawn."

"And if she's wrong, we all end up like Sacramento," another soldier said.

"I hope you know what you're doing," Victoria said. "If he doesn't back down and the warhead doesn't go off, he'll think we're weak, and then he might launch a full-scale attack."

Harris slipped his hand into his pocket, hoping the tablet would buzz. "Don't worry, it'll all go the way I planned, okay?"

THREE MINUTES REMAINED UNTIL IMPACT, and Quinn's gut had twisted into a knot. Ripley leaned against the charting table beside him and popped bubbles. He was tempted to ask for a piece of her magic gum to untie his bowels.

Three-One's status bar remained unchanged, showing six green icons in a row. They glared at the arming icon and willed it to change.

A faint ping echoed through the hull. "I think they saw us with that one, Skipper," the sonar operator called.

"Acknowledged," he said, watching the seconds tick away. He glanced at the missile track, which showed that it should be approaching Columbus, Ohio, and his gut tightened even more as the likelihood of failure grew.

The *Astor* pinged them again. "Twelve thousand meters, Skipper," Jackson said. "Screw aspect ratio shows they're coming straight for us. I don't know why they're even bothering with sonar."

"Acknowledged," Quinn muttered. He crossed his arms and suppressed the urge to scream at the monitor.

BIRD THREE-ONE'S SCRAMJET FLAMED OUT over Maryville. With no fuel remaining in the tank, the flight controller couldn't relight the engine, but its programming was clear about what to do next: Land in an open field so the warhead remained intact and recoverable. After turning for southeastern Ohio's vast farmlands, it activated its coded locator beacon and descended.

Its mission ended in a cornfield north of Lancaster, Ohio. The missile was still traveling at twice the speed of sound when it mowed through the late-season stalks and slammed into the muddy soil, ripping off the winglets and air intake. It furrowed the mud for three hundred yards until it rammed into a Producer, disintegrating both and covering the field with a fine spray of plutonium.

RIPLEY STARED AT THE GREEN ARMING ICON, chewing her gum even more furiously. She wasn't the only one studying the screen; the entire weapons team was crowding the Control Room and staring at her status monitor too, as were all the officers. Even the pilot sneaked a glance every now and then.

Quinn looked at the flight path map, which showed that Bird Three-One had just passed Columbus. If Ripley's fix was going to work, it would have to happen soon. She knew it; she was standing as rigidly as if she were carved from stone, her eyes glued to the screen.

He started to offer her some words of encouragement, but then she gasped. He looked up at the monitor and saw that Three-One's arming icon was flashing red.

"It's working," she whispered, leaning even closer to the screen. A few seconds later, every status icon turned gray.

"Skipper, telemetry lost from Bird Three-One," Durgan called.

Everyone in the Control Room whooped at the same time. Ripley jumped into the air and slugged an imaginary opponent, and then she bumped fists with Chief Bailey. The payloads techs slapped her back and punched her arm. Laughing, she punched them back.

When the fisticuffs were over, Quinn pulled her into his arms and bear-hugged her. "Thank you, Tala. I can't ever thank you enough. You were phenomenal."

"I did good, huh?" she asked.

"You did an awesome job. If it weren't for you –"

"Fish in the water!" the sonar operator called. "Active ranging, bearing 020, range 8,200 meters!"

Quinn let her go and strode to the front of the podium. "Tactical, shoot the Squid and the Mini-Me at heading 270 and enable the anti-torpedo batteries. Pilot, all ahead flank, maintain this heading, down bubble ten, make your depth two hundred meters. Comm, tell Julie Three-One is down, then retract the comm buoy and flash battle stations. Tactical, target Fish One and Two for the last location of the *Astor*, active ranging, wait for my order." He sat in the command chair and swiveled around to the helm. "Look sharp, sailors. Break time's over."

ADAM AND VICTORIA sat near the front of the plane and stared at the countdown clock on the screen. When it reached forty seconds, the

Presidential seal appeared, and Victoria climbed to her feet and clutched Harris' arm for support. She leaned toward him and whispered, "I just hope you're right this time, hero."

"So do I," he whispered back.

President Hayborn's tired and dusty face appeared on the screen, and he cleared his throat and peered into the camera. "My fellow Americans, I have recalled the 11th Armored Division from its operations in the state of California –"

Nobody heard the rest. They jumped to their feet and howled and hugged each other, and for the first time in fourteen years, Victoria wrapped her arms around Adam and kissed him. "You won, hero."

He forced a smile to his lips and pulled out his tablet. "Yeah. Feels good," he said.

"You don't seem very thrilled," she said. "What's wrong?"

"I'm not sure you wanna know." He tapped the screen a few times. "Listen, this is complicated. Politics is complicated enough, but machine intelligence is *really* complicated. It works in ways we can't even understand, Tori, and…" The tablet buzzed, and after reading the first line of the message, his face brightened with the largest smile Victoria had ever seen. He dropped the tablet into his pocket, wrapped his arms around her, and kissed her like it was their wedding day.

Victoria rested her head against his shoulder. "So you were saying?" she asked.

"Nah, it was nothing. The whole thing worked out the way I planned, Tori. Just like I said it would."

THE DÉBORDAN

Day 63
Tuesday morning, October 19, 2043
Sutter Shock-Trauma Center, Santa Cruz, California

Ada opened her eyes to see a white, featureless ceiling. She saw a small table to one side overflowing with flowers, and beyond it a window filled with deep blue sky. At the foot of the bed, a giant teddy bear stared at her with glassy brown eyes as big as saucers.

Why she was in this strange place mystified her. She remembered running across the dark, foggy causeway, but nothing after that.

She sat up and dangled her legs off the bed. The side of her head was bandaged and hurt to touch, but she was injured nowhere else. After a moment of dizziness, she stood, tightened the hospital gown around her waist, and checked the room again.

The bear and the flower display were so comically excessive that they had to be props to lull her into lowering her guard. Looking closer, the veneer of a bland hospital room disappeared, and she saw the true picture of the prison cell she was in.

The windows had no bars, but they also couldn't be opened more than a few inches, offering no way to escape. Even if she broke through the glass, she was a hundred feet or more above the ground.

The only way out was through the door, which was undoubtedly guarded. She tiptoed to it, looking up into the gigantic bear's eyes as she passed. The door was open a crack, and she saw the back of a man in green camouflage wearing a holstered pistol. It was definitely a prison hospital.

The Federal extractors would arrive soon, and she had to break out while they thought she was still asleep. She scanned the room for a weapon but found nothing except the slats in the window blinds, which seemed sharp. As she was walking toward them, she tripped over the bear's leg and stumbled into the flower-covered table, knocking over a vase. She caught it with one hand and smiled when she felt the cool glass surface.

She grabbed a towel from the bathroom, wrapped the vase in it, and then crushed the glass vessel under her pillow with a soft crack. Unwrapping the towel, she found a shard that fit her hand and returned to the door.

As she was planning her attack on the guard, she slipped on water from the vase and tumbled into the teddy bear's arms with a loud squawk. The door opened, and she scrambled to her feet while eyeing the approaching soldier. When he was in reach, she leaped at him and slashed, missing his hands by an inch. Instead of reaching for his pistol, though, he stood back and smiled. "Easy there, l'il anarchista. I'm on your side."

"Nobody's on our side, chump," she rasped through a dry throat. "Back off and I'll let you live."

"Yeah, the doc said you'd be disorientated when you woke up. I'll go get her and see if she'll give you something." He walked to the door and held it open. "In the meantime, you're free to explore if you want, but you gotta give me the weapon first."

She looked through the door at a hospital floor with nurses, doctors, and orderlies bustling from room to room. An elderly man coasted slowly by, leaning on a metal walker, and he winked at a wizened woman sitting in a wheelchair against the wall. "I'm not a prisoner?"

"No."

"Then why are you armed?"

"To protect you. Hey, I know this is all weird, but a lotta strange things happened last night, and the admiral didn't wanna take any chances. We're just here to keep the weird away. It's all for your own good."

She glanced out into the corridor again. "Where am I?"

"Sutter Shock-Trauma Center in Santa Cruz."

She nodded. "Near Stanford. How'd I get here?"

"We grabbed you off the island and flew you here. You were all unconscious, so you probably didn't know what was going on."

"*Who* grabbed me?"

"Us. Second Marines, Security Battalion Bangor."

"My father's base," she said slowly. "It's starting to come back to me..." Krista lying across Mark, trying to pull the pistol away from his head as a pool of glistening blood spreads around her nearly severed leg...Mark looking up, his eyes wide with fear, a bloodstain blossoming across his stomach...Micah wailing and clutching his brother's chest...Gilsig pulling him away, and prying the gun from Krista's hand and giving it to Mark...Gilsig lifting Krista off him, her leg dangling like a broken puppet's...leaving Mark behind and running through the fog...hearing the awful crack of a pistol and the maniacal shriek of missiles, and then flying through the air and hitting something hard. She slumped against the wall and slowly slid down to the floor.

"Hey, what's wrong?" he asked.

"It's starting to come back to me." She asked softly, "Is Mark Mason here?"

"Who?"

The glass shard slipped from her fingers, and then tears splattered on it. She buried her face in her hands.

"You okay?" he asked.

She shook her head, and he picked her up and held her until she stopped crying.

THE GUARD TOOK HER to see her friends. Gilsig had mostly recovered from his head injuries and his gunshot wounds were bandaged, but he was dizzy and needed assistance to walk; Micah had ruptured something in his middle ear and was being prepped for surgery; and Victoria was working in the emergency room, helping as much as a one-armed physician could. Krista had taken it the worst: She'd had hours of emergency surgery through the night and was recovering in Intensive Care. Ada demanded to see her, and the guard escorted her to a room in the next wing of the hospital, where a Marine stood beside a wide glass door. He slid it open for her, and she strode through and stifled a gasp.

In the center of the room, Krista lay on a narrow bed with tubes snaking from her arms to a machine by the bedside. She found a spot free of equipment and took her hand.

Krista appeared uninjured except for a black eye and a scrape on her forehead. However, her lips were dry and cracked; Ada found a pitcher of water, dipped a tissue in it, and dabbed them until they softened. She wiped the rest of her face, combed her hair back, plumped her pillows, and straightened her blankets, all the time avoiding the tangle of tubes running to the machine. When this was done, she thought she saw a faint smile on her friend's lips.

She sat in a bedside chair and held her hand again. A few minutes later, a middle-aged woman wearing a lab coat and a stethoscope walked in. "Finally, it is young Miss Lang," she said with a soft Creole accent. "You are hard to find, *zanmi*. I hunt you down and wear these shoes out, and my feet, they get enough work. Stay in one place."

"Sorry."

"Do not apologize. I am always a little *farfelu* in the mornings."

"Farfelu?"

"You have no English word for it. The word, it means to be bitchy and wacky at the same time." She smiled and held out her hand. "Dr. Baptiste."

Ada smiled back and shook her hand. "Ada Lang."

Baptiste arched an eyebrow. "It is not evident that I know who you are?"

"Wow, you *are* a little farfelu this morning," Ada said. "I have to remember that word."

Baptiste pulled a stethoscope from her pocket and listened to Ada's chest, checked the bandage on her head and looked into her eyes, and then declared her healthy. "The *sólda* say you have been disoriented. The head, it took a beating, and this is normal. But if you get dizzy, you let me know *byen vit*, no? I will give you medication, and you must rest. Try to save your energy, though, because you are taking a trip as soon as your ride comes."

"A trip? I'm there. We'll put the top down and cruise down the coast highway, find some monster waves…"

"You can wish, *zanmi*. The governor, he needs you to go to some secret facility where they're making Recombin and show them how you accelerated replication. Police captured two men this morning in San Francisco with Neovirus vessels, which they had not yet released," she looked up at the ceiling and made the sign of the cross on her chest, "but if we caught one team, there will be others, and we don't have enough of your vaccine to control an outbreak. You must help."

"No prob. They'll need a bucket brigade to handle the output when I'm done." Ada adjusted her hospital gown and sat. "So what happened? Last I remembered, we were in a war zone. That's over?"

"Yes, President Hayborn conceded right before you arrived here. The cost, however, was high. Many are dead or injured, and much of the South Bay is damaged." Baptiste dropped the stethoscope into a pocket and peered at Krista's monitor. "She is doing so well. I am told she was almost gone when she arrived."

"How is she?"

"As I said, she is doing well."

Ada winced. "I mean, what happened to her, what's the prognosis, that sorta thing."

"Oh, that." Baptiste pulled aside some tubes and sat on the gurgling machine beside the bed. "Ahh, these poor feet. Your friend here, she arrived with very serious injuries, and it took some time to stabilize her. Blood loss was her biggest problem, and of course, we have no blood, so we all gave." She smiled and pointed to a bandage in the crook of her arm. "Fortunately, she's AB Positive, so she can use anyone's blood. Her other problem was the leg. It was almost severed."

"I caught a glimpse of it last night just before the missiles hit. It was hanging from threads."

Baptiste nodded. "But the corpsman did excellent work. He iced the leg, and we were able to perfuse it until the surgeons arrived. It took seven hours to graft new nerves and blood vessels across her knee." She lifted the sheet and felt Krista's ankle. "The governor sent the best microsurgical team from UCLA. The surgery was a success, and the leg was saved."

"It sounds like she'll be as good as new once she recovers."

"Certainly better than she was. The surgeons also replaced her knees while they were working. She had advanced arthritis." She lowered the sheet and sat back on the machine. "But she will need emotional support. The pain, it will be considerable once we remove the spinal anesthesia, and she will need someone to help her through it."

"That'll be me. I'm on the case, Doc. Just say the word and I'll do whatever it takes, whenever she needs it. Krista and I go through everything together, and we've gone through worse than this, so don't worry. This'll be a piece of cake."

"Good, that is good," Baptiste said with a relieved smile. "It is critical to her recovery, and I am grateful that you will help. I am told she has no one, no family or friends."

"Not anymore," Ada said. "Except for me, of course, but I stay by her side no matter what. And we've had lotsa no-matter-what."

"Yes, yes, I have heard the stories, which sound very tall to me. That she survived all this, it amazes me. She is *débordan*." She snapped her fingers, grasping for a definition. "There is no word for it in English. It means to be filled so abundantly with life that one cannot be stopped."

Ada gazed through the windows with unfocused eyes, a half-smile coming to her lips. "That explains a lot. Maybe she was right all along. Maybe there *is* a Life Force." She shook her head and looked at Krista. "Débordan. That's another good word."

"It is a *zonbi* word. The Débordan are the only humans immune to the walking dead. They are too alive to die."

Ada laughed. "Zombies? Even better! Do you think I'm débordan too?"

"I think you are, but when we are done, we will find a zonbi and put it to the test, no? That will not be difficult. They are all on the Santa Cruz boardwalk taking pictures of the wrecks."

"Hunh?"

"There was a big sea war off the coast last night, and a Navy ship, the *Astro* or something, it drifted into the bay this morning on fire and sank at the end of the wharf. There is also a black submarine tied up on the wharf by Ragnaro's, and another in the beach."

"*In* the beach?"

"It must have been going very fast because the front plowed into the sand. It is low tide now, and you could walk out and touch it if those *maren* weren't shooing people away. There are hundreds of *sólda* and *maren* all over the beach and the wharf. And half the town is on the boardwalk taking pictures. Zonbis! Why do they need a million pictures when it is right there in front of them? Do their eyes not work?"

"You haven't gotten over that farfelu yet."

"And I will not. I haven't slept all night. Fah! With the ships shooting at each other, and the helicopters rattling the windows, and the dogs barking and the cats climbing the curtains, my nerves, they are frayed to tatters. And I had reservations for Ragnaro's tonight, and I won't be able to go because the *sólda* closed off the wharf." Baptiste's tablet buzzed, and she studied it for a moment and then slipped it into a pocket. "But back to my patient. I have seen *Freedom's Bell* and *Yearning to Breathe Free*, and she must have been severely injured even then. She has eleven cracked ribs that are partially healed…"

"Yeah, that happened after she blew up the dam, when we restarted her heart. Mark had to break her ribs or she woulda died."

"She also has crushing injuries throughout her right arm, with a significant loss of sensation…"

Ada noticed that Krista's lips were dry, and she stood and wet a tissue in the cup on her tray. "A house landed on her arm, but she probably didn't notice with all the rib pain."

Baptiste studied her face, an eyebrow quirked. "Yes, yes, a house landed on her arm, I see. This happens so often outside the Land of Oz. She also has two bruised kidneys, and she has bleeding in her right one."

"She got blown into a tree when Sacramento got nuked," Ada said, dabbing Krista's lips.

"And her legs are a study in traumatic injury, beginning with a crudely sutured laceration on the posterior."

"Sorry, I was totally ripped when I did that." Ada threw the tissue into the trash and leaned against the bed. "Will she be okay?"

"I believe so." Baptiste studied the monitors. "She is lucky. It is a miracle she did not lose her baby."

"Baby?" Ada's feet slid out from beneath her and she fell to the floor, landing on her rear with a squawk. Baptiste ran around the bed and helped her up. "Baby?" Ada grasped the bed rails. "She's making feet for kiddie socks?"

"Is this a problem?"

"Problem?" Ada gazed at Krista's sleeping face and remembered all the times she'd seen her resting her head on Mark's shoulder. There could be no coffin or urn of ashes for him; all that remained of Mark would be his child. "No, it's no problem. No kid will ever be more loved. I guarantee it."

"This is also very good." Baptiste slipped a large, pen-shaped object from her pocket and lowered the sheet to Krista's waist. "You would like to see?"

"Oh, yeah!"

Baptiste aimed the pen above Krista's navel and moved it around in small circles, muttering under her breath as she tried to find the embryo. Finally, she smiled and nodded at the screen. "There. Look close, it is hard to see."

Ada leaned forward until her nose touched the screen. "That smudge there? That's it?"

"That's it. Zoom in."

Ada tapped the monitor and the image grew bigger. "It looks like a little booger!"

Baptiste chuckled a light, melodic laugh. "A good booger to have, no?"

"Yeah." Ada smiled and touched the image. "Hey there, Booger. It's Auntie Ada."

"It is doing remarkably well. I see growth that was not there last night."

"How long has she been pregnant?"

Baptiste pursed her lips and studied the screen. "It is hard to say, but I would guess she conceived two or three weeks ago." She removed the pen, and the image disappeared. "I must go, but I will return in one hour. I have other patients that require my attention more." She straightened her lab coat and walked to the door. "When she wakes, please call the nurse. And please get her to drink water."

After Dr. Baptiste left, Ada sat in the bedside chair and held Krista's hand while watching the newsfeed reports on the war. One segment filmed just after Hayborn's announcement showed a reporter standing on the Southbay overpass, surrounded by dancing men and screaming to be heard over the thundering salsa beat, as the tanks of the 11th Armored Division backed away and turned around. A videographer on the Golden Gate Bridge had recorded the 81st Armored's rumbling, clanking arrival the previous night; the outbound traffic had stopped to watch the tanks, and people lined both sides of the road, cheering them on and taking selfies in front of the rolling armor. Another newsfeed focused on the extensive damage to the South Bay road network, and bravely tried to direct commuters through the wreckage and onto open roads, although nobody needed to go to work; most area businesses had already closed for the coming week. Tiara King of NewsPulse LA covered the emergency vaccination program the city had set up to contain a possible Neovirus attack.

Most of the other reports featured talking heads discussing Hayborn's capitulation and what that meant for the new California Republic. She grew bored quickly, and she rested her head on her arm while rubbing small circles into the skin above Krista's navel.

ADA WAS GAZING THROUGH THE WINDOW, still drawing circles with her finger, when Krista woke. "Stop. That tickles," she murmured.

"Sleepyhead! You're finally awake!"

Krista looked at the ceiling through half-open eyelids. "Where are we?"

"In a hospital. We're safe, don't worry."

"You're sure?"

Ada took her hand. "Yeah, you can relax. How are you feeling?"

"Drowsy. Why am I here?" She tried to sit up but then fell back to the pillow with her eyes full of panic. "Oh, shit."

"What is it?"

"They cut my legs off, didn't they? I can't feel anything down there. Did they...don't tell me." She closed her eyes and gritted her teeth. "Okay, tell me. I've got to get this over with."

"They gave you a spinal block. That's why you can't feel anything. Calm down before you pop a gasket." Ada pushed a button and raised the head of the bed. "Look – two legs, ten toes. All the equipment you came in with is still there, plus a little more."

Krista patted her legs. "Why am I all numb? What happened?"

"You had surgery on your leg last night, but it worked and you'll be better than new real soon."

"My leg?"

"Yeah, your leg got blown off." She poured water into a cup and handed it to her. "You need to drink water. Dr. Farfelu's orders."

"I'd rather have coffee."

"She said to drink water, so –"

"Coffee is mostly water, and it has healing properties too."

Ada pressed the cup into her hand. "Shit, you're difficult. Drink this and I'll go get coffee, all right?"

Krista curled her lip and sipped, wiggling her toes. "My leg got blown off? Seriously?"

"Seriously."

She wiggled her toes again. "Which one?"

"The right one. A bullet went through your knee. Ric sent half of UCLA Med up here, and they replaced the knee and grafted nerves and all that good stuff."

"I'll be sure to thank Ric, if he'll let me get a word in edgewise." She lay back and shook her head. "Huh. I guess I was out of it. I remember we were running, and then we were getting shot at, and then there was this huge boom."

"Yeah. That was from the missiles. It threw me halfway across the causeway into an anchor." She touched her fingers to the bandages.

"Are you okay?"

"I had a little brainburger last night, but I'm getting over it."

Krista raised the cup to her lips. "I remember now. You were there too, and so was Micah, and you were both yelling at me and Mark…" The cup shook and she turned quickly to look at Ada.

Ada saw the awful question in her eyes, one she couldn't bring herself to answer. She bit her lip and took Krista's hand, and although she tried not to cry, her eyes moistened. Krista drew a sharp breath and dropped the cup. "Mark, no…"

A tear fell on Ada's hand. "Krista…"

"No, oh God, no, no, no…" She drew another shuddering breath and let it out shakily, her lower lip quivering, and then she covered her face with her hands, the tears tracking around them and down her cheeks. Ada climbed on the bed and wrapped an arm around her shoulder, and she held her until they couldn't cry anymore.

KRISTA SWALLOWED THE COFFEE, shivered, and curled her lip. "It's pisswater, isn't it?" Ada asked.

"It's fine. Just don't dilute it next time."

"I didn't dilute it." Ada took the empty cup and handed her a fresh one. "Okay, it's pisswater, but at least there's lots of it. Just don't let Dr. Farfelu see you drinking that."

Krista sipped and gazed through the window at a clear morning sky, and then she looked down at the green band on her finger. "Blue sky, gray sky. It doesn't matter. It's dead to me, Ada. The world is dead, and it'll never come back. Keira is dead, love is dead, life is dead, and everything's just empty now. The world's empty, and all I can fill it with is shit." She lay back on her pillow and stared at the ceiling. "I want to go to sleep and never wake up. I wish I could have some of those Sanity Cells you've got in your mind. I'd crawl right into one and never come out."

"I know the space you're in, Krista, and it looks bleak when you're so far down that hole. But life changes constantly, and something better's always waiting around the corner. Good things come to those who move, those who keep going and always keep an eye out for the future. The people who stay still? Well, they just rust and wait for death."

"Ahh, bless you, Dr. Freud."

Ada took a sip of coffee. "Get used to moving. I won't let you rust away, sister."

"Splendid, just splendid. Like I need another drill sergeant in my life."

"You do, and we'll start drilling this afternoon. You're getting on your feet and walking today. Dr. Farfelu says there's a Charbucks across the street, and their Black Death Roast is so strong that she warns her cardiac patients to not even breathe the vapors. We'll stroll over there and get you some extra dark brew."

Krista's eyes glinted briefly, and then she sagged back to the pillow. "Even Black Death Roast won't fix me, Ada. Don't even bother. Good things don't grow in scorched earth. It just looks ugly till the weeds take over and choke it to death."

"Oh, c'mon, that's stupid and you know it."

"Life is stupid. I'm just trying to fit in."

"So it's stupid." Ada took her hand. "It'll get better, I promise. Someday soon, everything will change for you and it'll be good. You'll meet a guy, have a family —"

"I'll never have a family," Krista said. "I'd make a terrible mother. I'd screw up the kid even worse than me."

"I think you'll be an awesome mom, and I'll be an awesome aunt. You should plan for that cuz you're –"

Krista snorted and swirled the coffee around in the paper cup. "Don't go buying the 'Awesomest Aunt Ever' T-shirt. I won't be having kids, Ada. I'll never love another man in my entire life. I'm the youngest spinster in the world." She downed the rest of the coffee and reached for another cup.

"I'd get used to the idea of being a mother. You're –"

"It won't happen, okay?"

"Will you listen? You're –"

"Just let it go!" She grabbed a plastic knife from her lunch tray and started sawing at her wrists. "Get me something sharper if you plan to keep cheering me up, wouldja?"

"All right, all right." Ada took the knife away and threw it in the trash. "Hey, here's something positive – it's over! We made it and it's all over."

"Don't say that!" she hissed. "You'll cause an earthquake! It's the only thing that hasn't happened yet!" They sat motionless, listening for the inevitable rumble, but the earth didn't split open and swallow them. After a few seconds of silence, they let go of the breaths they'd been holding.

"Let's talk about something else," Ada said.

"Okay." Krista reached out and stroked Ada's hair. "It looks nice that way. It's so soft and touchable."

Ada touched the bandaged side of her head. "What way...omigod, they shaved my head? Am I bald?" She ran to a wall mirror and looked at her hair.

"It looks good. Kind of punk, y'know, sassy. Very flattering."

"Yeah, it *does* look kind of cute. Like Uptown Punk." Ada turned her head from side to side. "It'll piss my mom off too."

The door swung open, and Dr. Baptiste strode in carrying a large plastic bag. "My star patient, she is finally awake. And Miss Lang neglected to tell me."

"You must be Dr. Farfelu," Krista said.

Baptiste stopped in mid-stride and cast a glance at Ada, who covered her mouth and looked away. "Dr. Baptiste, please." She dropped the bag on a chair and pulled her stethoscope from a pocket. "Now let's take a look at…is that coffee? *Moun fou!*" She snatched the cup from Krista's hand and threw it into a trash can. "That is a diuretic! It is the worst thing you can drink!"

"Not that stuff. It's barely even coffee."

"Still, you will not drink it. Only water, yes?" She listened to Krista's chest, scanned her monitors, and checked her dressings. When all was in order, she sat on the blood machine and pulled off a shoe. "I hope you don't mind, but flat feet, they are a curse. Now, I am sure you have many questions, and there are things we need to discuss."

The thuttering of a helicopter rattled the windows, which grew louder until it sounded as if an entire squadron were hovering outside. Suddenly, the buffeting stopped and slowing turbines wound down.

"That is your ride," Dr. Baptiste said to Ada.

She walked to the window and looked down. At the edge of the parking lot, two gray aircraft sat side by side, each with long helicopter blades mounted to stubby wings emblazoned with MARINES. The blades on one were still spinning, and its rear ramp lowered to the ground. *"That's my ride?"*

"It is how all of you arrived here last night."

"We came in on *that?*"

"Yes, on that." Baptiste threw the plastic bag to her. "You will be leaving soon, so you should get dressed now. The *sólda* went shopping for you this morning. You may use the restroom over there to change."

Ada walked to a door in the side wall, reaching inside the plastic bag, while Baptiste turned back to Krista. She described the surgeries that had been performed and discussed every condition she had except one. She was getting to that when Ada sprang from the bathroom. "Look! They even got Anacondas!" She pirouetted in front of a wall mirror. "Do I look perfect, or do I look perfect?"

"Those pants will restrict your circulation," Baptiste said.

Ada stood sideways, examined her profile, and tried to slide two fingers down her waistband with no success. "No, they fit just right."

The Marine guard opened the corridor door, and two Navy officers stood outside, one a tall, slender man and the other a blonde woman with her arm in a sling. The guard snapped to attention and the officers stood to the side, and then a tall man wearing blue fatigues and two black stars on his cap strode into the room. He stopped short when he saw Ada.

Under the cap was the face in the wedding photo – older and paler than it had been years before, but it was unmistakably her father. She tried to speak but couldn't find her breath, and she only managed a shaky smile. He smiled back just as nervously. "Thanks for the clothes," she said after a few moments.

He looked her over from top to bottom and raised an eyebrow. "They fit?"

"Perfectly."

"Good, good, that's good. How are you feeling?"

"I'm fine." Ada noticed his shredded sleeve and the bandage beneath it. "Are *you* okay?"

"I got tagged getting you off that causeway. It's just a scratch."

"You rescued me?"

"Well, yeah, that's what fathers do, y'know, for their daughters, they watch out for…and…I…" He pulled off his cap and ran his fingers along the brim. "So Tori told me a lot of astounding stories about you."

"And you didn't run away screaming?"

"No, no, it's all good stuff. It's just a little hard to believe, y'know, the vaccine, the HIV thing, Los Alamos, all that."

She flashed him a bright smile. "I have weird hobbies. I take a little getting used to." Krista barked a short laugh and Ada shrugged. "I take a lot of getting used to."

He nodded slowly, fingering his cap's bill while looking at the floor; the room was still as all six hearts tried to beat quietly and not disturb the moment. He started to speak but then looked down at the floor again with a frown. "Hell, I don't know what to do."

"I know the feeling."

"All I've got is excuses. Pathetic, inadequate, laughable excuses."

"Don't worry. I won't bite you. Don't believe the rumors."

"You *should* give me a nip on the ass. I earned it." He worked his cap even harder, realized what he was doing, and then shoved it into a back pocket. "Okay, listen, I have no defense. I was absolutely and totally wrong. I was a fool, and I hurt you, and you never deserved that, and –"

"I forgive you."

"You do?"

"Yeah," Ada said. "So you blew it. Well, I've blown it even worse."

"Listen, Sacramento wasn't your fault."

"I don't care. I wanna forget that and focus on the now. And everything's okay now."

"It is?"

"Better than ever," Ada said.

"But I never –"

"The past is gone. Let it stay gone."

He nodded once, and the room fell quiet again. They stood rooted in place, unwilling or unable to move, and the moment would have become awkward if the blonde woman hadn't nudged him forward a step. Dr. Baptiste did the same, but she shoved Ada so hard that she stumbled and started to fall. Harris caught her, though, and she looked up into his eyes.

"All I want is another chance," he whispered. "This time I won't blow it, and I promise to be better. Just give me another chance, please, Ada, just one."

"I will, Daddy," she whispered. "I will."

12:43 PM

Day 76
Monday morning, November 2, 2043
The Capitol, Washington, DC

The nation's breakup passed its tipping point two days later. That evening, the USS *Alaska* glided through Gare Loch in a freezing rain and docked at Royal Navy Base Clyde in Faslane, Scotland. When the last submariner closed the hatch and disembarked, the commander turned over the boat to the bewildered harbormaster and then requested political asylum from the Scottish government for him and his crew. They granted it five minutes after the commander finished telling his story.

After issuing the launch orders to the *Alaska*, Commander Burke had sent a message to the boat's commander: PREZ NUTS. KILL MRCS. BURKE. It was the last noble act of the man's life, as Gavin Burke was shot and killed on the White House lawn minutes later. However, the *Alaska's* commander had known what the message meant; rumors travel beyond lightspeed in the Navy, and he'd already learned everything about Captain Bricker's crisis in the Pacific.

Like the *Henry,* the *Alaska* couldn't stop a launch by the Missile Release Control System after the twenty second abort window. Unlike the *Henry,* its MRCS and launch controllers were stowed in a closet behind the Control Room. The commander had ordered it disabled in the traditional Navy fashion – with fire axes – but made sure to preserve one controller to back up his story.

He turned it over to Scottish authorities to prove that the *Alaska* had been ordered to lay waste to more than a hundred West Coast cities the day before. A Witness in the Edinburgh government leaked the story and the *Alaska's* target list, and *Midnight Sun* published the breaking news while Washington slept.

The Activity's reprisal was swift and brutal. Within minutes of the article's posting, Warcode's hackers seized control of the national electrical grid's computers and diverted every watt in Texas to the city of Washington. Thousands of overloaded transformers exploded, rattling the sleeping city and its suburbs, and frightened citizens ran to bomb shelters convinced the Activists were bombarding Washington. When dawn rose and Civil Defense personnel told them they could leave, they checked their tablets for news on the overnight bombing. They only saw blank screens.

After crashing the power grid, Warcode took down every switching station, uplink site, and cell tower that was still operating – and then they unleashed a withering cyberstrike on government computer systems, focusing on the NSA's supercomputer complex.

Fort Meade's Cyber Command struck back, cutting the power to San Jose and much of California's Central Coast, yet Warcode wouldn't relent. After three hours of escalating cyberwarfare, Warcode breached the airlock of the NSA's core computer, Frame Complex One.

When Hayborn heard that, he ordered every government computer offline, and then he drove to Andrews Air Force Base to use Air Force One's communications suite, which was fitted with the only systems in Washington immune to Warcode's attack.

When the White House staff clicked on the big plane's monitors, though, they probably wished they hadn't: The first news item they saw was from Silverthorne, Colorado, where the governor was announcing that Colorado, Wyoming, and western Montana had seceded and formed Sagebrush Nation. An hour later, King Brigham declared that northern Utah would henceforth be known as the Kingdom of Deseret. Both nations signed mutual-defense pacts with New Columbia soon after.

The shocks kept coming throughout the afternoon. First, the Activist mayor of Cleveland announced that city and its suburbs had voted to become a city-state. The pro-Activist governments of Atlanta, Richmond, and Charlotte followed his lead, and the surrounding counties joined them by nightfall.

The next day offered Hayborn no relief. The New England and Mid-Atlantic states, along with the Maryland territory controlled by Sara

Hogue's Activists, joined Vermont on the 22nd and created the economic powerhouse now known as New America. They reminded the world that the new nation was still under a mutual-defense pact with Québec.

Minnesota and Wisconsin, together with Chicago and northern Illinois, seceded on October 23. Unlike Sagebrush Nation and New America, though, Heartland signed no treaties with nuclear nations. With Congress threatening impeachment due to the secessions of even more states than Cheyn had allowed, Hayborn decided to force Heartland back into the Union.

He ordered the 3rd Armored Regiment from Fort Bliss, Texas, to travel north and sack the Heartland capital at Minneapolis. However, the unit's commander informed him that he didn't have the forces to take down a preschool, never mind the Twin Cities; two-thirds of his tank crews had walked through the gate on October 19 and hadn't returned. Hayborn then ordered the 11th Armored at Fort Irwin to do the job, but their commandant explained that he'd lost thirty tanks in the aborted assault on San Francisco, and half of those remaining had been abandoned along Interstate 5 retreating from Northern California.

Hayborn tried to activate the Armored reserves at Fort Knox, Fort Hood, and Fort Benning, but few reservists answered his call. With no other options, he turned to the Watch Room and instructed the Collaterals to raze the Twin Cities, only to rescind the order an hour later.

History will never know the reason for this change of heart, as Noah Hayborn never wrote his memoirs, but students of that time believe that The Profit Joseph, the Grandson of God himself, ordered Hayborn to relent and accept an America comprised of seven nations.

Arista Molle had so much trouble remembering their names that she'd had Lin-Lin write them on her forearm in case Hayborn asked. She and the president sat in armchairs on the west Capitol steps watching the gallows crew, and she crossed her arms to conceal the cheat sheet. "I actually won't miss the show, Noah. My time was up. After all, once I get married, I can't very well call it *Stanton's Hill*. That wouldn't make sense. And besides, I'm marrying a doctor, so why work? I *will* miss the Capitol, though. How long will it be closed?"

"Indefinitely." Hayborn settled into his chair and watched the small crowd gathered on the Mall below. "The changes will be positive for everybody, Arista. We've all been wrapped up in the power game for so long that the hiatus will do us good. When we get back to business, we'll all be refreshed."

"Like a long vacation," Molle said. "I need a vacation."

"We all do, now that the trials and tribulations are behind us, and we walk together into a welcoming future. And it's been a great week – the Senate, in its last official act, confirmed my good friend Gary Kilmer as vice president. Ex-President Cheyn was captured and brought back to face justice."

"It was so unpresidential, hiding in a spider hole in Nogales, waiting for nighttime so he could sneak over the Unity Wall."

"Indeed. Such behavior weakens the dignity of the presidency."

"There's one thing I'd like to know before the show starts," Molle said. "Cheyn was never tried for his crimes. Can you really sentence him to death? I thought only a jury did that."

"He was guilty of crimes against humanity, Arista, and humanity tried and convicted him long ago. He's the worst mass murderer of all time, killing almost forty million Americans with his Neovirus. It's best that we put down this monster so the healing can begin."

"Will there be a funeral? I love October funerals. They're so somber."

"Of course. He was a president, after all. But he won't be buried in Arlington Cemetery. We'll inter the body in an undisclosed location so it won't be disturbed. The way public sentiment is now, we'd have to guard the grave around the clock if we didn't."

"Oh, and here he comes now. I see he's wearing a designer muzzle from that B&D boutique in the Georgetown Mall. That's great. I have a product placement scheduled for that."

Hayborn chuckled. "We tried everything, but he tore apart each muzzle with his teeth. This one worked better than anything the NSF had."

"Well, if you want quality, go to the fetishists."

"Right. You can be sure the thing's been torture tested."

"Why's he wearing a muzzle, though? Are you afraid he'll bite someone?"

"It's to shut him up." Hayborn watched as Cheyn was guided to the gallows. "He always tries to tell people his side of the story and spread his bizarre conspiracy theories."

At the bottom of the gallows, Cheyn stood with his hands cuffed behind his back as the hang team tested the contraption. The gallows rig was the most modern system available – the Hang Ten by Short Stop Corporation, a state-of-the-art, made-in-America disvertebrator capable of carrying out ten sentences simultaneously – which used a winch system to yank the feet of the condemned through the trap door while it also pulled up on the noose.

Short Stop guaranteed a quick and painless kill each time, although they'd never explained how a victim could make a claim, or how they'd make good on it if they did. Their technology seemed unimpressive today, though, since the trap door would only open an inch every time they'd tested it. A technician opened a panel and tapped on a computer screen.

"It looks like we have a few more minutes," Molle said. "So what do you think of our strange new world, Noah?" She glanced at the writing on her forearm. "It's so hard to get used to all these new countries – New Columbia, the California Republic, Sagebrush Nation, New America, and tiny little Deseret. And Heartland, of course. I like all the names except Heartland. It sounds like something from a country music album."

"I don't care what they call themselves. They're still states of this Union, and I'll refer to them by their proper state names."

"Are you saying the United States won't recognize them as separate nations?"

"Never. As far as we're concerned, these Separated States are undergoing a temporary autonomous period. Reunification will always be our policy." Hayborn tightened one hand into a fist, and the pen he was holding quivered. "Not that I lament their temporary separation from the Union. I never cared for the corrupting influence that the Godless, liberal states had on America. I'm glad we don't have to inflict Hollywood culture on our children anymore and treat it like free speech. I'm glad that we have in our Union the twenty-eight most God-fearing of the States, the most American of the States. They're good, clean, and pure, and each is loyal to God and the Union. I'm proud to have them."

"That faith will come in handy, Noah. The analysts predict tough times ahead."

"We'll have our challenges, no doubt. We're a lightly populated nation thanks to that man over there, and we have a weak economic base that doesn't compare to the stronger and more diverse economies of the Separated States. If we're to recover, we have long, hard days ahead. But we've culled the whiners from our congregation, and we have the strong backs and the willpower to do this job. With God as our guide, we'll prevail, and the Separated States can wallow in their indulgent, wasteful weakness until they decay from sheer lack of moral fiber."

"They do sound selfish. I'm bothered that the California Republic is making all this vaccine, but they're not sending us any. The Commonwealth, Sagebrush Nation, and Deseret are getting vaccinated now, but not a drop has made it here."

Hayborn leaned forward and patted her arm. "Now you see their true colors, Arista. They're self-centered and cruel, and we're better off without them. However, the Lord still stands with us, and we should sing praise that he's now making Neovirus less deadly. In the past week, infections rose but deaths fell, which proves that we still live in God's grace."

"I had a virus guy on the show a few weeks ago who said they just mutate all on their own." She noticed Hayborn's narrowed eyes and cleared her throat. "Obviously, he was wrong."

"Obviously. The Lord's invisible hand guides all of human life, and only a heretic would suggest otherwise."

The hang team gave the gallows another run just to have the trap door freeze again. Some device started beeping insistently behind a hatch, and when they opened it to check, thick blue smoke billowed out. Gabriel Cheyn stood to one side and tapped his foot.

"Just a few more minutes," Hayborn said.

"Well, at least the weather is cool and clear. It's weird, but I've noticed that the fug has been lighter lately. I can usually see only a few blocks down the Mall, but today I can see the radiation barriers over by the stub of the Washington Monument."

"The power plants have been working at forty percent capacity for the last few weeks. With almost a quarter of the population called home to Jesus, our energy demand is that much lower. Fewer trucks are needed, fewer cars are on the road, and there's less demand for everything. The planet has a fighting chance to achieve a balance and recover from the overburden of humanity it's been carrying for so long."

12:43 PM

Molle cast him a sidelong glance. "Funny, but you just sounded like one of those Aluminati, Noah." Hayborn smiled, but his eyes bored into her and she looked away. "I, umm…it was just an observation. Forget it," she muttered. "So this a smaller crowd than I thought. I expected something like an inauguration, but there can't be more than ten or twenty thousand people here."

"I guess these folks are here on their lunch break." He glanced at the gallows. "I hope we won't be keeping them waiting too much longer. This was supposed to happen at noon, and it's already ten after."

Molle squinted into the fug. "Some of them have cardboard boxes. What's up with that?"

NINO ROSSI WAS MANNING the Library of Congress main entrance security checkpoint that day. Bored and frustrated, he looked through the big doors at the east façade of the Capitol. He'd never see it again after today because the library was closing indefinitely at 4 PM.

Dr. Thomas Upton opened the door just before noon. Upton had been a regular at the library for the past week, and he recognized him on sight. He was easy to remember, because even though he was a history professor at American University, he had the physique of a triathlete. He could never recall his face, though.

Nino pulled his pants up over his paunch and waddled to the magnetic screener. Upton had already emptied his pockets and opened his brown leather briefcase for inspection. He saw nothing but papers and a book inside, as always. "Morning, Professor."

"Good morning, Nino." He handed over his driver's license. "Just a little research today, so I'll be brief. I found a reference to a Mayan codex from the Late Pre-Classic Period in an unpublished Spanish Colonial history last night, and I need to check Stanley's Index from the Harding Administration to see if any cross-references are registered. If there aren't, well, this could be a *most* exciting discovery."

"Mmm-hmm," Nino mumbled. He never understood a word the academics said and didn't ask for clarification. They'd bore him into a coma if he did. "Stand in the screener and hold your hands out to the side."

Upton did as he asked, and after his briefcase rolled out of the X-ray machine, Nino handed his identification back. "Squeaky clean as usual, Doc."

Dr. Upton smiled and pushed his glasses up his nose. "Of course, Nino. Cleanliness is next to Godliness. Isn't that what they say?"

HE WISHED NINO A GOOD DAY, sauntered into the Great Hall, and climbed the marble steps to the second floor. At the top, he turned right and walked along the gallery to the end, where he opened the doors to the Early Americas Reading Room. This was where Dr. Thomas Upton supposedly did his research.

He passed through the empty room, slipping on a pair of latex gloves as he walked, and unlocked a door in the corridor beyond it. The square room he entered had an iron spiral staircase in the center, and electrical panels lined the walls. He unlocked panel LP-47.

Instead of a row of circuit breakers, the panel held a briefcase identical to his, even down to the scratches on the leather, which was one of a hundred thousand Mal-Mart had sold the previous year. He pulled it out, set it on the floor, and wiped the fingerprints from the briefcase he'd carried in. However, this was unnecessary; a trace of his prints or DNA would identify him as an ex-Marine who'd moved to the Nunavut Territory two years previously. According to reliable sources, he'd planned to open a polar bear preserve, but the starving animals had devoured him on arrival and then squirted his remains across the Arctic tundra. No fall guy could be more untraceable.

He took off his jacket, hung it on the doorknob, and then pulled a pair of long latex gloves from a pocket. He slipped them over the pair he was wearing and taped them to his upper arms. From another pocket, he removed a thin silicone hood and slipped it over his head, which only allowed his eyes and mouth to be exposed. When that was done, he wiped down his old briefcase again and placed it inside the panel. After locking the door and wiping it clean, he picked up the other briefcase and climbed the spiral stairs.

THE TRAP DOOR SWUNG OPEN AT LAST, and the pulleys whirred. Arista's producer circled his finger over his head to start the broadcast countdown.

She repeated her mantra until two seconds before airtime and then snapped on a brilliant smile and looked into the lens. "Welcome to a special edition of *Molle's Hill*. We're broadcasting live from the west steps of the Capitol, which will be closed beginning today. This will be the last show we'll air for some time, because with Congress adjourned indefinitely, there'll be nobody to interview. Don't be sad – I'm looking forward to embracing change and moving on in this time of transition, as we all must.

"I'm here today with President Noah Hayborn, and before us are the gallows where ex-President Gabriel Cheyn will be hanged momentarily. How are you feeling about this auspicious event, Mr. President?"

"I'm feeling a number of things right now, Miss Molle. I feel sorrow at having to perform this duty, but also the anticipation of relief once it's done. I'm feeling pride for all the men and women who helped capture this man and make justice possible. I'm feeling optimism for the future of this country once this dark period is over."

"Thank you for those inspiring words, Mr. President. And now the former president climbs the gallows, making a final fashion statement with his Bishop's Secret Strict Leather muzzle. They offer devices for all sexual tastes at their Georgetown Mall location. With Christmas coming up, everyone will be happy to know they'll have extended shopping hours, along with a special Fantasy Experience to keep the little ones busy while you shop. The Bishop's Secret, for that little bishop in all of us! So while we're waiting for the hangman, will you tell us why you're closing the Capitol?"

Hayborn looked into the lens. "There's little need for Congress to regulate our nation with yet more laws, but there's a great and urgent need to balance our budget and support the dollar. Thus, I've adjourned Congress as an austerity measure. It saves eleven billion dollars a year."

"It has nothing to do with impeachment?"

"Of course not. It's merely a long-deferred act of fiscal responsibility, Arista."

"Congress regulated many facets of American life, Mr. President. How will those be managed now?"

"The Lord God Almighty will shape and direct our faith and morality, as the founding fathers intended, while our Corporate-Americans will shape and direct our capitalist economy as they see fit. It's an ideal and efficient solution."

"I understand that this is a temporary measure. Can you tell us when we might see a democratic system of government again?"

"Representative democracy was an anomaly we'd been keeping alive long after the patient was brain-dead, Miss Molle. I can't predict when, or if, it will be a robust enough system of government again for America. It's unknowable."

"Oh, and there he is! Today's hangman is Norbie Welton of Mishawaka Falls, who won the national lottery. I heard that was very popular."

"It raised over four hundred million dollars. Today's event will put a considerable dent in our deficit, and I think Cheyn is pleased that his demise helps fill the nation's coffers. Okay, it looks like Norbie doesn't plan to stand on ceremony. He's going right for the button."

The trap door opened, the pulleys screamed, and then they heard a dull pop from the gallows platform.

"I thought it was supposed to stay on." Molle's eyes tracked Cheyn's head as it rose high above the crowd. "Is that because of the muzzle?"

"The team needs to adjust the gallows," Hayborn said. "Wow, look at him go."

"Is that what you call hang time?"

"Puns are hardly appropriate, Miss Molle."

"No, I always get confused when guys say that…finally, it looks like he's coming down. For a second, I thought he'd go into orbit!"

Cheyn's head passed its apogee and fell toward the crowd below. It glanced off the shoulder of a small girl, knocking her to the ground and fueling decades of nightmares, and rebounded into the air above the outstretched hands of the crowd. Men elbowed and jostled to reach the landing zone, and at last, the head fell into the throng and disappeared. A pile of bodies grew, and it throbbed and thrashed as hands reached for possession of the prize.

Then a small figure shot out from beneath the scrum and sprinted for the radiation barriers surrounding the Washington Monument's stump. Bloodied men climbed to their feet and gave chase.

"This is like a rugby game!" Molle said, clapping her hands. "I wasn't expecting entertainment!"

"Well, that head's worth five million bucks to the one who delivers it to Warner. And the muzzle alone cost two tenpez."

Molle watched the little man dart into the trees, cradling the head in his arms. "Oh, I love to see people playing sports on the Mall! It's so American!"

NOAH HAYBORN STOOD IN THE CENTER of the Capitol Rotunda. Travis stood beside him as they waited for his staff to confirm that the building was vacant.

Hayborn crossed his arms and looked up into the dome. "I've been waiting for this moment for fifteen years, Travis. I spent too long in this House of Hubris repeating the mistakes of man. This place is a modern Tower of Babel, yet God's lesson is the same as it was then, and he has to repeat it every millennium because we're too stupid to learn that God will never let us conspire against him. Every law we passed in this pit decayed and corroded the word of the Lord and the teachings of the Profit, so I hope nobody's surprised that God has struck it down. It's long overdue." He nodded slowly and glared at the statuary. "It's about time the delusion of self-determinism was stripped from the common man's mind."

"The Profit Joseph chooses our role in life, and we only choose to comply or die. This is the Word of the Lord."

"That is the Word," Hayborn said. "No, it's not a house of hubris. It's a house of nightmares. It's fitting we're closing this right after Halloween." He scowled and shook his head. "Arrogance, sheer arrogance. Maybe we'll reopen it someday as the Museum of Human Folly."

"Let it collect dust, Noah. Let the weeds and vines take it down over the decades. Let the world see the symbol of self-determinism decay and be pulled down into the dirt. Let it die a slow death, like faith in God has over the past two centuries."

"I knew I kept you around for a reason, Travis. That's perfect. We'll let Nature reclaim it."

White House staffers walked from the House and Senate corridors and confirmed that the chambers and offices were empty. They gathered in the center, feeling the weight of the moment yet unsure how to memorialize the republic's passing. After a few moments, the silence grew uncomfortable.

"Ahh, screw it," Hayborn said. "Let's get lunch."

The group strode through the east lobby and met the rotund press secretary Buckman and the hatchet-faced chief of staff Parker on the front portico, along with four Secret Service agents. They gathered around the tall bronze doors for the final ceremony: Travis pulled a long silver chain from a cloth bag, and Hayborn looped it through the door's handles, slid a lock through the links, and snapped it closed. "It is done," he said loudly for the camera crews. "When God provides the key, we'll open these doors once again."

At 12:43 PM, he followed his Secret Service agents down the front steps.

JOSSELYN KERNS WAS HEADING the presidential security detail that day, and she was concerned. That was the nature of presidential guardians, but she was particularly on edge today. It was partly because Hayborn had chosen to perform a ceremony at the front doors of the Capitol and walk down the long stairs after. He'd be exposed the entire time.

She was standing by Goliath, the Presidential Silverback, when she saw the group leave the Capitol and gather on the portico. She began walking up the steps as they started down.

The six seconds that followed seemed to happen in slow motion.

When she was twenty feet from Hayborn, she heard a thud. Suddenly, he flew up the steps like he was being pulled back by a rope. A high-caliber rifle boomed in the distance, and then Parker, who'd been standing behind Hayborn, was also blown off his feet. She glanced at their bloody bodies and ran to Travis and Buckman. Travis jerked backward, spraying

Buckman with blood as the Press Secretary dove for the ground, and then the rifle cracked again and blew Buckman's head off his shoulders.

Kerns searched the area through her gun sight, but the Capitol was deserted. She holstered her weapon and called the medical team, although they could do nothing for the four men; the exit wound in Travis's back was as wide as a softball. Hayborn and Parker had been hit the same way, and they lay sprawled across the marble steps, examining the sky with a dead look of amazement.

She wheeled and peered at the roof of the Library of Congress, where her peripheral vision had caught movement. Tapping her headset, she ran down the steps and across the street.

BOB DOWNS CREPT BACK TO THE DOOR, unscrewed the barrel from his Dornitz, and dropped it into its foam niche in the briefcase. After that, he folded the stock, placed it in, and then slipped the scope into its hole. The yellow light on its side was blinking, signaling that the camera was still writing the video to the memory card.

He would have loved to sit across from Raphael and replay it, but he was gone. All the same, he could imagine what his friend would say, and tonight he'd replay the shooting and pretend that he was still with him. He needed a good laugh, and too, he wanted to be the first to tell Raphael that the Apostate was dead, and his murder had been avenged.

He pulled off his arm-length gloves, and then he stopped and listened; from far above the clouds, he heard the Archangels murmuring. Although a mere earthly being couldn't comprehend their words, he knew they were congratulating him for a job done well.

And it had been a great shooting, perhaps the greatest ever. They hadn't been wearing body armor, and the blood spatter was magnificent, spraying for at least ten feet. The only flaw was that Buckman moved before he made the fourth heart shot, but he didn't know that fat men could move so fast.

He gathered the spent casings, pulled off his cap, and then took off his latex gloves and wrapped everything into a tight ball. He dropped the bundle into a plumbing vent and listened as it rattled into the sewers four stories below. When all was in order, he snapped the briefcase closed.

At the bottom of the spiral stairs, he pulled on his tweed coat and clipped his researcher ID on his tie, and then he walked down the corridor whistling a pop tune.

WHEN DOWNS REACHED THE LOBBY, the Capitol Police were running through the front door.

They told him that the library was locked down, and he wasn't allowed to leave. The Capitol Police sealed the sprawling building in thirty seconds, and the Secret Service ran through the lobby shortly after and raced to search the roof.

Then the FBI arrived and immediately hobbled the investigation with pointless arguments over jurisdiction and authority. Downs leaned against a wall and watched the incompetence unfold, but he became tired after a few minutes, the strain of the past week catching up with him.

The Dornitz in his briefcase was getting heavier with each passing second, and he set it down on the floor and sat on it, resting his head on one hand as he listened to the police debate how to capture the assassin. A few agents broke away from the Capitol Police-FBI catfight and questioned people in the lobby, and one even swabbed his hands and hair for gunshot residue. They found nothing.

Just as the police argument seemed headed for blows, the front doors swung open and the NSF team strode through. The room fell silent when the nation's top domestic intelligence officer entered.

Cochon's gray uniform was immaculate, and the new 'A1' insignia on his high collar gleamed like it had been polished. It had, of course, because he'd known that the spotlight would focus on him after the assassination, and he was a stickler about his appearance. He took control fast, ordering the FBI to search the building and the Capitol police to corral everyone into the Reading Room for questioning.

Downs lingered near the door until the crowd wandered away. As Cochon reached the Reading Room steps, he turned and gave Downs the slightest of nods and the faintest of smiles. Downs nodded back, and then he stepped through the front door and into freedom.

He walked down the steps and began heading north to Union Station. The Capitol plaza was strung with crime-scene tape, and the area where the president's body lay was closed off with a curtain. Hundreds of people had already gathered and were taking pictures, despite having nothing to photograph. He stopped and joined the growing mob like an innocent man would.

He checked his tablet and saw it was already 1:45 PM. It was time to head for Union Station, where his kit and a new identity were waiting in a luggage locker.

After he changed, he'd catch the 2:30 express train heading west. In two days, it would make its final stop just inside the Commonwealth of New Columbia at Sandpoint, in what had recently been Idaho. He'd find another new identity and backpacking gear in a locker there, and then he'd hike to San Francisco and into Mexico, arriving sometime after Thanksgiving. Cochon had arranged for his travel to Gitmo from Tampico, and he needed an extended vacation before resuming his angelic duties.

If he was a brave man, though, he'd stop first in Tiburon to visit Miss Savu. He was tempted, but he wasn't sure he was *that* brave.

Whistling the tune from *Duck and Cover,* he started walking to the station. He had a month-long hike ahead of him; maybe he'd find the courage along the way.

IN A DARK-PANELED KREMLIN STUDY, two men sat in armchairs in front of a widescreen television, a fire roaring in the fireplace behind them. On the screen, President Noah Hayborn clicked a silver lock, and Premier Aleksei Rutskoy lowered his teacup and smiled. "Cheyn's Great American Century was somewhat brief, Dusan, was it not?"

"Perhaps he meant a century of days, not years," Dusan Nitskaya said. "We should have asked him before the Americans ripped his head off."

"Such spectacle. A bullet in the cranium would have sufficed, but they had to make a gory show of it."

"His head took off like a champagne cork. I've never seen anything like that."

"And, God willing, may you never again." Rutskoy sipped his tea and then shrugged. "I won't complain. American spectacle is so entertaining. Without it, life would be nothing but calculation and execution. And there, Dusan, there is where we go now."

"Disappointed?"

"Somewhat. The struggle was exciting for a time, no?"

"It was tiring more than anything else. And I'm disappointed in the results, given how much time and money we invested. California seceded right on schedule, true, and that was an unalloyed success. But whatever advantage we gained was nullified when the American Northwest seceded. Now nearly four hundred Lancet missiles remain deployed, even if in the hands of a breakaway state. That threat remains."

"No matter. Should the Commonwealth of New Columbia launch a first strike, it would be at Washington, not us. I believe that the threat has been substantially reduced, affording us the time to complete our own hypersonic stealth –"

Nitskaya snorted and rose from his chair. "*That* old sow? After twenty years, we can barely get it to hit somewhere in the correct latitude. Getting it to land on the right city will always be a futile quest. What we need is the Lancet, something that can strike its target within a millimeter, like the one that hit the Washington Monument. But we'll never achieve that with the teams we have. We'd be better off scrapping our rocket engineers and all our prototypes and just black-bagging the designers at the Jet Propulsion Laboratory."

"Intriguing, Dusan. Perhaps we should develop conduits into this California Republic and see if we can gain assets inside this lab."

"It's easier to kidnap them. And that Lang girl too, if we can locate her." He reached for Rutskoy's cup. "A warm-up, Aleks?"

Rutskoy handed him the teacup and then sat back, crossed his legs, and watched as Hayborn and his entourage began walking down the Capitol steps. "But more is required to win this struggle than fearsome missiles, Dusan. Look at the Americans: They know nothing of war other than the application of force. Cheyn should have read more Sun-Tzu. He would have learned that patience is not merely a virtue, not merely a strength, but a potent weapon. We only needed ninety years, not ninety billion dollars of stealth missiles, to shatter –"

Gunfire cracked on the TV. A drop of blood spattered on the camera lens and rolled down one side as the cameraman tried to record the melee. Rutskoy and Nitskaya leaned toward the screen.

More gunfire cracked, and suited men ran toward a prone body. The camera shook, and then it zoomed in on a fallen man and his bloodied chest. A woman pointed to a building in the distance and sprinted down the stairs. The crowd of men standing by one body parted, clearly revealing a very dead Noah Hayborn gazing into the sky.

"Hmm," Rutskoy said.

Nitskaya shrugged. "Good. Saves me the trouble."

Rutskoy pinned him with a piercing blue glare. "You were planning to kill him? This was not the plan."

"Money was involved, Aleks. Hayborn was skimming so much off the secession funds that I had to defer modernizing my aluminum smelters to offset the loss."

"Ah, well. Money." Rutskoy glanced at the screen again, where men were yelling into lapel microphones. "Never fear, Dusan. We have four billion remaining in the enterprise fund. We'll make you whole again. How much was it?"

"A substantial sum. That's all I can say until the teams return from America. It will take time to unravel what they did in the past few weeks."

"Time we have. Russia is eternal, as is war. We can be patient." A police officer ran toward the camera with a hand outstretched. Five fingers grasped the lens and the image shook, and then the screen filled with static. "The American spectacle. It was so entertaining."

EVENSONG

Saturday afternoon, June 14, 2046
Near Angel Island
Tiburon, California

Tiara and Timmie Topuha sat on a bench behind the Coast Guard launch's wheelhouse. Timmie peered across San Francisco Bay through his binoculars while Tiara scrolled down her tablet's screen.

"We'll be docking in Tiburon soon," he said. "Find something interesting?"

"They found the bullet," she said, hunching over the tablet to protect it from seaspray.

"Took 'em long enough. When was President Kilmer assassinated, like a week ago?"

"Well, the bullet went right through him and ended up in a tree across the Mall. It was so deep in the trunk, they had to cut down the tree to get at it." She scrolled down further and frowned. "The Ballistics lab says it comes from the same gun that shot Hayborn."

"In other words, they're planning to blame Krista and the Activists again." He focused his binoculars on Angel Island.

"Of course they are. She's the Arkie's Satan. They blame everything from hemorrhoids to hurricanes on Krista. But it doesn't matter. They'll never get to her here."

He zoomed in on a cliff-ringed peninsula jutting from the island and then at the base of the cliff, where a long dock extended into the bay. Two muscular men stood at the end, each with high-powered rifles slung over their shoulders, and one watched the launch through a pair of binoculars. In the woods above, Timmie spotted the nose cones of interceptor missiles beneath camouflage netting. "True. DaCosta's keeping her pretty safe."

"He wants to win the election. He won't let a single hair on the Anarchista's head get hurt."

The launch drew closer to the island. As they passed the cliff, he saw a long, green lawn at the top, where white tents fluttered in the breeze. A doe poked its nose into one and then ran for the trees when an angry chef burst from the tent waving his toque. "I didn't know there were deer living on the island," Timmie said.

"There weren't before she got there, but the first thing she did was import some. The tree huggers said the deer would upset the island's ecology, but they don't eat the foliage. She hand-feeds them every day."

The deer ran behind a white gingerbread Victorian house near the cliffside. A lighthouse with a widow's walk topped the mansion's west face, and a deep lemonade porch overlooked the bay. A few hundred feet away, a small house draped in a bright pink tarpaulin perched near the bluff's edge.

"So *that's* Pelican Point," he said. "Really, that's just magnificent – spectacular, even. What a setting! What a view!"

"DaCosta didn't let her buy the Commandant's Residence because of the view, Timmie. It was the only place to keep them all safe. Krista still has a Snuff Order out on her, and Ada and Victoria have outstanding warrants for murder charges, and the last thing DaCosta wants is for any of them to get snuffed on his turf. I think it's making Krista a shut-in, though. She hardly ever leaves."

"That's the way she prefers it," he said. "I talked to her a few months ago, and she said going out into the world doesn't scare her anymore. But once she got out and met people, she realized that most of them kinda suck."

"Maybe that's why she bought the deer," she said.

"Maybe. And I can see her point. I'd rather feed deer than put up with that hyperventilating Hollywood flakeshow all day."

"I don't get that. They're so much fun! Why waste your life on some serene, isolated island? She needs to get out and find a guy. She's Blind Billy's daughter, so she has her pick of California's most eligible bachelors."

"She says she doesn't want a guy she needs. She wants a guy she wants."

"Then she oughta get out so Prince Charming can find her, not hide on an island." She wrapped her fingers into Timmie's. "I think she oughta go to a rodeo. That's where I found mine." Timmie kissed her cheek, and she rested her head on his shoulder and glanced at the mansion. "Still, DaCosta *does* treat her well."

"He treats us well too. He's a generous producer. Timmie Topuha, lead cinematographer. I've always wanted to film a movie." She sat up and sighed dramatically. "Still disappointed you didn't get the part?" he asked.

"Well, yeah. I just don't get how I didn't. Does it make sense that I was too much like me to play myself in the movie?"

"Don't be offended. Krista and Ada weren't in it, either. I hear they're building a hospital with the money they got, but they didn't want anything to do with the movie after they sold the rights."

"They're not in the entertainment industry. That's different."

"I saw your audition, Tia. I gotta say, it was a little over the top."

"But that doesn't make any sense! I'm the perfect actress to play me." She pouted at the skyline of San Francisco as they chugged away. "I *so* wanted to be a Hollywood star."

"You're still a TV star, and you still have your own show. Besides, we have an exclusive today, and this is like a royal wedding. Our viewership will be astronomical. Maybe one of the TV producers will be watching, and you can get a series."

"That's true." She looked up at him and smiled. "Thanks. You always cheer me up, Tonto."

A cluster of gray concrete buildings appeared in a clearing as the boat rounded the island, and he focused the binoculars on it. "There's Ada's little paradise."

She peered over his shoulder at the new Angel Island National Laboratory. "I wonder why DaCosta sank nine million tenpez into this place. Nobody will say, and Ada changes the subject whenever I ask her. I think they don't want any attention."

He focused on the razor wire topping the complex's triple fence. "They won't get any with that much security." He put down the binoculars and wrapped his arm around her shoulders. "Angel Island National Laboratory. Now there's a problematic acronym for you."

KRISTA TURNED AWAY FROM THE WIND and lit another cigarette. No amount of nicotine would soothe her frazzled nerves today; she wasn't just chain-smoking, she was also chewing three pieces of Tala Ripley's gum.

Everything was going wrong. From where she stood behind Tiburon Unitarian Church, she could see Pelican Point a mile away, where the pink tarpaulin fluttered in the breeze and would undoubtedly blow off into the bay. That meant Ada and Micah might see their wedding gift on the way to the reception. They'd known she was building something on the bluff, but they didn't know it was for them, and now it wouldn't be a secret.

Worse than that, it wasn't even finished inside because getting contractors to work on the island was almost impossible. Victoria had been badgering them daily, and the house would still be a pile of lumber on the lawn if it hadn't been for her discipline. Still, it wouldn't be ready when they returned from their honeymoon next month, which wasn't much of a gift.

And that wasn't the day's only problem: Paparazzi had infested the Tiburon waterfront too. They floated out on the bay, circled in the sky, and dangled from tree branches while trying to get pictures for the tabloids. Thousands of spectators also shouted for attention from beyond the police barriers, too, just like in New York when she was young. And just like then, she hated it.

Then there was the catering disaster, which she was trying to forget because she could do nothing about it. The flower snafu was her fault, though, and she'd have to own up to that after the ceremony. She took a huge puff and inhaled down to her toes, hoping to suffocate the thought.

The day was already an unmitigated disaster, and it wasn't even over yet: After the reception on the island, she had to paste on a gown and a smile and attend a state dinner with the Japanese Prime Minister at The Presidio. She was already getting cheek cramps from smiling for the wedding photographer, and she'd have to do it again for three more hours tonight despite the risks – she feared that her face might freeze into a permanent Jokeresque leer like botched plastic surgery, and small children would point at her and snicker for the rest of her life – and if that wasn't enough torture for a single mortal, she was certain that the Prime Minister's chef would slide a slab of rotting fish in front of her and then stand back, smiling and wringing his hands, eager to see how much she adored blowfish marinated for five years in the saliva of Buddhist monks. And then the saké cups would come out, and then DaCosta would invite them to see The Head, and then they'd pile into the limos and drive down to Fisherman's Wharf. She saw more of Cheyn these days than when she was in his history class.

And if that wasn't creepy enough, the Japanese obsession with the busty Anarchista who took down the Evil Empire unsettled her. She didn't want to be the object of some Japanese rebel-porn fetish; she wanted to motor back to the island, fill her biggest mug with coffee, and then turn the air conditioning down to frost level and climb under the covers to read a good book.

However, she'd be clomping down the aisle on a peg leg today if DaCosta hadn't delivered when she needed him. Posing as his goodwill ambassador was the least she could do.

She lit another, thinking they might let her off the hook if she developed lung cancer before the Prime Minister's dinner. On the other hand, they'd probably have Ada zap the tumor and put her back on her feet just in time to go.

She was planning other elaborate escapes when the wind picked up and ruffled her short hair, making her shiver. The bow on her long green grown fell into the dirt, and it was coated in tan dust when she picked it up. She tried to shake it off, but that didn't work, and trying to rub it away only ground the dirt deeper into the silk. The result was a splotchy green and tan bow better suited for a battlefield wedding gown.

"Splendid, just splendid," she said, thumping her head against the clapboards of the old church. "Can this day get any worse?" She heard buzzing from the eaves above and looked up to see a swarm of agitated hornets flying toward her.

She shrieked and ran around the corner as fast as her high heels would carry her.

ENNIS QUINN HAD DECIDED TO TAKE A WALK and see the bayshore. He'd been standing outside the church with Tala Ripley, but she'd fallen into girl-on-girl bridal babble with Ada and Victoria. He'd made his excuses and wandered away.

Rounding the church's corner, he spotted a flash of green hurtling toward him – a tall redhead holding her gown up with both hands and running while looking behind her. He opened his mouth to call out, but then she stumbled and flew into his chest. The impact knocked a grunt out of him, and he lost his balance and staggered back a step.

They fell together into the rhododendrons and lay sprawled under a bush for a few heartbeats. When Ennis could breathe again, he asked, "Are you all right?"

She blew a leaf off her forehead. "I'm so sorry, but it was the heels and the hornets, and these knees, it's like running on marbles sometimes, I've never gotten used to them, maybe they put in trick knees…"

"I don't mind. Are you okay?"

She nodded and plucked leaves out of her hair, and he noticed a green band on her ring finger. "That I am. You did a splendid job breaking my fall. Thanks."

"You're welcome." He looked into her blue eyes, one with a fleck of green like his computer's screensaver. "Aren't you –"

"Krista!" Victoria called. "C'mon, the music's starting! Where are you?"

She smiled and climbed to her feet, and when Ennis stepped out of the bushes, Victoria was standing in front of them with her hands on her hips. "I don't believe you two!"

Krista brushed more leaves out of her hair and dusted off her gown. "I just tripped and used this nice man as my personal airbag."

"I'm sure you did. Now, could I bother you to be the maid of honor for a few minutes? Get in line." Krista walked toward the front door, but Victoria grabbed her arm and held out a tissue. "You girls and that gum. It's so undignified."

KRISTA TOOK HER PLACE in front of Ada. Ennis walked out of the bushes, dusting off his white Commonwealth Navy dress uniform, and her eyes tracked him as he climbed the steps into the church.

"I see you've met Ennis Quinn," Tala said.

"*That's* Captain Quinn? He looks like a schoolteacher, not the Submarine Swashbuckler. Where's his eyepatch and three-day stubble?"

"You watch too many movies. That's really Ennis, and he's the nicest guy you'll ever meet. I'll introduce you to him after the ceremony if you want." She nudged Krista in the back. "Maybe you can roll around in the bushes with him again."

At the church door, he bent over to wipe a smudge off his shoe, his uniform jacket rising as he did. Krista puffed out her cheeks and whistled. "Okay, that's just cruel."

"Are you getting a thing for him?"

"Let's just say I like the cut of his jib."

"Y'know, submarines don't use jib sails. The winds a hundred meters below the surface are pretty minimal…"

"It's only a phrase! Cut me some slack, wouldja?"

"All right, all right." She leaned forward and whispered in her ear. "He has a thing for you too, but he pretends he doesn't. Isn't that interesting?"

The door opened and organ music poured out, and the ushers walked down the steps. Adam gave each of the women a jittery smile as he walked to the back of the line to take Ada's arm. Victoria's hands fluttered over her wedding gown as she adjusted and primped everything adjustable and primpable.

The doors opened again, and this time two ushers held them open and nodded to the wedding party.

KRISTA FOLLOWED TALA UP THE AISLE. Tiburon Unitarian Church was small and austere, with a wooden plank floor and simple stained-glass windows set in plain plaster walls. Most of the pews on the groom's side were filled with Governor DaCosta's staff and other Republic officials. On the bride's side, Adam's staff from the Commonwealth Defense Department filled the back rows.

Micah stood at the altar in a white tuxedo, bathed in a polychrome glow from the stained glass, and watched the wedding party approach. When Ada walked through the door, he smiled and nodded to the organist. The processional music stopped in mid-note, and the organist switched to Blac Sacrament's *Another Freakin Love Song*, playing a rendition so awful and wheezy that even elevator music companies would refuse to play it. Ada snorted a laugh, prompting a quiet but stern warning from Adam.

Near the front, the groom's side held only Marissa. On the bride's side, Victoria sat with Jon Gilsig, and Julie waited for Adam at the opposite side of the bench. Jack and Elise Ripley, Tala's parents, sat in the second row with Ennis Quinn.

When Krista approached their row, a small red-haired head popped up over Ennis's shoulder and bellowed, "MAMA!" She gave Junior a little smile and a wave, and he broke out of Ennis's grip, scrambled over Jack, and had almost scaled Elise's bulk before Jack snagged a leg and kept him from jumping into the aisle. She kissed his forehead when she passed, which made him fidget even more.

THE PASTOR'S HOMILY couldn't have been more boring if he were reciting the tax code. Krista's attention wandered, and she glanced around the church.

Junior was fidgeting on Ennis's lap again, and neither was paying attention to the pastor. Ennis made a strange face and Junior giggled; Jack nudged Ennis and told him to be quiet, and the entire process repeated a minute later. One time when she'd looked, Junior was straddling Ennis' shoulders and pounding his head like a drum. Another time, she'd found Ennis holding her boy up by the feet and swinging him like a pendulum. The embarrassing display was disturbing the ceremony, and she tried to beam a thought into Ennis's head for him to stop, but a part of her wished he never would. Junior needed a father desperately, and even a few minutes would do him good.

IN WHAT SEEMED TO BE SECONDS, Ada and Micah exchanged their vows, kissed, and were married, and then the recessional music started playing. Soon after, she was standing in the sun at the bottom of the steps hugging the new Mrs. Wright. "I'm so happy for you," she sobbed.

"Mrs. Ada Wright. I like the sound of that," Ada said.

"You'll be having a great life, you and Micah. I just know it."

"And I owe it all to you." Ada hugged her hard. "You taught me to take a chance with love, and I knew you'd always be there to catch me if I stumbled. Without you, all of this would just be a fantasy." She reached up and kissed her cheek. "I love you."

Krista broke into a full cry. Micah handed her a tissue, and she dabbed her eyes and frowned at the streaks of mascara that came off. "I must look like the maid of honor at Frankenstein's wedding now."

Ada wiped the rest of the mascara off her face. "There. Now you don't look Halloweeny."

"Speaking of Halloweeny, I'm so sorry about the flowers."

"Oh, they're great," Ada said. "They're like zombie flowers! That's perfect for me and Micah."

"Still…"

"Still, I'll have a talk with the florist on Monday," Victoria said, laying a hand on Ada's shoulder. "Now both of you put your smiles on. You're in the receiving line, and these people are important. You want to make a good impression."

Krista blew her nose. "I do? Why?"

"Because it's a good idea to stay on everybody's good side, and because I said so." She took Krista's arm. "Now come with me. Adam and I can't stand next to each other because we're divorced. I need you to stand between us."

"Aye aye, Commander," Krista said as she was dragged to the head of the line. "Sure, use me as your personal demilitarized zone. Besides, I thought you got along with Adam's wife now."

"We get along *just fine,*" Victoria hissed.

"You want to hurt her, don't you?"

"Give me two seconds…"

Krista rested her hand on Victoria's arm. "On second thought, I'm happy to be your demilitarized zone."

"Good. Now smile and try not to say anything interesting."

By the time they were done greeting the crowd, Krista's smile muscles were spasming and she'd gone mentally numb. She started to ask Tala for a piece of her magical gum, but then Junior's voice drifted from behind the church. "FASTER, FASTER!" he yelled, and then he and Ennis burst around the corner, Junior perched on his shoulders and pulling up on his hair.

Junior spotted his mother and yanked the reins to steer his mount her way. When they arrived at the receiving line, he slipped off Ennis's shoulders and tumbled into Krista's arms. "You're all turned on there, Junior," she said, brushing the hair out of his eyes. "Have a good time?"

"He prefers to be called Mark," Ennis said.

"Is that so?" She rubbed the boy's cheek, and Mark Junior grinned and nodded. "You don't want to be a rebel, little man, not yet. Give me ten years of cuteness before you go anarchista, wouldja?"

"Thanks for letting me borrow him," Ennis said.

"Oh, no, thank you for the horsey ride. He loves those more than anything, and he's getting too heavy for me to lift." She kissed Junior's cheek. "And he needs to spend more time with men. He doesn't get the chance very often. His father died before he was born."

"I know." Ennis studied his shoes and cleared his throat. "You should know who I am. I'm the one who –"

"I know who you are, Captain Quinn."

"I'm terribly sorry. We wouldn't have released the missiles if we'd known you were still on that causeway. The observers said –"

"It's in the past," she said, brushing Junior's hair with her fingers.

"I just –"

"It's in the past and the ghosts don't haunt me anymore! Let it go, wouldja?"

A painfully awkward silence followed, and Krista was preparing to slink back to the island when Tala walked over and laid her hand on Ennis's arm. "Krista Warner, I'd like you to meet Ennis Quinn. He's the finest man alive," she said with a twinkle in her eyes.

He examined his shoes again. "Tala…"

"We made a deal, and I'm sticking to it," she said. "Now that I've paid up, I'll leave you two alone." She walked away to find her parents, leaving Krista and Ennis in an uncomfortable silence again.

"I'm sorry I popped off at you," Krista said at last. "I know you had a bad night on October 19th too. I went to the Independence Museum last year down on the Santa Cruz Wharf, and they gave me a VIP tour of your submarine. It looked like a tornado hit it."

"The *DuPont* ambushed us in Soquel Canyon after we hit the *Astor*, and I wouldn't be standing here now if the *Revere* hadn't come out of nowhere and drilled four torpedoes into her side. But she dumped everything she had on us before going under, and the aft compartments flooded. Our pumps gave out when we got back to Monterey Bay, and I had to ground the boat on the beach before it sank…" He looked away, the muscles in his jaw knotted.

"It feels like it just happened yesterday, doesn't it?"

"It feels like it just happened last night."

"Trust me – if you keep opening that wound, Ennis, it'll never heal."

"I know, I know." A gust of wind riffled through his hair, which he combed back with his fingers. "I just wish I could forget that whole damned night."

"Me too. I actually went to a hypnotist who said she could make me forget September and October of '43 like they never happened."

"Did it work?"

Krista shook her head. "I just got this weird urge to fry rubber bands for weeks after. Honestly, I think only early-onset Alzheimer's will cure me now." She rested her hand on his arm. "The only answer is to leave the horrors of the past behind and find the wonders that lie ahead. That's how I've coped."

He laid his hand over hers. "All right, let's try that. No more war stories."

"We'll change the subject. Now tell me why you're the finest man alive."

Ennis blushed and looked away. "Tala and I, we were cooped up, it was a stressful time, we went a little nuts…I wanted to get introduced to you, and she said she could do it, and…" He coughed into his hand.

"That's so sweet!"

His face suddenly blushed bright pink, eliciting a giggle from Krista. However, just seconds before he died of terminal embarrassment, Junior squirmed in Krista's arms and shrieked, "AUNTIE!"

Ada appeared beside her and took Junior from her arms. "I'll take him back to the island. You two can have all the time you want." She tousled Junior's hair, and he gave her a happy grin. "Hey there, Booger. How about a boat ride with me and Uncle Micah?"

They watched Ada and Micah climb into their launch, chuckling at Micah's yelp when Junior pulled his hair. Ennis rubbed his scalp and grinned. "I know what that feels like. The boy's got an iron grip. Wow, I thought he was going to give me a facelift right there."

"I'm so sorry," Krista said.

"Oh, no, he's a good kid. I don't mind at all."

"You don't?"

"No, no, that's what boys do."

They watched the launch motor away. After it rounded Angel Island, she started along a path following the shoreline. "I've got time before the reception starts, and I need to walk," she said. "Standing still too long makes my knees lock up. Would you like to join me?"

Ennis nodded and caught up with her. "So what did you think of The Movie That Shall Not Be Named?"

"Let's see." She tapped her finger against her lips. "It sucked dirty donkey balls? Would that be too strong a term?"

"Not strong enough. It was worse than *Mushrooms over Moscow*, and that was a mighty low bar to begin with. I think they threw the facts out and just made stuff up. Like near the end, when they showed the Anarchista wearing a low-cut leather bustier and racing across the desert in a tank."

She snorted and covered her mouth. "I kept waiting for her boobs to pop outta that thing."

"That's the only reason I watched it till the end, honestly."

He looked down at the path, and she tugged down on her dress, by chance exposing more cleavage. "You know what's so strange, Ennis? I really can't recall leading a phalanx of tanks into battle against an armored column planning to sack Reno. It's completely slipped my mind."

"Well, it was a hectic time. A lot was going on."

"True. I shouldn't expect to remember *every* little detail."

"Or maybe that hypnotist actually accomplished something? You never know."

She flashed him a sideways grin. "That must be it. Thanks for straightening that out. I feel much better now."

"My pleasure. I'm here for you anytime."

"So tell me – that really tense scene where you climbed into the missile tube and disarmed the warhead. Was that bogus?"

"Oh, God yes. We try hard to keep the sea outside, and putting thirty-six missile access hatches in a boat is pure idiocy. And no, my cabin doesn't look like a five-star hotel room, and I don't have a picture window where I watch the fish frolic. Subs don't even have portholes, never mind windows."

"That's a shame. I was hoping Blinky the Squid was real. He was adorable."

"Oh, yeah, he was the cutest thing ever, wasn't he? My crew bought a Blinky and stowed it over the helm console, and now everybody salutes him when they report to the Control Room."

"Junior has one too. He likes to hear it squeal when he yanks on the tentacles."

"Who doesn't? But I wouldn't mind how much they screwed up the facts if they hadn't hired that damned bodybuilder to play me. Now everyone expects me to be some muscle-bound hulk. I think they're disappointed to find out I'm just an ordinary guy."

"I'm not disappointed, and I don't think you're ordinary," Krista said.

Ennis grinned. "Is that so?"

She nodded. "But I know what you mean. Everybody expects me to be the bimbo from the movie, and sometimes I can't convince them that I'm really me. I guess I don't measure up to the actress that played me."

"You don't," he said. "You're a thousand times prettier."

"Is that so?"

"It's most definitely so."

Krista smiled softly but didn't reply, and a few steps later, she stumbled and fell against him. "Are you all right?" he asked.

"I tripped over a stone, that's all. I'm sorry, I just keep bumping into you, these knees…"

"That's okay." He glanced at the path behind them, which was free of stones, and suppressed a goofy grin. "Tell you what," he said, holding out his arm. "Hold onto me. I'll keep you on your feet."

"Thanks." She took his arm, and they walked past the rear of the church and along the bayfront. They found a bench at the end of the path and talked for hours.

THE BLUE SKY HAD DEEPENED into late-afternoon azure when Krista's tablet chimed. "I've got to be going soon," she said. "The reception's starting in an hour, and I need coffee before wading into that crowd again. Are you coming? We'll have some colorful guests from New Detroit there."

"From where?"

"It's a long story. Come along and I'll tell you."

"It's a deal." He stood and offered her his hand, and they began walking back to the dock.

"I'd like to ask you a strange question," he said. "It's actually a reasonable question, but you might find it strange."

"I can handle strange," she said. "Fire away."

"Are you Keira Kellen?"

She glanced sideways at him. "Why would you think that?"

"So you are?"

"How do you know me?" She examined every detail of his face. "I don't know you."

"How could you forget me? I nailed you right in the forehead with an iceball out in the resident's garden, and your bodyguard Seth got mad..."

"Copper?" She peered at his face with her mouth hanging open. "Omigod, you're Copper?"

He ran his hand through his hair and laughed. "Nobody's called me that since high school."

She took a step forward. "Holy crap! It *is* you!"

"It's a strange coincidence, isn't it?"

"The things I could tell you about coincidences. Wow, have you ever grown up!"

"I could say the same about you. The last time we met, you were just a little girl with a big mouth."

"The girl grew up, but the mouth didn't. That's how I got in so much trouble."

"We've had quite a journey from West 26th Street, haven't we?"

"That's for sure." She held out her hand. "Let's try this again. I'm Keira."

"It's a pleasure to meet you again, Keira."

"It's great seeing you again, Ennis." They started walking back to the church. A few steps later, she turned to face the bay and whispered, "Oh, you feckin blatherskite. He told me to move on, boyo, so why doncha shove..." She noticed Ennis watching her and blushed.

"Who are you talking to?" he asked.

"Just an old friend. I hear so much babble in my head, it's like Open House Day at the UN sometimes." She glanced into his eyes. "I'm nuttier than a squirrel turd, y'know."

"And you're okay with that?"

She nodded. "This is the way I am, like it or not."

"I like it. I spend my days with people so rational and predictable that the Navy entrusts them with the power to crush nations. In other words, they're boring as hell. If I didn't have Tala around to keep things weird, I would've left the Submarine Service years ago. Now, you never know what crazy people will do. They keep things interesting."

"*I* don't even know what I'm going to do, sometimes." She shrugged. "Whatever. I've gotten used to it."

A sailboat glided past, far out on the bay, and they watched until it passed out of sight. A cool breeze blew in from the ocean and riffled her hair. "The bay can get so chilly in June. It sometimes feels like winter's coming." She slipped her hand into his. "Sorry, but my hands really feel the cold."

"Mine do too. Let's warm each other up." He clasped her hand, and the green band that had been on her ring finger moments ago was gone; as surreptitiously as he could, he felt for it again and found it on her index finger. With a start, he realized why she'd moved it.

"Looking for something, Captain Quinn?" she asked.

He took both her hands and pulled her to him until their lips were close enough for a kiss. "Not anymore."

"Found what you wanted, have you?" He lifted her hand and gently touched his lips to it, and she looked into his eyes. "We should be having a cup of coffee, you and me, instead of standing out in the cold," she said.

"I'm always up for some good brew. Is there a place around here that serves a solid mug of the stuff? I'm no fan of weak coffee."

"I've got a French press baristomat at my house, and I guarantee you've never drunk coffee as strong as mine. I roast my own beans, and I roast them dark."

"How dark?"

"Black. Blacker than black," she said. "My coffee's so strong, you've got to use espresso to dilute it."

"Now *that* sounds like my kind of coffee."

She looked across the bay for a moment and then turned back to face him. "But I've got to tell you something, Ennis. It's a wild ride, and I wouldn't try it unless you're sure you can hang on. Would you take that risk with me?"

"I'm feeling a bit adrift here. Are you still talking about coffee?"

"Am I?" With a half-smile, she crossed her arms and tilted her head to one side.

He searched her eyes for a clue to the puzzle; he saw a challenge and a warning there, but also the hint of a promise. For several heartbeats, the enigma drew him in so deep that all he knew of the world was her eyes. They were as ever-changing as tropical seas, and as he swam in their warm blue depths, he realized what she'd meant. And he knew that he'd gladly walk into the unknowable future with her, no matter what perils he might face.

Suddenly, he realized that his life would never be the same. A delicious tingle raced up his spine, and he decided to step into Paradise at last and burn his boat down to the waterline. "I'll happily do that. You wouldn't believe what I'd risk for a great cup of coffee. Two sugars, no cream, please."

She smiled and took his hand. "I like a little cream in mine. Life's too short for bitter brews."

"Agreed. We'll try it your way."

They walked back to the dock, savoring the touch of the other's hand and listening to the seagulls squawk. As they stepped onto the launch, she said, "One thing you oughta know about my coffee. I can never tell how it'll turn out."

He laughed and squeezed her hand. "Nobody ever can."

EPILOGUE

Pelican Point
Angel Island, California
June 30, 2071

And that's how the Continental Divide actually happened.

I hope you enjoyed the ride. You almost didn't get the opportunity to take this journey with me, though. I had a hellish time getting this story out of my head and into print.

When I pitched this to my publisher, I told him I was writing an epic love story with nukes. He laughed for a full minute till he noticed I wasn't laughing with him. Then he said that was too ambitious a goal for a first-time writer, and I should stick to my day job teaching history.

He was right about the work – it took eighteen months to gather the oral histories and another twenty to write the story. Of course, I could have hammered it out quicker if I hadn't taken my mom's advice and flown up to the new Suncoast Resort in Nome to write without any distractions. It sounded like the perfect getaway.

It was perfect for all of two weeks, and then the beach bunnies came to town. Because the sun only set for three hours in summer, the party roared for three months straight, and finding my keyboard was devilishly hard with all those shapely bodies strolling the black sand beaches outside my window.

I guess I really am my father's son. In a way, getting laid constantly was like getting in touch with my inner Mark Mason. It was a kind of communion. Thank God so many girls up there are religious.

I'm a big proponent of climate change ever since my stay in Nome. So we lost the Miami Keys to the hurricanes – big deal. Alaska's got a thousand miles of undeveloped beachfront and a business-friendly government, which more than makes up for it. The Bering Sea is still too cold to swim in, but I have faith in humanity. We can pollute our way to paradise.

Besides, as it gets hotter, women wear less. Show me the downside. I dare you.

Anyway, I made up for the bacchanal in the winter. The weather turned chilly and gray, the sun peeked over the horizon for only a few hours in the afternoon, and ice floes even drifted by. The weather was perfect for writing: It was so depressing that I would have pulled a Hemingway and kissed my shotgun if I hadn't pounded away on the keyboard. I must have been desperate because I wrote a much longer manuscript than I expected that winter.

When I dropped the four-ream tome on my publisher's desk, he laughed even harder than the first time. After a truly uncomfortable few minutes, he said that he'd consider publishing it if I cut it in half.

I thought about it, but then I learned something that got me off the hook: A friend revealed that my hard-bitten, judgmental publisher had been that little refugee boy out at Hughes Airport in '43, the one with the endearingly trembling lower lip getting the first Recombin-B.

The next time I saw him, I said that I'd decided to cut all the Reno chapters. After all, who cares about the refugees' plight? You should have seen his face when *that* voodoo hit him. He shut up after that.

And anyway, the story of my parents is an epic, and it's impossible to cut it down without skewing their history. I'd never intended to write a fast-paced historical thriller – I was writing a love story about when my young and wild mother changed the world, and even more about the father I never met. By writing their story, I immersed myself in their time and shared their lives.

Most importantly, I shared my father's life. I built a model of Mark Mason in my mind, piecing him together from all my family told me, and it worked: I believe he actually spoke to me through my writing. Maybe I'm as crazy as my mother and I'm hearing voices, but I don't think so. It felt like he was there.

For a too-brief time, I walked along the sands with him, and we had the reunion I'd always yearned for, if only in my heart. It was worth all the work when my father began telling me what he'd say as I built his story, and he lived again in those moments. I learned so much about the man. More, I realized that I loved him, and I loved what he'd passed on to me.

And when he left on that dark and bitter December day, I believe he went away feeling proud of his son and the man he'd become. That aching moment will stay in my heart forever. But I'm my mother's son too, and I know we should treasure the moments we have and never yearn for the past. Now I don't, not anymore.

So this manuscript is the residue of that experience and a memorial to a man I'd always revered. Like all memorials, it just has meaning for those who want to remember, so I'd probably only sell a hundred books to history nerds. That's okay, though, because the reunion with my father was all I wanted, not literary success. Besides, I'm not planning to make a career out of writing. I have no more stories in me. I'm done.

I settle back in my big wicker chair on the west porch, happy with these realizations. I watch the fog retreat from the bay and drift away under the Golden Gate Bridge, and with it goes my tension.

I see Mom wander toward the trees where she feeds the deer. She's convinced that they're her spirit animal, and that they're attracted to her because they share the same gentle anima. Maybe that's true, or maybe they come because they like how my prize roses taste – Mom snips rose blooms from my garden before the feedings and thinks I don't know. Whatever the reason, I'd just planted more rose bushes to make sure she didn't run out.

The fabric of the big white tent on the north lawn flaps and snaps in the ever-present breeze. The caterers would be here with boatloads of food in a few more hours, and then the guests would arrive to celebrate my parents' twenty-fifth anniversary.

Theirs was a love story I'd always wanted to write but never would. Ennis had come for coffee after Ada's wedding and stayed for three weeks, only leaving for San Francisco on June 30 to marry my mother. I'd nagged Mom to tell me what happened because it must have been an absolutely atomic courtship, but she wouldn't. And Ennis can be as chatty as the Sphinx when he wants to.

The frustrating thing is that I was there when it all happened, but I don't remember it. I was only two at the time, and I still thought rolling my poo into little balls was a hoot. I missed it all.

They'd found their happiness here on Angel Island; in their separate ways, they'd always been seeking their islands in humanity's mad river. Aunt Ada and Victoria had wanted that too, and like Ennis, they'd probably stay forever.

However, Mom and Ennis will be spending the next few years in Japan now that she's been appointed as ambassador. Although she swears she won't go, I heard somebody playing one of those Learn-Japanese-in-a-Day programs in the upstairs library. The woman never could resist being around people that adore her.

The kitchen door creaks, and Aunt Ada walks through holding a coffee mug. She settles into the rocker beside me and looks across the water. The bay's a little hypnotic, and something out there always snags a corner of the mind and keeps it occupied.

Two yellow sailboats skid across the bay, heeling hard in a strong onshore breeze; men hang off the high side, and the gunwales ride no more than an inch above the water. Nevertheless, they make it across the bay without sinking, and we lose sight of them when they round Alcatraz.

"It's quiet out here," she says.

"Keira and Keriana wanted to see the city, and their kids wanted ice cream, so Micah took everybody over to Pier 39. He said to tell you he'll stop in Tiburon and pick up your brood on the way back, so you don't have to worry about that."

"Okay. I couldn't take the twins and all your nieces and nephews right now. It'll be a madhouse tonight."

"That's for sure." We watch the world float by for a few minutes. "Did you get a chance to read the manuscript?"

"I scanned through it, but I didn't have time to read every word. The thing's pretty freakin long, Booger." She sips her coffee, her eyes closed in reverence, and then she sighs and sits back in her chair. "Mostly the story tracks with what I recall, but there were a few jaw-droppers I didn't expect. I had no freakin clue the Reds were behind the Transition. It was depressing to find out they won in the end."

"Sara Hogue confirmed it. Cheyn had intelligence showing that they were funneling cash to the Arkies so they'd trigger California's secession."

"By the way, thanks again for calling me right after that interview and telling me about the kill chip."

"Really, you can stop thanking me."

"I can't thank you enough. I had no clue they put one in me, although it wouldn't have worked. They didn't harden it against an electromagnetic pulse, so the Sacramento bombing fused the circuitry."

"You're welcome. Anyway, I think you're wrong to say the Reds won. They might have won that battle, but they lost the war. When you look at the sheer power of the Coalition of North American Nations –" She snorts a horsey laugh. "What?"

"CONAN. What a cheesy name."

"It sounds better than SEA-nan."

"It's still cheesy. It's like we all live in some freakin awful barbarian flick. Is that the kind of image we want? What's Schwarzenegger now – a hundred and fifty? He rolls down Rodeo Drive in a gold-plated wheelchair with a built-in heart-lung machine and a cigar lighter, looking like Hawking on a Bacardi bender…"

"Auntie."

"…an IV with the blood of virgins dripping into his veins –"

"Auntie!"

"All right, all right, CONAN is awesome, got it."

"Well, it is, and that's where the Russian scheme failed. If they wanted to take down the United States, they should have let it stay together so the whole country collapsed together. But because they fomented secessions, smaller and more efficient nations rose in place of the United States, creating a more potent adversary than before. Look at CONAN's assets – California's strong Asian trade and New America's European business, Mexico's manufacturing prowess, the endless breadbasket of Heartland and the Canadian provinces, the throw weight and accuracy of Québec's and the Commonwealth's nuclear arsenals – together, we've been the world's undisputed economic and military superpower for twenty years. So I say the Reds lost that gambit miserably. In fact, they brought on the Great American Century they were trying to thwart."

"I'm not criticizing CONAN. I just think the name blows," she says. "There's one question you never answered in the story, though – did the Arkies know that the Reds were pulling their strings?"

Not only did they know, they were profiting off it: Hayborn skimmed nearly twenty million bucks from Dusan Nitskaya and used it to buy a seaside mansion in the Azores and a modest hundred-foot yacht. The leader of the Transition clearly expected it to fail and wanted to cash in while he could, which was breathtakingly cynical but also colossally stupid; Nitskaya was so pissed by Hayborn's treachery that he swore to nerve-gas him and everybody that even looked like him once the Transition was complete.

Downs relieved him of that chore, of course, but that was just coincidence. He'd known nothing about the Red skulduggery, and neither did anybody I interviewed from the Watch Room except Sara Hogue. And she only knew the bare outlines.

The sleazy tale of the Arkie-Russian collusion was riveting, gruesome, and newsworthy, and revealing it to the world would make this book a bestseller. In fact, I weaved it into the first draft, imagining all the plaudits and huzzahs the talk shows would shower on my worthy shoulders. But then reason returned, and I realized that publishing it would be irresponsible – as soon as Nitskaya read the story, he'd know who my source had been, and that person would be killed within days. Not only that, Nitskaya would probably whack me too, if just for shits and giggles. I wouldn't risk that to sell a few books, so I cut it all out.

It's ironic. Like my mom, the story of the century fell into my lap, and I couldn't write a word of it. It's indescribably frustrating to grab the shitty end of Irony's stick –

Ada snaps her fingers in front of my eyes. "Jeez, Auntie, can I have a bloody moment?"

"You're worse than your mom."

"Whatever. Look, I can't talk about the Russian angle without there being a body count, so let's change the subject."

"All right. So tell me – how'd you get Bob Downs to confess to assassinating Hayborn and his cronies?"

"I didn't. He gave up the secret himself on the last day of the interview, just as I was getting ready to leave. Maybe he's bored by living in Paradise and wants to relive the glory days."

"I can see that," she says. "Although now everybody will want to kill him."

"I think that's why he told me." Sitting in his little hacienda on the Havana coast, I got the feeling that he sees his end coming and yearns for that electric sense of danger once more. Even though he's over sixty now, he still works out every day and stays sharp. He'd take a few would-be assassins with him on the journey to his forever after.

And he'd also take with him the answer to my family's most enduring question: Did he boff my grandmother? He was too much a gentleman to say, and I know better than to ask Marissa. But he has scars on his neck and wouldn't say how he got them. And Marissa never remarried. Hmm.

I'd been mulling over the contradictions of Downs to get an angle on his psychology because it was more complex than any in the story. And that hasn't changed over the years – at one point in our interview, he told me he was still a mortal angel and expected a call to duty again. I didn't delve into that because you'd have to go completely loco to grasp the logic powering the Arkie mind, and I'm not *that* curious about their weirdnesses.

"So what I read of the manuscript is good," she says, "but like I told you years ago, nobody wants to read about us. We're old news. Nobody even remembers us, Boog. We can sometimes walk around without a security detail now."

"Still…"

"Still, you oughta write about your trip across the States. Now *that's* interesting. People would read that story."

"That's a subject for another time," I say. "I'd like to know what you thought about the Sacramento chapter."

"It was fine," she says to her coffee mug.

"I'd like to know if I got it right. You went to Sacramento a child and came away an adult, and since you wouldn't say what happened, I needed to create the emotional transitions, and I –"

"It was *fine*, I said."

"But was the pivotal moment when you were looking at the ruins from Mount Vaca? I know about your suicide attempt, but I know nothing about what drove you to it, and I hope –"

"Please, Boog…"

"I think you'd reached a crossing in life, and when you saw the ruins of Sacramento, it was easier to accept death than –"

Two yellow sailboats skid across the bay, heeling hard in a strong onshore breeze; men hang off the high side and the gunwales ride no more than an inch…I realize that I can taste my fillings, and a temporal translation headache is rippling across my brain. I look at Aunt Ada, and sure enough, that accursed Electric Donut is sitting in her lap. "Damn it! You timejumped me *again*? Do you know how inconsiderate that is?"

"What?" she asks with a chaste expression saints would envy.

"Oh, don't play innocent. That halo doesn't fit you. It just makes you look fat."

I see Mom over by the tree line rubbing her head. She was on the edge of the toroid's horizon, and her temporal translation symptoms would be intense. It'd be hours before she remembered her name, and we'd need a gallon of coffee to bring her back to normal before the party.

Ennis knew she'd need it too, and he'd headed straight for the coffeemaker after feeling that staticky time-travel shock. He yells from the kitchen, "Ada, dammit! You busted the baristomat again! The clock's running backwards!"

"It's not busted, it's just confused!" she yells over her shoulder. "It was just a two-minute hop. Unplug it and reset the time!"

"Yeah, but what time is it?"

"What time do you want it to be?"

I look at my mechanical watch, which isn't affected by the temporomagnetic fields generated during time travel. Being around Ada so much, I don't trust electronics. "It's eight minutes after two, Dad." I rub the top of my head even though the headache is gone. "How many times have I gotta tell you it's not a do-over button?"

"Of course it is, silly."

"Well, you shouldn't do it. It screws everything up."

"Not for me. It works like a charm for me."

"Gonna give me brain cancer or something," I say, sounding like the sullen loser I wish I weren't.

"Not with a two-minute hop, it won't. That's harmless, Boog. Besides, if you learned how to behave, I'd never touch the Donut at all."

"What'd I do to earn a reset?" I try to remember, but whatever offense I'd committed only exists in the timestrand I left behind. I just get a fuzzy sense of pissing her off somehow, which I must do a lot because she's hopped me across nine timestrands so far. No, make that ten.

"Oh, I don't remember."

"You were at the center of the toroid. Your memory is fine!"

"You know how it is with us old ladies – new ideas come in, old ideas get pushed out. We never hang onto anything. So we were talking about your trip across the States. Ever since the Arkies fried the communication satellites and closed the borders, nobody knows what's going on in there. What's it like now?"

I'm pretty sure we'd been talking about something else, but even my fuzzy sense had vanished. So, like sullen losers do, I give up. "All right, you wanna know about the Roadkill Republic. It's a failing, totalitarian, theocratic throwback to the sixteenth century, okay?"

"I know that. Everybody does. But what was it like?"

"God, where do I begin? For starters, it was creepy. It was empty and lonely and primitive, especially in the Midwest, which is still crawling with farm machines like Mom described. The interstates are abandoned, and some even had trees growing through them. And there are bones everywhere. The Arkies just left the virus victims for the vultures."

I look to see if that revolted her, but she has those dark eyes turned up to full power. I guess she wants to hear this.

"They had it bad post-war, and it shows wherever you go. The Arkies had a great plan for taking over the nation, but they never expected the secessions to work and that so many states would flip them the bird. And they certainly didn't figure on the Archangel Bob decimating their leadership. Downs said he not only assassinated Presidents Hayborn and Kilmer but also fifteen other members of the administration in the first two years."

"I remember. What little news we heard from the States back then was gruesome."

"Well, the assassinations certainly were. Downs showed me his scope videos, and I had to take a walk along the beach to stop shaking. A human sorta explodes when he gets hit with a fifty-caliber bullet." However, Downs was as proud of them as a new father with his baby, and he showed me all seventeen killings in high def, pointing out the blood spatter and how close he came to the aimpoint. I couldn't eat for days. "Anyway, without leaders or a functioning government – and with a worthless currency – the Arkie economy did a big swirly. Everybody was poor and hungry and pissed, and I heard they eventually turned on their own because they couldn't pick on California. Nobody I interviewed knew exactly what happened cuz the Arkies own the news, but one guy told me they 'strung up all the pinkoes and queers.' And he smiled after he said that. But another guy said the lefties and the minorities were just harassed till they left. He thought they moved to the Deposition Zone or Heartland or Sagebrush."

"Probably Heartland," she says. "Minneapolis was just cold and boring before the war, and it became the freakin world capital of the arts after. Best jazz on the planet now. Coincidence? Nope. That's where they went, I bet."

"Like I said, I'm not sure. I don't think anybody actually knows what went down in the first five years."

"Are they happy with their little paradise?"

"They seemed like it. I don't know why, though. Some parts I visited looked seriously Third World. The States never fully recovered from the post-war depression, and they only started pulling out of it in '50, when they formed the Corpus Council. The corpa run everything now and make their own laws and regulations – and since the Arkies own a controlling interest in all the corporations, they never make a law conflicting with Church principles. Even the justice system is run by corpa."

"Hmm. Hard to imagine making a business out of justice," she says. "How do you turn a profit on putting someone in jail?"

"They lease the prisoners to other corpa. If they can't do that..." I pantomime a noose being yanked. "They don't have a lot of people stewing in jail."

"Efficient system," she says, glaring at San Francisco.

"It actually works well, except that everybody seemed a little haunted, and they got a weird look whenever I talked to them – y'know, that face people get when they start talking about a person and then suspect that person is standing behind their back?"

Ada rocks a little faster in her chair. "I know that feeling well! So the NSF is still around?"

"I never found out for sure. I know that the local police watch everything cuz I got stopped a few times, and they gave me a lot of trouble. Once I showed them my Republic passport with the name 'Mark Mason', I had to answer lotsa stupid questions. After I got detained in St. Louis, I took back roads to keep from getting hassled again, but the locals warned me to stay close to the Arkie cities and the suburbs. The roads near the Deposition Zone are dangerous, and the Downwinders who still live there can be murderous. It's a wasteland where only the true scumbags could survive, and I heard they'll skin you for a cigarette."

"I'm surprised the Arkies tolerate them."

"They don't. If they catch a Downwinder, they'll either put them in Work-Lease or stretch their neck, but the Arkies are too scared of the radiation to go in and get them."

The rocker stops, and she gives a frustrated snort. "The fallout hit twenty-eight-freakin years ago, for chrissakes. The groundshine's gone now."

They might think three-hundred-foot-tall marshmallow men with glowing laser eyes wait in the wastes and hunger to boil their pure and virtuous blood. If you think I'm joking, you don't know much about the Archangelist psyche. They get a boner for the extreme or abnormal or self-destructive, so they'll believe anything that gives them a rise – and marshmallow monsters are definitely in their ballpark, trust me. And since they fear anything scientific, nothing keeps those suckers from sailing right off the Cliffs of Sanity. This appetite for the extreme is the engine of their religion's power and reach, but it can drive them to the most startling and incomprehensible acts.

Once, in Indiana, I found something horrific at a rest stop – eight recently severed left hands arranged in a perfect circle, small hands that had been lopped off children's arms. Do you really want to know the story behind that? And don't ask me about that asparagus thing because that makes no sense to me, either. You'd have to go completely loco to grasp the logic powering the Arkie mind, and I'm not *that* curious about their weirdnesses.

Wait a second. Didn't I just say that?

I swear I did, but I can't remember. This kind of crap happens when you have your synapses flung across timestrands: Little fragments of orphaned memories bubble up out of somewhen and drive you mad.

Ada waves her hand in front of my face and snaps me out of yet another rumination. "The fairies took you away again?" she asks.

"Right, right. So anyway, I came across a few tame Downwinders, and they told me interesting stories about how their communities have evolved. Some have gone agrarian and communal like New Detroit, but others went bad. You had to avoid those, and lemme tell you, I spent some tense moments on the interstates expecting post-apocalyptic savages to ambush me. I was thrilled when I finally got to Free Baltimore, and I could unclench my ass."

Her black eyes glitter, giving me a glimpse of the wild, sixteen-year-old Anarchista she once was. "You've *got* to write about this, Boog."

"But I didn't take any notes. The States made my visa conditional on not writing about current conditions or events. All I could do was interview the survivors about the past."

"And just because the States said so, you forgot what you saw?"

"Well, the people at the consulate in San Francisco were nice, so I thought I'd play it straight." Not only that, their visa officer sported one of the finest racks I've ever seen, and I would have agreed to a testicle piercing if she'd suggested it. "Anyway, it was two years ago, and I don't even remember half the trip. I just don't have the material for a book."

"That's a shame. It sounds like you had a real adventure." She rocks slower, returning to the demeanor of a responsible, middle-aged scientist again. "As I grow old, the colors drain out of life. Maybe it's my eyes, but they aren't as vivid as they once were. Maybe getting old saps your energy and makes you want to sit here on the porch and take it easy till the end comes." She wraps a blanket around her shoulders. "From here, I should see the end coming a long way off, Booger."

"That's a lot of melodrama. You're only forty-three, for chrissakes. Is there a point to this?"

"Oh, I don't know if there's a point. I think I'm just reconciling my life and bidding my childhood goodbye. It's a mid-life thing." She lets out a long sigh, and the hairs on my neck prickle because this is way out of character. "I have this urge to wrap things up, you know, visit the old haunts one last time."

"What old haunts? All your old haunts are in…oh, no! You wouldn't even think of that!"

She gives me the impish smile again. "I'd love to see what they did with the Washington Monument."

"They stuck a ginormous Sword of the Archangel on the stump, okay? It looks stupid, but you'll never see it. You still have a death sentence hanging over your head, y'know. Six of them, in fact. I know how those clowns work, and they'd reanimate your corpse and hang you six times. I think the virus killed off all the sane people and left the profundo bizarros behind. And that's assuming they forget about the lesser crimes, like sedition and treason –"

"You're right. It's dangerous, but I'll steer us around trouble." She looks both ways and then leans toward me. "Remember all those times in your book when Krista used the Life Force?"

"Yeah, I had fun writing those. They were a hoot. Really, that new-age crap…" I notice her vexed expression, and the angel on my shoulder screams *Dumbass! You're blowing it! Backpedal!* "…some folks say that new age stuff is crap, but I always thought there was something behind it."

"There was something huge and beautiful behind it. The Life Force is real, Booger."

"Really?"

"I've proved it in the lab. It's observable, measurable, and repeatable."

"She wasn't making all that up?"

"Nope, and that's why the Arkies won't catch me. I'll just steer us into the right timestrand and bypass trouble the way your mom did. If you do like Krista and listen to the universal consciousness, you can usually see what direction to take when you come to a fork in time. In Kentucky, that's how your mom knew that we should get out of a car that was about to be blown to snot by missiles. In Colorado, that's why we stopped at a bakery in the middle of freakin nowhere and met your future father. She can read the timestrands like a road map."

That makes sense of a lot of weird things in my life. Back in '69, I had a reservation on Flight 232, the one the Arkies 'accidentally' shot down over Arizona, but I didn't go. Why not? Because Mom said the Black Dog was on the plane, and she wouldn't let me board. After I heard the news, I wondered how she'd known, but now I see why: She'd sensed a fork in the timestrands, and the one I was about to take would kill me. Now that's a holy-shit skill, one I needed to learn fast. "That's kinda mind-blowing, like right out of a sci-fi novel. There's really some natural force you can tap into whenever you want?"

"It's really not a force, but a way of listening to the universal consciousness. And we all do it to some degree – when somebody says they made a choice by following their intuition or their gut, they're actually saying they bounced the idea off the Unicon and got a feeling for what's right. That works about seventy percent of the time depending on how strongly you believe in that outcome. That probably explains why prayer works for some people too." She looks into her cup and sighs. "Speaking of life forces, I'm out of coffee."

"I'm sure Dad's rebooted the baristomat by now."

"I'll go check. Be right back."

She walks into the kitchen, leaving me with a Times Square of big thoughts: Was Peter Pan right when he said that all we need is to believe? (I knew it!) And is God a quark? Or is God some dude on a cloud who subcontracted the prayer-fulfillment business to a super-sensitive swarm of sub-nucleonic particles? It would make sense for the Big Guy, being that everything else is automated anymore, and that fan mail's gotta pile up with the population growing by a million every day. But did the angels go on strike when their work was downsourced? Did St. Peter chain the Pearly Gates as indignant seraphim waved protest signs, their wings twitching in that weird way that pissed-off angels –

The door slams and Ada strides out holding a steaming mug. She drops into the chair and pulls the blanket around her shoulders again. "Anyway, if you're a cynic, the Unicon will also point the way to failure. It doesn't give a squat about your personal fulfillment or the greater good, so if you expect to fail, it'll help you do that too. And that proves Murphy's Law." She takes a sip of coffee and sighs. "That was my greatest breakthrough. I'd always wanted to prove it, and I finally did with the help of your mom."

"That's momentous. Congratulations, Auntie."

She smiles and toasts me with her coffee mug. "Thank you. I'm so proud, I'm having Murphy's Law pasted on the lab cafeteria wall – 'If you believe you'll fail, there's a seventy percent chance you will.' And below that I'll put Warner's Law: 'If you believe you'll succeed, there's a seventy percent chance you will.'"

"Who'd pick failure? That's pretty powerful stuff."

"It is. Warner's Law explains why placebo pills cure some patients, and Murphy's Law explains why effective drugs sometimes don't. And Warner's Law is even more potent for a débordan like me, or especially your mom." She leans forward and lowers her voice. "Wanna hear a juicy secret?"

I lean toward her, my pulse rising, because Auntie knows all the high-octane hush-hushes.

"Don't tell anybody this, Boog, but the débordan can use an even more powerful level of the Life Force. Sometimes we not only pick the right timestrand – sometimes we can also alter a timestrand's course and change its future. It's like Reality à la Carte. Hungry and thirsty in the middle of a desert?" She sits back and snaps her fingers. "No prob. We can fix that."

"Hunh…you mean that tumbleweirds thing that happened in Seven Up? That was for real?" She smiles and bobs her head happily. "Holy shit! I thought you made that up!"

"Nope. Krista made the reality she wanted."

My heart races, and I struggle to keep from turning cartwheels across the lawn and whooping like a fool. A discovery like this would change the world, and I had to learn all about it. And coincidentally, I wanted to be the first Terran Jedi. "So tell me about that."

She must have seen it on my face because she shakes her head and crushes my light-saber fantasies. "The Life Force isn't a toy for superheroes, Luke. Only a débordan can alter a timestrand, and it sometimes doesn't even work for us, and it only happens under exceptional circumstances – and only if the débordan isn't aware she's doing it. If she is, nothing happens. So you can't just pull the trigger and go *pew! pew! pew!* at your enemies."

"Right. Expecting the Life Force to work guarantees it won't. The only way to make it work is to expect it *not* to work."

"Exactly! You're getting it!"

I rub my temples. I'm not, really, but I won't say that because she might explain quantum paradox again. The last time she did, I had an icepick migraine for days. "Well, c'mon. That's obvious to anybody."

"Yep. Anyway, I can alter timestrands too, but I'm not anywhere near your mom's level. She changed the future at least three times just during the war – three times in three weeks! – and who knows how many times after. I've only done it twice in twenty years." She shivers and pulls the blanket tighter. "And I can still feel those chillybones. Whenever she changed the course of a timestrand, there was a nanosecond of quantum decoupling, and it felt like my bones turned into icicles. You never forget *that* feeling, trust me. But hey, I'm not complaining. She made water and gourmet food appear magically when I was starving, and I didn't mind getting a cold flash for that. Anyway, most people don't experience those sensations. For the rest of humanity, the Life Force is so weak that they never notice it."

"But she said it strengthened her at Highland Ditch, and she didn't get the chillybones, so she wasn't using that weird juju energy –"

"The only way the Life Force helped her in Highland Ditch was to point out that she had seven bullets in her pistol and seven Ironshirts in front of her, and the timestrand where she survived was the one where she took them on. The rest was adrenaline and bravery and a little Mad Monkey Disease, but that's the way Kick-Ass Krista rolled back then." She finishes her coffee and sets the cup on the side table. "Listen, I know you love me and don't want to see me hurt, but I have to go. Even if I don't have to change a timestrand's course, I'm a pro at reading them. I'll steer us around trouble. Trust me."

"But why even take the chance? Why do you have to go?" I think for a second and then remember something she mentioned during the interview. "Does this have to do with Big Sister? That was the only unfinished business you left behind."

She gives me the barest of nods. "It's been there for too long, and I have to get it out. Especially before you publish your book and spill the secret."

"I could just cut Big Sister out of the manuscript. No big deal."

She shakes her head. "It's time I got it out, and your publishing date is a good excuse for me to get off my butt and do it."

"Are you ever gonna tell me what Big Sister is? When I interviewed Sara Hogue, she said Cheyn thought you could make a monster bomb, and that's why he wanted you back. I'll bet it's that thirty-megaton silobuster –" Her laser look stops me, and I swear I can already taste my fillings. "But hey, you don't wanna get into specifics, that's cool. I can respect your boundaries."

"See, you're learning."

"Yeah, kinda the way Pavlov's dogs learned."

"Don't insult yourself. You're a smart boy, and you were always so sensitive and caring." She lays her hand over mine. "That's why I'm sure you'll want to come along and keep me safe."

I want to say how absurd that is, but I can't get the breath to power my words, so I just make fish lips and look stupid and surprised.

"It'd be a fantastic adventure," she says. "You could get all the material you need to write a new book."

My mouth still isn't working, but my mind is: That book would be an instant bestseller if I survived to write it. I'd call it something literary like *Travels with Ada*. Or something sci-fi like *Re-Anarchista*. No, no, I've got it – *Raiders of the Lost Arkies!* Wait, that sounds familiar. Did I say that in another timestrand too?

"What do you say, Booger? You wanted to know what it felt like to be there. Well, here's your chance. You and me, we'll pack up some shotguns and toilet paper and head on east. We'll figure it out as we go along. We'll get into tough spots and wiggle out, and along the way, you'll get all the stories you need and more."

"I could get killed!"

"So what? That's what makes it fun."

"Fun? You call that fun?"

"Oh, yeah, it'll be a hoot, Boog." She squeezes my hand. "You'll have the times of your life, I promise."

TERMS COMMONLY USED IN 2043

Aluminati: Pejorative slang for members of the Second Creation movement, an extremist group within the Archangelists. The term implies that they wore tin-foil hats, although there is no evidence this actually occurred.

Archangelist: a member of the Archangelic Church of the Son of Christ.

Arkie: Popular term for an Archangelist.

Base-M: A hallucinogenic street drug that was growing in popularity in the early 2040's. Due to eradication efforts, the drug disappeared by mid-century and is unknown today.

BoHo: Bohemian Homeless, itinerant urban artists of the working class.

Collateral Tactics Unit: The military arm of the National Security Forces, known popularly as the Ironshirts.

Corporate-Americans: Corporations. The 31st Amendment provided them all the rights and protections of human citizens, as well as exemption from taxation.

DeePees: A term for refugees, used by the California National Guard. Short for Displaced Persons.

Elders: Leaders of the Second Creation movement. See *Aluminati*.

Ellesmere A4: An enteric retrovirus weaponized by the US Army to incapacitate enemy forces. It readily mutated into the deadly Ellesmere A7 variant and was deemed too unstable for combat use. See *Neovirus*.

Executives: Elite operatives of the National Security Forces, often used for assassinations and surveillance.

Federals: Popular term for the National Security Forces.

Fug: A mixture of acidic coal smoke and ground fog, primarily affecting the eastern two-thirds of the country. The word is believed to be a contraction of the F-word and Fog.

Great Correction, The: A prolonged recession that eliminated the American middle class and placed all economic power in the hands of corporations.

Joe Slick: Navy term for the Lancet Missile.

Lancet Missile: A hypersonic stealth missile. See *Joe Slick*.

MRC: The Media Regulatory Corporation, a public monopoly formed to control the dissemination of news and information on the Internet and other electronic media.

MRCS: Missile Release Control System, an automated targeting and launch system installed on Patriot class submarines. It was intended to reduce human error and the amount of manpower required to operate a missile boat.

Neovirus: Civilian term for the RVE viruses Ellesmere A4 and A7.

NSF: National Security Forces, whose primary mission is to uncover and suppress domestic dissent. See *Federals*.

Patriot Class Boat: A guided-missile submarine originally designed to carry Warhammer cruise missiles. The submarines were retrofitted in 2041 to carry the Lancet missile with the new W104 nuclear warhead. The Pacific Fleet boats in 2043 were:

SSGN 807 – USS *Patrick Henry*	SSGN 814 – USS *Ethan Allen*
SSGN 808 – USS *Paul Revere*	SSGN 815 – USS *Nathaniel Greene*
SSGN 809 – USS *Thomas Paine*	SSGN 816 – USS *John Paul Jones*
SSGN 811 – USS *Nathan Hale*	SSGN 817 – USS *Seth Warner*
SSGN 812 – USS *John Adams*	SSGN 818 – USS *James Otis*
SSGN 813 – USS *John Hancock*	

Popobawa: Pejorative street slang for the National Security Forces, and particularly the Collateral Tactics Unit. It is believed that it was borrowed from the name of a mythical East African demon.

PRC: The Persian Regional Conflict, a naval and aerial war in which the United States sought to prevent the unification of Persian and Arab populations into one nation. It ended in a stalemate and an embargo on the shipment of Persian Gulf oil to the United States.

Ranks: The rank and file, or the lower class. This group once comprised skilled laborers but after the Great Correction came to include most of the surviving middle class as well. Also known as Breeders, Naggers, Mullets, or Working Class.

Recombin: A virophage engineered to attack Neovirus.

SAG (Special Activity Group): Action squads of the National Security Forces, often used for pursuit, capture, and localized suppression efforts.

Soviet Bloc: Also known as the Group of Sixteen, those nations allied with Russia to achieve nuclear parity with the United States.

Stiffer: A person who has died on the street from an untreated illness.

Tenpez: A coin containing ten grams of gold issued by the State of California in the 2020's. In 2043, its value was approximately one thousand dollars. The name is believed to be inspired by a candy popular in the mid-20's.

Transition, The: Archangelist euphemism for a hostile takeover of the United States government.

Transportation, The: The forced resettlement of the urban poor from Detroit and Cleveland after a period of rioting and urban warfare in those cities. See *The Troubles*.

Troubles, The: A period marked by the broad repeal of civil liberties and repression of public dissent, spanning from early 2024 to late 2027. See *The Transportation.*

W104: A strong-fission/fusion weapon, which pound-for-pound delivered 21.2 times the destructive force of its predecessor, the fusion-fission W102 weapon.

www.ingramcontent.com/pod-product-compliance
Lightning Source LLC
Chambersburg PA
CBHW021947170626
46808CB00001B/58